KABUKI-CHO CABARET

Ian McKinley

KABUKI-CHO CABARET

DOUBLE DRAGON

Part 1

Shinjuku, Tokyo, Japan

Chapter 1

My boss was squatting at the side of the hideously gutted corpse, bending over to search for fine details, nuances that might not have been picked up by the crime-scene technicians. I should have been following her head movements while the Chief Inspector methodically analyzed the victim but, instead, was trying to get a better view of the whale-tail exposed as her white silk shirt was pulled up and her low-cut denim jeans were dragged lower over her sizeable buttocks.

The CI was an impressive woman in many ways. Not only a legend throughout the Pacific Rim for her detective skills, but a veritable Amazon who appeared even more larger-than-life due to the contrast provided by the petite Japanese girls on our staff - or even myself, her lowly gofer. Stella Koide was a blonde, blue-eyed, epitome of the Teutonic dream, or maybe more a caricature thereof; with well in excess of a hundred kilos generously distributed over her two meter plus frame. A lot of those kilos were muscle and bone, but most of the rest seemed to be tits and bum. This provided yet another contrast to her androgynous female colleagues and endless distraction for males, or at least all of those who were not 100% straight gay.

I shook my head and tried to bring my attention back to the job, moving to the side for a better view of the brutalized body and, hopefully, fewer potential distractions. As I had already been provided with basic background, the contrast between the large breasts and beautifully made up face of the ladyboy and his, or was it her, well-dimensioned penis did not come as too much of a shock. What did cause me to gasp was the way in which the torso had been hacked open and, as far as I could see, all internal organs removed.

"Not as nice a sight as the crack of my arse," my boss commented, without pausing her inspection of the gaping wound. The woman had a reputation for having eyes in the back of her head and this seemed to confirm it yet again. "So, Watson, what do you make of it?"

My name is Holmes, Jim Holmes, but there was no way that the CI could give the impression that she was confusing me with the redoubtable Sherlock; so I had become *Watson* to her and hence to the rest of the department as well. I scratched my head to gain thinking time while I tried to come up with something that would avoid, or at least minimize, my usual humiliation. I decided to stick to safe ground. "Well, the deceased is a transvestite... "

"And just what makes you think that?"

Fuck! How could I possibly be wrong here? "Well, maybe a pre-op trans-sexual or a shemale, if you want to be pedantic. I'm not up on the distinctions involved. Is a shemale the same as a ladyboy?"

"You don't answer a question with a question! How many times have I told you that? Anyway, have a closer look and see if you can do any better."

"Well, the body has obviously been cleaned up and set out on display, no blood or... "

"Or shit, that's bloody clear. But you're drifting again! For Christ's sake, develop your thoughts in a logical, structured manner! You started off with the victim, so go with that thread first."

Fuck, Fuck, Fuck! This woman was a nightmare. "OK, the victim looks at first glance like a transvestite or some other form of person that possesses both fine tits and a rather large dick. How about that?"

"I could live with that as the basis of a first glance. So, now you've had a chance for a second glance, can you narrow down a bit on the range of owners of tits and dicks?"

"Well it's not a part of the community that I spend much of my time with," I retorted. I was aware that I was skating on thin ice here as the sexual proclivities of Koide-san were a continuous source of scurrilous rumor in the precinct.

"So, does the office scuttlebutt now also include me as the meat in a sandwich featuring a couple of chicks-with-dicks? Does that thought get you hard?" It didn't, but it certainly did, I thought to myself as the torment continued. "Is that why you're staring down my cleavage, instead of examining our victim's genitalia?"

Although I don't consider myself prudish and have seen a number of dead bodies in my time, the idea of examining a corpse's private parts made me distinctly uncomfortable. I prefer to leave all that stuff to the forensic pathologists. Not that this explained why the focus of my eyes had drifted towards the Grand Canyon, as it was universally referred to beyond our CI's range of hearing. The woman was evidently well aware of how distracting her massive bosom was and seemed to take efforts to show it off to best advantage.

I ignored the taunt and tried to determine what was being hinted at. Ignoring the butchery above the waist, I examined the victim's tackle as instructed. "I don't know what death does to prick size, but this seems to be equipment of above average size for an Asian." I glanced up at the undamaged face. "Maybe Thai or from somewhere thereabouts."

"Damning with faint praise!" my tormentor muttered. "So what else have your eagle eyes picked up? For fuck's sake: a willy, yes, but... ?"

"No balls!" I realized as I followed this lead. "So, he's castrated: a eunuch or a mid-op trans-sex!"

"Jesus suffering Christ, Watson! Your evenings of wanking over the thought of my admittedly delectable bod have actually made you go blind! I thought that was an urban myth, but you are the living proof thereof. I am going to fucking video your feeble performance here and put it on YouTube as a warning to the younger generation of the dangers of self-abuse!"

I let this tirade roll over me as I knelt to get closer to the focus of my boss's wrath. "Fuck me!" I gasped as the situation between the slightly spread thighs was revealed. "It's a hermaphrodite! Christ, there can't be more than a couple of them in Tokyo. At least we should be able to ID the victim PDQ."

"Finally! Yes, indeed, a hermaphrodite; although nothing like as uncommon as you're suggesting. There're actually quite a few of them in Kabuki-cho."

"You have got to be taking the piss here," I rashly interjected. "This must be some kind of really rare genetic abnormality, one in a million stuff."

"Natural intersex cases are much more common than that although, admittedly, most are handled soon after birth with corrective surgery. But we need to check if this is natural or engineered... "

"Engineered? Who'd engineer their parts... ?"

"Fucking hell, Watson, shut it for a bit! And don't fucking open your trap until you are certain, one hundred percent certain, that you know what you're fucking talking about!" A finger jabbing in my direction made it clear that this was a command beyond any further discussion.

I could feel myself blush as I was humiliated yet again. Every bloody time I disagreed with this woman, I ended up with a lecture that served the twin purposes of demonstrating how encyclopedic my boss's knowledge is and how fundamentally crap I am in every possible area.

"So, we certainly have a hermaphrodite. A rare condition, but one which will not only be reflected in many cases when you consider the fifty million population of the Tokyo megalopolis, but even more within Japan and worldwide." Another wave of her finger warned me not to interrupt.

"Most of the cases would be corrected in some way before adulthood, but many of those who didn't have this option would end up in places like Kabuki-cho, where their attributes assure them a prime position in the commercial sex trade."

My mouth opened, but closed again quickly as a glare in my direction warned me of the consequences of interrupting the great detective in mid flow.

"But that would probably be the minority. Selective assignment of intersex gender has been an option since the thirties and is popular with some parents who see this as setting their children up as big earners for alt-sex prostitution. Our victim here looks to have a real mongrel ethnic background; a really beautiful face with a lot of Thai and maybe some Philippines there. Just the kind of places where hookers are cultured over generations, until they reach a level where they can make the pilgrimage to Shinjuku, to finally make the big time."

I sensed that I was now allowed to speak. "Well, maybe you know a lot more about this than I do... " rolled eyes made it clear that I was stating only the obvious, "... but surely this will still be a very select subset of the knocking shops in this area?"

"Thank the great hairy fanny of the Goddess - finally!" C.I. Koide raised her eyes to the ceiling in an overly dramatic gesture that brought the edge of a large brown areola into view. Distracted by the hope that this might presage the appearance of one of her legendry nipples, I almost missed the next bit.

"This is where we're starting from, a top-end intersex courtesan is gutted and presented to us, carefully arranged, on the floor of a crappy soba joint; just where it would cause maximum impact when they opened up at about eleven this morning."

"And? What does this all mean? Who did it? And why put the body here?" The little restaurant was, indeed, rather shabby and the entrance zone was about the only place where the body could be laid out, even then requiring a cabinet presenting plastic models of the noodle set dishes available to be pushed back to block access to the back seating areas and the kitchen.

"Not the fucking foggiest! But, thanks to your brilliant and stunning good-looking superior, we at least know where to start. You can show your appreciation by buying me lunch in the pub I noticed round the corner; it looks like some pseudo-Brit thing, but it'll do for now."

The statuesque detective stood and stretched, causing her breasts to drop back into relatively secure concealment of a straining black silk bra. "No luck, Watson, maybe they'll fall into your lap next time." She grinned smugly and led our way back into the heat and humidity of Sakura-dori.

***

Shinjuku was bustling, with lunchtime queues beginning to form outside the smaller, cheaper eateries and shoppers blocking the pavement around a corner shop with ドン・キーホーテidentifying it in bright yellow kanji. This was "donki" - the emporium selling just about everything, if you could possibly find what you were looking for in its chaotic innards. A wall of sound was blasting from a huge video screen opposite, competing with the racket from a couple of pachinko parlors. Downtown Tokyo by day, just as foreigners imagine it to be - probably because it was such a popular background for news video crews. By night it was even busier - and even noisier.

A bell tinkled as I opened the door of the little bar, holding it for my boss to enter. A couple of young men sat at tables made out of large barrels in the front area of the pub, but the back, with a few longer tables along the left hand side of the narrow room, was empty. The CI glanced at a blackboard covered with scrawled katakana, announced that she would have fish and chips and a pint of Guinness, and then disappeared off in the direction of a toilet at the rear of the establishment.

I passed her order to a cute little barmaid and added a hot dog for myself, before having a more detailed inspection of the beers on offer in a wall of glass-fronted refrigerators. Ignoring the Belgian beers that seemed to comprise about three quarters of the selection, I narrowed down to English brews and finally selected a Young's Double Chocolate Stout. It is one of the great things about Tokyo, just about anything that you could imagine is available somewhere and, when it came to alcoholic beverages, most were on offer in Kabuki-cho, Shinjuku´s notorious entertainment quarter.

I carried our beers to the table furthest from the door and settled myself down on the inside bench, just before Koide-san emerged and plonked herself into the chair opposite. She lifted the bottle in front of me and grimaced. "Bloody poofter drink! If you're going to have a stout, why not Guinness? Or, at least, Murphy's or Beamish."

"*De gustibus non disputandum,*" I responded smugly.

"Jesus Christ, Oxbridge classics! Just as well you were turfed out and got a real job with the Met or you'd be just another over-educated but unemployable Pommie wanker."

As if it wasn't bad enough being a newbie Englishman in the recently formed Tokyo International Constabulary, I had the misfortune to serve under a part-Japanese woman who had been head-hunted from Sydney to lead the serious crimes division. The Valkyrie interlaced her fingers and stretched her arms over her head, her joints cracking like gun shots. This process also emphasized how gigantic her breasts were, while they threatened to burst from the confines of her shirt. "OK, thinking caps on. Let's see if we make use of the wonders of modern technology that we have at our disposal and crack this case before we finish lunch. In fact, why don't we make it more fun by letting you do the sleuthing? I'm supposed to be training up your useless arse, ain't I?

I groaned aloud and then sipped my beer as the torture continued.

"So, to make it easy for you, all you need to do is determine who our victim is and what this murder is all about. This will lead you to who dunnit and whether anyone else was involved. Then we go nick them. Right, I've now done all the sophisticated top-level planning shit, so you can fill in the details!"

I took a deep breath. "Fuck! OK, here goes. The victim, when clothed, would look like a rather stunning woman. With her Thai features, she wouldn't be at all unusual for this area, given its high density of hostess bars, brothels and soap clubs. With less clothing, could be mistaken for a ladyboy," I ignored the frown aimed at me and continued to break down evidence into minute pieces, "again in no way unusual for Kabuki-cho. But a bit more specialist, certainly, so the number of premises providing such services would be fewer. As we know, however, this is a well-endowed hermaphrodite that we're talking about, so, regardless of how many there actually are, would be likely to be working out of the very select, top-end of the flesh market."

"For example?"

While I had been speaking, my comm unit had been sitting in front of me in natural language mode and hence a holographically projected map with prioritized hits appeared immediately after this question was posed.

"How are these priorities set?" A long finger, with short, clipped nails painted a lurid scarlet, pointed at the top-rated hit, which also seemed to be the one closest to our present location. "Mmm... , just proximity, but that's interesting."

The map was replaced with a synthesis from the police knowledge base, complemented with material stripped from the electronic profile of a club called Pleasure Doubled. The visibility of this members-only club to the general public was minimal, but it featured on a number of rumor-monger sites and the availability of hermaphrodite prostitutes seemed to be an open secret among the hedonists who could afford its outrageous membership fees.

A red light was flashing just on the comm unit, indicating that any further details would require hacking into a highly protected server, with a significant risk of the intrusion being spotted.

"Well then, Watson, to crack or not to crack, that's the question. What do you think?"

Luckily I was given time to think by the arrival of our food. One swipe of my hand and the holo display vanished and I slipped the comm into my pocket.

I would have been happy to enjoy my lunch in silence, but that was not to be. "Come on now, time's a wasting. Which is it?"

"Hack their server!" I responded, showing my displeasure of this bullying by slamming the small unit back onto the table and concentrating on my hotdog while the pilfered information was summarized on the holo projection.

The Chief Inspector managed to eat her food one-handed while swiping her way through the PD database. There seemed to be a wide range of dubious, if not actually illegal, services available to the patrons of this establishment. On the surface it looked like a simple transvestite bar, but there seemed to a progression of increasing well hidden, and expensive, prostitutes available, that went through ladyboys to various surgically modified trans-sexuals and leading to a number of hermaphrodites at the top of the food chain. From the explicit depictions of the services available in each case, there seemed little to choose between some of the exotic surgical modifications and those claimed to be natural hermaphrodites, but the fees charged indicated an exponential increase in their attraction. To my great surprise, this single club had eight herms on offer.

Koide was methodically working up the list of increasingly expensive hostesses, peering at the holographic depictions of the provocatively-posed models, until she reached the top, causing me to choke on the last bite of my 'dog. "Yes! Miss Chrissy! Now we have a name, of sorts, and a work place to fit to our victim. Not bad for the time it took to drink a pint of Guinness." She raised her eyebrows as she wiped her fingers on a napkin. "Just what might we discover during a second one?"

I took the hint and wandered to the bar to order another Guinness, selecting a Traquair House Ale from the fridge for myself. When I returned, my boss glanced at my beer, but restricted herself to a grimace before she went back onto the attack.

"OK, we now have the *who*. We can fill in the details later, but there's enough now to let the data miners to do their stuff in the interim. So now the *why*. You're on again Watson."

I gulped the last of my chocolate stout and concentrated on pouring the ale to give myself time to get back onto track. "Well, the murder is so unusual that this might give us a way to start on that question." Once again I was refusing to let myself be rushed. "The victim was an exotic hooker working in premises in the immediate vicinity. The murder was certainly not a crime of passion; this looked more like a surgical procedure than anything else. It might be possible that the deed had been done in-situ and the place cleaned up afterwards, but I would guess our forensics would show this wasn't the case. The place was just too cramped. So she - or he, whatever you call it - was brought to the restaurant and left for us to find. Probably laid out would be a better term for it, as it almost looked like the body was placed for maximum impact on anybody seeing it."

"Maybe not wrong so far, but where was young Miss Chrissy actually sent to meet her maker?" CI Koide was tapping her fingers on the table top to hurry me along.

"Well, an operating theatre would be the easiest place to do something like that, if there was one in the vicinity." Immediately the holo showed another prioritized map, with a bright point located at the other side of Shinjuku station, in Nishi-Shinjuku.

The detective did not need to call up details for this one. "The University Medical Hospital. How would someone get access to an operating theatre there?" she mused, setting off the autonomous search machines to find an answer to her question.

"Apart from normal activities, there are two theatres reserved for demonstrations for some cosmetic surgical conference going on this week," I observed. "The shindig is based nearby, in the Hyatt."

"Which one?" The CI had her eyes closed and was evidently paying no attention to the output from our searches.

"The Regency."

"So, just across the road from the hospital. OK, get some plods with a forensic team over to have a look at those two theatres and check anyone who was supposed to be using them."

Koide twirled her thumbs, eyes still closed, while I followed her instructions. Then she continued, much slower than before. "There's something not kosher about all this. I've the spooky feeling of following a path that's been laid out for us. It all fits together too easily, too quickly. Cross-correlate conference surgeons with possible access to that operating theatre and membership of Pleasure Doubled... "

"This Japanese software is shit-hot," I noted as the output appeared almost instantaneously. "No direct match, but it spotted that a certain Professor Doctor Doctor Frick was a conference attendee who was brought into the club last night as a guest by a Tokyo University professor, who is a member."

"With all the titles, I'd guess this Frick guy is probably a Kraut. I'd also chance my arm by suggesting he left Dodge PDQ thereafter."

If I hadn't seen the amazing Koide in action before, I would have been simply gobsmacked by the match of her speculations with the data filling out the case file overview. Nevertheless, there was one minor slip, I was delighted to note.

"Yes, Prof etcetera Frick did indeed fly back to Munich this morning. However, not a guy: looks like a Frau Professor Doctor Doctor to me."

The CI finally opened her eyes to inspect the 3D image of the German surgeon that was rotating over the table between us. I had expected some sign of annoyance that her Sherlock performance had dropped below its normal level of perfection, but she merely smiled. "Tasty! I would have loved to be a fly on the ceiling to see what the dirty doctor got up to with the well-endowed Chrissy."

Somewhat surprised by this reaction, I waved my hands to expand the displayed image. Certainly not my type, but I could somehow see what my superior meant. The professor appeared to be in her late forties, but this could just as easily reflect expensive cosmetic surgery if the woman sampled her own wares. She looked the exact opposite of the female facing me: petite, raven haired, almost androgynous. If not for a certain aura palpable in this high-res image, one could almost call her elfin. But the woman radiated confidence that indicated a powerful, dominating personality. From that perspective, she was certainly much more similar to my boss. With the two of them in an S&M dungeon, who would be holding the whip?

My wool-gathering fantasies were rudely interrupted. "Stop drooling, Watson, she's not that tasty! Anyway, your task now is to list at least five reasons why we shouldn't get Interpol to pick up the pervy professor and charge her with murder."

The question was enough to set the web-crawlers off, so I had a bit of help ghosting up in front of me while I struggled to respond. "Well, the first problem would be motive. Why would a high-flying, rich surgeon kill a prostitute? If something did happen during their encounter in the club, why this gratuitous butchery? Given that the murder seems to have been carried out in such a complex manner, why move the body back to Kabuchi-cho, instead of getting rid of it elsewhere. Thinking about it, hospitals have incinerators, so that would be an obvious option. Even if transported back, why this formal presentation in a bloody soba house right next to the club?" I stopped and peered at the holo in desperation.

"That's four. What about the kicker that the meta-analysis is throwing up for you?"

"The motive-opportunity link?" I hazarded, then continued when no objection was raised. "The logistics for something like this would be tricky, to say the least. It appears that Frick has never visited Japan before and her contacts with the Japanese professor who took her to this establishment seem to be restricted to a week that they spent together in Berlin a couple of years ago." It was only as the information map filled out, I finally noted that the Japanese professor was also a woman - and one with a reputation, albeit well hidden, for indulging in the wild side of the sexual encounter spectrum.

"And so?"

"Unless Frick is part of a much larger operation, there's no way that she could have set up something like this. The entire show is some kind of diversion."

"Indeed! From a first look at the corpse, it was clear that this was a carefully planned caper. I suspect, however, that we weren't supposed to see through it - or, at least, not as quickly.

"And how do you come to that conclusion? How can you know that you're right?"

"I think the fact of two armed heavies heading in our direction has just answered that last question."

Chapter 2

Tokyo has, at least so far, weathered runaway global warming much better than other mega-cities. Nevertheless, the manpower needs for the massive engineering of coastal defense projects combined with an aging population led to huge influxes of foreign workers and some major social restructuring. Specific areas of the city were now set up as Special Administrative Regions, with infrastructure tailored to a multinational community - such as our police department. Although colloquially referred to as *gaijin ghettos*, these were islands of affluence and stability compared to the continually degrading situation in less developed or less well-organized nations.

Japan has always had a low rate of gun crime but, learning from the foreign civil unrest as populations gradually realized how political inactivity had caused the ongoing environmental catastrophe, the Japanese government acted quickly to reduce risks by introducing draconian laws to prevent any form of gun ownership. It had been a shock for me to realize that even the police were unarmed in the SARs and this must have been even more so for CI Koide, coming from the battlefield that is present day Sydney.

The term *heavy* well described the man now leading the way into the bar. He was about two meters tall and built like a bull; with a physique like a steroid-enhanced professional wrestler that was little concealed by the baggy grey tracksuit he was wearing. I absently noted a Nagoya Dragons baseball cap crammed onto long, greasy blond hair, but my attention was mainly focused on the heavy machine pistol in his right hand.

After the brightness of the street, the bar was dim and the gunman was taking his time to let his eyes adjust while he scanned the pub, apparently oblivious to the cries of shock from the two barmaids and a couple of customers up front, who were now diving for cover.

A little late, I started to struggle to pull the taser from its holster on my belt. Then all hell seemed to break loose: it sounded as if every alarm in every shop, bar and restaurant in the vicinity went off simultaneously. Although evidently a professional, the big hit-man was momentarily distracted by the cacophony and that was enough for the CI to taze him in the face, causing him to spasm backwards into his companion and slam him into the fridge door, which smashed in an explosion of glass and beer bottles.

I could now see that the second gunman was much smaller, but notably broad across the shoulders and clad in a matching baggy tracksuit and baseball cap. He was struggling to get his gun arm free when Koide screamed at me above the racket. "Fuck's sake, taze the bastard! On max and make sure you hit his face!"

I then realized that I was already pointing my taser in the right general direction, but it took a special effort to go against years of training and flick the voltage restraint off and deliberately aim at my victim's face. Nevertheless, as his gun began to swing in my direction, I fired as ordered.

His spastic reaction to the huge shock was enough to lift both the tangled bodies into the air and, despite the background noise, I heard a tortured scream before the man lapsed into unconsciousness.

Just then the alarms cut out, leaving my ears ringing but able to hear the cries and shouts of fright and confusion from both inside and outside the pub. I was also able to hear Koide using my comm to calmly order uniforms over from the neighboring crime scene and call external reinforcements to secure the area.

Responding to a vague wave of her hand, I took over organizing details with our desk sergeant, who would then liaise with Tokyo HQ as required. As soon as this was set up, I shoved the little comm projector into my pocket and followed the CI over to inspect our attackers, under the watchful eyes of two shocked-looking cops, who were now standing just inside the door with tasers at the ready.

It was almost a repeat of my view at the murder scene as Koide squatted down and bent to inspect our unconscious assailants. I tore my eyes away from temptation and concentrated on our attackers. The bigger man had been slightly turned as the barbs hit and had rather messy wounds around his ear and right eyebrow. The smaller guy had, however, come off much worse and one of the barbs had burst his right eyeball.

"Fuck!" I muttered. "Why did we have to shoot them in the face? This kind of damage is exactly... "

"Shut it, Watson, for fuck's sake!" The CI had sprayed a sealant over her hands and was now pulling open the Velcro seal of the larger thug's tracksuit. I could see what seemed to be a lurid Mickey Mouse T-shirt below.

"I guess they intended to just dump the suits after the hit," I observed.

"That's not what you're supposed to be looking at to find an answer to your original question." She peeled back the grey material, separating inner and outer layers while I squeezed beside her to look more closely, forcing myself to avoid a sneak peek down her cleavage.

"That looks like some kind of fine mesh, maybe taser-proofing?"

"Exactly, they're walking bloody Faraday Cages. A regulation shot to the torso would have done sweet fuck all, even at maximum voltage."

"Right, but how could you have possibly known that in advance?"

"We'll have a discussion about that later, but the key fact here is that these fuckers were set up to take out cops."

"OK, that explains the head shots, but why take the voltage limiters off? Those guys are going to be really fucked up."

"Dead fucking right! Their brains will be mush, if they ever come out of their comas. That's the message we're giving: anyone coming with guns against unarmed police officers isn't just going to get deported, they're going to suffer a fate worse than death."

"But we probably won't be able to interrogate them, so they can't give us any information about what this is all about."

"Oh, but they already have - a lot. We just need to tease it out, which will be easiest done in the cop shop. Remember, just about anywhere else in the world we'd have real guns, not these poofy tasers. From now on, keep the voltage limiter off. You'd also better program a panic button like I have - it worked well don't you think?"

I suddenly remembered the diversion that may well have saved our lives. "So that's what happened?"

"What did you think it was set off all the local alarms, a convenient act of God?" She confirmed smugly, then stood and stretched, making way for a couple of paramedics and a crime-scene technician who started to fuss around the bodies in the preliminaries for the usual turf war. Not our problem, I decided as I followed her out, making my way over broken glass and puddles of beer towards the door.

***

Another great thing about Tokyo, I mused as I settled into the chair opposite the CI, is that you can forget that most of the rest of the world was going to hell in a hand-basket. OK, diversion of resources has meant that technical progress since the first decades of the century has been a bit limited. But at least it is not slipping backwards, as is usually the case elsewhere.

I looked at Koide as she waved her hands into the hologram above her desk, mumbling instructions that caused strange morphing of the view presented. This was a summary of the case file, constantly updating as the crime-scene tech and forensic data were added. It was automatically structured in the form of a prosecution case so that, when we had identified and apprehended the murderer, together with anyone else playing a role, we could simply pass this on and let the lawyers do their thing. It was very high tech and formalized compared to what we had in the Met, but a typical Japanese response to widespread criticism of their police earlier in the century. Their suspiciously high success rate, most of which associated with confessions from the accused, seemed too good to be true. Of course, it was, because it wasn't, as proven by a number of high profile scandals.

"What are you daydreaming about, Watson?" The question woke me from my reverie and made me realize that my boss had stopped playing with the case summary and was now staring in my direction. "How the fuck am I ever going to train you up if you doze off instead of watching a master at work?"

"Master: is that correct?" I objected pedantically, trying to gain time so that I could check on her progress with sorting out the new information. "Shouldn't it, formally at least, be mistress?"

"In your dreams!" she smiled, a little ferally I thought. "Anyway, what's your take on this now?"

I leaned forward to check the exec sum. "Well, the heuristic analysis hasn't contributed much."

"And you expected it to? You think there'd be a pile of similar cases of hermaphrodites being butchered that would lead us directly to the perp?"

"Maybe not, but you usually get a much higher confidence level in the main case components. We've over ninety-five percent for identification of the victim, but there's little else that even goes into double figures."

Now the CI's smile had widened, almost to a grin. "Yes, indeed. Doesn't it make you feel lucky to be a detective, working in one of the few fields where you can't be simply replaced by a chunk of silicon?"

"Well, I'm not sure... " I started, before being stopped by a frown.

"A rhetorical question, you know what that is?"

"Yes, of course, it's... " The frown had turned to a glare.

"Also a rhetorical question! For fuck's sake Watson, pull yourself together! Anyway, your little diversion gave you some time to think about the executive summary output. What does this tell us?"

"That we don't have much of a case?" I ventured hesitantly.

"Christ, glass half empty Pommies! The low confidence in the autonomous synthesis, tells us a lot in itself. Doesn't it?"

I was obviously missing something that should have been staring me in the face. "The probability of the kinky German prof having a major role just scrapes above ten percent, so I guess we don't put Interpol onto her?"

"Watson! That's just the murder: have you forgotten what happened thereafter?"

"The two maniacs with the guns... " I flicked the holo to bring up details. "Well, it seems that they're US citizens and known mercenaries. Both have managed to stay out of jail so far, but lots of links implicating them for assaults and, possibly, assassinations. Freelance hit-men, I'd say."

Eyes raised to heaven indicated that my superior was praying for the patience to deal with incompetent underlings. "And, and... "

"Well, it was very strange that they attacked the pub just then... "

"The point at last: although, typically, you have it completely arse to tit! The timing was perfect and gives us both a better feel for what is going on and, even better, a way to prove that we are right. Of course you understand that, when I say we, I mean me," she added as unnecessary clarification.

I suffered her smug grin as long as I could before conceding. "OK, great detective, pass on your knowledge to this, your most unworthy of serfs."

"First thing you've uttered that's sensible," she responded with a satisfied smile. "Do you remember what I said just before our lunchtime beers were so rudely interrupted?"

My frantic search through the auto-stored audio files on my comm unit answered that question. A side panel on the holo showed the low res record of the blonde detective as she stated, "... it was clear that this was a carefully planned caper. I suspect, however, that we weren't supposed to see through it - or, at least, not as quickly."

A light seemed to dawn, finally. "So, this thing has something to do with a diversion; it's all much more complex than it seems. The attack on the pub was directed at us, as a response to the progress that we were making." I stopped for a moment as the obvious inconsistency hit me. "Which is very difficult to explain, as we had just come to that conclusion."

"I had just led you by the nose along the trail leading to that conclusion, yes indeed. So this inopportune diversion means what?"

"That the tacky pub must have been bugged in some way and the heavies had been on standby the entire time! Not only was the murder set up to lead us in a specific direction, advanced preparations had been made for the case that we diverted from this course. Shit, this would have required a huge amount of preparation. How could anyone have known that we would go to that place for lunch?"

"They couldn't possibly have, so this means that... ?

"The body was placed to be found just before lunch. Not much effort required to bug all potential eating houses in the vicinity, if they had considered a chance that we'd talk over progress there." I stopped, but a raised eyebrow indicated that more was expected. "Maybe even the chance of us going for something to eat wouldn't be difficult to predict, if it was realized that you'd be the detective in charge."

"Indeed! If I had been planning something as complicated as this, I would certainly check who does what at the cop shop and what their typical behavior would be. It wouldn't take a lot of effort and would be well worth it, if the reputation of the extremely clever CI Koide had gone before her."

"Extremely clever but not very modest," I muttered under my breath.

"Modesty is for those with nothing to boast about," the CI smirked in my direction. "Anyway, this caper clearly has wheels within wheels. So how about picking up the evidence that we're going in the right direction?"

I was momentarily nonplussed, but then remembered what had led to the explanation of the attack in the bar. "The bugs! In the place we had lunch and scattered around."

"Very easy to hide, but not difficult to find if you know that they're there in the first place. It's possible that our opponent might have something set up to recover them if needed, but we still have our bar closed off. Have the plods do a quick check and, for further confirmation, also look in another few nearby eateries. In fact, just for the sake of completeness, run a few joints that don't open for lunch: you shouldn't find anything there."

This rapid change in direction had diverted me from the main murder case summary, but nothing significant would get past Stella's eagle eyes. "Mmm.., well that's a *where* nailed down. I guess we were expected to find that, but not nearly as quickly."

It was the report from the team at the University Hospital. Both of the operating theatres examined had been comprehensively cleaned and video logs erased, but there were enough traces on an air ventilation filter for a DNA scan to show that one of these was the probable location where our Chrissy had been carved up.

"So we know where the murder took place... "

"Not so fast! This is very probably where the organs were removed, but we still don't know if that was where Miss Chrissy actually met her maker. So let's get the search machines going... "

While she spoke, her specified actions appeared on a side window of the case file as an itemized list:

1. How, when and by whom was the operating theatre accessed and how did they manage to clean up so well afterwards?

2. Is there clear evidence where Crissy was killed and what was actually responsible for death?

3. When was Chrissy last in action in the club and how did she get from there to the hospital?

4. How did the body get from the hospital to the Kabuki-cho noodle shop?

5. What happened to the missing organs - and why would anyone want to take them in the first place?

6. Is there any way of finding out who planted the bugs and where this might lead?

7. How do they know about how things are run in our Shinjuku cop shop and are there any indications of an insider being involved?

8. What is the role, if any, of the German and Japanese professors who have a kink for hermaphrodites?

9. Why might we be getting pushed in the direction of this PD club: has its clientele or their sex choices any link here?

"Well," I commented, "that seems fairly comprehensive."

"Yes, it's the stuff that smart software can start sniffing out. Lucky that we are here to carry out the more difficult part: determine who dunnit, why and what's behind this Machiavellian complexity."

"And just where do we start?"

"The morgue seems as good a place as any. Let's look in there before Doc Nakayama has finished carving and see what gems forensic pathology has for us. If nothing else, it will keep you busy for a few hours until the main action commences."

"A few hours? What's going to happen early this evening?"

"A certain dubious club will open and we will then hire ourselves a hermaphrodite."

"You have got to be joking!" I gasped. However, from the gleam in the CI's eye, I was dead certain that she wasn't.

***

The police morgue serving our SAR was located in Shibuya, which we could drive to in about twenty minutes or easily reach in about the same time using the JR Yamanote line. CI Koide had other ideas, however. Our division was based in the old police station in Nishi-Shinjuku, just at the edge of the skyscraper district and it was only 5 minutes' walk to the University medical hospital. We strolled past it while the tall blonde set out her plans for the rest of the day.

"We are now in the process of killing a number of birds with one stone," she started off in a thoughtful manner - as if there were so many birds were lined up that she had to count through them. "Clearly we get a look at the body, which I think will be instructive, especially as I have our good Doctor Nakayama running the most detailed internal and external multi-spectral 3D scans that he can manage."

I said nothing, but clearly my confused look was spotted. "Maybe as importantly, this gives us some exercise in the fresh air, which might speed-up the mechanical relays they obviously installed in your cranium in place of neurons."

"Fresh air," I muttered under my breath, "some chance of that in Tokyo!"

Koide pretended not to hear me as she stomped confidently into the Hilton, ignoring the Hyatt Regency opposite, which sported a large banner advertising the *25th Pan-pacific symposium on reconstructive and cosmetic surgery* - an event that evidently ran until the end of the week. "Further, we get a chance to check my suspicions on who the mole in the copshop might be and test just how far our opponents would be prepared to go to stop us."

"Would this have something to do with me wearing this bloody protective vest?" I enquired, feeling my suspicions crystallize.

"Mmm... , yes, could have. I let the three prime candidates have different details of my proposed walking route, so we can see if anything happens at any of these points."

"So you have a team shadowing us?"

"Why would I do that? Fuck, Watson, this bloody place is like Disneyland compared to Sydney. How about afternoon tea?"

Within the lobby of the Hilton, the Marble Lounge sported a large banner advertising a Teatime Viking. Spotting my confused look, Koide explained. "Viking is just Jenglish for a buffet - so it's tea and coffee and as much cake as you can manage."

"So that explains why the clientele is predominantly groups of Japanese women," I observed. "Although I don't know where these little ladies put it all - have you seen the loaded plates that they're bringing back from the buffet?"

"Lots of healthy carbs - just needs a high metabolic rate to burn it all off," she responded while a waiter led us to a table at the far side of the busy lounge within the atrium of the hotel. She did not even bother looking at the proffered menu, being clearly well at home here. "It's fixed price for buffet and tea or coffee - but extra for beer or champagne."

"Just a black coffee for me. I'll skip the buffet."

My boss looked at me as if I had farted out loud. "What the fuck? You're skinny as a rake and need some bulking up. Some carbs now, then a serious work out in the gym. So what size of beer do you want?"

"I don't want any... "

With a dismissive wave in my direction, the CI turned to the waiter. "Two buffets with black coffee, a King's cup for me and a Queen's cup for my nonce underling."

"But I don't... "

"Just sit on your arse, have a guess who the mole is back in the copshop and wait while I have a quick mooch around the buffet."

As the towering blonde joined the gaggle of diminutive Japanese women swarming around the piled displays of confectionary masterpieces, I waved over our waiter and got my beer cancelled and the coffee replaced by a triple espresso. I knew I was asking for trouble, but I felt that, at some point, I needed to stand up for myself - and it was definitely easier when my overpowering boss was not actually present.

Koide returned with two plates piled high with cakes and biscuits, which seemed to focus mainly on the themes of strawberries, caramel and chocolate. Lots of chocolate. One of these was unceremoniously plonked in front of me. "Go on lad, get that down your neck!"

"You have got to be joking," I groaned. "I'd be dead of a heart attack if I consumed even half of that sweet shit."

"Worry you not, just keep going until you're about to peg out. Then I'll finish the rest for you."

She had just started on a small pile of chocolate-dipped strawberries when our drinks arrived. I held my breath as the single beer was first place in front of me - then moved to its correct position after a theatrical cough and a severe glare in the direction of the waiter.

I was surprised by the grin I received after my espresso was served. "Well, Watson, maybe you've dropped a bollock. I wondered when you'd have the guts to stand up to me." She obviously spotted my relief as she added, "... of course, this applies only to non-work stuff. For the rest, just do exactly as you're told."

I sipped my coffee, noting that the shaking of my hand died away as the realization dawned that I had made a first step in establishing myself in this rather weird job. I treated myself to a large profiterole - realizing halfway through why I avoided such sickly deserts. Anyway, I had also made a gesture here: another grin from my boss as she annexed my plate and proceeded to polish off the lot.

As she paid the bill, Koide checked her watch and smiled. "Just right on the time plan. Our mysterious opponents should have had enough time to get set up by now."

We left the hotel and set off in the direction of the Tokyo Metropolitan Government buildings. "Set up for what?" I mused aloud, looking at the bustling streets around us.

"Well, there are two obvious approaches after the first attempt to stop us failed - either up the odds against us in a direct attack or try another way to divert us from the track we're now taking in this investigation."

"So, with a bit of luck, someone will show up with a pile of high denomination Yen and suggest that we back off a little."

"Possible, but I'd actually bet on the other option. What do you think, Watson? We fucked-up two brutes with guns - what can we expect now?"

I rolled my eyes theatrically, which was lost on the CI as she stared in admiration at the TMB Number One skyscraper, its upper floors touching some low-lying cloud, somehow making it look even more like something out of Fritz Lang's Metropolis than it usually does.

"What about a sniper? That's what I'd use if I wanted to stop someone."

The woman smiled enigmatically. "You'd think so, wouldn't you? But if just stopping us was the concern, a sniper could've been used in Kabuki-cho. No, there's a lot of theatre involved here. I'd guess it'd be heavies again - just a few more of them this time."

"And you're betting your life on this?"

"Actually betting your life on it also, Watson," she pointed out with a cheery grin. "But it's nothing that we didn't handle on a daily basis in Oz."

"OK, but in Sydney you had bloody heavy-duty firepower."

My boss smiled at me in a distinctly smug manner. "Let's just see how it goes. Anyway, we'll leave the SAR here and cut through Chuo park," she announced, leading the way towards an automatic transfer gate through the fence that surrounded the international Shinjuku zone.

The gate cycled us through together, the multispectral biometric scan identifying us as police officers with open transit permits. We turned right, avoiding the TMG building entrance and followed a path across a bridge and into the small park. Despite the fact that it must have been about twenty centigrade, I felt a shiver down my spine when I noted that Koide's posture had altered in a subtle manner, her head held slightly downwards as if she was inspecting the ground in front of her feet. It may have been involuntary, but I remember having been trained to increase my peripheral vision in this manner when defending against multiple attackers in the dojo.

The small park was quite busy, the usual homeless encampments of blue plastic sheeting below the trees and the paths scattered with young mums, courting couples, perambulating pensioners, dogs and staggering toddlers. It was an uneventful transit, made in silence - a feature that, more than anything else, made me very aware that this was more than a normal walk.

As we exited the south side of the park, my boss continued as if there had been no hiatus in our conversation. "Yes, it's a bit trickier to stage something outside the SAR, especially on short notice. Anyway, that's probably young Takahashi-san off the potential mole list."

"Takahashi? Isn't that the young guy who was transferred to us last week?"

"Indeed it is. I didn't actually request him and assumed that he was the usual case of somebody being assigned to us for failing to fit into the real Tokyo police force. However, he seems a bit brighter than the average Tokyo cop, so could be a plant."

"So how did you test him?"

"Simply asked him the best route through Chuo park if I was heading for Shibuya."

"Right - so now I know why we're taking this bloody walk! Why didn't you just tell me in the first place?"

"What and spoil your afternoon tea, what kind of horrible boss do you think I am?" A feigned look of shock transmogrified into an uncharacteristic titter as she added, "I also can´t miss a chance to wind you up a bit! You're such a fucking pussy!"

I glowered at her and sank into brooding silence, which was completely ignored by my companion as she chatted away with an endless stream of trivia about the area of Yoyogi that we were now walking through. After passing the Tokyo riding club, set incongruously with a view onto the rather hideous DoCoMo building, I noticed again the change in the CI's posture and my sulk vanished instantly.

"Who was it this time?" I inquired, recognizing that we were checking on another of our potential moles.

"Little Shoko, the communications tech."

"Shoko Kita-something, looks about twelve years old?"

"Yes, Shoko Kitayama. She's thirty five and has two kids."

"You're joking! I thought she was probably straight out of the Academy."

"Thirteen years on the force, with eight of those vice in Shinjuku."

"Shoko in vice, that I can't believe. Anyway, if that was the case, how'd she end up a comm tech."

"Usual move to a desk after maternity leave, I'd guess. In any case, she had lots of opportunity to get to know the type of folk who seem to be behind this caper."

We had now entered the grounds of the Maiji shrine and were crunching our way along a wide gravel pathway towards the Imperial Treasure Museum. I spotted a group of young men ahead wearing black hakemas and white judo kit and realized where we were. "Isn't this where the Aikido headquarters are? I did a bit of that at uni and thought it would be nice to get back into it now that I'm in Tokyo."

"Yes, the Aikido dojo is just over there," a wave of her hand indicated somewhere off to our left, "but I don't think that's where these guys are going."

"Why's that?"

"They seem to be carrying swords... "

"Well, that's quite possible: there was lots of practice with bokken, wooden swords, when I was doing my Aikido."

"Those don't look wooden - and that mob certainly seem to be heading in our direction." This observation was confirmed by the flashes of steel as

41

blades were withdrawn and scabbards tossed casually aside.

"There's eight of them, so a couple of tasers aren't going to get us out of this!" I was looking around anxiously, checking escape options. I had spotted that our opponents were all wearing zoris, traditional sandals, so I reckoned I'd have a good chance of outrunning them.

"Yup, eight. They also look like they know what they're up to with those swords." Despite the seriousness of our situation, the woman sounded calm as she slipped on a thin pair of black gloves. "You've got those earpieces in, I assume?"

"Yes, you gave me them at the same time as this bloody flak jacket, though I don't see how either is going to help against a katana. An Uzi would be more like what I could use at the present moment."

"Well let's just see if we can make do with what we've got." There was a wicked gleam in her eyes as she pulled out the two small bars that telescoped into tonfa side-handle batons.

As she moved directly towards the approaching group she called out. "Police officers! Do not come closer or we will use force against you!" This was followed by a burst of Japanese which I guessed conveyed the same message, causing an eruption of laughter from the young men.

I sneaked a glance at my chosen escape route and then, with a sigh of resignation, drew my own batons.

"Right, Watson, hit really hard and go for soft bits," my boss hissed over her shoulder, before charging directly at the swordsman.

My initial surprise transformed to shock as the feeling of being slapped on both ears was followed by complete silence: I had gone stone deaf. Simultaneously, two of our attackers dropped to the ground as if poleaxed and the others staggered about, cramming their hands to the side of their heads.

Seconds later, the mighty detective was in their midst, lashing out savagely in all directions. By the time I had recovered sufficiently to follow her, the apparent leader of the hit squad was collapsing from a blow to the groin, a very tall man to his left flying backwards as his nose exploded in a plume of blood and a stocky youth to his right gasping for breath after a baton was driven into his solar plexus.

I started to shout a warning as one of the remaining attackers swung his sword wildly at Koide's neck, but she blocked this easily with her right baton and swung the left to smash into the side of his head. Now I was close enough to notice a spark as the truncheon made contact and catch a whiff of burning flesh.

I lost track of the action for a moment as one of the prone forms in front of me made an attempt to grab my leg. I dropped onto his stomach with both knees and my baton walloped his forehead, resulting in a squelch that seemed to indicate a seriously fractured skull. The other assailant who had been dropped by whatever it was that the CI had done lay nearby, so I smashed him over the head also, just in case he wasn't as unconscious as he looked.

By the time I got to my feet, the Valkyrie was speaking into her comm, evidently calling up a pick-up detail. Or, maybe, some ambulances, considering the amount of gore on the grass and the lack of movement of the bodies strewn about on it. I was relieved to see that, at least, she seemed a little breathless. So not completely superhuman.

"OK, now we're cooking with gas!" she grinned. "There are at least a couple of these young chaps who'll survive after a bit of patching and be fit for interrogation when we get back to the nick. We also have little Shoko getting prepped as we speak. We could continue our little perambulation through Yoyogi park, but there's probably little point as I don't suppose we have two in-house rats. What do you think, want to give it a try anyway?"

I pretended to ponder on this question. "Um, as we have a lot to do and you're a bit blood-spattered at the moment, maybe we should pass on this."

"Okey dokey," she smiled agreeably, seemingly more relaxed now after this bit of mayhem. "I can hear the cop cars, so we can get a lift over to Shibuya."

***

Our button cams downloaded automatically as soon as the police vehicles came in range, as Maiji Jingu was one of the few places in Tokyo without ubiquitous wifi broadband coverage. This complemented the brief reports that we had already made to the local Tokyo commander and so we were already underway before all bodies had been loaded into ambulances for transport to a secure hospital or, in three cases, directly to the police morgue.

In the back of the police cruiser which, despite flashing lights, crawled only slowly towards Shibuya, I finally had a chance to quiz my superior while she cleaned up with a box of wipes provided by our driver.

"So, just what happened there? You couldn't have done the alarm thing again, so what did you hit those guys with?"

This question was greeted by a theatrical roll of her deep blue eyes. "How did I prep you for this?"

As I thought on the question, I was aware of a residual buzz in my ears and pried out the ear buds. "These I suppose. Ear protectors?"

"Military spec anti-noise. Used for anti-terrorist actions together with... "

"Sonic bursters! So, a more sophisticated version of the same trick you pulled in Kabuki-cho!"

"Well, yes, but this needs a bit more preparation. You'd also have been flat on your back if not for those ear buds."

"But this is military spec, though. How'd you get a hold of that?"

Her grin would have made a Cheshire cat jealous. "You know that I was specially recruited for this job... " She waited for my nod before continuing, "... and you know that I agreed to stick to the prohibition of use of firearms." Again she waited for my nod. "Didn't it occur to you that I might have added a few conditions in that case?"

My look of bafflement was clearly sufficient answer. "Well I did get a few special clearances for use of what they term *non-lethal* weapons. Of course, this stuff can be as lethal as you want it to be, if used properly. You never know, with a bit of luck you may get a chance to play with some of the others."

I sincerely hoped that she was, for once, wrong on this.

Chapter 3

The morgue was in a sub-basement close to Shibuya JR station - apparently part of one of the tunnels constructed for a Tokyo Metro extension before funding for such pork barrel projects dried up in the forties. Access involved a long drive down a tunnel starting somewhere around Omote Sando and passing by a host of side drifts, which were generally guarded by police or military personnel.

"Mainly disaster management stuff," commented CI Koide, stating that which I already knew. She did however read out the names of the different organizations as we passed, "Tsunami warning and recovery, volcanic eruption prediction and impact minimization, nuclear incident rapid response, pandemic monitoring and control,... " The list went on and on.

"They certainly seem well prepared for just about any natural disaster," I observed.

"You'd think so - but have you spotted what's missing?"

"It can't be something major: they've even got meteorites and extra-terrestrial hazards covered. Invasion by aliens?" I guessed.

"I think that's actually included as an extra-terrestrial hazard," my boss laughed. "No, it's integrated hazard management. Even after the many catastrophes that have hit this country since the beginning of the century, they still focus on specialists and have very few generalists."

"Don't tell me that you're also an expert in natural hazards," I groaned.

"Not an expert in anything, a generalist. All good detectives know a little about most things, which provides the overview that you need to see the links needed to solve a tricky case. The Japanese have all the high-tech supporting specialists they could possibly need, but not the generalists who are the really great investigators."

"Well, just lucky that they have you," I responded sarcastically.

"Yes, indeed; lucky little buggers that they are," my sarcasm like water off a duck's back. "Anyway, you have a chance to see what I mean now: we're now approaching the realm of the extremely bright but totally unimaginative Nakayama-sensei."

***

Morgues and dead bodies don't particularly bother me - it's more the casual behavior of pathologists when they dissect corpses with power tools and carve out choice bits for subsequent analysis. In this case, however, most of the dissection had already been done for us by the murderer and a lot of the interesting bits were already gone. The remains of Chrissy were displayed on a slab in the center of what looked like a cross between a state-of-the-art operating theatre and an industrial robotics laboratory.

Nakayama-sensei had obtained his PhD from Stanford and his English was flawless - at least from a west-coast US perspective. "Ah, the redoubtable Chief Inspector Koide and her sidekick Watson! Good to see you guys. You certainly get all the interesting murders in Shinjuku. All I usually get elsewhere are old guys with knifes in their backs and the wife's prints all over it - or vice versa. This really is a nice change."

I tried to avoid grimacing at anyone who could call the gutted hermaphrodite a nice anything, but it probably would have made no difference anyway, as the dapper Japanese in the white gown clearly had eyes for the CI only.

"Good to see you, Hiro," my boss replied. She was the only person I had encountered in the department who addressed the pathologist, who was also a professor at nearby Ookayama University, in such a casual manner. "So what do you make of this? It's all a bit Ripperesque."

I was momentarily confused by the last statement, but Nakayama was unfazed. "Yes, indeed, surgical precision involved and removal of inner organs. A bit neater than would have been the case with the tools available in old London, but definitely the work of someone medically trained."

"You think so? What about someone with access to an advanced surgical expert system?"

The professor seemed initially taken aback by this question, but recovered quickly. He peered quickly into the open chest of the corpse and then, with a flurry of hand gestures, called up a 3D scan of the cavity within, which appeared to rotate in the space above it. More waving of hands and various sections zoomed in to micron-scale resolution for an instant of inspection, then vanished.

This process continued in silence for almost five minutes, before the doctor waved the display away with an audible sigh. "OK, Stella, how could you have possibly known that? On first inspection it just looks like the job of a very good surgeon but, if you know the signatures of current ES packages, it's unambiguous. The job is one hundred percent pre-programmed."

"But you'd need both top-level software and hardware for this, wouldn't you? The kind of stuff you'd find at the University Hospital in Shinjuku?"

"Yes, of course. The uni hospital would be just the place. But how did you know in advance that it wasn't a surgeon?"

"Because someone went to some effort to set up a surgeon as a fall guy - or actually fall gal in this instance. In fact, this entire case is such a mess of wheels within wheels, smoke and mirrors, that it's difficult to distinguish the clues that we were supposed to find from the ones that we weren't. Anyway, was there anything else from the full body scans?"

The pathologist conjured up a blurry, eye-watering image of the entire body. "This is the raw compilation of the multi-spectral scans. What do you want to do with it? It's the usual mess of redundant information that you get from throwing the entire toolkit at the problem."

"Well, let's start with the missing organs; could you put up the internal vis scan for a start?" The image transformed immediately. "So, this is the starting point. What did the organs look like when they were in place?"

"Ah, so we need to use the external scans to determine the amount of contraction post excision and then compensate for that. Check the network of blood carriers - put those in and also main nerves. Now also associated plumbing. Interesting in this case as the database on intersex cases is a bit sparse... " The pathologist was clearly talking to himself as the image gradually transmogrified, acquiring resolution and overlays of different structural components.

After ten minutes the process was complete and the final structure rotated slowly in front of us. "Hot Damn! Now where did they come from?"

My bafflement did not extend to my companion. "Two full sets of operational wedding tackle, you don't see that often."

"You don't see that at all," the Japanese corrected my usually infallible boss. "However, as far as functionality is concerned, from a hormonal point of view that wouldn´t be on the cards. Nevertheless, we clearly have not only the usual penis and internal testicles, but also a womb and fully developed ovaries."

"So that isn't normal?" I asked, causing Nakayama to start, indicating that he had completely forgotten my presence.

"Not only not normal, but fully developed ovaries are unique as far as I am aware, my dear Watson. Or would be unique, anyway, if we are looking at a fully functional human hermaphrodite, with no traces at all of chimerism."

"No sign of surgical intervention?" my boss interrupted the lesson in intersex biology.

"Not possible to say with complete confidence, as we are looking only at a computer simulation of

51

the missing material, but looks unlikely to me. Nevertheless, this seems also very unlikely to be natural, so I'd guess gene engineered."

"What about blood work, hormone profiles?"

More arm waving and the missing organs were replaced by a complex assortment of 3D graphics. The analytical software had already highlighted and identified a number of anomalies. "Well, chemistry is consistent with the initial crime scene estimate of time of death late last night: about midnight or slightly later. Recent consumption of alcohol, probably champagne, just before that. Also recent use of a couple of top-end recreational stimulants. Even for a trans-sex, hormones are all over the place. Under normal circumstances, I would guess that supplements were being taken to maintain or enhance secondary sexual characteristics."

"And, under abnormal circumstances?"

The normally confident professor hesitated, clearly unwilling to take the step he was being forced towards. "Well, given the extraordinary physiology of this person, the hormonal signature could indicate that she was pregnant."

This bombshell seemed to go beyond whatever Koide-san had been postulating. "Interesting. I wonder if this was something that we were expected to find out or not?"

There seemed to be no answer to that very good question.

***

Thirty minutes later we were in a SAR patrol car, heading back in the direction of Nishi Shinjuku. Before I could ask, the CI explained, "I knew that if anyone went for the bait, we would be attacked on the way here. No reason why we can't travel back to the nick in the comfort of a jam sandwich." The driver, who had clearly been listening to the famed CI, turned with a look of bafflement on his face, causing her to grin and thicken her accent, more South England sitcom now than anything from East Oz.

Anyway, I want to have a chance to chat to both Shoko and a couple of our attackers before we head out for our evening of sybaritic pleasure."

I wasn't keen about the last bit, but certainly wanted to know more about whoever was behind all this mind-fuck activity. "Do you think Shoko will actually know something?"

"I'd say a lot more likely than the youths who had a go at us in Yoyogi. I'd guess they're just a yakuza hit team, typical rent-a-thugs."

"But why swords, wouldn't firearms be a more sensible option?"

"With the odds that they had in their favor, pointy sticks would have been sufficient if we hadn't been properly prepared for an attack. In fact, for such close-up work, swords are probably a lot more effective, with less risk of collateral damage."

"Collateral damage? That didn't seem to be a concern when they went after us in Kabuki-cho."

"Exactly: in the SAR they didn't give a shit. But maybe our nemesis doesn't want to cause too much of a ruckus outside in Greater Tokyo. Had we been taken out by a squad of nutters wielding katanas, the local plods would automatically assume yakuza and all efforts would go in that direction. Firearms in a shrine would be something totally different, they'd be forced to think a bit outside the box."

"You don't think they were yakuza?" I asked.

My boss gave a typically smug smirk. "I'm pretty sure they were. Yamaguchi-gumi from the tattoos I spotted on a couple of them. The Daimon is quite characteristic."

"So this is all some organized crime thing?"

"Certainly not under Yamaguchi lead; this is far too gratuitously complex for that mob. I'd guess they were contracted only for the hit on us. Probably provided with no background at all on us, which made them so easy to take down."

I vividly remembered the shock of fear that had flooded me when I realized that the swordsmen were about to attack and felt that our survival owed a lot to luck rather than an easy target being presented. Nevertheless, there was no way in which I was going to admit this to my overpowering boss.

"Anyway," the overpowering boss continued, "I don't expect much from the hired muscle. Young Shoko may be a different kettle of fish, however. She must have been a resource in place before the murder occurred, so could know a lot more."

"Maybe we could put a trace on her and see where that leads?" I suggested.

"That would give us a lead only to the girl's body: I wouldn't give five Yen for her chances of surviving ten minutes outside the cop shop. So she's currently in high security protective custody."

"Maybe even that isn't going to be enough. If the mastermind behind all this could put one mole in our organization, he could well have two or more."

"You're not totally thick, Watson." A pleased smile took the bite from her words. "You're finally beginning to pick up at least a little of the paranoid nature that you need in this game. This had also occurred to me and so I've had little Shoko moved to a safe house that's usually used for cyber-crime witness protection. This was handled personally by the SAR police commander and the cyber-crime minders, who have no idea what this is all about."

"Well, that goes beyond even my paranoia," I noted with a feeling of relief for not screwing up this time. "How did you manage to get our political clothes-horse of a commander to do something useful for a change?"

"Not a respectful way to talk about your boss's boss," I was rebuked, "no matter how perceptive the observation may be. Anyway, she owes me a couple of favors and, in any case, she would also go a long way to avoid anything nasty happening during her watch."

"OK, that's us here now," she pointed out as we drew up in front of a small apartment block, which I guessed must be situated just about on the border between Yoyogi and Shinjuku wards.

We passed through a narrow alleyway leading to the door of a ground floor apartment and I rang the doorbell while Koide faced directly towards the camera, which was obvious just above the post box to the left of the door. With a click, the door unlocked and I followed in her wake as my superior stormed through the minute hallway and into the small, sparsely furnished sitting room. As I had expected, the diminutive communications tech was sitting alone on the single sofa, facing a barrage of tiny cameras and scanners mounted on thin stalks. She looked very neat in a dark blue trouser suit, with her shiny black hair caught up into a tight bun. The minders would be in the next flat, monitoring every move that she made and ready to intervene if anything untoward happened during our interrogation.

"Good afternoon, Kitayama-san. How are you doing today?"

Rather than relaxing the little woman, this polite enquiry seemed to make her even more uncomfortable.

"You know that we have given you a suggestion enhancer and the monitors here will detect immediately if you are anything less than fully truthful to me."

The tech nodded mutely and the CI continued. "You've been passing on information on our activities to a third party, haven't you. Most recently, indeed, you let your contact know details of the route I was taking for my walk to the morgue."

The young woman looked completely terrified now, but managed only a slight nod in answer to the question. Sweat was beading her brow and her eyes were like saucers.

"Your husband was also a policeman - in vice - but he left a few years back to become a security consultant, didn't he?"

I wasn't sure where this line of questioning was going, but I had seen Koide quickly scan through Kitayama-san's file during our short drive and guessed she had picked up something there.

"So the first question is whether it is just your husband that you are leaking information to, or is someone else involved?"

The small Japanese woman started to sob, making me feel sorry for her, despite the fact that she was probably responsible in some way for both attacks against us. "Only my husband." The whispered response was barely audible, but was enough to elicit a satisfied smile from her interrogator.

"I suspected that this might be the case. Now you need to tell me a bit more about what's going on."

"I don't know, I really don't."

"Well I don't need to look at the monitors to see that you're not telling me the complete truth. You're an experienced cop and smart to boot. So even if you don't know everything, you've got some ideas or suspicions."

"I don't know anything, can't say anything." Although still whispered, there was now an evident air of panic about this response.

"We can extract all knowledge you have, one way or another - but maybe it would be quicker just to put out an open call for the arrest of your husband on suspicion of involvement in both of today's incidents."

"No, you can't do that!" The shrill cry was accompanied by a distinctive, acrid smell and I realized with embarrassment that the woman had wet herself.

My discomfort was not reflected by my boss, as she continued relentlessly. "You know very well that the people involved in this case play hardball. If word gets about that your involvement is known, I doubt that we could pick up your husband before they got to him. Isn't that the case?"

"They'd go for the kids... "

"... and probably also your parents, who look after them during the week." The CI was flicking through holographic comms images while she continued upping the pressure. "So, you see how important it is that tell us everything - and do it immediately. There's only a small window of time before someone spots that you aren't where you're expected to be and draws the obvious conclusion from that."

Kitayama-san was clearly completely broken. "You've got to get them into protection, but avoid using anyone from Nishi-Shinjuku," she begged.

"So there's a second mole in our office, then. Do you know who it is?"

"I don't... " she started, but stopped in response to a glare from the CI. "I think it's maybe Detective Miyahara."

The tall blonde snapped her fingers. "Shit! So, if we had continued through Yoyogi park, we would have had a second welcome awaiting us. Maybe just as well we didn't, though, as those acoustic bursters are single shot devices and I only had the one to hand. Anyway, back to the key issue: whoever it is behind all of this."

"But you've got to get my family into protection first! Please, please, Chief Koide-san!"

"Not the way things work, Shoko. First everything you know about whoever is running the spies in our nick."

"Anony-maus," she whispered.

"Anonymous? You've got to do better than that! Remember we don't have much time to save your kids."

"No, it's his name," she cried, spelling it out, including the hyphen. "He always contacts us by video-messaging, using an anime avatar. It's like a mouse with a kind of mask on."

"Would this mask happen to be a white, smiling face with a thin beard and moustache?" I asked, causing Kitayama-san to start as if she spotted my presence for the first time.

"Yes, I suppose so. I think I have seen it before somewhere, but I don't know where."

Koide was looking at me quizzically. "Would you care to enlighten me on this?"

"Often called Vendetta masks, after an original comic book. Widely used in protest movements around the turn of the century and also by a hacker collective that was called Anonymous."

"Ah, yes, I remember now. Very well done, Watson. And you have this information immediately to hand because... ?"

"English lit project at the uni," I confessed.

"Should have guessed that," she groaned, theatrically.

"But my family, you've got to do something now, quickly!" Little Shoko was completely distraught, shaking with fear.

Finally my boss took pity on the young woman. "It's OK, Shoko, I had them picked up already by the same crowd that are looking after you now."

As Kitayama slumped in her seat, her tears turning to sobs of relief, Koide continued. "You're in a bad position, that's clear, but if you and your husband quickly tell us absolutely everything you know, I'll do what I can to minimize the consequences." She now addressed herself into space, talking to the hidden watchers. "OK, get this girl cleaned up, with fresh underwear and trousers. We'll do the rest of the questioning remotely."

With a pleased smile, the CI turned to me. "Right, now we're getting somewhere. Have Miyahara lifted and the same procedure as here with his family. You set up the interrogation and I'll do the same for the least battered of the yakuza hit-men. We can do it while we drive to the cop shop."

Even with a SAR control point and Shinjuku traffic that would take only 10 minutes, so I was already working on my comm unit as we left the room.

Chapter 4

My interrogation of Detective Miyahara yielded nothing new: just another link to Anony-maus and some indications that the aged detective had been on the take for some time. We would undoubtedly get the entire story from him later, but I would bet it was linked to his divorce nine years previously, when he was also part of the same Shinjuku vice division as Shoko and her husband.

It was six pm when I was summoned to the CI's office for a status review. The holographic case argumentation model was rotating slowly above her desk and clearly the focus of her attention as she silently waved me to the seat facing her.

"You've seen the stuff from the yakuza?" she mumbled in my direction, not looking at me.

"Yes, nothing much apart from a bit of gratuitous police violence."

This caused her lips to curl in the faintest trace of a smile. "You think anyone'd give a shit about what happens to a bunch of yakuza thugs who attempt to murder a couple of cops in a shrine? I was just softening them up prior to handing them over to the Tokyo cops; then they'll really find out what a beating means."

"But it didn't give us anything we didn't already know."

"Just one or two little nuggets. For example, the leader of this team recognized the name Anony-maus."

"You could have picked that up easily from the monitors. You didn't need to keep hitting him in the groin. My God, after you walloped him in the goolies this afternoon, one of his testicles was already the size of a bloody grapefruit!" My eyes watered at the very thought.

"Of course, but it's good to keep your hand in. You never know when you might need some critical information and you don't have a lot of high tech equipment to hand. Anyway, that wasn't all that I picked up."

I flicked through the relevant area of the hologram to check what I might have missed. As the links from our attack in Maiji Jingu expanded, I picked up a thread that exploded like axon terminals as it connected to the Nishi-Shinjuku knowledge base. "What's this, an ambulance?"

"Looks just like a private ambulance, of the type that rich bastards use, but this is what was used to transport the yakuza team from Ginza to Yoyogi. As soon as I extracted this information, it was easy enough to pick it up on CCTV."

"I wonder why - seems a bit strange?"

"Maybe quite sensible if they were expecting to take some hits. Easiest possible way to pick up some damaged bodies and transport them rapidly to a hospital."

"But all these links to Nishi... " I ground to a halt as I saw the pattern emerge. "Bugger me, so that's how Miss Chrissy was moved about!"

"Well, whether or not you are buggered later is completely up to you," the CI laughed. "Nevertheless, it's clear that the same ambulance can be seen in camera shots from Shinjuku last night. When you check carefully, you can see that all key CCTVs around the uni hospital and Sakura-dori have been edited for critical time blocks but, after we spot these, we can search around for unedited records in the neighborhood. Then it's obvious that this vehicle was en route between Kabuki-cho and Nishi-Shinjuku at around 11:50 and on the way back an hour later."

"Where did it go after that?" I peered at the model as it expanded in response to my query.

" Ginza," Koide replied before I could read the answer for myself. "When you do a trace through all the cover companies, it's owned by a small medical insurance company which, in turn, is owned by Yamaguchi-gumi."

"Yakuza again. Looks like they're heavily involved here."

"I'm sure we're expected to think that," my boss frowned in concentration, "but is that one of the false trails that's been set up for us to find? Anyway, let's have a quick look at my original question list." This immediately materialized between us.

1. How, when and by whom was the operating theatre accessed and how did they manage to clean up so well afterwards?

2. Is there clear evidence where Chrissy was killed and what was actually responsible for death?

3. When was Chrissy last in action in the club and how could she get from there to the hospital?

4. How did the body get from the hospital to the Kabuki-cho noodle shop?

5. What happened to the missing organs - and why would anyone want to take them in the first place?

6. Is there any way of finding out who planted the bugs and where this might lead?

7. How do they know about how things are run in our Shinjuku cop shop and are there any indications of an insider being involved?

8. What is the role, if any, of the German and Japanese professors who have a kink for hermaphrodites?

9. Why might we be getting pushed in the direction of this PD club: has its clientele or their sex choices any link here?

"Well, we seem to have nailed down four and seven - and come a fair way with two and three," I observed.

"So you do concede that crushing the balls of that yakuza bastard did actually serve some purpose?" she asked smugly.

"Possibly," I conceded grudgingly, "but I suspect we could have obtained the same information without inflicting as much pain on the poor bastard."

"Poor bastard? Have you forgotten he was swinging at us with a fucking sword. I want to ensure that anyone who does that kind of thing passes on the news that even surviving an encounter with me is going to be an extremely painful business."

"And decrease your chances of ever having children," I pointed out.

"Reduce your chances to zero! I told the Tokyo plods that these guys knew we were cops, but didn't know we were SAR. I reckon the old bolt-cutters will be in action tonight."

"Oh, come on, surely that doesn't happen in this day and age?" One look at my boss's grin and I quickly decided to change tracks. "Anyway, back to your list. The data-miners seem to have filled in some other gaps." An explosion of color-coded links appeared, coupling the list to our case model.

"It looks superficially consistent, doesn't it?" my boss mused as she waved a hand to expand links to the first question. Both operating theatres had been booked for the entire evening for cosmetic surgery demonstrations of scar removal technology, focused on cases of post-operative infections. The Japanese company responsible could again be traced back to expose yakuza links. "So, not only assures that they would have access, but also explains a team carrying out a rigorous clean-up after use," she concluded.

"Seems that that ties up also place of death," I noted, moving the focus to the second question. "From the time profile, it's almost certainly the hospital."

"Any more on that?"

I groaned, sensing that I was being tested again. "Well, there's no evidence of defensive wounds, so this means that our Chrissy was either persuaded to go to the hospital, willingly or not, or wasn't in a state to object." I waited for a response, but the silence simply stretched on as I scanned through the database. "The blood work doesn't preclude some kind of designer date-rape drug, especially in the small concentrations that you'd need on top of the booze and stimulants that she'd already taken. Of course, a threat might have been enough - a gun held to her head or something similar."

"I'd guess something similar," Koide offered cryptically. "What about cause of death?"

"Tricky, as there's so little evidence of trauma. If she was in an operating theatre, however, maybe something in the narcotic?"

I was awarded with a slow clap of her hands, which I took to be a good sign. The case model expanded with a slew of chemical formulae while she explained. "As always with this trace chemical analysis of blood work, there's so much information, that it really only helps if you know what you're looking for. In this case, exotics that could be easily added to a general anesthetic. The individual components of this particular mixture are innocuous enough, but together would certainly cause heart failure. Normally, we'd confirm this with analysis of the heart itself, but of course that's missing along with most of the other internal organs."

"Convenient - but not enough on its own to explain the Ripper-style butchery."

"Definitely not, but maybe the heart and lungs were included in the organ harvest to muddy the water an extra bit." The CI was clearly deep in thought as she closed the pathology database and leant back in her chair with her eyes staring unfocused at the ceiling. "I'm sure that the message being made here was centered on the removal of the internal sexual organs and getting us to focus on what is going on in this Kabuki-cho cabaret."

"So, you're still planning to visit it tonight?"

"Just after it opens at eight. This'll give us time for a quick snack beforehand. In any case, we can kill two birds with one stone, as we're meeting Professor Toyota there at eight thirty." Koide noticed my look of confusion and waved a distant branch of the hologram open. "The To-Dai prof who invited our German professor doctor doctor to the club."

"So I'm on overtime for this?" I asked, hopefully.

"Overtime? Overtime? You've got to be joking! I'm taking you to one of the most exclusive dens of iniquity in entire Kabuki-cho and you're expecting to get paid for it? You should be paying me!"

"Well, it's not my choice," I retorted, churlishly. "I don't expect to get anything out of it!"

"Education, lad, education: that's what you'll get out of it. I'll guarantee that, or your money back."

"Money, what money?"

"The money that you're going to spend buying me dinner. So, go get your jacket and we'll be off. I think I fancy tempura tonight. I know a great little place in I-land just around the corner."

I left to pick up my stuff from my small office while she was still rabbiting about the tempura restaurant, but caught her last sotto voce remark. "... and you may not only learn a thing or two, you may even enjoy yourself."

I was sure of the former but, somehow, seriously doubted the latter.

***

It was a couple of minutes before eight when we pushed our way through the bustle of Sakura-dori to face a rather bland door that was embossed with the ornate logo of Pleasure Doubled and otherwise sported only a brass plaque announcing that this was a private members' club. There was no obvious bell or knocker to announce our arrival but, as we approached, the door swung open to allow us access to a small but luxuriously fitted lift. As I looked into the mirrored wall facing me, a disembodied voice seemed to come from the center of it. "Welcome, Chief Inspector Koide-san. This elevator will take you to our reception on the fourth floor where mama-san is waiting for you."

There was only the slightest sensation of movement after an inner lift door slid silently closed and then, shortly afterwards, the mirrored wall opened to give us access to a lounge that seemed to have been taken directly from an early 20th century Berlin bordello. It took a second before I spotted that the high ceiling with its ornamental plasterwork and glitzy chandeliers must be some kind of holographic illusion. The rest of the room was dominated by red and gilt, including the thick pile carpet, the satin-covered settees and painted walls with their *trompe-l'œil* views onto landscapes populated with capering nymphs and satyrs.

Only when Koide-san moved forward to present her business card, did I spot the small Japanese women who had been hidden by the CI's robust frame. The mama-san bowed deeply before exchanging her own card for my boss's. I had known in advance that this was a top-end brothel but, even then, the outrageous costume worn by its manager distracted me completely. The black waspie, tanga knickers, suspenders, fishnet stockings and stiletto heels would have been spectacular on their own, but the diaphanous material of the bustier left nothing to the imagination, showing clearly that her large earrings were matched by equally large rings through both prominent nipples.

A theatrical cough from my boss shook me out of my daze and I recovered enough to proffer my meishi with hardly a handshake. As was expected, I accepted an expensively engraved card with two hands, examined it carefully and then bowed. "Very pleased to meet you Kurokawa-san."

The mama-san seemed amused by my discomfort. "Michiko, Michiko, darling, call me Michiko." Her voice was deeper than I had expected from her diminutive stature and the perfect English seemed to contain traces of a German accent, which was eminently suited to the surroundings.

"Can we talk to you in your office?" The CI's question abruptly reminded me of our purpose here.

"Let's just sit together here," the little woman gestured at a pair of sofas facing each other. "Nobody else will be here for a half hour, until Toyota-sensei arrives. Would you like something to drink? Some champagne, perhaps?"

"Not yet," the CI answered for us both. "First of all we have some very bad news for you."

The mama-san looked confused. "I thought you were just coming here to discuss membership before your rendezvous with Toyota-sensei."

"I would love to discuss membership of your esteemed establishment," Koide responded to my surprise, "but now we are here in an official capacity. As you know, we are detectives in the SAR police force."

"But of course, it was your commissioner who recommended you. She has been a member for some time." If the CI had surprised me, this bizarre revelation shocked me to the core.

"Yes, but I'm afraid that we are here as representatives of the serious crimes division, as part of a murder investigation."

"What, you think one of our members has murdered someone?" The Japanese woman was clearly shocked and her German accent vanished, her English becoming much more British-sounding.

"Maybe, but I'm sorry to say that one of your staff has been the victim of this murder."

"Oh no!" Tears brimmed in her eyes. "Who is it, who?"

"Chrissy."

"Miss Chrissy! Oh my God! That can't be - she was working here last night!" The mama-san now broke into tears that racked her slim frame.

The CI settled Kurokawa-san onto one of the sofas and cradled the distressed woman in her arms. "Yes, it was certainly Chrissy," she murmured as she stroked the courtesan's perfectly trimmed, page-cropped, jet-black hair.

"What happened? Who did it to her?" I could barely make out the questions mumbled into Koide-san's massive chest.

"We don't know the answers to those questions yet, but I'm sure that we soon will. We are, however, fairly sure that she didn't suffer. But I need to ask you some questions to help us catch her murderer. Can you handle that?"

The madam pulled herself free and used a tissue from a box on a side table to wipe her eyes. There was a catch in her throat, but the woman showed impressive inner strength as she clearly enunciated, "Yes, certainly, Chief Inspector. Just let me know what I can tell you."

"Well, for starters, I'd like to know who Chrissy had for clients last night and which members were present between about ten pm and midnight."

"I can tell you who was here yesterday, but I'm afraid I can't tell you who saw Chrissy."

This announcement clearly surprised my boss. "How can that be: surely all arrangements in this place are logged in some way?"

"Well, only to the minimum extent possible. We try to maintain as much anonymity as is possible in this present day and age. Members are identified by the door management software, along with any guests that they have with them: such visits are always reserved in advance. When they enter, members are assigned a room and can go directly there, unless they choose to visit this lounge, where they might meet other members. They can see which of the hostesses are available on the screen," she indicated a discrete panel set into the side table and made a swiping movement to bring up a holographic display that listed a half dozen names, all of which were highlighted on a green background.

"Of course, very few of the girls are here so early in the evening. Normally we would have a couple of dozen in house and about ten or more would be available at any one time." The woman seemed to have recovered her composure and was evidently proud of her establishment. "You just select who you want and any other special services, drinks or stuff like that, then costs are automatically deducted from your prepaid account."

"But this means that there are records of all transactions, surely"

"Not at all, for our own records we keep a note only of who has visited us so that we can plan to optimize our services. When we close each morning at three am, all account statuses are updated - client accounts, girls' accounts and house books - and past records deleted. So I can tell you which girls were here and how long they spent at work. I can also tell you which members were here, but not the times that they came and went."

The CI was not happy with this development. "We have a lot of forensic IT kit, maybe we could recover the deleted files."

The Japanese woman shook her head decisively. "Not if our IT consultant is to be believed. We use a UV burst to delete an optical memory chip, then simply dump it in the regional recycler: he says it's completely impossible to recover data, even if you could find the chip."

Koide looked at me and I shook my head: not a chance.

"OK, what about if we just interview all the girls who were on last night?"

The mama-san looked uncomfortable. "I would really like to help you however I can, but the girls would not normally know the names of clients. You could probably dig out the information you need if you could access file information on all of our members, but you would need a court order for that. Many of our members are in positions of power, so I think that might be very tricky."

I suddenly remembered that our commander was a member and realized that tricky might be an understatement of the challenge involved. In any case, it seemed likely that our hack this morning had probably accessed just about everything that was available from this source.

The CI was evidently also aware of this situation. "No problems, Michiko. You've had enough of a shock for now and I don't want to add to your problems. But could you tell me when Miss Chrissy left?"

This reminder of her girl's death brought tears back to the madam's eyes, but she responded immediately. "I know exactly when that was, as she logged out here in the lounge while I was sitting on this very spot with a couple of our older members and three other girls. Our records show only that she worked... " her fingers flicked through the air and a table with Japanese characters appeared, "... three and a half hours. I saw her leave at twenty to twelve, so she must have started at around eight."

"Isn't that a bit early? I thought things don't get going until a bit later?"

"Not really. Several of the top girls have repeat clients who come on regular days and have special requirements. They can organize these directly with the girls, who may need a bit of time to get everything sorted out."

"What kind of special services might these be?" asked the CI, taking the words right out of my mouth.

Kurokawa-san raised her eyebrows as if this was a strange enquiry. "Well, that's really limited only by the imagination and assuring the safety of both client and courtesan. There are various kinds of group activities and role playing that need props and preparations. Depending on what is going to happen, you may want to have a full bladder - or ensure that it is empty. You know what I mean?"

I felt that the question was being addressed to me and I could feel myself blush. "I can kind of guess," I mumbled uncomfortably.

"Well, again, I am very sorry for your loss and please pass our condolences to all of your staff." I was relieved to note that the CI seemed oblivious of my embarrassment. "Please also ask them to contact me if they have any information that they think might help our investigation and assure them that anything of this sort will be treated in full confidence. We will probably need to come back again sometime, but I will try to avoid any disruption of your staff or their clients."

The madam bowed deeply. "Thank you very much, Chief Inspector. I greatly appreciate your kind understanding and consideration. You are still meeting up with Toyota-sensei as arranged?"

"Yes, should we wait here - it's still about a quarter of an hour before she is expected?"

"As you like. Either here or in room Bismarck. If you go into the elevator, it will take you there automatically."

"Maybe best if we go to the room then. I'm sure you have other things to see to."

The mama-san bowed again. "Yes, you are correct. Thank you once more."

I could see tears start to flow again as the small woman turned to leave us. She had covered it well, but it seemed that her heart was breaking.

***

The room Bismarck was one floor higher and the door into it was the one of three facing us that lay ajar. I guessed this system reduced the risk of members accidently bumping into each other. The room appeared large and airy but, like the lounge below, much of this was holographic illusion. The center of the room was dominated by a huge bed, which was covered by a black silk sheet. Two large leather wing chairs that looked to be antique stood against the far wall, bracketing a leather sofa and a low coffee table.

Koide marched around the bed and dropped heavily onto the sofa, leaning forward to wave at the inlaid panel that activated the holographic menu. "A beer while we wait?" she enquired.

I noted that this was a rhetorical question as I spotted the confirmation for two bottles of Yona Yona ale. Seconds later the quiet tinkle of a bell announced the arrival of the drinks in a hatch above a shelf in the left-hand wall of the room. I fetched a beer and a frosted glass and carried them over to my boss. She didn't look up as she took the bottle and sipped a mouthful directly from it. I shrugged my shoulders and took the glass back to the delivery hatch, where I poured my own beer into it.

By the time I returned to the settee, my boss had moved onto the list of available girls, which had now increased to seven. "She's tough, the mama-san," she observed. "She's clearly broken up and must have lots of admin stuff to handle, but she's here at the top of the list ready for service. I guess it's probably because she thinks she owes us and spotted you salivating the moment that you first saw her."

I ignored this dig to point out the obvious incongruity. "Why should she be on the list? I thought this was a ladyboy brothel - do they have normal services also on offer?"

My boss looked totally gobsmacked, before she burst into guffaws of mirth. "Jesus suffering Christ on a bicycle! Watson, you really aren't safe to be out on your own! Or, anyway, at least not in this neck of the woods."

I was dumbfounded and this was clearly obvious to my tormenter. "So, you have a kink for piercings have you?"

"Well, nothing against them, I suppose. Can't say that I've encountered a lot of women with them." This caused another burst of laughter, which deepened my confusion.

"And what about a Prince Albert? Have you encountered a lot of women with them?" she smirked.

"Well, as I don't know what a Prince Albert is, I wouldn't really know."

"Have a look here," the CI waved her hands to conjure up an enlarged holographic image of an erect dick with a ring through it. I could feel my testicles contract at the very thought of the required piercing.

"Don't be stupid, that's a... " my objection died as the image zoomed back to show the proud owner of this ornamented tool. "Fuck, it's little Michiko! Where the fuck did she get a willy that size?"

"I'd hazard a guess that she's always had it," Koide laughed, "although maybe a bit smaller in the days of her youth. A more relevant question might be where her perfectly formed little tits came from."

I was going to object that the tits were far from little, but then recognized that it all depended on your viewpoint. Compared to Koide's humungous boobs, I suppose Kurokawa-san's breasts might be considered modestly dimensioned.

Koide wasn't going to let up, I could see. "So, in your time at the Met, did you never work with anyone from vice? I seem to remember that your CV was a bit sparse in terms of hands-on cop work."

I was sure she was leading me on, but I could not get out of some kind of response. "OK, I was fast-tracked from uni into serious crimes intelligence division, but it was mainly white-collar stuff... "

"So you pushed paper... "

"Not all the time," I protested feebly, "I was involved in a number of raids. We closed down quite a few big operations, which is probably why I got this job."

"So, a few encounters with the hard cases of the banking and finance communities," she laughed. "I guess this does explain a lot!"

I was spared further torment by a subtle buzz as the door to the room opened. I turned to inspect the tall, slim Japanese woman who was entering, before immediately wondering if she might also be a shemale.

My boss had jumped to her feet and hurried around to greet our visitor. "An honor to meet you, Toyota-sensei," she gushed as she proffered her meishi. "I am Chief Inspector Koide and am very grateful that you have agreed to meet us here."

"I am happy to be of help, Koide-san," she passed over her own business card. "... and also Holmes-san," she added in crisp Oxford English as we exchanged cards. "I am, however, very surprised that you wanted to meet here. In fact, I don't know how you could have even known that I was a member."

"All of this is linked directly to a murder investigation," Koide answered, adroitly avoiding the last question. As the professor raised a quizzical eyebrow, she continued. "The victim of the murder was a hostess here, a certain Miss Chrissy."

"Oh my goodness," the woman looked shocked. "I have never actually met her, but, from her pictures, she was very beautiful - and supposed to be very talented. How could this possibly happen?"

"We're in the process of clearing that up now. But an important bit of information for us is the fact that you've never met her. Now, before we go further, please sit down."

"Well, I wouldn't say it was by choice," Toyota-sensei stared at the hologram of a fully exposed Kurokawa-san in an unfocused manner as she took a seat beside the CI. "Miss Chrissy was an extremely popular entertainer and very difficult to get an appointment with. Also very expensive. I don't live on my professorial salary but, even with the inheritance from my late husband, Chrissy would be a treat that I could consider only for very special occasions."

"You were here last night, though?"

"How would you know that?" the svelte academic now sounded very suspicious. "You haven't been following me or something, have you? What's this all about? You surely can't think I have something to do with a crime?"

"Actually, I'm now sure that you had nothing to do with our case," Koide assured her, clearly trying to sort out ruffled feathers. "The thing is, someone has set up a trail that seems to be tailored towards pointing us in your direction. Why would that be?"

Toyota-sensei spluttered, evidently shocked at this news. "Someone wants to blame me for a murder. A murder of one of the girls here? That can't be correct!"

"I assure you that it is. So can I ask you again about last night?"

The professor shrugged in a resigned manner. "Well, if you know so much, you're probably aware that I visited with a guest last night."

It was clear that a response was expected and Koide nodded in my direction. "Yes, you were here with a Professor Frick. As far as we are aware, you know her only from some time you spent together in Berlin."

The CI frowned, implying that I had been a bit too open, but Toyota-sensei seemed amused. "Well, so much for privacy. If you know all of this, what do you need to ask me about?"

"This club is very discrete and goes out of its way to assure that members leave the absolute minimum of a digital spoor. We don't know when you arrived here, who you were entertained by and when you left."

"Well, that's nice to know." To my surprise, she seemed happy with this, but not as relieved as I might have been in her place. "As you noted, Angela Frick and I have previously met only once, but we have known each other for a longer time as we share common interests." I noted that she pronounced Angela in the German manner, with a hard g. Then she looked directly into my eyes. "I guess you would call it kinky sex..." she smiled a little at my discomfort and continued, "... exhibitionism, voyeurism, group encounters of interesting kinds."

The CI sported a matching smile. "I guess your contact was previously within an internet social

80

group, based on highly encrypted messaging via a secure server."

"Yes, in fact that's how I ended up a member of this club: I was sponsored by a friend with similar interests that I met through this group. Angela and I have shared a lot of experiences electronically and she took the opportunity for us to have real world contact when I had a conference in Berlin a while back. I was very happy to repay this during her visit to Tokyo."

"So, if you don't mind, could you tell me more about last night?" This was the question that I couldn't wait to have answered.

"Well, we met about seven thirty at Angela's hotel, the Hyatt Regency, and went over the road for dinner in I-land. Some kind of steak grill place in the basement - Sakura something, I think. It was about nine when we took a taxi over here."

The professor seemed unsure how to continue, so the CI piped in. "Who did you meet here? What did you do and when did you leave?"

The little Japanese woman seemed to consider how to answer this before she continued. "Angela and I selected Miss Lee and Mistress Domino. Do I need to go into detail?"

The tall blonde shook her head, but clearly wanted to get as much background as possible. "You certainly don't need to say anything at all without a lawyer present, but I would really appreciate any information at all that you can give me. I can assure you that this will be kept completely confidential and I'll set up a formal interview if I think I ever need to use anything that you have provided. I do, however, really want to find out why you were being set up here and how this is linked to Chrissy's death. I am aware, of course, that some people judge others in terms of the extent to which they deviate from the expected behavior of the hoi polloi. I can assure you that I'm not one of them and, in fact, my own sexual preferences lie more on the unconventional side of the street."

This admission caused Toyota-sensei to visibly relax, her rigid posture slipping as she slumped back into her seat. "OK, well we hadn't decided anything in advance and just scanned through the available girls until we found a pair that would fit our mood. Lee and Domino were ideal."

"Which of you was with which of them?" I blurted out, momentarily surprised that I had actually spoken the question that was foremost on my mind.

My boss groaned audibly. "I'm sorry, Toyota-sensei, ignore my underling: he is an idiot and just doesn't get out enough. Just continue in your own time."

"Yes, well as I previously mentioned, Angela and I share interests in group encounters: watching and being watched. Domino is a very butch, but extremely well-endowed ladyboy while Lee is a mid-op trans-sex. This gives lots of interesting combinations - and we tried quite a few of them last night. We had one of the BDSM rooms, so Domino ran the show after we outlined our preferences. It was actually a really excellent evening and I know

Angela was having a great time. It was a terrible shame that we had to leave early."

"Why was that?" I enquired, spotting Koide's frown.

"Just before we left the restaurant, Angela got a message that a huge grant had come through to support her research. From some kind of foundation, but unexpected. Anyway, she had to get the first plane back to Germany this morning. It meant that we had to be careful with our time, but, on the other hand, she was elated by this surprise and I'm sure that contributed to the fun that we had. I must say that she's a completely wild and uninhibited woman. I just hope we have a chance to meet up again in real life," she smiled wistfully.

"Would you have a record of this fun encounter?" the CI asked.

"Of course. This is available to clients with the agreement of the girls - guaranteed no copies for anyone else. I have a hard copy in a safe at the university."

"Very sensible," my boss smiled, "you don't want to trust anything to be secure if there is any chance of it ever being linked to the net. I wonder, though, if I could look at a copy: either at the university or if you could provide me with a single read only chip."

The academic hesitated, then responded with a shrug of her shoulders. "Why not, I'll send you a one-read chip. If there's anything you need to follow up on, I can meet you at my apartment in Shiodome. How would that be?"

"Excellent, Toyota-sensei. I can't tell you how much I appreciate your trust here. I know keeping personal life truly private is very tricky nowadays and I will do everything possible to minimize the fallout from this case."

"Don't worry about it. I am well aware that there are already rumors circulating about me. Luckily I'm not prominent enough for this to be of great interest to anyone, except some of my bloody nosy students. Anyway, is there anything else that I can help you with or are we done now?"

"Actually there is one thing," my boss responded, much to my surprise as I had thought that we were now finished with the professor. "I know that you've never met the deceased, but you are a member here and must have a better idea than us about how things work. If we wanted to know more about Chrissy's private life, who do you think we should ask?"

"I don't think the girls are encouraged to form bonds at work, but the other herms will certainly have been close to her. All the really big rollers are looking for herm-on-herm action as part of the play-line. This is probably especially the case because a good proportion of the members who can afford this kind of treat are old men, who probably only watch anyway. Just think what Angela and I could do with a pair like Miss Chrissy and Dame Elizabeth... " she licked her lips salaciously, then realized that she was maybe revealing a lot more than was necessary.

"Elizabeth, she's the second most expensive pros... , ah, well, entertainer here," I spluttered to a halt, aware that I'd stumbled into a social faux pas.

Toyota-sensei frowned at me and put on what sounded like her professorial lecturing voice. "Please have a bit of respect here, young man. The courtesans here are highly skilled professional entertainers, on a par with the very top geisha. To demean this with the term prostitute would be like comparing a lab tech to a Nobel laureate. They both do a job for money, but one is pedestrian and the other outstanding on a global level. I have nothing at all against prostitutes and have made use of their skills on many occasions. They perform a valuable service and, if in control of their own fate, are probably happier and more generally useful than most civil servants." There was a distinct glare at me accompanying this statement. "The girls here, however, are the creme-de-la-creme of the commercial entertainment business in which sex is only one component."

"Sorry, I'm very sorry," I groveled. "No disrespect meant, it's just that this is an area that I really don't know anything about."

"Painfully obvious, Watson, so leave the rest to me," my boss whispered. "Yes, I'm very sorry that the younger generation of Englishmen have such narrow and rather provincial views of the world outside their coddled university system."

"You don't have to tell me that," Toyota-sensei smiled, "I spent three years at Oxford. What a bunch of wankers! Their ideas of alternative sex seem to revolve around transient, drunken, lesbian flings for the girls and pederasty for the older males. Anyway, as you are going to be seeing a lot more of me than I'd allow most people, you should just call me Yoko."

"Yoko, that's great. Please call me Stella. I'm sure we'd get on well together so we should try to keep in touch even if this case doesn't require it." The physically contrasting women were looking into each other's eyes as they gave matching nods, apparently sealing the agreement.

The Japanese woman waved a hand over the table and conjured up the updated list of currently available courtesans. Top of the list was Lady Jasmine. "This is probably who you should talk to: Dame Liz is second on the price list because of her experience and notoriety, but Jasmine is actually much prettier and, although she's quite young with limited skills, she must have been paired with Chrissy a lot. I'm sure she'll be booked solid later tonight, but she's free for the next hour.

"Sounds good to me. Say, would you like to come along? You never know, we may have some spare time after talking to Jasmine and could maybe sample her wares."

"Well, that's very tempting Stella. But what about your boy?" she nodded her head in my direction.

"No problem at all, it's well past his bedtime anyway. Off you go then, Watson, I'll see you tomorrow in my office at about nine. Just don't get up to any mischief in the den of iniquity outside."

I could feel their condescending smiles bore into my back as I retreated through the door, letting it close behind me without a backwards glance. I had travelled down to the ground floor in the elevator and then out into the bustle of Kabuki-cho before I finally relaxed with a sigh and wondered if I was annoyed or relieved by my dismissal.

After standing motionless for a couple of minutes, allowing the crowds to pass around me in a babbling flow, it dawned on me that I was just a couple of hundred meters from an ancient Scottish whisky bar, which always had an interesting selection of craft ales on tap. OK, happy it was! I strode off in the direction of this watering hole with a definite bounce to my step.

Chapter 5

I had been waiting in CI Koide's office for almost 15 minutes before she finally appeared, rubbing her eyes in a sleepy manner. "Had a nice night?" I enquired cheerfully as she slumped into her chair with a groan.

"Don't push your luck, Watson!" she glared at me from somewhat bloodshot eyes. "Just make yourself fucking useful by buggering off and getting me a triple espresso - with two sugars."

"Two sugars? Must have been a heavy night," I grinned as I scurried out, sure that a death stare was following me.

By the time that I returned with her coffee, the CI was working on the case model, flipping through sub-directories and zooming in and out of the central holographic network, which now looked like a color-coded neural map of the brain. I remained silent while the espresso was sunk in two inelegant gulps, followed by an even less elegant burp.

"Well, to answer your previous question, my night was a great success. I've already added the key stuff from Jasmine to the model, but I'll walk you through it, so that you can hone your sleuthing skills on the associated interpretation." Ignoring my grimace, she expanded a branch that was labeled *employees-PD*. "Jasmine hasn't had a session with Chrissy for a couple of days, but they're very good friends and, in fact, live very close to each other."

"I remember that Chrissy stayed in a luxury apartment block here in Nishi-Shinjuku: Platinum Mansion, I think, twelfth floor."

"That's the one; Jasmine is immediately above her on the fourteenth floor." I was momentarily confused until I remembered that, like the US, many Japanese buildings don't have thirteenth floors, almost missing the next key message, "... and they regularly meet up in the block coffee lounge for a late breakfast, around ten am."

"Isn't that a bit early, if they are in action until the early hours of the morning?" I wondered.

"This happens only when they both leave the club with a member, to spend the night elsewhere. Seems to occur quite regularly, even if this is very expensive for the punter involved. In most such cases, this is arranged in advance... "

"Although, such arrangements would have already been deleted from the PD database," I finished.

"Yes, but Chrissy had actually arranged to meet Jasmine yesterday morning... "

"... so she had planned in advance to spend the night with a client!" I suddenly saw where this was going.

"So, Watson, pieces are beginning to fall into place. What do you make of it all?"

I expanded and contracted links from the Jasmine interview while I struggled to find an intelligent-sounding start. As Koide began to fidget, I was forced to blurt out, "Well, we have a clear link to a member of this kinky club. We can't tie anyone explicitly to Chrissy, but, in addition to a full membership list, we know everyone who visited the club on the night in question and also names of any of their guests." Three lists ghosted into existence above the desk. "Well, actually, we don't need the membership... fuck! Look who is at the top of that list!"

The list in question expanded and highlighted an entry close to the top: A. Maus.

"Watson, you jammy sod! A cleverer person would have simply focused on the members present the night before last. I hadn't picked this up. Not conclusive in any way, but definitely a very interesting link."

A wave of my hands expanded the second list. It contained about fifty names but, apart from Toyota-sensei, none of them rang any bells. Then the guests, which I was surprised to see actually outnumbered the members.

"Looks like a few corporate bashes," Koide commented, as if she had read my mind. "Big bosses from above the clouds entertaining clients and government officials, I would bet. Here's our Angela Frick, but I am sure that many of the other names are just covers: there are an awful lot of Satos and Suzukis. And here's someone who's just down as Akira."

"Doesn't anyone here need to give their real name?" I wondered.

An associated block of the case model automatically expanded to provide the information I was requesting. Members had to be proposed by an existing member and provide a name and address with associated bank account details. As long as the bank account was bone fide, nobody seemed to be bothered about how genuine the name was, which I guess made sense for a club of this nature.

Things were even looser for guests: as long as the member vouched for them and paid all associated costs, there was no specific requirement to assure that names given were correct.

While my boss cursed under her breath, I idly scanned down the guest names, identifying the obvious aliases. I grinned when I spotted a Peter Parker, but then froze when my eyes drifted upwards to an E.V. Hammond.

"Fuck me, is this bastard really pulling on our chains or what?"

"What has your eagle eye spotted, Watson, I already saw the Spiderman guy."

"No, not him, this E.V. Hammond. Couldn't this be Evey Hammond?"

"Who is?"

"One of the main characters from V for Vendetta. Remember, we were discussing it yesterday."

"Oh, yes, the comic that you did a dissertation or something on."

"I would actually prefer to refer to it as a graphic novel," I retorted. "Anyway, it could be a link of some kind."

"Who introduced him?"

"Well, if linked to the story, Evey would actually be a woman," I explained, aware that I was being a bit pedantic. "Anyway, the member is Val Page."

"So this is another V link?"

The name was familiar, but I couldn't bring it immediately to mind. A quick Wiki-cheat brought it back: "Valerie Page! That's it. She was a lesbian in the book, prosecuted as being a sexual deviant."

"Sounds like a nice book," the CI observed sarcastically. "It does, however, definitely indicate that several people are playing games that all link up with this Anony-maus character. All too much to be simple coincidence, but not very illuminating in terms of our quest to find the murderer of Miss Chrissy."

"Yes," I agreed, "it's hard to see a link between someone using the name of a hacker collective and a top-end perv bordello."

I thought my boss was going to dress me down for my description of her new favorite night spot, but she had been diverted in another direction. "Yes, we think of hackers as generally poor young males who lived in squalor and get their sexual pleasures by tossing off to internet porn," she mused, in a thoughtful manner. "But what about the earlier generations, who were active when these comics of yours were coming out? Those young rebels have grown old and I would bet that many have gone over to what they would once have called *the dark side*. They would now move in the highest echelons of software engineering, corporate security and cyber warfare: so are rich old bastards who are part of the system. I wonder if it is so strange that an ex-geek could be a member of one of the top entertainment houses in Tokyo?"

"I suppose it's not impossible," I conceded. "Might explain some of the silly names, but doesn't really give us a motive."

"Oh, that: I thought we nailed that down yesterday. Our amazingly fully functional hermaphrodite was pregnant, so there must be a lot of potential motives arising from that fact."

I pondered on this throwaway comment. "You mean something like blackmail?"

"Well, it could certainly be blackmail gone wrong. Punters would naturally ignore precautions to assure inadvertent pregnancy in their relationships with a hermaphrodite. Someone rich and powerful may be extremely pissed-off to find that he had an unplanned heir."

"Which could explain removal of the womb, to remove DNA trace back," I realized, suddenly seeing an explanation for this grotesque act beginning to develop. "However, with what we know now, we could look for fetal cells in Chrissy's blood and run the DNA."

"Already on it: rather early stage of pregnancy and extensive exsanguination will make getting a DNA photo-fit challenging, but let's see what Nakayama-sensei can do with all that high tech crap at his disposal."

"There's a problem with this explanation, though," I mumbled as a glaring inconsistency came to mind. "The corpse was... "

"Presented in a way guaranteed to attract our attention and focus it on Pleasure Doubled." My boss took the words out of my mouth in her usual annoying manner. "While a less brilliant detective might easily have missed the pregnancy, a much safer option for the body would clearly have been the hospital incinerator. What do you think?"

I was so caught up in this mystery that I didn't notice that I was back in the spotlight. "It's all like a gratuitously complex game: a murder that should head us in a certain direction, but with preparations already in place to nobble us if we don't follow the script."

"Or just move too quickly," Koide grinned. "I love this shit! Old Nakayama was right, we do get all the best cases!"

"Or the most bloody dangerous ones!" I reminded her.

"Pussy! This caper hasn't even begun to get dangerous. In fact, I suspect that the attacks on us were more diversions; intended to put on the frighteners and maybe delay us a bit, but not actually intended to kill us or halt the investigation."

"Well, a few months in intensive care would certainly slow us down a bit, but I still remain to be convinced that thugs with machine pistols or samurai swords were intending only to frighten us a bit."

"As you noted earlier, a sniper would have been a much more efficient way to take us off the case permanently. This stuff is all theatre, just like all this nonsense with the comic book names."

"Do you really think we were expected to spot that?" I wondered out loud.

"Maybe not as quickly as we did, but it looks like an unnecessary risk. Unless, of course, it was all part of a message, which wasn't actually aimed at us." The CI closed her eyes and plucked her lower lip with the index finger of her right hand, allowing me to spot that her nail varnish was chipped, in contrast to her normally impeccable manicure. "What if this is all about a message to a third party and, in fact, our activities are part of the message?"

Risking answering another rhetorical question, I felt I had to contribute my tuppence worth. "This makes it a very high stakes game, with a perp who is extremely confident that he can lead us by the nose for his own purposes, rather than the clues ending up with him in the nick."

The blonde's grin got even wider. "I think you have it there in a nutshell, Watson." She waved at the case model hologram, causing it to expand and fill the entire space above her desk. "This is an outline of what Anony-maus wants us to do for him. We now need to find a way to look behind the curtain and see what the wizard is really up to."

While I was processing this revelation, wrapped up in an Oz metaphor, a feeling of *deja vu* overcame me. "Shit! If Anony-maus has this place bugged, he'll now know what we're thinking on this!"

"Worry not, Watson, already ahead of you on this. Both our offices, several meeting rooms, the canteen and all the interview rooms contained micro-pin cameras. They were exactly like those in the Kabuki-cho pub and emplaced by our moles about 2 weeks ago. These have all been stripped out and my office has now military spec active and passive security systems. I'd never bet a system is un-crackable, but this is probably as close as you get."

"What about my office?"

"Well nothing exciting ever happens there, does it? Anyway, just be careful and make sure that we discuss any mission-critical stuff here."

I swallowed a retort and forced myself to return to the case model. "So, this is all artifice, the storyboard of an egotistical puppet master."

"I'm beginning to think so. But, if so, we have the great advantage of knowing that this is the case."

"How does this help us?"

"Well, instead of trying to work immediately through to who dunnit, we first have to define exactly what the message is and who it is aimed at. This would be the critical step towards identifying the brains behind this malarkey."

"Yes, well, if the Vendetta storyline is part of the message, it could fit in some way. Part of this involves concentration camp experimentation on inmates, sort of Mengale-type stuff, which might be linked to artificial production of fully functional hermaphrodites," I speculated. "There are also links to prostitution and a brothel cum cabaret, which could also fit in."

"Links spotted by a sad person like yourself," Koide pointed out, "not quite as direct as a gutted hermaphrodite put on display in the vicinity of her work place. Nevertheless, you do have a point of sorts. How could the impact of this brutal murder be increased by linking it to this story?"

I shrugged my shoulders, but a glare in my direction reminded me that I was still being tested. "OK, let's assume that we were supposed to follow leads from Chrissy back to the club, but get diverted by the apparent link to Toyota-sensei and her pervy pal. We would, sooner or later, become aware that Toyota was a dead end and then chase up anyone at the club that evening and also some of the other hookers. I guess this could get uncomfortable for some of the members, especially those where this kind of entertainment would be a hazard to their public persona - politicians, clergy and the like."

Koide silently raised her eyebrows, evidently expecting me to continue. I waved frantically at the case model, looking for inspiration as the members and visitors lists expanded over the desk. "Or, I guess it could be one or more of the visitors. If visits to this club are associated with some kind of corporate or political jiggery-pokery, a police investigation could make things very uncomfortable."

"Jiggery what? OK, I know what you mean anyway. But I doubt that this would fit in with the butchery of a pregnant herm."

"True, that's the tricky bit of this fucking jigsaw puzzle." I glared at the hologram as if it was responsible for my lack of understanding of what was going on here. "If we can identify the father, that would certainly help. Do we have any idea when this information would be available?"

"As I mentioned, it'll be tricky and, even if we get something, we will have to treat it with great caution, given the games that Anony-maus plays. In any case, we should have first results this afternoon. Until then, we should try to push this investigation forward, keep our nemesis on the hop."

"Well, we could get the search engines working on these lists, see what we can get out of them. We could also link them up with any CCTV from the vicinity over a relevant time period. See if anyone of interest appears. Even if of no use, it may indicate to Anony-maus that we are now following his lead."

"Yes, Watson, that's step one," I began to feel pleased with myself; then the sentence was completed, "it's already running now. I started it while you were getting the coffee. The interesting bit is step two... "

"Fuck, I don't know!" I exploded, annoyed at the way in which I was being toyed with. A sneer indicated that I was missing something obvious. I closed my eyes and rubbed them hard. "Chrissy's apartment," I hazarded a guess, "have a look around it?"

"Exactly! You're not as dumb as you look. Let's get a move on. Forensics have it on their to-do list, but there's little chance that they'll get to it within the next day or so. We'll be able to have a snoop about before they bugger things up."

I settled for this back-handed complement and didn't even consider mentioning that visiting a potentially relevant scene without techs was a breach of protocol. I was actually more interested to know what the CI expected to find there.

***

The Platinum Mansion was a top-end apartment block only a couple of hundred meters distant from the cop shop. Koide again ignored protocol and did not register our visit in advance; she simply used her police ID to over-ride the entrance security system and browbeat a meatbot concierge, who was dozing in an entry lounge that seemed to double as a self-service cafe.

Chrissy's flat was huge by Tokyo standards and was located in a corner of the block, with large windows facing south and west. The entrance led through a small hall directly into an airy, open-plan lounge-kitchen-dining room that must have been about a hundred square meters or a bit more, I estimated. An open door evidently led into an equally over-dimensioned bedroom.

We had both already sprayed our hands with sealant, so the CI immediately started to rummage through a pile of magazines on a coffee table in the center of the living room.

"What exactly are we looking for?" I finally asked, feeling like a bystander in this operation.

"Something incongruous," was her rather unhelpful reply. "This Chrissy isn't anything like the streetwalkers that you think of as whores. She is a highly educated courtesan, probably with a better degree than you have."

"What, there are degrees in fucking now? I knew I went to the wrong university," I responded sarcastically.

"Don't be a prune, Watson! This is a professional who gets paid as much in an hour as you get in a week. Didn't think of that when fighting you way into your classical tripos," she laughed.

As I slowly turned around to build an impression of the room as a whole, my boss expanded on her assessment of the fruits of the commercial sex trade. I let the words wash over me and concentrated on the bottom line: it was likely that someone smart enough to earn megabucks in a top-end knocking shop would also be smart enough to know that getting pregnant was a risky thing to do, especially given the power wielded by the clients in that particular establishment. In such a case, some form of insurance would be sensible. This could well be something in the hands of family, a friend, a lawyer or some other third party: but could also be something hidden close to hand if it was sufficiently difficult to find.

I let the background information on the victim run through my head. She had entered Japan almost two years ago and registered as an entertainer under the loose regulations for foreigners in the SAR. I guess she was specially recruited, as she had worked at Pleasure Doubled from that time. The first three months were probably an initial probation period, when she stayed in a hotel in Kabuki-cho. Then she moved into this luxury abode and had been here ever since.

Given that she had lived in this flat for such a long period, the living room had little trace of any personal input; just the standard furnishing and generic ornamentation provided by the rental agency. Koide had already unearthed a tablet computer buried under e-paper magazines and had cracked the simple biometric access protection. I wandered into the bedroom and gazed at the circular bed that dominated the room, with its almost surrealistically smooth silk top-sheet. Everything in the apartment was so neat and tidy that I was sure that maid service was responsible.

The decor looked similar, but a picture caught my eye. It looked like a standard framed twentieth century movie poster: Barbarella, queen of the galaxy, I read. A quick wiki-cheat and I had all the background. Apparently known for some suggestive sexual scenes, by the standard of the day in any case, and also some classic quotes. So maybe, something personal of Chrissy's I guessed. I mumbled some of the lines from the film out loud, trying to nail down the connection. "A good many dramatic situations begin with screaming. Make love? But no one's done that for hundreds of centuries! De-crucify the angel!"

As I uttered the last sentence, the poster transformed into an e-picture frame and started cycling a series of photos which I guessed to be friends and family. "Hey, boss, you should maybe get in here," I shouted as I stared at the images, noting the tropical background in some cases that would be quite consistent with some parts of Thailand or the Philippines.

Koide entered the room with the tablet still clutched in her hand. "So, what've you stumbled over here?"

"Hardly stumbled," I objected as I explained how the picture function was accessed.

"Stumbled!" she over-rode my protestations. "The chances of a structured room search coming over that must be negligible."

"Aren't we doing a structured search now?" I inquired irately.

"Well, I was actually referring to the group who went over this place before we got to it."

"And just what makes you think that this happened?"

"Well, it's subtle, but the entire content of this tablet has been cloned. There are also some blank memory blocks, where content has been scrubbed by tools that the average Joe just can't get a hold of. You wouldn't spot it unless you were looking for it."

"... and had some tools that the average Joe couldn't get a hold of," I added, receiving only a cryptic grin in response.

"Anyway, this place has been professionally turned over, but I guess they didn't pick this up," she waved at the picture. "Somehow, it's the kind of thing that I'd expect from a smart cookie like Chrissy."

"So you think this is more than family snaps?"

"I'd bet on it." The CI looked around the room then set her comm on a bedside table. "I'll record the photos first just to be on the safe side, then I'll find the memory for this display and see if I can crack it."

"Shouldn't we wait for techs. There's a good chance that the memory will be well protected."

My warning was met by a typically smug snort. "The tools I have here are as good as anything that the techs will have."

"Let me guess, military spec?"

"See, Watson, you're learning just from being in my presence!"

"So why don't I get access to all the kit that you have?"

"That's obvious: if I have it, you don't need it. And, anyway, nobody in the department is really supposed to even know about this kit, so I can hardly give it out like sweeties."

I limited my response to an exaggerated roll of my eyes and focused my concentration back on the family snap slideshow. An older couple with their arms around a somewhat younger Chrissy could well be parents and a couple of very beautiful children could well have been siblings. They looked like teenage girls but, thinking back to Chrissy, could also have been hermaphrodites for all we knew.

After about ten minutes, I began to recognize the pictures. "Well, that looks like the entire show; about thirty or so pictures, I'd guess."

"Thirty-seven," my pedantic boss confirmed. "I wonder if other output is also voice-activated. You got the text from the movie?"

"Yes, it seems that it was some kind of kitsch classic of the last century. Although, now I think about it, it's strange that this kind of activation wasn't tied to a voice-print. It would make it a lot more secure."

"A key phrase on its own would indicate that it was intended to be accessed by others in addition to Chrissy. The link to the poster makes it easy for someone who knows what is going on to remember or recover the phrase, without risking writing it down. Nevertheless, the chance of anyone just blundering over it by chance would be negligibly small." The tall blonde was inspecting me minutely as if I had been exposed with some bizarre mutant abilities.

"It was just a fluke," I insisted, feeling distinctly uncomfortable under her gaze. "Just the kind of thing that my past interest in the cultural significance of graphic fiction at the millennium transition might pick up."

"I thought it was this Vendetta comic that you studied."

"Yes, that was one of my projects. But it was one example of a quite high impact movie based on a rather obscure graphic novel. Barbarella was an earlier example."

"Was it now? It wouldn't, by any chance, have links to brothels and kinky sex?"

I had to revert to a cheat in order to confirm that kinky sex was a focus of both the movie and the associated comic and, although maybe not a brothel, a sexual den of iniquity featured prominently in the movie.

"This is coming together in a weird sort of way, isn't it Watson? Chrissy set up this display to be accessible to an anorak like you, exactly the kind of nutjob who would make the links to all the Vendetta shit. What're the chances of that?"

"Well, this is Japan, where manga and anime are completely embedded in national culture in a way that is very different from the West. And, if we are looking at those with an interest mainly in the darker, sexual side of this medium, maybe not so surprising that the rich ones end up in a club like Pleasure Doubled."

"A bit simplistic, Watson, but maybe you've got a point in there somewhere. Looks like we might be getting a handle on whoever is the target of Anony-maus's messages."

"Chrissy's friend? Whoever it is with potential access to these pictures, I mean. Well, I guess there's more to it than the pictures, there must be something beyond this family album. Maybe there's sound or something. Volume!"

To my surprise - and, by the look of it also my boss's - a background soundtrack cut in. I immediately recognized the bizarre techno-metallic tune as something that I had heard before, but couldn't put a name to it immediately. All very interesting in its own way, but somehow not what I'd choose for slideshow music: certainly not when it was mainly family and friends. My comm put a name to it immediately: *Absurd*, with a link to a YouTube titled *Nancy and Hartigan*. Then it clicked, before I needed to search further. "Sin City!"

My boss looked confused by this outburst, then smiled. "Let me guess, another comic turned into a movie..." I nodded and she continued, "... with links to brothels and kinky sex, I would hazard."

"Definitely. Although what we're supposed to do with this information, I'm not quite sure."

"Any of the characters particularly significant?"

I struggled to remember the films and how they related to the graphic novels. "Well, the character Nancy linked with that tune was memorable:

attacked as a child by the pervert son of a corrupt top politician, I'm sure. She ended up as a star act in a bar or brothel after being saved by an incorruptible policeman."

"Smart and street-wise?"

"I would say so."

"So this could be Chrissy's comic analog, with the plot providing us with the information that she wanted to pass on."

"Under threat from the son of a prominent personality would be an obvious message, I'd guess."

"OK, we have enough for the search machines to get on with. Right, Watson, you're on again: any other bright ideas before I go for a hack on the memory that must be embedded in this poster, somewhere or other."

I reverted to wiki-cheats. "The classic line seems to be *Skinny little Nancy Callahan. She grew up. She filled out.*" I don't know if it was the entire phrase or just a component of it, but the slideshow froze. Then the display went blue with a counter in the upper right corner and two lines of text in the middle of the screen:

... memory burn initiates in 10 seconds

I am a dame...

"Fuck!" my boss cursed as the counter ticked away ... 9, 8, 7...

"To die for!" I surprised myself with my own outburst, not sure where it came from. Nevertheless, the counter stopped at 5 and the screen flashed three times in quick succession before being replaced by a dense page of small script and embedded images.

I started to move forward to examine it more closely when I was roughly pushed aside, ending up on my back on the hard but surprisingly comfortable bed. "Don't get in the way, you tool, I'm scanning this."

"Shit, so that's all the thanks I get for cracking the code. And under time pressure too!" I complained, feeling rather hard done to.

My boss ignored me completely. "Only the one page," she observed as the screen flashed again and was replaced by the original Barbarella poster. "The recipient would have had to be prepared for that, scanning the image like I was. Now let's see if anything else is recoverable." She retrieved her comm and mumbled into it.

I pointedly ignored her while scrambling to my feet and heading over to the en-suite bathroom, which I estimated was about the same size as the living room in my apartment. A large bath, an open shower, toilet and bidet still left lots of space for a massive sink which was combined with some kind of makeup table. This seemed a bit strange, as I had noticed a vanity table to the side of the bedroom. I sat on the stool in front of it and saw that this immediately activated a 3D holographic image of my head and shoulders along with a menu that was clearly related to hairdressing. Top-end robot barber, I guessed. I waved at the scanning options and the image moved lower and the menu morphed; evidently including a range of options for pubic topiary.

I pondered for a moment and then selected a memory function that sat to the side of the main

107

menu. A list of dates and times appeared, the latest being 4:40 pm on the day that Chrissy had died. Immediately after selecting this, a hologram of the victim appeared, sitting on this stool in a very relaxed manner. Especially relaxed considering that she was buck naked.

Over the last day I had been increasingly referring to Chrissy in the feminine, but the view of a sizable flaccid penis reminded me of how incongruous this was. The system was completely unprotected, so I could download the image directly to my comm.

"Getting into kink porn, Watson?" I jumped at the voice behind me, unaware that my boss had followed me into the bathroom.

"Downloaded and sent over to Nakayama-sensei to help him polish his model of the missing bits," I responded smugly. "I know that he had already something from the PD website, but this is very much higher resolution. You can easily make out individual pores," I illustrated this by zooming in on the image - unfortunately with a center of view on the pruned pubes above the hermaphrodite's prick.

I was just about to close the display when I was pulled out of the stool and the CI plonked down in my place. I cut off a curse of complaint to peer over the large blonde's shoulder while she scanned the victim's flat stomach at high resolution. "So, what are you looking for there?"

"Any small trace of a scar," came the indistinct response as Koide tried to simultaneously stifle a yawn.

"Wouldn't Nakayama have spotted that?"

"Not if it was right where the incision was made when poor Chrissy was gutted," again blurred by a yawn.

"Ah, right, that's a possibility." I noted now a faint shaded overlay on the image. "So you're checking along a profile downloaded from your comm."

"Well, I couldn't do it from memory at this resolution. Image analysis will get the confirmation, but I think this is the trace of a small incision, just about where the left ovary would lie based on the forensic visualization of the missing organs."

"Weird," I commented, "but how did you know to look there? What's it all about?

"No idea on the latter and, in response to your first question, I was only browsing to see if there could be additional reasons for carving up our victim in that way. Looks like there could be."

I pondered on this strange development for a bit, but couldn't see any way in which it would help us nail down the murderer. Nevertheless, the progress that we were making suddenly made me feel uneasy, reminding me of what happened only a day earlier in Kabuki-cho.

"Boss, I wonder if we should be discussing this here. It has just occurred to me that the place could be bugged."

"Luckily it occurred to me as soon as I entered the place. Three high res video pins in the main living room, two in the bedroom and one here in the bog. They weren't taking risks of missing anything." I looked startled, but this caused only a smug smile.

"Off course, I fried them all immediately and set up a broad spectrum white noise generator to cover any other options that Mister Maus might have up his sleeve. In any case, we'll have the techs go over the place just on the off chance there's something we've missed, but I have a feeling that we have the lot."

"So, our opponents suspected that Chrissy had hidden something here: they couldn't find it themselves, but set up a watch to see if we could do any better."

"That's how I read it," the CI confirmed. "Think we might have a reception committee waiting on us?"

"Oh, fuck! You don't think that knocking out the spy cams will have put us on the hit list again, do you?"

"Well, what would you do if you were in Maus's shoes?"

"Of course, we don't know that it was his team that searched this place," I responded pedantically to buy myself some thinking time.

"Right enough, Watson, but let's just consider this as a worst case."

"OK, then I guess what he does depends on how sure he is that there was something concealed here in the first place, how confident he is that we would find it and whether he really thinks that he can obtain this knowledge from us. After all, his hits have a hundred percent failure rate so far."

"That's only based on two attacks on us," the CI responded equally pedantically, "he did manage to take out Chrissy without leaving us much to go on - and we don't know how much else he has been up

110

to. I suspect that, from the ease with which he has been able to pull together these professional thugs, that he's no stranger to the criminal world."

"Point!" I conceded. "Additionally, these head games that are being played with us might indicate that he could well set up another confrontation regardless of if he is sure that it would be successful or not, as it would keep us off balance in any case."

"Yes, that's the argument for having a go at us. What would cause him to leave us alone?"

This change in tack threw me for a bit as I tried to reorganize my mental picture of our nemesis. "God, this wheels within wheels stuff is doing my bloody head in! OK, if I was the mouse and thought there was a chance that we would find something hidden here, I wouldn't attack us if it was something that we were supposed to find and act on."

I waited for the usual scornful criticism, but instead received a look of surprise. "Indeed, Watson, I think this would be the case. So we learn a lot just by leaving this flat and strolling back to the office."

"But what if there's a mob with guns and swords waiting for us?" Even to me I noted that my voice pitch had increased, betraying my fright at the thought.

I received a condescending pat on the head. "Don't bother your little head about it. If there is a mob, we just beat seven shades of shit out of them and bang-up the survivors when they get out of intensive care."

This answer surprised me not at all - and provided exactly no reassurance. Probably as was intended, I guessed.

Chapter 6

Our brief walk back to the SAR police station was a complete anti-climax, nothing in the least bit threatening, although my nerves were like taut cables the entire time. I breathed a sigh of relief as I closed the door of Koide's office behind us and slumped into the visitor's chair.

Even my redoubtable boss was unable to hide a trace of tension being relieved as she settled down opposite me and rubbed the back of her neck. "Always nice to avoid agro, but this then implies that our opponent isn't worried about what we found or, indeed, wanted us to find this stuff in the first place. Anyway, let's have a butcher's at this stuff that Chrissy was hiding."

My boss had accumulated slang from throughout her travels, which I was just reminded included a year with the Met in London. Sometimes I struggled to follow her English, which ensured that many of the Japanese staff were constantly baffled - but, of course, much too polite to say anything about it. If anything, this probably contributed to her mystique.

The text grabbed from its brief appearance in the victim's bedroom was projected above the desk as an expansion of a node of the case model. "Did you get anything at all from the associated memory?" I enquired, remembering that the CI was working on this when I entered the bathroom of the apartment.

"Not a sausage. It really was read once and fry. Volatile optical holographic memory with a UV

113

flash built in for good measure. I doubt even these smart Jap techs will be able to extract a Dicky Bird from it. Anyway, I think we may have enough here," she waved towards the displayed material.

The list was labeled Nomura-san payments and contained 25 numbered entries. Each had a date - the first being twenty years ago and the second five years later. A third was ten years ago and the rest within the last 2 years at approximately monthly intervals. The last entry was six days ago. The next column was headed XCD and contained numbers with many zeros - giving something in the order of tens of thousands for the earlier entries and tens of millions for the later ones. "XCD?" I mumbled aloud.

"East Caribbean Dollars apparently," my boss glanced at her comm, evidently cheating it. "Originally floated, but tied to the US dollar a few years ago. One is now worth ten Yankee bucks."

"US bucks, but those are toilet paper! There's, what, about a hundred to a New Yen."

"Ballpark, so that means that the latest payments are in the order of a million NY: quite a tidy sum."

I thought about it. A mega-yen would probably rent Chrissy's very smart flat for a year, so there was indeed a sizable flow of cash here. "I guess someone like Chrissy is very well paid, but not that level," I commented.

"There're also these earlier payments: this Caribbean dollar was then about one to one with the US version, but that was a lot more valuable then, before their ecosystem was totally fucked."

I found it weird to think that it was only two decades ago that the US economy started to go tits-up, hit by the perfect storm of reduced rainfall due to climate change, pollution of major aquifers by fracking and a political system reduced to impotence by the power of uneducated religious fundamentalists and right wing gun-nuts. Of course, climate change both giveth and taketh away: the losses of the US were matched by gains in Canada: transforming it into a super-power that is one of the world's bread-baskets. The US is now really just a supply of cheap labor for its northern neighbor and would be much better off if it tied its battered currency to the mighty Canadian dollar. But, due to the incompetence that caused the US's problems in the first place, there seemed no chance that such a sensible move would ever happen.

My wool-gathering was interrupted by my boss. "So, Watson, what does it all mean?"

"Fucked if I know," I responded irately, to be met by a glare that indicated I wasn't getting off that easily. "OK, if we knew who this Nomura guy was, we would be a bit further along the path," I waved in the direction of the main axis of the case argumentation model.

"So, who might he be?"

"Maybe there's something in the images embedded with that list." These now expanded up. "Looks like photos of hand-written entries in an account ledger to match the payments. Based on the running total, nothing has been spent; this pot of gold has just been continually increasing, with some strange way of calculating accumulated interest that

I can't work out. Why on earth would anyone write down this stuff on paper? I suppose it could be digitally created, but why do that?"

"Jesus, Watson, would you stop asking questions and answer some for a change. You can start with Nomura: how do we find him?"

I scratched my head. "Well, from the recent payments, could be someone who is a member of PD, paying for special services rendered. The mama-san said that happened, didn't she? The members pay a fee to take a girl for the evening, but the rest is between the hooker and the punter."

"Seems a sensible place to start, although we will also need to find an explanation for the earlier payments. OK, we have something to go on there. So, now, what about the images of hand-written pages - what could be behind those?"

I racked my mind as I skimmed through a range of argumentation branches. In desperation I tried to stall for time. "If the message is for Chrissy's mysterious friend, it could be something that would make sense only to him or her. Just like the codes to access this stuff, most people wouldn't have a chance of cracking that even with the most sophisticated of tools. It's actually a bit like the brothel," I spoke slowly as the idea began to emerge, "not very sophisticated tools, but used in a way to provide an extremely high level of security. Actually, I wonder if that's what the accounts ledger is all about. You can crack just about any normal bank account if you have the right tools, but an account recorded on hard copy can't be touched unless you can find it physically, which could be very hard if stored in an out of the way place."

"Like one of the tax havens in the Caribbean! Fuck me, Watson, you're picking up this stuff really fast. Did someone slip something into your Twisted Thistle last night?"

"Fucking hell! How on earth could you possibly know that? Did you have someone tailing me?" This last thought was annoying but, in some ways, offered a bit of comfort in that we may not have actually been as exposed during the previous day as it had seemed.

This reassurance was quickly quashed. "Don't be silly, Watson, why on earth would I waste resources tailing you? Anytime you're in Kabuki-cho late in the evening you always gravitate to that pseudo-Scot dive and you always start with a pint of draft Belhaven. Not a great feat of deduction to make that prediction."

I spotted that I was getting diverted from extremely unusual words of praise, probably deliberately as the CI tried to cover up her slip.

"So the numbers in whoberry dooberry Caribbean Dollars fit with the snaps!" I grabbed the image of the earliest entry and blew it up so that the page extended from ceiling to desk top. "Multi-spectral," I commanded, initiating differential filtering to improve contrast. There seemed to be a trace of a watermark on the plain, lined page. "Edit out text and enhance," the writing disappeared and the diagonal watermark was now clear - CIBC St John's.

Koide had been following this closely and already had the cheat to hand. "It's the First Caribbean International Bank in St John's, which seems to be the capital of the island of Antigua."

"Antigua? Well that's a bit of a coincidence."

"What kind of coincidence?"

"Not so much really, I suppose. Just I have a mate that lives there now."

"Your mates have got to live somewhere, so it really isn't much to do with our case."

"I suppose not, it's just that this guy was pretty well responsible for getting me out here to Japan in the first place."

Now my boss looked startled, an expression that I couldn't recall having previously seen on the face of this self-possessed woman. "Well, maybe that is an interesting coincidence after all. Let's put it into the case model for the expert system to work on and we'll come back to it after we've nicked Nomura-san."

***

I was sent off to get another coffee while Koide took a toilet break. It was about fifteen minutes later when the detective finally returned to her office, clearly having showered and freshened up somewhat. She sank her coffee in a single gulp, then glared at me as if it was my fault that it was stone cold.

"OK, Nomura. Nobody of that name on the lists of members or regular guests, but let's map days when Chrissy had short shifts at the club with

118

members vising on those dates... " A histogram showed a ranking of matches, with A. Maus amongst the highest ranked.

"Looks like Mister Maus may well be Nomura," I observed, "but he wasn't at the club the night before last, so might not be the murderer."

"Yes, well this looks like what we were expected to find. Let's get this linked into image analysis of all CCTV records from the vicinity for all evenings that Maus visited over the last two years."

"Couldn't Shoko have edited them?" I asked, as a linked branch showed that interrogation of our comms tech revealed that she had done the editing of the records to hide the ambulance transfer of Chrissy's corpse.

"She claims not to have touched any other records and, in any case, has been with us only six months since her last maternity leave and wouldn't have been able to modify older records after they go to the archive vault. Anyway, the analysis will take a while, so we can run other threads in parallel."

"What've you got in mind?"

The big woman smiled mischievously, making her seem suddenly much younger. "Well, I thought we would start by hacking a bank account."

"That's not exactly legal," I pointed out.

"Yes, well we're only going to have a quick peek. If there's anything dodgy, we'll get a court order and do it properly."

"We'll get into trouble if anybody catches us at this."

"Don't be such a poofter! Anyway, if we did get caught, you can always claim that a big girl made you do it!"

I risked a quick glance into the Grand Canyon: she was indeed a very big girl. "OK," I gave in with a shrug, "what do I need to do here?"

"Hopefully bugger all at all. But the voodoo shit you do with geek passwords has already come in handy, so just be ready to perform whenever needed."

I started to complain that nothing that I had done could be classed as any form of voodoo, shit or otherwise, but realized that the detective was paying me no attention and had already cracked into the Pleasure Doubled server. The security protecting client accounts looked impregnable, but Koide's tools cut through the firewalls like butter. I made a mental note to remove everything that I had on the cloud that was remotely sensitive and burn it onto stand-alone hard memory. Koide was frighteningly good at hacking.

The client details for A. Maus appeared. Address was given as Prudential Building, Akasaka, without further details. Linked account was with the Akasaka Mitsuke branch of Credit Suisse. I groaned as Koide started the hack into the bank. This was not just small fry like PD, she was fucking about with very big fish here - sharks who would have her blood if she made one small mistake.

Even with the super tools that the CI was using, hacking into CS took time. As we already had a name, address and account number, getting into the system was quite straightforward, but checking account details without a biometric-linked password was tricky.

"Yes, got you, you bastard!" my boss punched the air in delight as account details scrolled through the air between us. I had difficulty noticing anything but the size of the balance, an eye-wateringly large number that hardly seemed to be perturbed by either payments or withdrawals of huge amounts of cash.

"This can't be set up only for illicit dalliances at a brothel," I observed, "regardless of how expensive the hookers might be."

"Indeed, Watson, my boy: the Akasaka mouse has seriously fucked up here. This looks like a general purpose dirty dealings Konto, the kind of thing that often ends up buried in a Swiss bank. Now let's just see... " a subset of the entries became highlighted in red, "... and now you are indeed fucked, Nomura-san. That's a one to one match of the payments that Chrissy had listed over the last two years, taking into account the conversion rates from Yen at the time involved!"

I felt strangely deflated, with a general sense of anti-climax. All the labyrinthine complexity of this case and then, with a single page of numbers from Chrissy's flat, the entire thing seemed to be unraveling.

The display vanished and then was replaced by another ongoing hack: a Ginza branch of BTMU. "Jesus, what now?" I groaned. "Shouldn't we quit while we're ahead?"

"This is called a winning streak, boy. Just watch a genius at work - and try not to piss yourself."

This last remark made me think back to poor Shoko, reminding me of the terror invoked by the people that we were now going toe-to-toe against. Maybe pissing myself would be a completely normal reaction.

The hack went quicker than I expected, as the CI was clearly basing it on a file that the Tokyo police organized crime division kept on yakuza gangs. Literally hundreds of accounts from a weird diversity of cover companies and individuals were integrated and mapped against Maus's Akasaka account over the last week. Seven withdrawals and three payments matched. "Why would Yamaguchi-gumi be paying the mouse?" I wondered aloud.

"Refund in case of job fucked up," Koide responded immediately, showing a match between three withdrawals and equivalent fifty percent repayment.

"God, these guys work fast! I normally pay within thirty days and, if anything is wrong, I count myself lucky to get repaid within six months."

"Money moves fast in the criminal world: in itself the speed of these transfers indicates something fishy."

"OK, so we could now formally go for a court order to access these accounts. But we still don't have a direct tie to Nomura."

"Well, let's see how our image mining has been going." One wave of the blonde's hands and a complex 3D graphic linked to video files appeared. From the exec sum, it seemed that many of the members could be linked to video with a reasonable degree of confidence. Two images most closely

122

matched Maus's visits to the club, although both of these were also linked to a visit the night before last, when we knew that Maus was not logged in.

I checked the back-links, the similarity of the matches was due to the fact that two members always visited the club together: A. Maus and Val Page. I expanded a couple of the most recent images, from two nights ago. Two good-looking, expensively dressed, middle-aged Japanese women, caught walking arm in arm in both cases. Then a couple of very similar images from ten days previously, when both Maus and Page were logged in. In both cases the taller of the two was sporting a canary-yellow scarf.

The penny dropped. "I think I know what happened on the night in question," I announced. Our Miss Maus was actually at the club, but in the guise of a guest of Page - the V-linked E.V. Hammond."

"Yes, of course," my boss sounded unimpressed at this piece of masterful deduction. "We have both of them now: first Miss Fumiko Nomura, the scion of a mega-rich Tokyo clan with fingers in industrial developments everywhere," one of the images expanded. "Here she is with her notorious lesbian lover, Michiko Saito, ex-porn actress with reputed links to yakuza." The other image now enlarged.

"Not Yamaguchi-gumi, perchance?"

"Indeed: apparently had a strange relationship with both the Kumicho - the big boss - and his wife."

I called up recent wiki-paparazzi snaps of the two women that the CI had identified. "I'm not sure that I can see the resemblance here - apart from the fact that the women are again holding hands." The couple on display were certainly striking, the taller with very short cut hair dyed an iridescent purple and the smaller with a completely shaved head, tattooed with a spider's web."

"Yes, the wigs would have made a forward search tricky, but I was matching images picked up against prominent Nomuras. The biometrics are clear: it's a perfect match."

"Fuck! And again Nomura-san is wearing something yellow." In this case it was a sash that seemed to be an integral part of the black dress that she was wearing.

"This is significant in some way?"

I grinned, feeling quite pleased with myself. "The persecutor of Nancy Callahan in Sin City is referred to as the yellow bastard."

"So everything is pointing clearly towards rich bitch Nomura as the perp. It's all a bit too neat."

"The pregnancy stuff is a bit up in the air though," I pointed out. "If Nomura had been a bloke, he could have been the father. Fumiko is off the hook here."

Koide stroked her lower lip, eyes focused somewhere in the distance. "I wonder if that is actually the case, when you've eliminated the impossible... " She was obviously talking to herself and this quote from the Great Detective certainly needed no response.

Chapter 7

I spent most of the rest of the morning alone, chasing up on a murder that had occurred a week previously in a karaoke joint in Shinjuku-sanchome, just by the JR station. This was much more like our normal murders, which occur about once or twice a month in the SAR. An altercation between a bunch of drunken construction workers on who's turn it was to sing next resulted in one of them getting knifed. Probably just bad luck that the stab hit an artery; the crowd seemed so legless that it was unlikely to be deliberate. Indeed, if they had immediately called for help instead of spending so much time fumbling about in an attempt to stop the bleeding themselves, their colleague could probably have been saved. This did, however, provide plenty of time for the attacker to make himself scarce.

The men interviewed had been very reluctant to name the perpetrator, but between a description given by the three girls in the party and a visit to the construction site where they all worked was sufficient to identify the prime suspect as a certain James Brooks, normally referred to as Jiggy. The Scot had been in the SAR only two months, but already had a reputation as a bad-tempered bastard. Nobody seemed to like him, but they put up with him to avoid potentially violent confrontations.

He had gone to ground without trace, but had been informed on this morning by the girlfriend he had been living with, apparently because he had been roughing her up. The girl led us to her tiny apartment in a low rent block and handed me the

125

key that opened the front door. I led the way in, followed by a trainee detective and two beat cops, and we literally caught him with his trousers down: wearing only a vest, he was pissing into the sink of the kitchen corner associated with the tiny bed-sit.

"What the fuck're you cunts doing. Marie, is that you there, you fucking evil little bitch! You grassed me up, you cunt, I am really going to fucking cut you to ribbons for that!"

Ignoring the urine still dripping from his dick, he grabbed a large bread knife from a rack by a chopping board and lunged at me, slashing at my stomach.

As I had my taser ready, it was no problem to shoot him point-blank in the center of his chest. The result was spectacular: he shot backwards, the knife flying from his hand as his spine arched and the back of his head cracked against a pseudo-granite work top. He was unconscious as he slumped onto the floor, a curl of smoke wafting from the scorched front of his wife beater.

I heard a shocked gasp from the trainee behind me and turned to see his look of amazement - and the grins on the faces of the two plods. The voltage limiter: I realized that I had followed Koide's command and left it turned off.

Damage limitation time, I decided. "Now, you know that, of course, we set voltage limiters on the taser at all times, and keep them on for normal crowd control or unarmed confrontation situations," I ad-libbed, watching all three of my colleagues nod. "The situation is different when you or an innocent bystander are attacked directly by someone with a deadly weapon. The key thing is to ensure that no harm is done by the attacker so, if it seems justified, you may turn the limiter off. CI Koide has made this very clear to me, something that may have saved our lives over the last couple of days."

The guys seemed to swallow this, but were immediately diverted in any case as Maria squeezed past them, lifted her T-shirt to expose bruises on her side and stomach, and started kicking the groin of the prostrate man. "You, you're the evil cunt! This is what you did to me, you fucking Glasgow bastard, fucker, fucker!"

I didn't move and none of the others seemed inclined to stop her. With the damage that the taser had done, it seemed unlikely that he'd have much future use for his genitals. With the evidence that we had, Brooks would be convicted even if he did not regain consciousness. Murder conviction of someone in a coma would move very quickly to euthanasia. The Japanese were very pragmatic in such matters.

"OK, Charles," I addressed the bemused looking trainee, "I think you can run with the ball from here. Calm the girl down, which should be a bit easier after she's got this out of her system." The girl was, indeed, already running out of steam and now crying more than kicking.

"Sure, boss, I've already called for a meat wagon to transport the suspect to our secure hospital wing. That is, assuming that there is any space there," the young Taiwanese grinned cheekily, "it seems to be full of guys who have run into Koide-san."

"CI Koide to you, you disrespectful young bugger," I responded automatically, but unable to keep amusement out of my voice at the mental image of a ward packed with those who had experienced a close encounter with the formidable detective's take on non-lethal weapons. Presumably there would be an equivalent over-crowding problem at the morgue.

The junior detective's grin just got wider. "Man, you work with the CI Koide crime-busting machine, how awesome is that? What's it like, isn't she a genius or something?"

"Or something," I agreed, trying to change the subject. "Anyway, you know what to do now, so get on with it."

As I left the room I could hear Charles rabbiting to the plods. "CI Koide she's like this tall, blonde goddess, but one with truly huge tits... " I was grateful when the closed door cut off further waffling from someone who was clearly one of the many members of the Koide fan club.

***

I had just settled into my office after lunch when I was summoned into the presence. I decided to avoid being sent off like a tea boy and pre-emptively pick up a coffee for my annoying superior en route. The tricky bit was anticipating her desires. I went for what should be a safe option, a long coffee with a shot of espresso added and sachets of sugar on the side.

CI Koide accepted my offering with a nod of her head, which could possibly be interpreted as some form of thanks. She was working on a part of the Chrissy case model, so her question caught me off guard. "So you whacked Jiggy Brooks, did you? He's in intensive care, but effectively brain dead so they'll be turning him off sometime soon."

"Fuck! I didn't mean to do that. It was the fucking voltage limiter on the taser, still switched off after... "

"Stop wittering, Watson. I was just in the process of telling you that you did a good job." She was continuing to work on the model and her voice was uncommonly soft. "Went at you with a knife, did he?"

"Yep, the little shit. A fucking typical Glasgow ned - knifes and razors. How the fuck he ever got an entry permit I do not know."

"Apparently a shit-hot waldo operator, especially for tricky welding jobs. Seems to trump his record of continuous GBH since his teens. Anyway the world is a better place without a shit like that in it. Kicking his goolies to fuck was a nice finishing touch, by the way."

"I had nothing to do with that... " I started to protest, then noticed Koide's grin, "... as you probably well fucking know! You're just winding me up again!"

"Yes, I know I shouldn't, but it's like shooting ducks in a barrel - such fun that I can't resist it."

I suspected that Koide was again slipping off target to cover her uncharacteristic complement, so

129

I decided to help her. "So, boss, what's new with Chrissy?"

"We've got a couple of fetal cells in remnant blood and Nakayama has done a sterling job of analyzing the buggery out of them."

I leaned forward to peer at the data linked to the forensic block of the model, excited by the thought of nailing down the father of Chrissy's baby, which might completely break the case.

I scratched my head in confusion. "I can't be reading this fucking ex sum right, it's got Chrissy as the bloody father! It must be all this trans-sex shit that's messed up the expert system producing the interpretation."

"That's what I initially thought, so I got Shinji to run over the data himself," I had a great view of the Grand Canyon as Koide leant forward to highlight a linked note from the pathologist but, for once, my attention was completely on the case.

I read the short note through twice - then quickly checked my watch to ensure that it wasn't April first. No, safely on April third. "Is Nakayama-sensei taking the piss?" I finally asked, as this seemed the only possible explanation.

"Nakayama? He hasn't the imagination to come up with anything nearly as bizarre as this on his own."

"But this says that Chrissy, who was carrying this fetus in her womb, must have been the father, not the mother."

"And that's not even the weirdest part," she confirmed.

"But, but... " I spluttered, "... but how the fuck can there be DNA from another mother?"

"Not just another mother - two mothers! The ovum that was fertilized by Chrissy's sperm has genetic components traceable to both Miss Nomura and her lesbian lover. Ain't that a thing?"

I just couldn't get my head around this. "Wait a minute, it isn't you taking the piss here, is it?" I didn't need my boss's glare to answer that question. She would never fuck about with a murder case file. "OK, so the data and interpretation are kosher. This has got to be gengineering gone crazy."

"Yes, well some form of genetic manipulation has certainly occurred to create the ovum, on top of whatever was required to create Chrissy. Tricky enough now, but biting edge when Chrissy was conceived twenty-one years ago. Interestingly enough, however, a leader in this field over the last three decades has been a certain Nomura Human Life Sciences," she opened a website link, "part of the empire belonging to Miss Nomura's clan."

"Well, even though I haven't a clue what all this DNA crap is about, we must have enough now to nab Nomura-san and her rug-munching partner."

"Even the dyke partner would be tricky and we would need a lot more to risk touching Miss Nomura. Her father is the seventeenth richest man in Japan and he has the political clout to go with it. We would need a water-tight case before we could even consider touching little Fumiko." My boss was very seriously pissed off.

I traced back through the case model links. "Why did it have to be this Nomura?" I mused. "If it had just been Mistresses Mouse and Page, we could have just got steamed in."

I jerked back in shock as the CI appeared in front of me, grabbed my shoulders and planted a kiss on my forehead. "Out of the mouth of babes and innocents! If I didn't know you were dumb, I'd think you were fucking brilliant!"

"Do what?" I stammered in confusion. "What did I say?"

"See what I mean," the blonde grinned. "Totally clueless: takes genius like mine to interpret your cryptic Delphic utterances."

I was now beginning to get annoyed. "Will you stop bloody congratulating yourself and tell me what the fuck you're on about!"

"Ah, you hit the nail on the head and didn't even know that you had a hammer in your hand." I glared as she drew out my agony. "As you said, it would be easier if we didn't know who our prime suspects really are. We could just arrest them, use suggestion enhancers under medical supervision to get a confession that would stand up in court and then Bob's your uncle."

"But we do know: it's in the model and that's time locked. We can't possibly pretend that we didn't know."

"Yes indeed, the case arguments are time locked - but look at this fucking thing... " a fully expanded summary model filled the entire room. The case file logs the time that everything is added and all links made, but ninety-nine point God-knows how many nines percent of that is autonomic generation. There is no record at all of what we looked at and when we did so."

"So we would need to lie if questioned?"

"Not really a lie, more a little fib. Anyway, it'll come up only if we don't make a completely stonking case."

"So it's all or nothing, with my career probably on the cards?"

"Something like that. So, when do the lesbos usually go to the club?"

I flicked through the model while Koide glared at the ceiling, deep in thought. "Fridays: the last visit was evidently an exception."

"Every Friday?"

"Whenever they're together in Tokyo, it looks like."

"Are they here now?"

"No indication that they've left that I can see."

"Right you are. We now need to line up all our ducks before we go into action tomorrow night."

This just confirmed my premonition that she was going to say something like that.

***

I was given the job of extending background checks on all of the identified PD members and guests, setting up the search engines in a way that didn't seem focused on Nomura and Saito. With extended CCTV capture in and around Sakura-dori in the relevant time window, grouping of images picked up on different dates, elimination of known workers and so on, we had identified with reasonable confidence almost a half of the active members and about a third of the regular guests. To my great surprise, the split was about fifty-fifty men to women.

The guests were a mixture, with a tendency towards high functionaries in government and commerce, but the members were a select group of the rich, tending towards the extremely rich. Even our seemingly humble professor, who claimed unable to afford the most expensive courtesans, had inherited a considerable fortune. I seemed to remember seeing that sixty-seven out of the hundred richest Japanese were women, so maybe the sex ratio was not so strange after all.

Suddenly it dawned on me that there was one anomaly in the identified members: our own commander. She was clearly well-connected and, if her kink went in that direction, would fit well into the profile of guests, but was not even close to having the wealth typical of other members. I expanded the search to check that my boss's boss hadn't won a lottery or come into a great inheritance, but there was absolutely no indication of anything of that sort. In any case, this seemed to have nothing to do with our investigation; so I simply appended a comment on this, noting also that it was a bit of a coincidence that someone from the SAR police force would actually be a member of this club.

Any police records of identified visitors to PD were also automatically linked to the file. Unlike some other countries, such records were never expunged in Japan for any offence, regardless of how trivial it was or how long ago. This led to extensive files on almost all citizens, including traffic violations, petty teenage indiscretions and even cases where they had reported a crime or registered lost property. Links were also included to internal security files, with education, employment and residence histories, records of foreign travel, rumored sympathies for dubious organizations or political parties and a host of other related material.

This could easily look like the records kept by a repressive regime but, in the case of Japan, it was more a matter of search engine and data archiving technology running loose without any clear legislative control. Personal privacy was treated in a different manner in the West, where even prosecution of terrorists and mass murders could be blocked by their right to privacy. Oriental culture was more pragmatic: unnecessary invasion of privacy resulted in loss of face by the perpetrator, causing serious damage to their standing in the community. The more time that I spent in Japan, the more I appreciated this approach.

Probably as a function of their wealth, all security files of club members were very large, so I focused on the police records alone, ranking them by size. Here there was a lot more variation, but the top ten were all more extensive than might be expected from the great and the good.

I first scanned the largest file, a prominent industrialist who had dabbled in politics on a number of occasions, but without much success. Tetsuo Ishikawa was the only son of a shipping magnate and had been a hell-raiser in his youth, at school in Japan and at university in the USA. I looked at a 2D image of the young man from the turn of the Millennium: small, wiry and radiating attitude. It clearly cost a fortune in lawyers' fees to keep him out of jail. Indeed, even when he took over as patriarch of an industrial empire on the death of his father, he had continuous scrapes with the law: ranging from the results of his violent temper when drunk to his dubious business practices. Now in his eighties, he had passed on management responsibilities to a son and a daughter and seemed to have finally calmed down. His record was, however, continually expanding due to use of his influence to protect a grand-daughter from coming to grief as the result of a lifestyle which made his own teenage years seem tame by comparison. Here the acorn had not fallen far from the tree.

With a better feeling for the lifestyles of the mega-rich, I moved on to Fumiko Nomura's file, ensuring that it was read-only, so leaving no record of my analysis of it. In terms of size, it was number eight on the list, so I was not surprised to encounter the history of yet another misspent youth. Initially, however, Fumiko was recorded as the reported victim of sexual abuse by her older brother, Sumio, when she was only ten years old. Although the evidence seemed compelling, the case never went to court. The justification for inaction was based on extensive psychological assessment of both Fumiko and Sumio but, reading between the lines, I would guess more due to political pressure from their father.

By her mid-teens, Fumiko was going through a spoiled rich brat phase, with a host of minor drink and drugs misdemeanors being punished by admonishments or token fines. She also came out as lesbian over this time and several complaints were registered of her stalking or showing obsessive behavior towards female teachers. Complaints were dropped in every case before they could lead to any prosecution, which I could identify again as the trace of a paternal guardian angel.

I skimmed through sparser records covering her time at university; typically in the USA, at Stanford. The US police were much less meticulous in documentation of trivial offences, which could be covered by a spot fine, or recording complaints that did not lead to prosecution. I was amused to note that, during three years in California, she did get arrested twice and even spent a night in jail; in both cases due to charges of public indecency at cosplay conventions. Despite separation by the Pacific Ocean, the long arm of her father was evident, having charges dropped and records removed from the US system, even if they had already been copied to a vault in Tokyo.

After Miss Nomura's return to Nippon, her behavior was much improved, at least as far as her formal police record was concerned. Nevertheless, she was linked to a number of incidents where investigations were focused on her assistants, drivers, bodyguards and other lackeys. Clearly fall guys, I guessed; or, in Fumiko's case, fall gals as they were women in every example that I looked at.

It was a decade ago, when she was in her late thirties, that Nomura-san's file first contained a link to the notorious Michiko Saito. In terms of size, Michiko's file was number three on my list, so I expected yet again to start with a debauched childhood. Not a bit of it: a completely clean record until her early twenties with notes only of her having been interviewed but cleared during an investigation of schoolgirl prostitution and again during an investigation of a failed arson attack on a Catholic convent, where she had been a novice nun.

There was no record of why Michiko left the convent, but her file exploded with detail when, aged twenty-two, she appeared out of nowhere in a hard-core porn ring run by Yamaguchi-gumi. Links showed graphic examples of the product in high resolution 3D. Over a period of a couple of years the ex-nun acquired her trademark tattoos and a range of rather uncomfortable-looking piercings. She was also, I noticed, increasing typecast in the role of dungeon mistress in BDSM fantasies.

The material produced was certainly pushing the limits of legality, but not quite extreme enough to merit prosecution. The file was full of evidence supporting allegations that this pornography front covered prostitution activities of a kind not allowed by even Japan's rather liberal laws, but again not enough to lead to a court case.

Saito-san's widely rumored links to the upper echelons of Yamaguchi-gumi were well supported by surveillance material, which traced how she quickly worked her way up the ranks: generally first building relationships with wives or girlfriends, which then led to menage a trois with the male partner. Although within two years she was living with the capo di tutti capi of the yakuza, she still seemed to maintain relationships with a number of his underlings.

The transition from yakuza moll to life partner of a prominent socialite was sudden and mysterious. As with all major Japanese companies, there were numerous hints of links between Nomura holdings and the yakuza, so contact between the pair could have occurred via a business connection. Miss Nomura was, however, also well known for frequenting establishments catering for clients partial to the weirder fringe of sex, so this was also a possible contact point.

However it happened, the two women were suddenly inseparable. The relationship was peculiar enough that, despite Nomura's power, it was a constant source of speculation and innuendo in the gutter paparazzi websites. Nevertheless, there was little more of direct interest in either of their police files after they paired up and no link at all to Chrissy or Pleasure Doubled.

I sat back and closed my eyes, trying to draw some kind of pattern from this deluge of information. We had a lesbian couple who seemed devoted to each other, with common interests in kinky sex. Although they did not try particularly hard to hide their visits, their membership of PD was concealed by comic-related pseudonyms. Given Fumiko's cosplay past and time spent in the States, it was not unreasonable that she may have also encountered western graphic novels.

The elephant in the room, however, was Chrissy's pregnancy. How did this come about and how on earth did this link to her brutal murder? It certainly wasn't unusual for homosexual couples to want children, but there were many ways in which that desire could be satisfied. Even if, for some bizarre reason, they wanted a hermaphrodite to be the father and someone else to carry the baby to term, the procedure involved here seemed gratuitously complex.

I desperately wanted to find out more about Nomura Industry's genetic engineering branch, but could not think of a way to set this up without making it evident that we were already focusing investigations on Fumiko and her lover. While pondering this problem, I idly threw up a breakdown of the occupational histories of all members, which also linking to their academic qualifications. As I had expected, lots of industrialists, politicians, lawyers and bankers, matched to appropriate degrees in management, politics, law and accountancy. Also, being Japan, a fair number started off with qualifications in various sub-disciplines of engineering. Michiko mapped into a sub-group with no higher educational qualifications: generally those who inherited wealth or married into it. I was surprised to see that Fumiko had been placed with a small number of top scientists and doctors as, apparently, her degree from Stanford had been in molecular biology.

To my surprise, I discovered that Fumiko was actually Doctor Nomura, with an external PhD from the highly prestigious University of Tokyo. This was certainly something that wasn't common knowledge. I felt my hands shaking as I leant forward to flick on the link to further information, but, at the last moment, forced myself to sit back and leave it untouched. I had just remembered that my office could possibly be bugged and, even if the chances were small, I could not risk allowing our hidden puppet-master the chance to follow our progress.

I struggled with the frustration caused by my conviction that I had serendipitously stumbled over a key to cracking the case and the prudent need to avoid immediately following up on it. Finally I shrugged my shoulders and set up a meeting with CI Koide at her earliest availability, which was in forty minutes. Until then I would just have to stem my impatience.

**

My boss was visibly annoyed when she stormed into her office five minutes late, evidently due to an over-run of her previous meeting with our Commander. "What's up, Watson?" she growled. "It had better be good, as I'm not the happiest of bunnies at the present moment."

I refrained from pointing out that she was stating the obvious and, instead, gave a quick summary of my findings to date as the case model morphed to back me up. "I'm fairly convinced that Nomura-san's doctorate has something to do with the case, but I didn't want to go any further until I was sure that I was secure and there is no way that whoever is behind this circus can follow what we're doing."

The tall blonde dropped into her chair and gave me a quizzical stare. "You seem very sure of yourself here. What do you think you'll find when we open the box? Could it be something quantumy: a kind of Schrödinger's link which will solve our case or be totally irrelevant, but we won't know until we open it."

For a moment I had no idea what the woman was gibbering on about, then I caught the slightest trace of a smile. She was winding me up! At least, I seemed to have taken her mind off whatever had occurred during the encounter with her boss.

She was obviously intending to continue in his vein, but I rudely interrupted her. "Fuck this! Just have a look for yourself." I hit the link and leaned forward, suddenly aware that I might just have shot myself in the foot.

I did not have to even look at the appended precis of the work, the title of Nomura-sensei's doctoral thesis said it all: *Investigations of the genetic basis of non-chimeric human transsexual development.* "Jesus suffering Christ on a fucking bicycle, well there's the link we were looking for!"

Koide-san looked bemused. "So, Watson, you are not only a detective but a poet to boot. I couldn't have expressed that any fucking better myself."

Chapter 8

We played around with the case knowledge base for about half an hour, being careful to keep any updates generic for all identified members, but with our attention focused on the material output for Doctor Nomura. The research that formed the basis for her PhD had been carried out at Nomura Human Life Sciences main research lab in Kyoto. Reading between the lines of linked documentation, it looked very much like Fumiko had been more of a team leader and had been directly responsible for little of the associated technical work. Nevertheless, she was awarded the doctorate for the dissertation produced, although she graduated in absentia and there was no record of her ever using her doctoral honorific.

Typically, it was Koide who noticed an apparently trivial footnote mentioning that the head of the HLS lab committed suicide by eating a cyanide-laced apple on the day that the doctorate was awarded. "What do you think of that, lad?" she inquired as the text was highlighted in read-only mode.

"Looks like an irrelevant coincidence... " I replied cautiously, "although the thing with the apple is ringing bells somewhere."

"The brother... " she hinted, raising her eyebrows in a most annoying manner.

"The brother, the brother... " I stalled as the knowledge base software did its thing, "Fumiko's brother also committed suicide by eating a poisoned apple. The brother who raped her," I expanded.

"Mmm..., poisoned apples - a bit of a history there from Snow White to Alan Turing," my boss mused, "but a huge coincidence of two being closely linked to Miss Nomura."

"You know, there's also another coincidence here," I pointed out, indicating an autonomously generated link, "the date of submission of the thesis is within a month of the first payment to Chrissy."

"It gets even better," my boss grinned, clearly intending to play a trump, "it's also on the day of Chrissy's birth. So I wonder how she managed to set up a bank account from the womb."

**

I cursed myself. It was evident from Koide's self-satisfied smirk that the last throwaway line was a piece of information that she had been sitting on for some time. Nevertheless, my new information opened a different perspective on this discrepancy. I opened up the exec sum of Nomura-sensei's thesis. "Looks like blue sky academic research," I commented, "but this is a commercial lab, not a uni. What were they doing this for?"

"A good question, Watson. What about following it up with a good answer?"

I scanned through the displayed text, looking for clues. "Well, it's claimed that the findings would help both early identification of the probability of intersex children based on parental genetics and also sex assignment in cases where intersex offspring are inevitable."

"So you think that this wasn't just the theoretical research that it's presented as, but was actually being implemented on test subjects? All rather illegal, that." As usual, my boss had reached the conclusion of this thread while I was only halfway there.

"Well, it would fit. In fact, it would be illegal most places, but not... "

"In the Philippines! Good lad!"

"I was actually going be less specific, as there are quite a few places that have not signed the international conventions banning experimental engineering of human genetics. Nomura doesn't happen to have a lab there does it?" I enquired, suspicious that the CI had being doing a bit more digging into the background of the Nomura woman than she had admitted to as yet.

"No, but there is a large research contract with the University of Manila, which covers all of the Nomura medical and life sciences institutes."

"But there's more, isn't there?" I queried, suspicious of the gleam in my boss's eyes.

"Could be. It also appears that the Nomura-funded research is coordinated by a Professor Meg Aquilla, who just happens to have studied at Stanford at the same time as our Fumiko."

"Did they share classes?"

"No, Prof Meg was doing her PhD while Fumiko was an undergraduate. But there are suggestions that they knew each other - and not in the Platonic sense."

"I can't find anything about this on the case model... " I was frantically chasing links to see where it could be secreted.

"That's 'cause nothing's in the database about this so far."

I was horrified. "You can't do this. If this is discovered you'll fuck up the entire prosecution case."

"It will all be added in good time," she tried to reassure me, "immediately after we're finished having our chat with Miss Nomura."

I groaned aloud and offered a silent prayer that Koide's security system was as good as she claimed it to be. I felt as if I could almost smell bridges burning. "Anyway, how did you find out about this Meg?"

"It's quite interesting, because I wasn't looking into Fumiko directly, more following leads on the gengineering technology used to produce Chrissy and how it could have been further modified as the basis of the fetus that she was carrying at the time of her death."

"And just how did this bring you to the Philippines?"

"Apparently it's the go to place for quasi-legal genetic modifications: those of the non-medicinal, cosmetic variety."

"Shit! What does that involve?" I wondered aloud, trying to imagine why someone would do something like this.

"A lot is fairly trivial: ensuring eye and hair color, height and physiogamy of children of a chosen sex. Then again, there are also designer sexual characteristics - a huge penis for your son or giant boobs for your daughter."

I couldn't help an automatic glance at my boss's bosom in response to this last comment. "Don't worry, Watson, these beauties are completely God-given, miraculous as that may seem." She laughed aloud at my discomfort.

"Anyway," she continued, "this led on to tailoring of kids destined for top-end brothels - or even arranged marriages. Very rare until around twenty years ago, but now big business in a specialist niche market. I haven't been able to find anything about fully functional hermaphrodites, although there are certainly rumors."

"Jesus fucking Christ! I remember you mentioned something like this when we were at the crime scene, but thought you were exaggerating - or taking the piss."

"*Moi*, taking the piss?" The CI appeared to be trying to project a cow-eyed picture of naive innocence, which failed completely.

"Anyway, so this is probably where Chrissy came from and you think Nomura is responsible for it?"

"I'm fairly sure that the toolkit came from their human gengineering division and that they're definitely still a big player in this field, constantly raising the bar on what is technically possible. However, there's no hard proof: technology comes from the University and is spun-off for commercialization by a host of small companies in a local science park."

"How does Nomura make money out of this?" I wondered, certain that support of an academic institute would not be altruistic.

"That's quite clever, actually. On the surface, it just looks like profit sharing on all patents and licenses resulting from Nomura-sponsored work. This alone produces more income than the funds Nomura provides for sponsoring research. Then there's another twist. If you fight your way through a labyrinth of dummy corporations and holding companies: most of the small companies making big money out of these developments are actually owned by Nomura."

"So you hadn't actually picked up a direct link to Fumiko?"

"Not yet, but I would have, of course. You've just saved me a bit of time with your further stroke of luck."

"Luck," I spluttered, "there was no way that this was just luck. I was systematically... " I ground to a halt as Koide burst into peals of laughter.

"Don't get your bloody nickers in a twist, Watson, I'm only winding you up. However it happened, the aforementioned ducks are lining up in a most pleasing manner." She glanced at her watch and nodded. "Anyway, time to celebrate: you can buy me a drink."

***

There were a couple of nearby Sapporo beer halls that the cops tended to frequent on the occasions of drinks parties after work, but the CI preferred a smaller Ebisu bar in I-land plaza. As we sat in strained silence over glasses of creamy-top stout, I wondered what was bothering my usually imperturbable boss. She sank two thirds of the beer in a long swallow, sighed and then got straight to the point. "Commander Levich wants to take the lead on this investigation."

"You have got to be kidding me! I don't remember her ever doing any real police work; just committees, strategic planning and all that admin crap."

"Well, I must concede that she's good at the admin crap stuff, but I'm fucked if I want her crashing about here - especially as she is already linked to PD. She should know fucking better!"

"Yes, well her membership of that perv club is very strange... " I started, before my boss broke in.

"I expect that you may consider it very strange for a senior police officer to have interests in less-conventional sex, but it isn't a crime and the Commissioner has made no attempt to conceal her membership... "

"It's not that," I interrupted, impolitely, "it's more how she can afford it? Folk like the Commish should be guests, not members."

"I'd already asked Helen about that. She told me that it was her husband who received the membership from a rich client as a gift after a very big deal went through: he's an accountant specializing in company takeovers. They have an open marriage as he travels abroad about eight months per year, so he had the membership transferred to her. Apparently she has visited the

149

club on her own or with a girlfriend only a couple of times. As a special treat, she takes her husband as a guest once or twice a year."

I felt a bit deflated by this explanation, but it still did not completely convince me. "So you think it's nothing but a coincidence?" I challenged.

"Well, it's certainly an anomaly that we want to keep in mind - but maybe something we shouldn't add immediately to the case model. So what's your take on it? Think the well-dressed Missus Levich is part of the murder conspiracy?"

"I wouldn't go that far, but it would be interesting to find out a bit more about who this gift membership came from."

"Mmm... , you know, Watson, that's not a bad idea. Even if there's nothing at all to it, I could use this to delay letting Helen mess with our case for at least a day or two. This could be all that we need to take down Fumiko and Michiko."

"So how do you want to play that?" finally getting to a question that had been bothering me for some time.

"Well if the lesbian duo turn up at the club as expected tomorrow, we'll provoke them into doing something stupid. They're always accompanied by at least two bull-dyke bodyguards, who shadow them to and from the club. If we can trick them into intervening, then we can wheel the pack off to the nick for a bit of chemically-stimulated interrogation, under rigorous supervision. One slip from them and they're done for."

"This, of course, assumes that they're both guilty and prepared to confess this under a mild suggestion-enhancer. Some pharmacological counter-measures or even focused mental training could get them past anything that we're allowed to use."

"That's certainly the case and would happen if we went through normal channels and attempted to arrest Miss Nomura or her Sapphic bedmate. If we can catch them unaware, however, I think we've a good chance. In fact, I think that this is what will happen, because it's the path planned by whoever is running this entire game."

I pondered this for a couple of minutes as a second round of drinks were served. "So you think these women are being framed?"

"I think they'll go down for murder and probably well deserve it. But it's not the entire story, I know it in my water."

I was suddenly sure that Koide's water was right on the mark.

***

Three hours later I staggered home to my tiny bachelor flat in Shinjuku-gyoemmae. As a result of bullying by my boss, I had stayed in the pub for some snacks and more beers than I really wanted. I had walked home, hoping that the exercise and an unseasonably chilly wind would burn off some of the excess alcohol in my system.

I sat with a double espresso and tried to get my mind sorted out for the day ahead. Oddly enough, it wasn't the risk that I was taking with my career that bothered me. We were pushing our luck with concealing our actions from the case record, but I had every confidence that Koide would manage to sort all of that out. It was the planned confrontation with the bodyguards that I was concerned about.

My previous studies of Nomura-sensei's police record had shown that she was no stranger to trouble, even if in recent years she seemed always to have underlings to take the rap. She appeared hyper-sensitive to anything that could be considered disrespect; either of herself or her partner. The resulting altercations often led to violence, with the other side inevitably coming off worse. I remembered photos of some of Nomura's guards - not women that I would like to come home to with a broken pay packet!

I had also looked at a few photos of victims of such confrontations: in all cases examples of gratuitous mutilation, especially of the face. Slashed by knives, carved up by broken bottles, pulped by blunt objects: it was almost a signature of falling foul of Miss Nomura. Even though such damage could be repaired by cosmetic surgery, the psychological impact must be awful, which was probably the entire point. I don't know if it scared others, but it certainly terrified me.

Chapter 9

The next morning it was me who was summoned to meet with Commissioner Levich, but this was just a formal session to pass the case file on Jiggy Brooks to the Prosecutor and confirm that we supported the proposal of euthanasia, based on the clear evidence of guilt for murder, assault and attempted murder of a police officer. The last was a bit tricky to justify, but having already stabbed someone to death, attacking a policemen with a knife seemed enough to form the basis of the charge. As the perpetrator had already been certified as brain-dead, we were basically just going through the motions to assure that the case could be tidily closed.

In other countries, anti-government do-gooders and ambulance-chasing lawyers would probably have made a circus out of this, claiming police brutality and suing on behalf of distant relatives who probably never had any contact with the deceased. Once again I was convinced that, although it looked a bit like a Big Brother approach, the Japanese system was infinitely preferable.

***

It was mid-morning by the time that I was called to CI Koide's office, expecting to be grilled on my non-existent progress with Chrissy's murder. To my surprise, I was welcomed with a smile and a coffee she had fetched for me. Such anomalous behavior immediately put me on the defensive.

"Sorry, boss, not much to report. I've been with the Commish most of the morning and... "

"Yes, Helen; I guess she's trying to clear her priority admin jobs out of the way to free up time to take over our investigation. As yet, she doesn't realize that this is not going to happen." The blonde was evidently very pleased with herself.

"Are you sure?" I wondered. "This morning she actually asked me how things were going with this case."

"I trust you were suitable vague?" In response to my nod, her smile brightened further. "Yes, well we can certainly exclude any further interference from Helen as soon as we nick Miss Nomura and identify her as prime suspect in this case."

"How can you be so sure?" I repeated, sure that this circumlocution was specifically aimed to annoy me.

"Because I've managed to trace the generous client responsible for the gift to Helen's husband... "

"That's what I suggested," I pointed out.

"Whatever. In any case, it was another silly mistake by Nomura-san. The client involved was a property developer with a history of rather dubious dealings with the yakuza - Yamaguchi-gumi in particular."

Koide san was clearly waiting for a comment from me - or maybe just words of praise for her investigative skills. I thought this argument through for a moment: it actually seemed a bit weak to me. "OK, that's a link, but it isn't so convincing. Almost all big companies have been linked to the yakuza at some time or other."

I had obviously walked into her trap. "Of course, but the key evidence involves Nomura-san's silly mistake... "

"Shit! This is another of your bloody tests, isn't it?" A grin was all the confirmation I needed. I moved to pull up the case diagram, but then froze as I remembered that Koide-san had decided not to add anything related to our Commissioner. "OK, fuck, a mistake by Nomura-san rather than the company that the husband was working for. I assume that you hacked the bank account of the property developer and it didn't give you anything."

"I would have done, but didn't need to." The sphinxlike grin was really getting on my tits now.

"Fuck me, I don't know! Why do we have to go through these fucking mating dances anytime that you make progress with a case?"

"All part of training up your flabby arse to make you a less-crap detective! OK, another hint: all I needed to do was check dates of members being admitted to our favorite Kabuki-cho nightspot... "

I grimaced in concentration as I tried to talk my way through the conundrum. "You didn't hack the account of the firm that paid Levich's membership, but you've nailed down a link that'll disbar her from the case, something a lot stronger than just vague rumors about yakuza." No response, so presumably I was going in at least roughly the right direction.

"You have the date that the Commish became a member and we know how much that costs: you could hack your pal Helen's bank account to show... Wait a minute, that's not it: you checked Nomura-

155

san's dirty tricks account, didn't you. Don't tell me that the stupid bitch paid for it directly!"

"I don't really need to tell you, do I? Yes!" Koide punched the air in a gesture that said more than any words could.

***

Although this surprise development solved my boss's most immediate concern, it did not help explain just what Nomura-san hoped to gain by having our Commissioner as a fellow club member. Blackmail would have been one option, but that was rather scuppered by Levich's open declaration of her membership in her conflict of interest records. Maybe Helen's recent move to take over the investigation had something to do with it but, if so, it indicated some very long-term planning. In any case, something to follow up when we finally get around to questioning Miss Nomura.

I was assigned the job of following up on the coincidence of the poisoned apple suicides, to be done in Koide's office to ensure that my inspection of the case model would be untraceable, either by our mysterious nemesis or by future defense lawyers who might attempt to trace the history of development of our case against Nomura-san. The CI left the office immediately after laying out my work plan, vaguely muttering something about getting some kit sorted out as she disappeared.

The tricky part of my task was to input the databases that I needed into the case model without making it obvious that we had already identified

Fumiko as the prime suspect. I decided to start by linking our list of all identified club members and guests to suspicious deaths of disappearances of any sort. This vague specification resulted in a vast file, which I then subdivided by category - solved murders, unsolved murders, suicides, and so on. The category of suicides was larger than I originally expected, but then I remembered that this cause of death was much more common in Japan than in the West.

Again to make the focus of my investigations less obvious, I then subdivided all categories of death by cause, which produced a suicide coupled to poisoning sub-class. To introduce a further smokescreen, I introduced a multi-attribute comparison of all identified murders involving mutilation of the corpse with Chrissy's case. To my surprise, this produced one highly ranked match, which automatically expanded in front of me. I caught my breath, dreading that it would link to one of our suspects. However, a quick scan showed that it was a false alarm, the girlfriend of a son of a top government functionary; a regular guest of several different members, certainly reflecting his role in managing funds for environmental remediation.

The son was evidently a total nut-job: murdered his fiance and kept the body in his fridge while he gradually dismembered and ate it. Apparently he thought this would be the perfect crime and would also give him revenge following her revelation that she was pregnant with another man's child. It hadn't seemed to have occurred to him that he would be an obvious suspect as soon as the woman was reported missing and that cadaverine would be detectable even in the minute quantities that were present in his penthouse apartment. He committed suicide before the case came to trial, with suspicions of this resulting from pressure by his family. In any case, looked like a sad bastard whose genes were best removed from the pool and with no connection of any sort to our case, despite the superficial similarities.

I then returned to a read-only view of the suicides by poisoning. The majority involved carbon monoxide or overdoses with either prescription or recreational drugs. Fumiko's brother was listed, with death due to potassium cyanide injected into an apple. Found dead in bed by his housekeeper. The case for suicide was clear as the syringe used to inject the poison was found in his home office and it showed only his fingerprints. The event had occurred just a couple of days before his twenty-first birthday and was interpreted as a result of stress caused by his imminent planned transition to a more senior management role in the family company.

Although it was noted that Fumiko benefited from this death, becoming sole heir to the family fortune, there was no suggestion that there could have been any link as she had been in school in Kyoto while the rest of her family lived in Tokyo. The linked details on the private, residential school were vague but, reading between the lines, I guessed it was a special institution for problem rich kids. I made a mental note to check on this further after Koide opened the case file for explicit investigation of Nomura-san as prime suspect.

I checked on further poisoned foodstuffs. The Nomura Life Sciences division head was too remote a link to be included on this list, but one further poisoned apple did appear - again featuring potassium cyanide and again the suicide of the son of a wealthy family. The father had been the senior partner of a major Tokyo law firm, but was now retired. It was actually his twin daughters who were club members; both lawyers who now jointly held the helm of the practice.

I checked the dates: young Saito was a law student who had committed suicide just over eight months after Nomura, under identical circumstances. This had actually been noted in the police report at the time and attributed to the fact that the two young men had been acquainted with each other at Tokyo University. There was even some speculation that they may have had a sexual relationship, but this was not followed up on, no doubt due to family pressure.

There was no specific link made to the Saito-twins, probably because the main beneficiary in this case in terms of inheritance was an older sister. She was, however, a medical doctor who was already married to another doctor living in Okinawa. The investigators had not spotted the fact that it was the sisters who gained in terms of taking over the law firm.

I nervously looked over my shoulder, as if I would be able to spot if someone had managed to bug the CI's office. Again read only, I flipped the node containing PD members' security records. Scrolling down to Akiko Saito, I grunted when I saw my suspicion confirmed: she had attended the same Kyoto school as Fumiko, together with her sister Yoko.

I blanked the holo display and sat back in my chair, eyes closed. This case just kept getting more complex. It was not at all obvious how it could have been done, but it looked a lot like Fumiko together with the Saito girls were involved in the deaths of their brothers, made to look like suicides. Even if I could explain this puzzle, however, it did not seem to be leading me any further with explanation of the murder of Chrissy.

***

A tap on the top of my head shocked me into awareness. "Having a nice snooze, Watson? I thought I left you with a fucking job to do!" My boss did not sound pleased.

"Not sleeping, trying to fit a great number of loose ends together. Anyway, I think you'll be pleased with what I've discovered."

"This better be good," she glowered at me. "Have you linked the deaths of the brother and the Life Sciences guy?" I had forgotten about the Nomura scientist and the guilty look on my face must have given this away. "Jesus suffering Christ, Watson, I can't leave you alone for five minutes and you're dossing off."

"Will you stop talking and fucking listen for a second!" The sharp tone in my voice silenced my

160

dominant boss. "I couldn't see a way to access the suicide of Nomura-san's colleague because it's not linked to her files in a way that it could be accessed in a generic manner... "

"Suicides and suspicious deaths of colleagues of members and guests of PD?" responded the CI with a smug grin.

"OK, smart arse, I might have eventually gotten round to that. But what I did find was much more interesting." The blonde rolled her eyes, clearly skeptical, but slumped into her chair to hear what I had to offer.

I opened the case file and explained the relationship between Fumiko and the Saito twins and the links to the identical suicides of their brothers. Koide was silent throughout my entire presentation, but she leant forward as the picture began to come together and peered at the network of holographically linked nodes.

"Watson, you must be the jammiest sod that I have ever encountered," she sighed. "Every time you do things wrong, you manage to come up with the goods. I just can't believe it! OK, the Saito-twins, what monikers do they use at Pleasure Doubled?"

"They are amongst the minority who don't use pseudonyms," I reported as the appropriate case node expanded. "They're spinsters who live together and their firm specializes in corporate law, so I guess that they don't feel that they need to conceal their membership. It must be quite well known in any case, as they are amongst the group that most regularly bring guests to the club."

"What kind of guests - do we know that?"

"The guests names are often false, but we've identified a number of senior executives from major Japanese and foreign companies. In all cases women," I grinned, "so looks like more beaver-eaters."

"Fuck, what a simple view of the world you have! I guess the twins may be straight lesbian, but I'll bet most of their guests are happily married women."

I quickly checked the linked nodes: the CI was correct in thirty out of thirty three cases where relevant information was already in the case file. "How on earth did you know that?"

"Very powerful women - and men too for that matter - tend not to be conventional in their lifestyles. Simple heterosexual monogamy is OK for the hoi polio, but not for the makers and shakers."

I paused to let this information sink in while my boss flicked through the autonomically-generated connections between the two suicides. "You'd better watch that," I warned, "this is very close to a record that we are already focusing on Nomura-san."

"I know, I know, we're definitely skating on very thin ice here. But the chance to nail this bitch to further murders is too good a chance to miss."

"How do we know it was Fumiko?" I objected. "This could just as well be the work of the Saito sisters."

"Regardless of who did what, the case for the three girls conspiring together on the deaths looks convincing. Plus we have the Nomura Health guy."

"Shit, yes, Doctor Yoda his name was. I keep forgetting about this guy, because he doesn't seem to have any clear link to any of the other stuff going on."

"Why do you think that? He was head of the lab at the time Miss Nomura was doing the research that seems to have resulted in creation of Chrissy."

"And that would be enough to kill a guy for?"

"Well she appears to have killed her own brother when she was only fourteen, so I would think that it wouldn't take a lot to cause her to eliminate a colleague if she thought he was a threat to her."

I could not disagree with that, but it made me worry yet again about what we were going to be letting ourselves in for this evening.

***

I spent the rest of the afternoon in my own office, trying to sneakily access background on the death of Yoda-san without making it evident that our investigations had narrowed down to Nomura-san. The CI's suggestion provided a first link to his suicide, but yielded only the most superficial information on the death. The discovery of a letter to his wife apologizing for his cowardice, but admitting to gambling debts that could be covered only by his life insurance made it an open-and-shut case. Despite the letter, it was noted that Nomura, who also covered his insurance policy, paid out in full although they could have easily fought against it. This was explained as recognition of the stress

163

under which top managers worked, but explicitly without admission of any direct liability.

I was thinking over this when I was interrupted by a news flash on the internal comlink. The latest US president - Hunt or Hurt or something similar he was called - had been assassinated. That made the fourth president down in six years and boded for trouble in the SAR. Two of the earlier presidents killed had tried yet again to control universal availability of firearms - and had been gunned down by NRA nutcases. The latest victim - and one of the previous ex-presidents - had supported free access of citizens to all weapons of self-defense which, in the madhouse that was the USA, included ground-to-air missiles, landmines and even chemical and biological agents. Both had been taken out with the very weapons they supported: the earlier one when Airforce One was hit by a missile during take-off from Dallas Fort Worth and the latest by weaponised plague, which had taken out half of the White House staff as collateral damage.

The internal squabbles in the States were of no direct interest to me, but we had a large number of US nationals resident in the SAR and such events usually sufficed to touch off the pent-up violence between the pro- and anti-gun headcases. The great difficulty of accessing firearms in Japan would restrict the consequences of this - a mere firecracker compared to the firestorm that would erupt in US of A - but it was certain that all police leave would be cancelled and that patrols throughout the SAR would be increased in strength by drafting in support from the Tokyo metropolis SWAT and special action teams.

I buzzed Koide-san, feeling a bit of a coward to be so relieved. "Hi Boss. I suppose you've seen that another Yank president has gone the way of all flesh."

"Way of all flesh? I sure as fuck hope not! Of all the options on my list of how I don't want to die, bio-weapons are in about the top ten places."

"Not quite what I meant," I responded automatically, before realizing that the CI was probably just pissing about with me again. "Anyway, I guess that our plans for this evening are now scuppered. We'll be out with the rest of the squads tranking unruly Yankees."

"And why do you think that you're going to get off so easily?" I could almost hear her grin. "Homicide stays as backup for these events and we can do that just as easily from the middle of Kabuki-cho as sitting around here. Better, in fact, as that'll certainly be the epicenter of all the action."

"But it's going to be dangerous in Shinjuku tonight. Do you think a rich bitch is going to be just waltzing about there?"

The snort of derisive laughter was a clear answer. "Remember what our Fumiko is like," my boss expanded, talking down to me like a kid. "There is absolutely no way that she is going to have her chosen path deviated by a millimeter due only to a bunch of drunken gaijin, who will, in any case, be fighting with each other. I'm sure she will strengthen her security team and that they'll be on hair triggers, but that only makes our job easier. Just shows you that these wankers in Washington have their uses, even if it's only when they're pushing up daisies."

I groaned aloud, then broke the connection. Just when you think everything cannot get worse, it does. I wondered if this was one of Murphy's Laws, or something more specific to Koide-san.

***

At six pm I was commanded to the Ebisu bar for a last check of our plan for the evening, inevitably lubricated by several creamy-head stouts. Our comms allowed us to follow the trouble as it was slowly building up in the SAR. First of all scuffles at construction sites and the surrounding bars, then altercations in stations, trains and the metro. More of a nuisance than anything else, but a forewarning of how things would develop when the idiots got more alcohol and other stimulants in them later this evening.

Koide seemed amused rather than worried. "The Nips really have it easy, don't they! If this was Sydney - or even London or Paris - they'd be knee deep in body-bags by now."

"I don't think that's a fair comparison," I protested. "Sydney's the fucking Wild West, like Chicago or New York; there's no British or French city with violence like that!"

"Sidney's wild, possibly, but not very west. Then again, Chicago is kind of central and New York is definitely also in the east."

"Christ, are you always this fucking pedantic? It was a general point that I was making," I retorted with a glare in her direction.

"Oh, a general point was it? What about the per-capita murder rate in Cardiff or Belfast?"

"That's not Britain, they're fucking Wales and Ireland!"

"But, as I understand it, still components of the United Kingdom of Great Britain and Northern Ireland."

"Just a few percent change in a couple of referenda and that'd all have been different," I muttered under my breath as I struggled to find a thread of conversation that would dig me out of this hole. "Anyway, even if it isn't going to be the fire-fights that we get elsewhere, it is going to get chewy in Kabuki-cho this evening. It's not just the Yanks; all the Brits, Ozzies, Kiwis and anyone else looking for bother will be stirring the pot: aggro is inevitable."

"Certainly," the blonde smiled unconvincingly, as if trying to cheer me up, "but it'll mainly be a load of pissed young lads and lasses looking for a bit of bovver. Only the fundamentalist Shermans will be out to do serious damage to their opponents."

I was confused for a moment by Koide's rhyming slang: where I came from, a Sherman was self-abuse rather than an American, but from the context her meaning was clear. "Whatever... we'll still have a much crazier than usual Kabuki-cho to deal with before we even get to the killer lesbos and their tooled-up dyke bodyguards from hell."

167

"God, Watson, you make our job sound like so much fun! Why don't we celebrate with a steak in the place that Toyota-sensei and the kinky German prof doctor doctor ate in. It's just nearby. I'll tell you what, I'll even buy you dinner."

This all sounded good until she had to add, "... and, if all goes tits-up, at least your last meal will have been a good one."

That did not help my digestion one little bit.

***

The steak was, indeed, excellent and actually, after we started eating, conversation drifted away from the evening ahead and onto the Tokyo professor and her exotic love life. Koide had now watched the time-logged recording of the two professors with the pair of ladyboys and seemed rather bemused by it all. "Mainly voyeurism," she summarized, "the two professors touching each other while they watched the professionals going at it hammer and tongs, then one masturbating while the other was tied and bound as part of a transvestite sandwich. OK, a little bit of group action at the end, but all rather tame."

"Tame?" I spluttered. "Two senior academics involved in a kinky orgy: that's hardly what I'd call tame!"

"Yes," she grinned, "spoken like a prude with no sexual experience to talk of." I tried to interrupt, but she continued to talk over me. "This is all completely harmless stuff: consenting adults in private. As Toyota-sensei said, of interest only to some of her prurient students, but nothing that would bother grown-ups."

I could almost see my boss's viewpoint, but it somehow didn't seem viscerally correct. "Yes, I see that... But, if that's the case, why all the pseudonyms and secret identities. It doesn't seem to fit in with a club offering harmless amusement for aesthetes."

"Watson! You're again hitting the nail on the head; but I bet you don't know what it is though! The pseudonyms are natural for anyone in the public eye who doesn't want their proclivities to become common knowledge. But the spectrum of members... "

I racked my brains, determined to wipe the supercilious smile off her face. "It's almost as if there's a club within a club," I mused, fighting for time.

Koide's eyebrows shot up in surprise. "Right in one!" I struggled to hide my surprise, but it was evidently spotted by my eagle-eyed boss. "You haven't really worked it out yet, have you?" she grinned.

"I'm getting there," I bravely lied, attempting to fit this revelation with what we knew about Pleasure Doubled. "There's the kinky sex club that seems to be the scene experienced by Toyota-sensei, the Commish and most of the corporate guests. I guess this focuses on the girls who are regularly available. But there must be something more to draw in real extreme pervs like Fumiko and Michiko. I suppose this mainly involves the top-end hermaphrodites like Chrissy."

The CI leant forward and patted my hand, I'm sure intentionally presenting a fine view down her vertiginous cleavage. "You know, lad, you continue to amaze me: one minute you're a rabbit in headlights and the next you've seen through a smokescreen of chaff to pin down key clues in the case. I'm actually beginning to think I can make a real detective of you."

She leant back in her seat and stretched, threatening to pop the already over-strained buttons on the front of her blouse. "It certainly isn't evidence, but if part of the club is a front, it would explain why the Commish - or her husband - might be given membership. As it is situated in the SAR, this diverts any suspicion that the club may not be kosher."

"So that's the cover side of the club, but what's hidden behind it?"

"Not a clue as yet, but you can be sure that it must be extremely perverted and almost certainly illegal," the big blonde grinned salaciously. "In any case, there's a good chance that we're going to find out soon. Let's off to the cop shop, gird up our loins and head off into the fray!"

As I left the restaurant in the wake of my heroic boss, this call to arms was ringing in my head, reminding me that we still had to face a team of black-belt bodyguards with a penchant for physical mutilation before we were likely to get any further with the case.

Chapter 10

We had just passed under the railway bridge, walking along Yasukuni-dori towards Kabuki-cho, with its flashing neon and crowded streets, when we were reminded of the trouble expected this evening. A group of six young men were heading towards us, evidently drunk and looking for trouble. The apparent leader was singing, "... six green presidents lined against a wall, six green presidents... " emphasizing the position stated on his t-shirt *The only solution to a bad guy with a gun is a good guy with a fucking bigger gun!*

The flow of pedestrians in the busy street was diverting to leave a safety margin around this pack, but I groaned when I saw that Koide was making straight for them. "Police!" she called out when we were about three paces away. "Will you kindly shut the fuck up and stop trying to start a fight or do I need to run you in?"

The short, rather skinny thug looked the tall blonde up and down and licked his lips. "You're an Ozzie, ain't yer," his accent betraying him as a countryman from the antipodes. "You should just keep yer nose out've this, it's a fuckin' free country and I'm... "

His challenge ended in a high pitched squeal as Koide lunged forward and grabbed him in the groin, lifting the screaming man clear of the pavement before slamming him into one of his friends. "Right, you stupid fuckers, are you going to fuck off home or are we going to have to do this the hard way?"

171

I sincerely hoped that they would back down, but the damage that Koide had done to their leader's wedding tackle had been enough only to make him even more aggressive. Given the difference in their sizes, taking a swing at the policewoman was either an indication of bravery or stupidity. In any case, he clearly hadn't spotted the baton that smashed into the side of his face, covering a couple of his fellows in a spray of blood and teeth.

The largest member of the gang, probably as tall as the CI although not as robustly built, then decided to get involved, rushing forward with a bottle clutched in his right fist. Focused entirely on my boss, he had not even spotted me. I actually had a moment to wonder about anyone who went out looking for a fight while wearing flip-flops, before I stepped forward to take hold of his right arm while stamping down on his right foot.

Tonight we were not in usual civvies, but basic summer riot gear. Padded, kevlar-lined shirts and trousers and heavy boots. The boots were designed to protect our feet and, thanks to ceramic studs, assure grip even when riot-control foams were used. It was thus no surprise that my attack resulted in the sound of breaking bones and a scream that cut off only when my lock on his arm lifted him off his feet and slammed him face-first into the pavement.

I spun around to see that two of the yobs were sprinting off in the direction of Shinjuku station, while the rest were strewn on the ground, either groaning or motionless. Already a couple of uniforms were rushing towards us, indicating the high density of patrols this evening.

Koide was not even breathing heavily. "Just taze these bastards to put them out of their misery and get them wheeled off," she instructed the plods when they arrived. The policemen cheerfully complied with her orders, happy to be mopping up after the famous CI Koide, I guessed. "Incitement to riot, attempted assault of police officers, resisting arrest, it's all logged," she muttered towards their backs, "so if they were dropped a couple of times or fell down stairs, that'd be OK."

"You shouldn't be suggesting that kind of stuff," I whispered in her ear, anxious to avoid being overheard.

"Don't worry, Watson," she responded with a smile. "We now have it as policy to respond harshly to attacks on police officers in the SAR."

"But that's your policy," I pointed out. "It hasn't been confirmed from above the clouds."

"It hasn't been countermanded either! This couldn't be official policy, anyway, that'd be police brutality. It's a bit more in the way of operational guidance."

I couldn't really argue against actions intended to reduce threats to the police or the pragmatic way that such issues were handled in the SAR, so I brooded in silence as the CI set off again in the direction of Sakura-dori.

***

We had only one further altercation en route, this time a fat American couple with matching t-shirts claiming *The second amendment was not intended to arm lunatics!* What was it about t-shirts as a medium for provocation? Had it always been this way or did this just replace bumper stickers in an environment where nobody had cars, I wondered.

The CI was her usual diplomatic self. "Police! Cover up those fucking shirts and get the fuck home before I run you in for incitement to riot!" She had actually walked past them, assuming that they would obey her orders, when the woman spat at her back. Despite the din of the busy thoroughfare, Koide heard this and span like a top, backhanding the chubby visage with a blow that felled her like an ox.

"What the fuck're you doing, you stupid fat slag. Spitting is classified as assault and I'm a fucking policewoman." She kicked the crying woman lightly in the stomach. "Now are you going to... "

"Get away from my wife, you bitch!" the fat yank intervened, grabbing Koide's arm.

Nobody ever sees me when the CI is about, I thought as my steel toecap smashed into the side of his knee. His leg buckled and he fell heavily on top of his better half, his hefty carcass probably doing more damage than anything inflicted by my partner.

Both of the obese Americans were now crying and forming the focus for a growing circle of rubberneckers. At that moment the tall blonde removed a knife from a sheath on her belt, causing an intake of breath from the audience, including myself. The knife had also been spotted by the man on the ground, who had stopped crying and now lay

174

still, his eyes as big as saucers as Koide bent towards him.

"Boss, you can't... " I started to object before the blade flashed and a large chunk was cut out of the triple X size t-shirt, exposing a very unattractive area of pallid lard.

"Wipe this shit of the back of my shirt, would you," she requested as she straightened up and tossed the rag to me. As I complied, the uniforms had appeared. "If I was you, I'd walk these fucking whales to the paddy wagon and taze them there," she advised them. "Otherwise you're going to need a fork lift to move the fat bastards," she finished, casually kicking the terrified man somewhere around his kidneys.

"Not only politically incorrect in every possible way," I sighed, "with all played out to an audience of bystanders."

"Public health warning," she grinned, "shows that fucking about with SAR cops is dangerous for your health. Also shows you can't expect any preferential treatment just 'cause you're a fat fuck." She nudged me in the ribs to ensure I caught her gratuitous sizeist comment.

***

We were in position in a bar with a view of the entrance of Pleasure Doubled about thirty minutes before the expected arrival of Mistresses Maus and Page. We now completely ignored the provocative yobbos, leaving them to the other police squads. The fact that central Kabuki-cho was completely pedestrianized at night would make intercepting our targets easier, as they could not simply be deposited at the door by a limo. Based on past video records, the pair would be dropped at the north end of Sakura-dori but, to be on the safe side, we had placed Koide-san's military-spec micro video bugs to cover both ends of the street.

Bang on nine thirty, a brutally over-dimensioned stretched SUV pulled over as expected and five black-clad women piled out and formed a cordon, roughly shoving any curious passers-by to the side. Fumiko and Michiko then descended like visiting royalty and proceeded to stroll in our direction, the calm eye of the storm of humanity crowding the narrow street.

"Five! She's got five bodyguards with her! Fucking dead bastarding president: this has screwed up all our plans!" I couldn't understand how my boss could look so unperturbed by this.

"No, Watson, you've got it arse to tit. This is good for us: they are going to be fired up for trouble, so it'll make it even easier to provoke them into doing something stupid."

"But that's five: five professional toughs with records of grievous bodily harm we're talking about here. At the very least, we could intercept the lesbos on their way home. They'll be strung up on alcohol and other stuff, so easier to manipulate. The hard team will also be tired by then and, in the interim, we could move in a bit more support."

I could almost feel the scorn dripping from the tall blonde's gaze. "Don't be such a fucking wimp! Five girls and you're ready to call the whole thing off. You're a big tough guy and now you have a chance to prove it."

"But, later might be better because... "

"Don't add stupidity to cowardice: it's got to be now because that gives maximum time before our Miss Nomura will be noted as missing and several squads of hotshot lawyers set off on her trail. So, stop moaning and choose your targets. What about that really wee one?"

The amazon that my boss was pointing out on the small vid monitor was indeed rather short - I guessed about one meter sixty. She seemed, however, about as broad as she was tall, reminding me of our first attackers in the English pub. "No thanks," I responded, "I think I'll take the two tall, skinny ones."

"Are you sure? They look pretty mean to me."

I peered again at the tiny screen. The two women that I had identified stayed at the back of the pack, evidently using their height to check how things were going. I zoomed to check my original impression: yes, they were both wearing boots with thick platforms and ridiculously long stiletto heels. I had no idea how they could even walk in such things and hand-to-hand fighting would be out of the question. "Yup, I'm certain. If we've got to do this, I'll look after that pair if you can handle the rest of them."

The CI chuckled as she shrugged her shoulders. "Fine with me. It's your funeral if you've drawn the wrong cards."

I just wished that she hadn't used that particular expression as I followed her out into the bustling street.

**

Koide planted herself just in front of the door to the club and let the tide of humanity flow around her. I moved a couple of meters to the side and placed myself with my back to a lamppost, watching our targets approach.

The small, wide woman formed the vanguard of the flying wedge of bodyguards and headed straight for my boss. "Excuse me, could we please get past." The soft polite voice sounded as if it had come from a posh finishing school somewhere and so seemed completely out of place coming from this bruiser.

"Actually, I am waiting here for your employer." I had never heard my foul-mouthed boss sound so sweet. "Chief Inspector Koide," she presented the holo from her regulation comm unit, before clipping it back to her belt. "Now, if you would please let me past... " while speaking, she wormed past the bemused bodyguard to stand face-to-face in front of Nomura-san.

"My name is Koide," she repeated with a slight bow of her head and proffered her business card.

Nomura accepted the card as a conditioned reflex, but did not even glance at it. "So, Koide, why are you disturbing me?" she commanded arrogantly.

I expected the CI to explode as a result of this deliberate rudeness, but she appeared completely unperturbed.

"Just a couple of questions to start with: you are Miss Maus and your companion is Miss Page, is that correct?"

"No, we're... " Michiko started to respond before she was silenced by a glare from her partner. It was clear who held the reins in this relationship.

"Your names are Maus and Page and you are members of this club, Pleasure Doubled, is that not correct?"

If looks could have killed, the CI would have been dead on the spot. "Yes, that is correct," Nomura spoke English perfectly, with a distinct west-coast USA accent. "Now fuck off back to your koban and stop being a pest."

"OK, I'm glad that we've got that out of the way. I am now going to charge you both with murder, so I would appreciate if you would let me cuff you before I go through all the formal warnings and stuff. You can also send the heavy team home, we'll look after you for now."

Michiko looked shocked, but Fumiko was spitting mad. "Who's this we? I don't see any police squad."

"We? Oh, that's me and young Watson there," she pointed vaguely in my direction. "I mean, you're just a bunch of lesbos after all," she laughed in Fumiko's face. "What're you going to do, cover me in chocolate and lick me to death?"

The crack as Fumiko slapped Koide's face was enough to draw the attention of the crowd, although anyone catching sight of the bodyguards tended to lose interest very quickly.

A talon-like nail had cut the CI's cheek and she dabbed a trickle of blood with the tip of her index finger while she smiled contentedly. "Well, you just seriously fucked up there, Miss Maus. No more good cop now."

Uppercuts are rarely used in street fights, but they are spectacular when they catch someone unaware. I heard the crunch as Nomura-san's teeth smashed together and saw the spray of blood as she flew backwards into the arms of one of her retainers. Then all hell broke loose.

As all attention was on Koide, I was able to taze one of the tall guards before anyone was even aware that I was there. As I wasn't actually being attacked at the time, I had turned the voltage down a little, but it was still enough to knock the woman out of action.

The second woman in high heels was now facing me, with a look of savagery on her face that froze me to the core. I could certainly outrun her, I thought, before she spun in a blur of motion and I felt a blast of pain across my forehead while I stumbled backwards into the surrounding crowd. I crouched and dodged to the side, blinded by a flow of blood from my forehead.

Remembering the sealant cream on the back of my hand that the CI had insisted on, I smeared it over the wound while I continued to push my way past screaming bodies. Gradually my vision cleared and I spotted that my erstwhile opponent was now heading off with the lesbian lovers, forcing her way through the throng with Fumiko over her shoulder and Michiko in hand. I guessed the others were trying to hold the CI back.

It was hardly chivalrous, but I gave no warning as I charged up behind the tall ninja and aimed a two-handed blow of my baton at the back of her head. The stick made contact with a loud crack but, instead of instantly dropping my victim, it caused her only to stagger forward and drop the load from her shoulder. Some kind of surgical armoring I guessed, realizing that maybe I had not chosen the easiest opponents after all.

Once again we were facing off, with bystanders struggling to clear an area around us. She looked at me with undisguised contempt. "You were very lucky, little man. One centimeter lower and your eyes would already be gone. But now I'm going to cut you up even worse."

"Do it, Yu, do it!" Michiko was now crouched beside her lover, a look on her face that could only be interpreted as lust. She's getting off on this, I noted; she gets turned on by the thought of me getting carved up in front of her eyes."

The tall woman, called Yu apparently, shoved her hands into pouches on the top of her thighs and brandished the results at me. The streetlights were not bright enough to see details, but the glints of razor sharp steel were unmistakable. Once again I wondered if I couldn't at least outrun her.

Koide's shout pierced through the surrounding din. "Stop posing, Watson, take the fucking bitch down!" Galvanized by this command, I dropped the baton and threw myself forward and tackled the woman at waist level, bowling her over the prone body of Fumiko and onto Michiko.

We landed in a sprawl of bodies and I could feel blows pummeling into my sides and back, but it seemed that the Kevlar was holding. My head was jammed against her bodice, which felt like leather but was probably something synthetic and much stronger. It did, however, zip up the side. Like Koide, I had a ceramic knife on my belt which I fumbled loose with my left hand while my right maintained distraction by punching towards her groin, without any sign at all of an effect.

I caught the zip between my teeth and pulled it upwards as the blade slipped into the exposed triangle of white flesh. The resultant scream was followed by a release of pressure as the woman pushed back and rolled away, before flowing to her feet, a hand clamped to her side to stem the flow of blood.

I was still on my knees, but close enough that my knife stabbed right through her hand and into the open wound. She attempted another back roundhouse kick at my head, but she was a little off balance and I was in a better position to take out the leg she was standing on, causing her to fall again on top of semi-conscious Fumiko. I was on my feet in an instant, kicking viciously at her face and head while I drew my remaining baton, and used this to fell Michiko, who had been attempting to squirm away.

Protective head armor can do only so much. Crush zones will protect from a single blow, but not repeated impact at the same location. The tension gradually disappeared from Yu's body as she lost consciousness, blood flowing freely from her mouth, nose and ears.

I hardly felt the tap on my shoulder, but jumped from Koide's voice in my ear. "OK, Watson, I think we can call that one done. Maybe had mush between the ears to start with, but she certainly has now." I turned to look in amazement at my blood-splattered boss, who looked happy as the proverbial pig in shit.

"Are you OK?" I inquired, holstering the bloody baton and looking her over carefully. There seemed to be several cuts to her clothing, but nothing that appeared to have penetrated the Kevlar.

"Not a problem," she confirmed. "None of this blood is mine, except for this little trickle on my cheek." She pointed to a small scar that had already scabbed over. "But that's the good one, it lets us do what we want with this pair of cunts." She reached down and pulled a quivering Michiko to her feet, waving back a couple of plods who seemed eager to taze her. "OK, guys, police assault for the bodies that you see scattered about, so don't hold back. These ones are ours, however, and we want them in a state to talk."

I started to shake as the adrenalin began to wear off and saw the almost complete lack of reaction as the prone form of Yu was tazed. Another brain dead one, I guessed. This case had turned into complete carnage, the initial murder dwarfed by our body count.

"Stop daydreaming, Watson, you dozy bugger. Pick up Miss Maus and let's get back to the nick.

We've got a lot of interrogating to do before the night is over."

I groaned as I heaved Fumiko onto my shoulder and staggered forward, now impressed that Yu had done it with such ease. Koide had cuffed the still-dazed Michiko and was hustling her along with a savage wristlock that caused repeated squeals of pain. Dully I noticed that I felt no sympathy for her at all.

Chapter 11

During the short drive to the station we reviewed our plans. Assault charges were laid against Misses Maus and Page and their companions, who would be identified while they were processed for any required medical treatment. As standard procedure, a search was made to confirm that no legal representation was already specified for these persons - an option that allowed those and such as those to avoid defense by an expert system during preliminary interviews. As we knew in advance, there were no links at all for Maus and Page and, given that they had freely acknowledged their identities, we were not obliged to include a DNA search.

The question was whether to interrogate Fumiko and Michiko sequentially or in parallel. The advantage of the former was that we could try a good cop / bad cop routine, while the latter gave us the option of playing them off against each other if we used the case file as an interface between our two interviews. Koide was certain that breaking Nomura-san was the key to the case, so I let myself be convinced that the parallel option would be the best bet.

To stack the cards in our favor, the CI had come up with a ruse that, although not actually illegal, certainly did not represent standard protocol and could lead to problems if it was spotted. We would have the interrogations in neighboring rooms under expert system legal supervision, but Koide had placed a laptop displaying a large digital clock as screen-saver to the side of the plain desk set in the middle of her room. This was set up to be forty-five minutes fast.

I placed a small bud in my ear that received audio from the holographic case model, which was automatically displayed over an identical desk as soon as I led Michiko into the room. As we sat down on opposite sides of the table, I spotted the very small window displaying a dazed Fumiko being settled in in a similar manner. Our gamble was that neither of the prisoners would notice these windows within the huge complexity that comprised the total hologram, especially as a much larger window was set to loop through a replay of our scuffle in Kabuki-cho.

My instructions were to follow Koide's lead, following up lines of enquiry that she identified. This would be a bit of tricky multi-tasking, but benefited from taking things very slowly, which I guessed would be especially effective for my victim, who was already squirming under my silent gaze.

Koide requested a paramedic to bring Fumiko to full consciousness and administer the suggestion-enhancer. This could not force anyone to speak if they were completely against it, but tended to encourage guilty parties who felt some form of regret to confess their misdeeds. For those who felt no regret, it was less effective, although often encouraged the arrogant to boast of their crimes. With some warning, there were a number of pharmacological and mental training techniques that could nullify its impact, but we were gambling that our surprise action would have avoided these.

Michiko had already been dosed and was silent as I repeated the description of her rights and had her formally acknowledge the support that she had from the expert system. I was not required to tell her that she could also access the audio links that I had to the hologram before her and she clearly did not think to request this.

Koide was having problems with Miss Nomura, who was demanding access to her lawyer. Despite being told that, having confirmed her name as Maus and this being supported by bank and residence details, this was the identity under which she would be interrogated, the woman was trying to browbeat the CI into changing this formally to Nomura. Here Koide was simply acting dumb, pointing out that her alias as Fumiko Nomura had been formally logged and tied up to a DNA match, but her primary identity was automatically time-logged into the case file as Maus and this was unalterable.

While this was being nailed down, I started the interview with Miss Page, who seemed to have transformed from the harridan calling for my blood to a passive wraith, who now appeared more like I would have expected from an ex-nun.

When I formally asked her to confirm her name, she admitted without prompting that Val Page was a nickname that she used only for membership of Pleasure Doubled and some other clubs and internet communities. Her legal name was confirmed as Michiko Saito, born in Nagoya and aged thirty-seven. All this information was provided in beautifully enunciated Oxford English, marking her as one of the generation who grew up with English as a second language, when the use of Japanese by professionals began to decline at the beginning of the 21st century.

I noted that Koide had now managed to force Nomura-san along to a similar stage of the interview, showing a one-to-one match of all Michiko's membership of exclusive clubs and select chat groups, but with the addition of a few others that were more clearly meeting places for top-level executives. I could see the tiny image of the CI lean back in her chair and stare pensively at the ceiling. "Interesting, the same list as we got from Saito-san with addition of Roppongi Hills, the American Club and ExecLinkedin," she mumbled indistinctly, but evidently clearly enough for Fumiko to hear as, for the first time, a look of uncertainty crossed her face.

Koide now casually asked where Nomura-san's strange alias had come from, so I asked Miss Saito the same. As Nomura tried to avoid the question, my interviewee simply replied, "I've no idea. Michiko suggested it, I think, when she introduced me to these places."

"Do you know that Val Paige is a character from an old graphic novel; like Maus, your friend's membership name?"

"I seem to remember that Fumiko-chan said Val was a famous lesbian; she was into that old Western manga shit. Always going on about it when she was chatting to our friend Bev."

"Bev?" I was already searching the PD membership file by use of subtle hand motions.

"Would this be Beverly Grove, who is also a member of Pleasure Doubled?"

"Yes, Bev Grove. I don't know if that is a real name or not. We always called her Bev, but she used our real names: well, first names anyway, we were never very formal."

"Interesting," I responded as the associated search results came up. "It seems like Beverly Grove is also an old graphic novel character from something called Black Kiss."

Michiko shrugged her shoulders with a smile. "Wouldn't surprise me, especially if it involved a lot of wild sex."

I quickly scanned the Wikicheat. "Seems to be the case. Violent rape, hermaphrodite vampire, transvestite anal,... " I read off the key words and noted that, for the first time since the interview commenced, Michiko actually showed signs of interest.

"I've never been with her in real life, but some of the stuff she posts... " she grinned in a disconcerting manner that said more than words.

In the interim, my boss had used my input to put pressure on Nomura. In response to prevarication over the source of her nickname, Koide glared at the woman in exasperation. "You've got to get it into your head, Miss Maus, that you're in very serious trouble. We have evidence that could form the basis for prosecution for crimes that carry the death penalty. Your cooperation could make a big difference when it comes to sentencing. We have input already from our interview with your partner," she glanced as the display showing the incorrect time to imply that this had already been completed, without actually perjuring herself.

Nomura was obviously perturbed by this statement. "So let's cut through this shit and get on with it," Koide smiled as she continued. "Let's just assume that your alias resulted from discussion with your friend Beverly. How did you get to know her?"

The woman's defiance seemed to evaporate as she slumped back in her seat with her eyes closed. "I've known Bev since we met on line, maybe ten years ago - in a group with similar interests. She actually introduced me to that club: PD, I mean."

Michiko was looking at me strangely and I tried to remember where we were in our session, now aware that this parallel interviewing was going to be even more challenging that I had previously expected. "OK, Miss Saito, could you tell me a bit about how you came to leave the convent and end up a yakuza porn actress."

I had expected some reaction to this question, but Michiko seemed completely unperturbed as she related the story of her life. She was the only child of Japanese parents who had been devout Christians, Catholics, who had encouraged her to join the convent. Miss Saito blandly confessed that this pressure, especially from her father who was rabid in his condemnation of the sinful ways of contemporary Japanese youth, had been one key factor in her vocation. The other was the increasing awareness of her Sapphic inclinations, which made the idea of an enclosed life with a like-minded group of women seem particularly attractive.

While Michiko reminisced on her various lesbian encounters at the convent, I checked on progress with her current lover. The CI had proceeded directly to the murder of Miss Chrissy and Nomura-san's links to the victim. Fumiko had freely admitted to being a regular client of the hermaphrodite, often paired up with one of the other herms or a ladyboy to make up a foursome. It appeared as if she was trying to shock the CI by giving gratuitous detail of their sexual encounters, but this ploy was clearly failing to produce the desired effect.

"Fine, but how does this link to the long-term payments that you've been making to Chrissy," the CI cut in to Fumiko's rhapsody on the joys of simultaneous vaginal and anal penetration while her partner sat on her face, shocking the woman into silence.

"How the fuck can you possibly... How did you get... " she spluttered as soon as she had recovered her composure. Then lapsed again into silence as she began to realize just how much of her secret life might have been uncovered by us.

I drew my attention back to the woman in front of me, who was now calmly explaining the problems resulting when the mother superior found out about her numerous trysts. It did not seem to be lesbianism as such that was the problem, rather the wild group encounters that Michiko had been organizing, with their increasing focus on rough sex which expanded to domination, punishment and humiliation fantasies at the extreme end of the SM range. She was forced to confess to a bishop and

191

two older priests who then, as form of penance, brutally raped her.

Again the wistful look appeared on Michiko's face as she described this abuse, it was as if she was reminiscing over a pleasant experience. Indeed, her decision to leave the convent had not resulted from the rape, but the constraints then placed on her love life. A little internet surfing and she quickly saw that she could not only live as she wanted, but actually be well paid for it through the yakuza vice activities. The transition had actually been a lot smoother than she had expected, as her status as an ex-nun provided cachet to her role as dominatrix prostitute and video star. Almost as an aside, she mentioned that she had no further contact with any of her family since she left the convent and was quite happy for it to stay that way.

Little further nudging was required to get the woman to describe her yakuza career. I was not sure if this was due to the suggestion enhancers or the pleasure she showed when describing this to me, clearly well aware at how shocked I was about it. I hazarded a guess that this may have been exactly how my scheming boss had planned it.

The CI had now completely broken Nomura-san. Koide was actually doing most of the talking, guiding the way through our evidence of our suspect's involvement in both Chrissy's creation and her eventual role in Kabuki-cho. When forced to make a statement, Fumiko simply nodded or grunted a confirmation to the material that was presented. The match between the payments recorded in Chrissy's secret file and in Nomura's bank account were unambiguous. Nevertheless, it was the DNA match with Chrissy's fetus that was the final straw, destroying her resistance and opening the floodgates for a torrent of self-justification.

"Whatever may or may not have happened, you can't convict me of anything," she stated bluntly, glaring at the CI as if challenging her to contradict this statement. In the absence of a response, she continued in a neutral tone, "I admit that I created Chrissy: my team did all the gengineering required using seed sequences from myself and Meg Aquilla. I also hired the surrogate mother, who both brought her to term and raised her until we took her back in her early teens. I set up an account for her, which ensured that she was fully recompensed for everything."

"Both your manipulation of her birth and later services rendered?" the CI queried.

"Chrissy was created for a purpose: to break the tyranny of Japanese fathers and sons who control our greatest companies. Wives and daughters have roles only when the male line is broken, but I've created the solution, a female line that additionally assures that only the best, most successful characteristics are passed to progeny. What could possibly be wrong with that?"

I was shocked by this hubris, but my boss was cleverly exploiting it to encourage Nomura-san to incriminate herself further. "You engineered both Chrissy and the fetus that she was carrying?"

"Of course, that was always the plan. The child, my daughter, will also be a fully functional hermaphrodite."

I had to force my attention away from this revelation as Saito-san mentioned her partner for the first time. I had missed the beginning of the sentence but it continued, "... and after that Fumiko became my most regular client. Together we developed the most extreme SM dungeon in Tokyo, which is saying a lot for Japan," she proudly boasted. "We also spent increasing amounts of our free time with each other. I moved on about ten years ago, left the business side of clients who pay for pain to Yamaguchi-gumi and settled in with Fumiko."

Somehow I was sure that this transition was a key to explaining what was behind the murder. The problem was that I could not quite put my finger on what the loose end was. "So your SM fantasies became more extreme, leading on to murder?" I speculated wildly.

The woman looked surprised, seemingly reading my question as a statement. "How did you find out about that? Actually, I suppose that I always knew that it would come out sometime. In the Yamaguchi dungeon, we combined business with pleasure, handling those within the organization requiring punishment and also contract jobs for wet work. They were all people that really deserved everything that we did to them."

I couldn't believe my ears. This ex-nun was calmly confessing to torture and murder, her only emotion shown by a smile as she relived some of her past experiences of brutal savagery. I had been looking for a link to our single murder case and, serendipitously, stumbled over something that was very much bigger.

"And how did you get rid of the bodies?"

"Oh, the yakuza do that. They've been using the incinerator in the Shinjuku Uni hospital for decades."

Yet another link to Chrissy's death had emerged, but I was more interested in Saito's use of the present tense in her statement. If she stopped running a commercial dungeon a year ago, why wasn't that past tense. Then the penny dropped. Anyone into the extreme perversion, of the kind that this pair were, would not just suddenly stop. They were still doing it, but entirely for their own pleasure rather than as part of a yakuza vice ring.

"And Yamaguchi-gumi also supply the victims for you?"

"Yes, of course," she seemed surprised by the question and a bit discomforted, as if she had just spotted that we did not know as much about her activities as she had originally assumed. "Nowadays many are actually criminals on the run from the police. The yakuza offer to smuggle them out of the country and make them disappear. Well, at least the last bit is true," she grinned in a rather frightening, feral fashion. "Fumiko and I always make the punishment fit the crime, it's part of the game. The rapists and pedophiles are best... "

I tried to block out the serene description of the way their victims were tortured to death to catch an update of the CI's progress. Koide had used the

195

information that I had picked up to break into Nomura-san's justification for her blatantly illegal and immoral genetic manipulation. "So, why did you murder Chrissy? Was it linked to the others that you and Miss Saito tortured to death for your perverted pleasure."

Fumiko looked completely shocked by the question, the color draining from her face. "Fuck! How the fuck did you... ?" She then stopped, realizing that she was digging herself deeper into shit.

My boss glanced at the time display again and grinned. "Your partner in crime was happy to boast about what you've been up to - both in her yakuza days and since then. We know everything that you've done. All we're doing is trying to tie up a few loose ends and give you the opportunity to confess, which is about the only possible chance you have of avoiding the death penalty."

"That fucking stupid cunt! She just likes talking about everything far too much. It was always the same in the fucking chats, although I always assumed that everyone would think it was fantasy."

I could see a search initiated to break into likely community groups that could be hosting such chats, but the CI continued without waiting for results to emerge. "So, Chrissy was carrying your gengineered heiress, so why did you kill her and why brutalize her in that way?"

"I don't know how Chrissy found out about our playroom, probably that stupid fucker Michiko talking too much again. We usually started an evening with Chrissy and one or two of the others, just to get into the mood before we went to play. I was sure that nobody except Bev knew about the basement, much less what went on there."

A link sprang open to show drawings of the building hosting Pleasure Doubled, but there was no evidence of a basement. Trace-backs did, however, show that both this building and that directly opposite across Sakura-dori were actually owned by a company that was a well-hidden subsidiary of Nomura Holdings. The building opposite was shown to have a small basement linked to the Thai massage parlor on the floor above.

"So did your friend Beverly also join in your games?"

"She set up the dungeon for me, but I don't know if she ever used it herself. She was just a good friend."

"What about in PD, did you do things together there?"

"No, Bev wasn't into groups, she was extremely private. We shared a lot virtually, but never in real life."

I was wondering where this line of questioning was going, when Koide suddenly gave one of her annoyingly smug grins. "Well, I think we have everything nailed down now. Chrissy was blackmailing you about your ultra-sadist activities and you decided to kill her and transfer the fetus to a surrogate. This was another of your engineered herms, and your pal Bev recommended that kill two birds with one stone and display the body in a way that would ensure that nobody else would dare to

197

threaten you again. You don't like being threatened, do you? Your brother found that out to his cost."

Nomura was now not only showing shock, but also fear. The edifice of her lifetime of privilege and immunity from the law was collapsing about her and she now was slowly becoming aware that even her great wealth and political power was not going to get her out of this.

Saito-san was still reveling in descriptions of extreme torture, focused on anal rapists, which seemed a particular bugbear - possibly due to her own rape in the convent. I interrupted an almost lyrical description of fisting a pederast priest with a spiked gauntlet before filling his arse with molten lead in order to fill in a gap for my boss.

"So, you have tortured a load of total bastards to death. But not Chrissy, even though she was blackmailing your lover."

"Chrissy wasn't evil, just fucking stupid. We had to take it gently so that we could transfer the baby to Liza, then we just let the narcotic take her out. We just let the medical waldos do their stuff, although the dissection was quite interesting."

This last description of brutal butchery made me finally realize just how totally fucked in the head this mild-sounding woman was.

"You know, there's no way that you're going to avoid the death penalty here," I pointed out.

"Do you think I give a fuck?" she smiled in a way that chilled me to the core. "It was worth it, every minute of it, and I'd do it all again even if I knew that I was going to end up here."

I couldn't think of how to possibly follow that. "You are being charged with multiple counts of murder, full details of which you can access via the case model. You are free to continue to use the expert system to develop your defense or to pass this information to you solicitor. Interview terminated," I sighed and called for a uniform to take her to an isolated holding cell.

***

Koide was also close to wrapping up the interview with Nomura, summarizing the charges against her. The list went on for a while, including an undefined number of aggravated murders in the torture chambers, the murders of Chrissy, her brother and her colleague at Nomura Life Sciences, multiple offences against human genetic manipulation laws, assault and conspiracy to assault Tokyo police officers. Fumiko demurred only when this last charge was mentioned, which Koide had clearly expected.

"Oh, yes, I forgot about that. Funds from your account were used to pay for two attacks against my colleague and myself, but you had no idea about it did you?"

The look of confusion on the woman's face was answer enough for the CI. "Interview terminated," she stated, "I'm sure that you will have a mob of lawyers to support you very soon, but it's not going to do you a bit of good. You may delay it for a bit, but you and your evil bitch fuck-buddy will never experience free air again until you're executed, which will be as soon as I can possibly make it."

Koide faced Nomura's glare of hatred with a grin. "And I'm also going to ensure that Liza's pregnancy is terminated and every one of your bastard creations is sterilized. So I'm not just destroying you, I'm taking out your entire legacy."

Nomura's scream of rage was still echoing in the small room as the video cut off.

Chapter 12

I was summoned to the CI's office ten minutes later for a quick debriefing. As soon as I entered, she looked up from the case model hologram, which was producing a map of the input from my interview with Saito-san, and gave me an appraising stare. "You did very well there, lad. The key was picking up just how far their SM games had developed. Just how did you do that?"

I scanned the map to remind myself how the interrogation had progressed. "Well, Saito was clearly very susceptible to the suggestion enhancing drug. I guess it was because she really enjoyed describing what she had done. As soon as she started, she just got further and further into the details, getting off by seeing how shocked and disgusted I was. I don't know what Nomura is like, but I'm sure that Saito focuses as much on psychological as physical torture. She really loved to see me squirm as she described castration, disembowelment, mutilation,... "

"Well, at least I got it right by putting you in with her," she responded, pensively. "But drawing her out to confess multiple counts of murder was a bit of a leap of faith."

I looked again at the case model and tried to see how I could present this to my best benefit. Finally, I decided to confess the truth. "Actually, it was more of a misunderstanding than anything else. I was trying to lead Saito towards Chrissy's murder, but she mistook this as referring to her past activities in the dungeon, maybe because she doesn't really consider Chrissy's death as a real murder."

"But, then you linked that up to what was still going on at Pleasure Doubled."

"Well, that was use of the present continuous in her... "

"Fucking English students! I might have known," she raised her eyes to heaven for dramatic emphasis. "OK, so basically you lucked out again."

I started to protest but she cut me off. "Never mind, not a bad bit of interview work in any case. I guess it must be about your bedtime now. Care to join me for a nightcap?"

"I'd love to but, after tonight, I'm completely wrecked. I don't know what was worse, the fight in Sakura-dori or interviewing that totally fucking evil lesbian clone of Myra Hindley. Maybe tomorrow evening... " I responded as I scuttled out of the office.

I grinned as the torrent of derision was cut off by the closing door.

***

Next morning I had an uninterrupted hour in my office, which was entirely spent tidying up my interpretation of the output from the previous night's interview and cross-checking links between it and the material that my boss had obtained. The biggest job was to try to identify some of the victims of this psychopathic couple. The list of missing persons who were suspected as possible yakuza assassinations was too long to provide much help, especially given the method used for elimination of the bodies. Nevertheless, I compiled a file of all associated DNA records available.

The potentially more useful tie-in was to criminals sentenced to execution. Japan had one of the highest capital punishment rates in the world, but this still amounted to only about a hundred and fifty cases per year. Lethal injections were videoed and logged along with the official death certificates and records of cremation. I set up a forensic expert system to critically review all video records and added linked medical records to my DNA file.

I stretched as the current case file hologram rotated before me. I was trying to assess it from the viewpoint of defense lawyers, who I was sure would be the best that money can buy. The confessions plus the evidence from Chrissy's autopsy should be enough for conviction, but assuring a death sentence might be tricky. We really needed to tie them to the other murders.

Just then I was buzzed to Koide's office, which I suspected would lead to another grilling. In any case, I picked up a coffee for my boss en route, aiming again to pre-empt being sent to fetch one.

To my surprise, the case hologram was not on display and the CI was perched on the end of her desk, mumbling into her comm unit. She accepted the coffee with a grunt, which could be interpreted as thanks, waving me back in the direction of the door. "Morning, Watson. Don't get settled down, we're just going over to Kabuki-cho."

"Good morning to you, boss," I replied cheerfully, trying to hide a feeling of relief, as I realized that my examination had been, at least, postponed.

Koide gulped down the coffee as she headed out of the office, then handed me the empty cup to dispose of when she met with a team of about a dozen forensic techs who were bunched just outside, almost blocking the pavement. I was impressed: this must be just about every free tech to be found in Greater Tokyo. The CI must have pulled a lot of strings to have them all assigned to this case.

I tailed the tall blonde as she strode the short distance to Pleasure Doubled, chatting animatedly to the head crime-scene investigator. The area around the club had been cordoned-off since early morning and a couple of guys borrowed from Tokyo Water had used ground-penetrating radar to confirm the existence of an unrecorded basement that could be accessed both by the lift in the PD building and directly from the basement of the massage parlor opposite.

A couple of plods met us at the barrier of yellow tape that kept back a small group of rubbernecking civilians and confirmed that both buildings were empty, pretty much as you would expect in this entertainment district during mid-morning. Koide instructed them to contact all those working in either building and inform them that they should stay clear for at least the next twenty-four hours.

"Well then, Watson, what would be your preference? Do we enter via the club or the soap house opposite?"

I thought for a second. "I guess the gruesome twosome would always enter via the PD lift, so that's the way I would go."

I received a hefty slap on my back, which knocked me one step forward towards the entrance of the club. "That's the way that I'd go too. Good lad! Get your hands covered and we'll get started," she added as she tossed a sealant spray in my direction.

"Can we jinx the lift so that we can use it?" I enquired as the CI's comm opened the front door to the elevator accessing Pleasure Doubled.

"How do you think that'd work?"

Fuck, I hadn't escaped my daily test after all. "OK, if access needed to be completely secure from this side, I'd guess something biometric."

The CI was already using some hacking app in her comm, which suddenly produced a hologram in front of the small camera facing us. "Miss Nomura's retinal scan; I recorded it last night," she explained.

A disembodied voice immediately responded. "Welcome Maus-san."

We waited for a few seconds, but clearly a command was required from our side. My boss passed me her comm. "Use this, it'll synthesize any response in Nomura's voice."

I tried Basement, Cellar and Dungeon, but without any success. I racked my brains, trying to recall my interrogation of Saito. Then it came to me: "Play room!" the unit commanded in Nomura's arrogant tone and the lift smoothly descended and the door opened to a small anteroom. A heavy steel door faced us, with standard doors leading off on both sides.

I opened the door to the left side, which revealed a spacious room with a wall of cupboards and drawers and two massive dressing tables loaded with diverse cosmetics. The CI slid a mirrored cupboard door aside to reveal an array of black and scarlet leather rig-outs that must have included just about every dominatrix fantasy option. "What do you think of these, lad? Does this get your juices flowing?"

I grimaced, remembering the casual descriptions of obscene tortures from the night before. This feeling of revulsion was reinforced when I opened a drawer to expose a display of gloves and gauntlets adorned with vicious spikes, studs and, in one case, what looked like razor blades.

As we looked through the rest of the room, uncovering a bewildering range of underwear, clothing, boots and masks in leather and latex, Koide muttered instructions into her comm for the forensic team who were waiting to follow us.

We then looked into the room opposite, which was a bathroom with a toilet, bidet and a huge open shower area that was clearly big enough for the couple to use together. A shelf was stocked with soaps, shampoos and deodorants, while a rack contained about a dozen white towels of various sizes. A large wicker chest was lined with a thick black plastic bag. This was now empty, but I guessed was used for discarded clothing.

"Thoughts, Watson?" The question woke me from my reverie.

"I guess the evil lesbians came in from this side, but the place is serviced from across the road. Whoever did the cleaning up must have been completely aware of what was going on, but probably had no contact with the perps. Probably the same crew who were involved with Saito's earlier dungeon: Yamaguchi-gumi."

"Yep, that's also my take on things. The forensic team will have to go over this place with a fine toothed comb, especially the drains. So, are you ready for the main attraction?"

My boss was already striding towards the metal door, which slid aside silently as she neared. "Christ, this must be about six inches thick," she observed. "I'd bet you could explode a good sized bomb in here and nobody would be any the wiser."

I checked my own comm. "Also active noise cancelling. All set up to hide the screams of their victims," I shuddered at the thought.

I followed my boss's large frame into the dungeon, trying to prepare myself mentally for what I was about to see. As I scanned the large, white-painted room my first reaction was relief, its cleanliness gave it almost a clinical feel, emphasized perhaps by the faintest trace of an antiseptic smell. Then details began to register: a large cross equipped with buckles and chains and a similarly outfitted operating table and something that looked like a gynecological examination chair. Then I noticed that the plastic-sealed floor sloped gently towards a drain in the center of the room and I began to feel distinctly queasy.

To my amazement, Koide seemed completely unperturbed and was carefully examining a tray of implements beside the operating table. It was like a toolkit from hell: surgical implements, power cutters and grinders, knifes and saws. "Just don't be sick, for Christ's sake!" she commanded, without turning.

I gulped and looked away, unfortunately catching sight of a rack containing an array of whips, clubs and devices that were some form of strap-on dildo, the last ranging from large to gigantic and studded with spikes, blades and what looked like shards of glass. I closed my eyes and struggled to control my reflexive hyperventilation, which was making it very hard to obey my boss.

I jerked in surprise as a hand gently touched my elbow. "Just relax, lad. Slow breaths and think of something nice: like my beautiful body."

I had never heard the CI speak so gently and this, more than anything else, helped me to calm down. "Thanks, boss," I sighed as I opened my eyes. "Sorry for being such a wimp, but this place really gets to me. I just can't imagine anyone getting pleasure out of inflicting such pain."

"Not a problem. The one thing that makes it easier for me was the justification given by this pair of twisted fuckers: that those they were torturing all deserved it."

I started to object, but was waved to silence as Koide continued. "I don't mean that torture is OK under any circumstances, but I've worked on a couple of past cases where children were the victims and those were a fuck of a lot worse."

A distracted look came over the detective's face. "Actually, such violence is usually against children and women, often accompanying sexual abuse. In cases involving males, the psycho is usually gay and often trying to hide it. As far as I can make out, these women got their rocks off together or in their group encounters with hermaphrodites and transvestites. I'm sure a psychologist could probably dream up a sexual link, but they basically seem to enjoy inflicting pain on men for its own sake."

This dispassionate analysis helped calm me further and I risked a grim smile. "Right, we can get on further now. The forensics team will have a lot to do here, so I guess we should see how the bodies were cleared out."

"Yes, they'll be into the drains again here. But what about that?" she pointed to the rose of small lenses that, when you knew what to look for, could be discerned in the middle of the ceiling.

"Shit, yes, these fuckers were bound to record everything going on here." I tried to imagine how this could be done most securely. "Probably directly encrypted onto a chip that they took with them, a variation of what is done upstairs in the club. I assume that we've a search warrant for their apartment in Roppongi, so we should have a look there. Somehow or other, though, I doubt that they'd leave that kind of evidence lying about, unless it auto-burns if disturbed."

"We'll keep that in mind when we go over there, probably as soon as we're finished here." She strode towards a plain steel door opposite where we entered but, in this case, it remained stubbornly closed.

It was five minutes before my superior, swearing like a trooper throughout, finally managed to hack the door lock. The large room that we entered was probably double the area of the dungeon, with a much higher ceiling, looking like a cross between an equipment store and a garage. A circular platform was clearly used for turning vehicles, dimensioned to allow a van to be handled. "Mmm... , I think Yamaguchi's ambulance would fit on that," I speculated aloud.

"It would indeed," she agreed. "This is all starting to come together." A holo from the GPR survey of the vicinity was projected from her comm. "They could drive from here onto a ramp that will take them into a warehouse two blocks away. Medical supplies it says. Want to bet that it's another yakuza front?" she asked.

I took that as a rhetorical question, as I had already worked that one out by myself.

***

During our drive to Roppongi, through traffic slowed by an intense downpour, I could not help being surprised by Koide's apparent lack of any sign of tension. "We've got a lot of circumstantial shit on these bastards, but aren't you a bit worried that we won't be able to get something really hard? This

Nomura bitch is mega-rich and we will need a cast iron case against her."

"Worry not, lad, we're certain to get everything we need. I predict that there'll be a defect in the system that they used to clean that torture room that'll allow us to get incriminating DNA. That is assuming that their snuff porn video collection doesn't fall into our hands."

"But how can you be so sure? They've been at this for a long time and we haven't had the slightest inkling of it, so they must be good at covering their tracks."

"No doubt about that," the CI agreed with an annoying grin. "So why am I so confident that it's going to be downhill all the way from now on?"

"Shit!" I cursed, realizing that I had brought this quiz on myself. "OK, well we only got a first inkling after Chrissy was murdered and the evidence was presented to us on a plate. So... " I ground to a halt as jigsaw pieces began to fall into place. "It's the fucking hidden manipulator: he set the whole thing up for us to nab Nomura and Saito. So he'll also ensure that we get all we need to truly nail them to the cross."

"You've just about got there, but clearly missed a key clue," she smirked in a way that made me really want to slap her face.

"How do you know I missed it," I retorted angrily.

"Grammar, my dear Watson, your own specialty. Use of the masculine to refer to our nemesis."

Then the penny dropped completely. "It's Beverly Grove! She's been conspiring to destroy her friend Fumiko from the very start!"

"Indeed. So all we have to do is take care of all the loose ends that'll ensure these psychopaths get their just deserts and then we can concentrate on fucking-up the mysterious Bev."

"You seem to be taking this quite personally," I noted with surprise.

"'Course I fucking am. This Bev is the one who set the hit teams on us and has also been leading us around by the fucking nose. Dead fucking right I'm taking this personally."

Just then I decided that I really would not want to be in Beverly's shoes when the CI finally tracked her down.

***

A single uniformed policewoman was guarding the door to the private lift accessing Nomura's penthouse apartment in Roppongi Hills, caught in the middle of an animated conversation with two young men in expensive-looking matching grey suits. The rapid fire Japanese died immediately the CI announced herself and informed the woman that we were going to carry out a quick inspection before the forensic team arrived. The taller of the two men then rudely pushed in front of us and demanded to see our identification.

"Fucking lawyers!" Koide muttered under her breath as her comm displayed her holo-ID.

"And yours also," he glowered at me as I responded to what I was sure was a deliberately impolite command.

"You can't enter this property without a warrant," he stated, opening his arms as if he was going to physically block our passage.

"Actually, we can," the CI responded with admirable calm. "The owner has been charged with a capital crime and we have a blanket authorization to search any and all property belonging to this woman."

"Show me this authorization!"

I could tell from her body language that this arrogant solicitor was really beginning to get on my boss's nerves, but again she responded with polite restraint. The authorization is logged in the SAR police headquarters in Nishi-Shinjuku. I'm sure you could access it on your comm if you went to the bother to check.

"If you enter this property, I demand that we accompany you," the man changed tack instantly, clearly already aware that our search authorization had been granted.

"I think not," the CI responded with a smile. "For that you would need a special warrant, which I know you don't currently have."

"I demand that you remain here, while we apply for this warrant." The man was clearly instructed to try everything possible to hinder our investigation.

"OK, I've had enough of this fucking nonsense," the change in the blonde's tone made it clear that her patience had been exhausted. "Get out of my way, right now." She turned to the policewoman and added, "... and this officer will arrest you if you attempt to follow us."

As we pushed past, the man grabbed my shoulder. "You can't go in there, I demand... " His demand changed into a high pitched scream as the aikido wrist lock drove him to his knees. His companion moved towards us as if intent to come to his aid, but dropped like a puppet with cut strings as the policewoman's baton slammed into the side of his head.

"No tolerance for attacks against police," the young woman smiled at the CI, who grinned back.

I released the lock, allowing the lawyer to slump back onto his haunches. "Book them both for police assault and obstruction of an investigation," I commanded, trying to hide my own smile as I followed my boss into the lift.

***

We spent two hours wandering through Nomura's apartment, which extended over the entire top two floors of the building, with one further floor below including servants' quarters and a roof garden that featured an Olympic size swimming pool. I had never even considered luxury on this scale anywhere, much less in the city with the highest property prices in the world. Chrissy's flat had impressed me, but this was a completely different order of magnitude. I was totally bemused, with no idea how a couple could possibly use so much space.

The sheer size of the place presented our biggest challenge. Decades of video records could be stored on a chip the size of my fingernail, so this would be a tiny needle in a really huge haystack. There were eight luxurious bedrooms on the upper floor, of which seven appeared completely unused and only the largest contained clothing in the attached dressing room and a more personal range of toiletries and cosmetics in the massive en-suite bathroom.

Koide sat on the edge of a large circular water-bed, which was the focus of the master bedroom, and glared around her. Evidently this search was not going to be as easy as she had expected. "I'm sure that anything stored here would be in this room. If they were going to view their past atrocities, it would be here, in their bedroom."

"But the video file wouldn't need to be stored here: it could be on the private server that they use to run this place," I pointed out.

"I doubt that very much," the CI rubbed her face with frustration, "anything with links to the outside could potentially be hacked. It'll be a stand-alone memory unit linked to a screen or, more likely, a holo display."

"Can you find controls of the entertainment system, there must be one in this room?" I enquired as my boss worked her way through the advanced hack apps on her comm.

"Jesus fucking Christ! I can see the holo system in the apartment schematics, but no indication of how it can be accessed."

"Maybe code words again," I guessed, flicking through a wiki-cheat. "Sin City, Black Kiss, V for Vendetta,... " I enunciated carefully, reading from a list of related graphic novels from roughly the same time period.

After five minutes, I had almost decided that I was barking up the wrong tree. "Bite Club, From Hell... " I gasped as a holo menu appeared in the air in front of us.

"From Hell? What the fuck's that?"

I had to consult the wiki again. "Seems that it's a Jack the Ripper tale."

"Lots of kinky sex and violence?"

I scanned the precis. "Doesn't seem to be much sex, but there is all the known ripper murder and mutilation."

"Well that seems to fit then," Koide conceded as she used gestures to run through the list of videos available. "This seems like the most recent one, from the evening of Chrissy's murder. It's been paused midway."

I settled on the edge of the bed beside my boss as the hyper-realistic, full-scale holographic image appeared. This had evidently been recorded in Pleasure Doubled and the action commenced from where it had last been stopped. Chrissy was naked, spread-eagled on the bed with Fumiko in a soixante-neuf position, grunting as she attempted to get as much as possible of a huge erection into her mouth. Simultaneously, Chrissy's vagina was being rammed by another large penis belonging to an individual with enormous, pendulous breasts: either another herm or a ladyboy, I couldn't tell which.

Koide waved her arms to rotate the point of view, showing that Michiko, who was clad in a painfully-tight looking leather corset, equipped with a strap-on that sported double dildos, which were deeply penetrating her lover's cunt and arsehole. The CI froze the action and zoomed the image until we could make out part of Chrissy's face, her tongue pressed against Fumiko's engorged clitoris.

"Well, we can now see what the dirty duo get up to at the club and, at this point, there's no evidence that Chrissy was anything but a willing participant. Let's see what else we have here." Koide returned to the menu and selected another file.

Over the next quarter of an hour we viewed a half dozen further examples of kinky group sex from Pleasure Doubled and a number of older records from other locations, which could well be the dungeon that Michiko had run for the yakuza. Hermaphrodites and transvestites featured prominently, with men appearing only in the SM fantasies. These latter showed savage beatings and extreme degradation as victims were pissed and shat on, but nothing that approached the mutilation and murder that we had been looking for.

"I don't think there's anything here," my boss eventually sighed, turning the display off with an abrupt wave of her hand. "And if it's not here, I don't know where it would be."

This had been bothering me also, but mainly because it hadn't seemed quite right that Nomura-san would keep anything extremely incriminating in her main residence. She was a serial killer whose

217

victims must number in the hundreds: a scale never before seen in modern Japan. Such a large number of murders could be readily concealed in the third world, but would require extremely rigorous precautions somewhere like Tokyo. Like Koide, I was fairly sure that our hidden puppet master wanted us to have the evidence we needed to tie down our case, but the strange feeling that we were looking in the wrong place had been building up continually since we arrived in Roppongi.

"You mentioned it before," I mused aloud, "there seems to be a strange disconnect between this pair's bizarre sex and their murderous sadism activities. Maybe this extends to how and where they view them."

"Well rich-bitch Nomura certainly has properties scattered around the world, but this is where she lives most of the time; all of the time when she's in Tokyo."

"Yes, this is Nomura-san's pad, but what about the apartment in Akasaka Mitsuke, registered to Miss Maus?"

"Shit! Why didn't I think of that?" My boss looked really annoyed with herself, something I had never seen before. "OK, have this place sealed until forensics eventually get here, which I guess isn't going to be for a day or two. Also block access to the Akasaka flat. Let's go."

I followed in the wake of the tall blonde, carrying out her commands as I walked.

***

218

The apartment in the New Prudential Tower was also a penthouse, but on a more modest scale, with neutral decor that reminded me of Chrissy's place. The main feature was a huge, sparsely-furnished, glass-fronted living room that offered an unusually clear view of Mount Fuji, the air probably cleared by a recent rain shower. There were also two bedrooms and a well equipped kitchen / dining room, but these had a virgin appearance that indicated complete lack of use.

The CI flopped onto a black leather sofa that faced Fuji. "This is the only piece of furniture that shows any sign of use," she noted, pointing out slight scrapes on the surface that could have resulted from clothing sporting metal studs or zips. "From Hell!" she commanded, but nothing happened. "OK, smarty pants, you're on now."

I sat down next to her and thought for a moment, refusing to be rushed. As I vacantly stared at the ceiling, I noticed a rose of camera lenses, almost identical to those in the PD dungeon. "Could you use Nomura's retinal projection again," I pointed at the lenses, "and use the voice synthesizer for the vocal command."

This time "From Hell!" resulted in the windows immediately darkening while a holo menu appeared before us.

The last entry was a high resolution documentary of the butchery of Chrissy in the uni hospital operating theatre. It commenced with the hermaphrodite being led into view, already clad in an open-backed hospital gown. She was clearly drugged, offering no resistance as she was strapped to the table and completely docile as a mask automatically descended to cover her face.

The operation was carried out by ceiling-mounted waldos, with an older, white-clad man closely following the proceedings and the evil lesbians standing by as rapt spectators. Koide fast-forwarded until Chrissy's womb was removed from a small incision and placed in a refrigerated carrier by the man in white, who then immediately scurried from the theatre. From the slow rise and fall of her breasts, Chrissy was evidently still alive at this point.

Another fast forward and then I gulped as a scalpel cut the herm from throat to groin, the chest cavity was opened and the internal organs were removed one by one. Initial gushes of blood stopped together with the beating of a then-exposed heart. I could see that both the organs and drained blood were packed together into a large drum labeled biohazard - plasma incinerate. There was no way that we would be getting anything useful from the residue of that process, I was sure.

"OK, let's see what else there is." The menu reappeared and the detective selected a file from a folder called *playroom* with a swipe of a finger.

I recognized the dungeon that we had visited this morning, but now a naked young Japanese man was bound to the St Andrew's cross-shaped frame. The women then moved into view, clad in matching black leather bodices that were connected by suspenders to thigh-length leather boots with high stiletto heels. Neither of them were wearing pants and their shaven clefts were openly displayed. I could just feel the first twinges of involuntary tumescence, when I noted the large hunting knife in Michiko's leather-gloved hand; about the same time as their victim did, I guessed from his scream of terror. There was thereafter nothing that could elicit emotions other than fear and disgust.

A hand gesture from my boss silenced the sound track, but the man was clearly screaming himself hoarse while Fumiko used barbed wire to form a kind of tourniquet and then her partner hacked his right arm off at the elbow. The poor guy was certainly in shock as his eyes rolled and he lapsed into unconsciousness. The women laughed at some silent joke, then Fumiko injected something into his neck, bringing him awake in time to experience Michiko cauterizing his wound with a blowtorch.

I closed my eyes, only occasionally risking a quick glance to confirm that the systematic mutilation was still in progress. After both arms and eyelids had been removed, a drip was attached to his neck, which seemed to prevent further loss of consciousness. Then the two women went to work on his genitals and anus. I felt sick to my stomach, despite the man now having been identified by Koide as a known serial rapist.

"Got you now you despicable cunts!" I turned to see the rapturous smile on my boss's face: completely incongruous given the events we were watching. "We'll need to be extremely careful digging out the memory here, but just my comm record will be sufficient to ensure a death penalty for even someone as powerful as Nomura.

"Can we go now?" I requested in what, even to me, sounded like a whimper.

"Let's just record a couple more examples, then we'll be on our way." The image vanished and, after a quick flash of menu, was replaced by the same room but, in this case, with an old, fat man who looked more Chinese than Japanese tied into the gynecological chair. "In any case, we'll take some of the team off the dungeon and get them started here as soon as we're finished.

I needed only one glance of the spike-studded baseball bat in Michiko's hand to decide that I just couldn't take any more of this. I screwed my eyes tight shut and prayed that my boss would get this done as quickly as possible.

***

The next week passed in a blur as we integrated huge volumes of video material with the steadily accumulating forensic evidence from Kabuki-cho, Akasaka and Roppongi. As a precaution, thousands of hours of holograms had been rapid scanned from the two apartments before attempts were made to access the source memories - successfully in the case of their bedroom porn, but resulting in triggering a sophisticated autodestruct in Akasaka. This was, however, merely an inconvenience as far as the case file was concerned.

Although the hidden basement at Pleasure Doubled had been cleaned by professionals, a number of traces of DNA had been obtained from nooks and crannies, particularly after the major items of bondage equipment had been removed. The real treasure trove, however, came from the drainage system. Stainless steel drainage had been rigorously flushed with strong alkali, but a crack in a concrete sump had allowed seepage of blood into surrounding soil prior to such washing, building up a mixed trace that had been linked to over a dozen individuals so far. Could be regarded as bad luck for the perps, I mused, but not really unlikely given Tokyo's active tectonic setting.

Somewhat to my surprise, CI Koide had transferred copies of the case files to both the homicide and organized crime units of the Greater Tokyo force as soon as we had hit the jackpot in Akasaka Mitsuke. Jurisdiction was extremely complex, but it was clear that investigations would extend to both yakuza links and also internally to determine how death row prisoners managed to get into the hands of this pair of psychopaths.

After an internal bun-fight, a GT police commissioner was appointed to lead an interdepartmental team and we were assigned a supporting role, focused on crimes committed within the SAR.

Using an expert system search engine and the file of missing persons that I had already compiled, I had quickly established identities for all but three of those tortured to death below PD. These John Does were all gaijin, from the audio analysis two being identified as American and the other either Indian or Pakistani.

Koide had followed up on the yakuza team who had supplied the victims and cleaned up afterwards.

Three men and two women had been identified so far, both women having part-time jobs at the Nishi-Shinjuku University Hospital and one of the men registered as working for a private company that was contracted to support maintenance within the high security wing of the central district Tokyo prison.

As a final action before the GT team took over custody of our prisoners, we carried out a further interrogation together with the commissioner himself and his two deputies. In this case, however, both Nomura and Saito were each accompanied by two top-level solicitors.

We interviewed Nomura first, presenting video excerpts from our case file to emphasize how hopeless her position was. The woman followed her legal advice and was completely unresponsive throughout, staring blankly at the holo depiction of the atrocities that she had committed. There was actually more response from the lawyers who, case hardened as they were, clearly had difficulty watching such gratuitous brutality.

The interrogation of Saito was a completely different matter. She became animated as soon as we presented the first clip and, against repeated remonstrations from her council, happily reminisced on the crime, explaining how the torture had been tailored to fit the victim's past history of crime. She freely acknowledged both her culpability and the involvement of her partner, further salting the wounds of the lawyers who both looked as if they were about to be sick as the videos were shown.

***

It was late morning and I was checking a video to confirm that the latest case of a drunk falling in front of a Yamanote-line train in Shinjuku station showed no indications of foul play when I received the urgently summons to CI Koide's office. I was glad that I hadn't stopped to pick up coffee when I saw the look of thunder on her face.

"Those fucking incompetent GT wankers! Not only did they allow the yakuza to regularly wander off with prisoners from death row, now they've let those bitches off the hook."

"Christ, they can't have escaped, can they?" I responded in surprise.

"No, they're not quite that fucking useless. But look at that!"

The holo image showed the naked bodies of the sadistic lesbians entwined together on the floor of what appeared to be a standard police interview room. The image zoomed in on Fumiko's face, showing the glazed look in her eyes. "Poison?" I guessed.

"Fucking fugu - blowfish toxin. Their legal team had insisted that the prisoners had the right to meet together to develop their defense, but someone must have greased a palm somewhere to allow them into a room accompanied only by two lawyers with all monitoring cameras off."

"The lawyers must have been in on it."

"Certainly, but it turns out that the ones present are only junior interns: cannon fodder who will be amply recompensed for any time that they end up serving. There's no record, but I'll bet the attorneys simply brought in the poison and stood back while the women did their thing. Waited until there was no chance of resuscitation, then called for assistance."

"What a cluster-fuck! At least, we've already passed on all responsibility for this."

"Yes, Watson, you're certainly a glass half full sort of guy. I suppose there are some up-sides to this. Top GT brass will be up to their eyeballs now, given the links already established to Interpol on Nomura's activities in the Philippines." A section of the current case file, now a multi-exabyte monster, appeared over the CI's desk.

"Also US cops, now chasing up a couple of suspicious disappearance cold cases from Nomura's time in Stanford," I pointed out. "I suspect that we're probably well out of this."

"You could be right," she conceded, reluctantly. "Actually, before this bombshell emerged, I had been intending to give you some good news."

I stared suspiciously into my boss's eyes, aware of a mischievous glint. "What good news would that be?"

"You're going off on a nice, all expenses paid, Caribbean vacation."

"I am?" Now I was even more worried, noting that Koide had brightened up considerably as she teased me by drip-feeding her news.

"Well, actually we are. What could be more perfect than that?"

"I'm going on holiday with you?"

"Well, you could, at least, pretend to be pleased by the prospect. I can tell you that I cut quite a figure in a small bikini."

I refused to be diverted by that thought. "So where and when is this all supposed to happen?"

"When? That'd be setting off in a couple of days. As to the where - you must be able to work that out for yourself."

"Oh, not another of your fucking annoying quizzes," I groaned as I opened Caribbean as a search in the case file. Even as a mesh of links exploded throughout the exec-sum level, the answer to the riddle became clear to me. "Antigua, that must be it! You're going after this mysterious Beverly!"

"We're going after Bev," my boss corrected me pedantically. "We've accumulated a huge number of Brownie Points by both cracking the case and then passing it on so that GT can take most of the credit. I just thought it was worth cashing some in - so we get a well-deserved vacation and also the chance to tie up some of the loose ends that have been getting on my tits."

I involuntarily cast a quick glance at the CI's huge boobs, causing her to grin wickedly. "Yup, there's even a nudist beach on the island - what do you think of that? Your beloved boss in all her wondrous glory."

I tried to force that distracting thought from my mind, with limited success, as I mused over this unexpected development. "Do we really need to go all the way to the other side of the world? We've got electronic access to just about everything these days."

"That's exactly the point," she grinned and I realized that my test had not yet been completed.

I grimaced and closed my eyes, going over how we first established a link to this exotic location. "The reason that this murder spree continued for so long, was that all the key evidence was kept isolated from the internet. The material that we did access was mainly provided by Nomura-san's enemy, either in the persona of Bev or Anony-Maus. Fumiko certainly screwed-up with the bank account that we were able to access but, given that Bev was also able to use funds from this for the yakuza attacks, I wouldn't be surprised if she was also involved in setting this up."

I interpreted Koide's grin as indicating that I was going in the right direction, but missing something important. "Bev meticulously planned Nomura's downfall, but managed to remain in the background throughout. What mistake might she have made, that provides us with a clue to her whereabouts?"

I used a mixture of gestures and code words to highlight in the case file the first link to Antigua from Chrissy's hidden ledger of payments. "If we were intended to use this only to move the focus of our investigation towards Nomura and not identify the bank location, it could be a clue... "

"A bit more than that: can't you remember your comment when we first uncovered the Antigua link?"

"What? There's nothing in the case file that I can see."

"You thought it was a coincidence... " she hinted.

"I can't think of anything, only that I had a mate that lived there."

"Exactly!" she grinned triumphantly. "This is the key to the entire business."

"Are you having me on?" I enquired, baffled by this cryptic statement.

"Not at all. We couldn't have accessed the material that cracked the case if not for your bizarre ability to decode comic-related puzzles. I don't think this was a coincidence: the stuff was set up for you to solve."

"Come on, this can't possibly be the case. How could anyone plan something like this, which must have been developed over a period of years, and know that I'd be involved in the investigation."

"There is one possible way, of course," she interjected.

"Only if I was part of the conspiracy, which I'm definitely not," I protested.

"I considered this option, of course, but I'm now fairly sure that you're completely clueless... "

"I'm sure you could express it better than that... " I interrupted.

"... not knowingly involved. But you were manipulated into playing your role here, nevertheless. What was the name of your pal from uni who encouraged you to move to Japan."

"David McNeill," I responded automatically, unsure where this was going.

"David McNeill - who I think we will find is also known as Beverly Grove."

Part 2

Antigua, West Indies

Chapter 13

To get to Antigua from Tokyo, the options of flying east or west were roughly the same in terms of travel time and cost. Koide and I were in agreement that options involving flying via the US were not worth bothering about, so we narrowed our choices down to BA via London or Air Canada via Toronto. London would involve the annoyance of a transfer from chaotic Heathrow to slightly less chaotic Gatwick, so this led us to the Canadian option. Koide had, somehow or other, managed to wangle us business class, so the long flights would be significantly more comfortable.

By the time that we arrived at the V.C. Bird international airport, just outside of St Johns, I had briefed Koide on everything I knew or had been able to subsequently dig up on my friend David. I recalled him as a quiet, somewhat older, mature student; so more restrained than most others I associated with, who were frantically enjoying a first taste of freedom from parental reins. Although only in his late twenties, he referred to himself as retired, having made enough in his first job as a currency trader to fund a few years out to pick up a hobby degree in English and Fine Arts.

A bit of research confirmed the impression that he always gave of being scarily intelligent.

Although he had never mentioned it to me, he had completed parallel first degrees in accountancy and computer science before his twenty-first birthday and was head-hunted directly as senior consultant to a Swiss private bank. Despite his stellar position, he had managed to maintain a very low internet profile prior to Cambridge and, even there, his digital footprint was minimal: mainly records of him topping the class in every examination that he took. He had been a member of a science fiction discussion group and a cosplay club, but I could find no trace of any close girlfriends.

Thinking back, I remembered him as both shy and slightly effeminate and, at the time, had wondered if he could be a closet gay. In any case, there were also no indications that he had any close boyfriends.

After leaving university, he had spent a year in Tokyo before moving on to Antigua. There he had purchased a massive villa and, through a strange program that seemed to be called Citizenship by Investment, had obtained Antiguan nationality. He seemed to be a bit of a recluse, rarely venturing out of the country, but occasionally embarking on long cruises in the floating gin palace that he owned, which was otherwise docked at the *English Harbour* marina.

I could find little indicating a link between him and Nomura and nothing to support Koide-san's conviction that he was behind the Bev character who had it in for Nomura-san. The one exception to this statement was the fact that his first degrees had also been obtained at Stanford and he had overlapped six months with Fumiko's time there. Nevertheless, this was a huge campus and there was no indication that his accountancy and computing would bring him into contact with Nomura's bioscience.

Koide had also been digging into his background, using her hacking tools to access material that was not in the open domain. She had discovered that his specialty in Switzerland had been trading New Yen - which she considered significant but, to me, was peripheral at best. She also picked up that he had an older sister who had lived in Antigua for a couple of decades, running a massage parlor there. This could explain his move to the island as, following the death of his parents fifteen years ago, she was his only close relative and now lived together with him in his mansion.

One extremely anomalous fact about David was that Koide could find absolutely no trace of his medical records - in the UK, Switzerland, Japan or Antigua. All searches led to lost or corrupt files, indicating that these had been systematically doctored. Not proof of anything, of course, but maybe an indication of his hacking skills.

***

We disembarked from the plane at mid-afternoon local time on a beautiful sunny day. I had opportunity only to glance into the tiny terminal building before Koide led me to a pair of policemen who were standing at the end of the jet-way. The thin man and stocky woman both had flawless ebony skin that was well displayed by their white short-sleeved shirts and shorts. "Welcome to de island, Chief Inspector," the woman greeted us in a thick Caribbean accent, with an open smile that showed off her gleaming white teeth. "I'm Kempf and I'll be sorting out anyt'ing you be needing here."

"Thanks a lot, captain," my boss responded with a matching smile as they shook hands, "I really appreciate the help that you're giving us here."

"Dass all sorted out by de Interpol guys," she confirmed, while I shook hands with Sargent Scott, her deputy. "We also got de OK to skip de immigration, so we'll log you's visit to de island only when you leave."

Koide had explained this last detail when we had booked the flights under the names of James and Linda Hamilton. Given the way in which Bev - or David - had manipulated our investigation, we were clearly well known to him. If he really was such a hacker wiz, he may well have search engines that check names on flights to Antigua or registered by the immigration service computers against a watch list, which would certainly include us.

David seemed to value his privacy, but the question was just how much effort did he expend to guard it. This would depend both on the extent to which he felt under threat and his natural level of paranoia.

We confirmed that we had hand luggage only, a benefit of the larger allowance of business class, and were led through an unmarked door which led directly into a garage area. As usual, my boss was the center of attention, especially as our case had been a headline for the news media since the arrest of the pair now generally known as the *Kabuki-cho Killers*. Although she had played down our roles, our names were inevitably linked to this investigation. Or, more often, her name; I was the invisible sidekick.

After we boarded a marked police all-terrain vehicle - strangely with left-hand drive even though traffic drove on the left side of the road - Koide provided the goggle-eyed police officers with a condensed overview of the state of our investigations. She did not identify our target on the island, merely noted that we were chasing a suspect who was involved in financial aspects of the network of criminal activities that we had uncovered. This was readily accepted, as money laundering seemed to have replaced tourism as the major industry in the Caribbean.

During the thirty minutes required to drive to Falmouth Harbour, I appreciated the type of car used by the police: the condition of the road was appalling. The speed-bumps, which were scattered at seemingly random locations, were superfluous given the ruts and potholes in the normal road surface.

The island was hillier than I had expected, undoubtedly a great advantage given rising sea levels and the huge storm surges that accompanied regular super-hurricanes. Despite the very high annual rainfall figures that I had seen, the inland areas were parched by a sun that blazed from an almost cloudless sky. Small villages featured colorful wooden houses, which usually seemed to include wrecked cars as a kind of garden feature. There was also a proliferation of small churches belonging to odd-sounding Christian sects and roadside stalls selling local fruit and vegetables. I couldn't think of anywhere that would present a starker contrast to central Tokyo.

As we descended a hill looking onto Falmouth Harbour, the view was breath-taking, a hundred different shades of blue resulting from whatever lay beneath the crystal-clear water contrasting with the gleaming white of boats anchored throughout the bay and moored at the large marina at the other side. Captain Kempf pointed out the large cruiser by the Antigua Yacht Club that was our destination. "We confiscated dat beautiful ting jus a coupla weeks ago," she explained. "T'aint got no crew at all, but fully stocked wit anyting you'll need. Will dat be OK wit yous?"

"Just perfect," the CI confirmed. "Has it got secure comms?"

"She's a drug-runner, so got all de security dat money can buy," the captain grinned as Scott drove us into a car park beside the marina office. "If you wants a rental car, just pop over der," she waved across the road at a sign for Titi Car Hire, "it's reserved in me name, so you don't have no paper work to sort out."

Scott reached into the glove compartment and produced a chip attached to a small orange float. "Dis de key fo' de ship, so you can even take it fo' a likkle sail if you wanta," he smiled as he turned to pass it to me.

We piled out of the car and, for the first time, experienced a blast of raw Caribbean heat. I guessed it would have been a bit over thirty degrees and sweat broke out on my brow immediately. We unloaded our luggage, which the police officers insisted on carrying for us as we were led along a jetty and onto our floating accommodation. I noticed that it was registered in Rhode Island and named Halliday's Happy Endings, which I hoped might be a good omen, despite the fact that the eponymous Halliday was now in the clink.

***

We boarded over a gated gangplank, which opened automatically as we approached. This led onto the stern deck area, featuring a central Jacuzzi that was surrounded by sun loungers. Again bay doors opened as we neared, granting us access to the chill of a huge, air-conditioned cabin fitted out as a dining room on the left hand side and a bar to the right. Koide made a bee line for the latter and opened a glass-fronted refrigerator. "Beer, anyone?" she enquired as she popped the cap off a small bottle of local Wadadli lager.

The captain politely declined, although I could sense that her partner would have happily taken up this offer. Our friendly colleagues then made their excuses and left, after providing us with details that would allow us to contact them at any time in case we needed any support. Koide shoved a beer in my direction and opened an app providing an interactive layout of the ship - an extremely valuable tool for a vessel of this size. "Well then, hubby, where'll we dump our kit? The master stateroom looks very swish," she raised her eyebrows suggestively while she pointed out its features on a holo display.

"I'm sure that you'll be very comfortable there," I responded with a smile, "but something less grandiose would be more to my liking."

"Pommie poofter!" she muttered under her breath as she chugged the last of her beer. "OK, a quick shower for me and then we can go over our plan of action - back here in the bar in twenty minutes, say."

I sat by the polished granite counter and took a trial sip of my beer. A little sweet, but very refreshing after the heat outside. Just then I glanced again at the holo of the luxurious bedroom, saw my boss enter and realized that it was a live monitor feed rather than a simple display image. I knew that I should switch it off, but the voyeuristic temptation was too great, especially after my boss had dropped her two shoulder-bags on the floor, kicked off her sandals and started to unbutton her white silk blouse.

I could feel my breathing deepen as the shirt was casually chucked onto the bed and the tall blond reached back to unclip her straining bra. Feeling like a Peeping Tom, I rotated the image to get a better view of her gigantic breasts and large brown nipples. I watched as she undid her belt and unzipped her hipster jeans, almost choking on a sip of lager as she pulled them down to her knees and dropped backwards onto the bed, legs in the air

238

while she struggled to remove her tight trousers. Again I guiltily rotated the point of view to get a close-up on the minute black tanga that strained to cover her pudendum. At that moment there was a blur as her briefs were whipped off, exposing a shaved vulva and a flash of gold that indicated some form of labial piercing.

I could feel myself blushing with shame as I zoomed out and watched my boss bounce to her feet and stride off in the direction of the en-suite bathroom. My left hand hovered part way through a gesture that would cut the feed, but my right seemed on autopilot as it moved the image to follow her into the shower and present the best view as she washed.

I seemed to wake from a daze as the blonde started to dry herself with a large white towel, noting that ten minutes had already passed. I killed the holo display, located the nearest guest bedroom and scurried off to quickly attend to my own ablutions.

***

Back in the bar by the appointed time, my hair still wet from the shower, I scanned the wide selection of Caribbean beers on offer while I waited for my boss to appear. Spoiled for choice, I grabbed a Presidente from the Dominican Republic and then almost dropped it as a voice whispered in my ear. "That'll do fine," Koide observed as the bottle was twisted from my grasp.

"Jesus, how do you manage to sneak up on me like that?"

"It wouldn't happen if your senses weren't dulled by self-abuse," she grinned. "So, did you enjoy your little bit of voyeurism?"

I kept my back to my tormenter, sure that guilt would show on my face, selecting and opening a Presidente for myself to gain time while the question hung in the air. "I'm not really sure what you're talking about," I finally responded, this sounding lame even to myself.

"Oh, so you cut the video feed immediately I left, did you?" she teased.

"How did you know it was a video, looked just like a static display to me?" I attempted to change the subject.

"Play of light on the ceiling, look," she commanded, waving the display back into existence as I turned to obey.

"Fuck me!" I muttered, realizing that it had defaulted to the last used point of view, which was the bathroom shower.

"So who's a dirty dog, then," she scolded me, waving a finger in a schoolmarmish fashion, the impact of which considerably lessened by her wide grin.

"OK, I'm sorry, I don't know why I did it... " I stuttered, to her evident amusement.

"Christ, Watson, I'm only kidding. I was only fucking about with you - I knew the monitor was live and could have set the privacy setting at any point. So it was all just a little treat for you, a reward for your good work on the case."

I was completely disconcerted by this revelation. "So, you perform strip-tease shows regularly as rewards for your downtrodden underlings?" I asked, petulantly.

"Not very regularly, but I has been known," she laughed, clearly continuing to fuck with my head. "You have to learn to relax a bit - and also lose some of your fucking Brit body-shyness. I was thinking that we could maybe relax on a beach tomorrow, as there's a nudist one somewhere on the island." A wave of her hand and the bathroom view disappeared, replaced by a map and an arrow indicating the location of Eden Beach.

"I thought we were here to work," I interrupted.

"Yes, but we're here undercover, so need to look at least a bit like tourists. We are also supposed to be man and wife, so you can't get tongue-tied every time you get a glimpse of a nipple."

At that point I became aware of what my boss was now wearing. Rather than her standard blouse and jeans, she had poured herself into a skin-tight white t-shirt, which made it very obvious that she was not wearing a bra. This was complemented by what looked like tight white shorts, but which could just as easily have been some kind of sports knickers. I could feel my eyes goggling as I stared openly at the goods on display.

"Now you've just gone and proved my point," she laughed aloud, delighted with the impact of her unsubtle wardrobe.

"Christ, boss, how the fuck am I supposed to concentrate if you flaunt yourself like that?" I eventually recovered enough to respond.

"It's all good training for you, lad. You never know when you may need to do some work, despite having a hard on."

I involuntary glanced down to see if my state of arousal was that obvious, causing a further peal of laughter. Although the sight of Koide's breasts had indeed had an effect, nothing was apparent given the baggy khaki shorts that I was wearing and the loose blue shirt which completely covered the area of my groin.

"Very funny," I muttered in annoyance. "Are you just going to have a laugh at my expense or are we going to work out how we can nail David aka Bev?"

The mention of Bev's name brought a more serious look to the CI's face. "Yes, well we've got two main tasks here." She slaved her comm to the ship's display and the case model appeared, showing a new branch from the labyrinth of our Tokyo investigations, labeled Antigua in lurid scarlet text. This evolved automatically as she spoke.

"The first job is to rigorously confirm that the anime Anony-Maus, Beverly Grove and David McNeill are actually one and the same person - and determine if there are any other aliases under which he or she operates." Koide looked at me as she settled onto a barstool.

"I think we have Anony-Maus and Bev pretty well tied down," I commented as I sat next to her. "Bev was hacking Nomura's sin account and used the Anony-Maus persona to organize the attacks on us, knowing that this would help us identify Nomura via her PD nickname."

"OK, fair enough," she conceded, "but we need to have hard proof that your uni mate David is playing the role of Bev. To me, the circumstantial evidence for you playing a pawn's role here is convincing, as are the links from you to David, but we really need something that would stand up in court."

"Hardly a pawn," I objected, feathers ruffled by the apparent disparagement of my important contributions towards solving the case. "How would we have managed if... "

"OK, placed as a pawn, but progressed into a position to change into a queen," she conceded, elbowing me gently in the ribs in what seemed intended as a conciliatory gesture. The fact that this caused a hard nipple to rub against my bare arm seemed completely unintentional, but I could never be sure with this conniving woman.

"Well, this would probably be something where we'll need the best hacking tools that you can get your hands on. David has done a shit-hot job of covering his tracks, so anything digital will be bloody hard to access," I contributed, swallowing a large mouthful of beer to help keep my mind off physical distractions.

"If there's one thing that we learned from the investigation so far, it has been that our puppet-master doesn't make anything openly accessible unless he wants us to see it." Koide rapped an empty bottle against the bar top and I heaved myself up to get a replacement, letting her try a can of Banks from Barbados as a change.

"But he will have records on a stand-alone system," she continued, "which will be located somewhere in his villa here. Could be that he also has a backup on that ocean-going cruiser of his, which is even bigger than this monster," she cast her eyes around the cabin as if to emphasize the latter point.

"What are you thinking, try to get a search warrant?" I hazarded.

"Completely pointless, even if we had the jurisdiction, which we haven't."

"We could go through Interpol, the case is high profile enough," I pointed out.

"It'd be a complex process and I don't think we have a hope in hell of carrying it off without your David getting wind of it. I'm sure that, if he was forewarned, we would never find anything incriminating in his abode." The blonde slurped some beer, wiped her mouth with the back of her hand and burped inelegantly.

"So what do we do, then, break into his villa and steal his memory chips?" I enquired sarcastically.

"That's a good idea," she smiled in her most annoying manner, "but why don't you let me sort that out. You can get on with task number two, finding out what other mischief your mate has been up to."

"Why are you so convinced that he's up to anything at all?" I enquired, allowing myself to be diverted from my Boss's plans for criminal burglary."

"Stands to reason, doesn't it?"

She looked at me in a quizzical manner and I groaned. "Why do we have to go through all of this here, I thought we were on holiday?"

"We're on holiday as soon as we get Bev locked up. For the moment, we're still working and I'm still training up your pallid arse."

"How do you know that my arse is pallid?" I enquired, hoping to divert the interrogation - or, at least, buy myself some time.

"Do you think my shower is the only one with a video monitor?" she burst into laughter at the shocked look on my face.

"But you can't... That's fucking... " I spluttered, shocked.

"What's good for the goose is good for the gander - or vice versa," she smiled, smugly. "In any case, back to the question: why might I think that David must be up to his neck in dodgy dealings?"

"Well, if David was really playing as Bev in Japan, he has been hacking accounts and has links to the yakuza," I started uncertainly, finding the appropriate cross-connections in the case model. "More importantly, he must have known about the murderous activities of Nomura and Saito for a considerable time, but has only now passed us the information that we needed to stop them."

"That's the key," she swung back and forth on her stool, ignoring the repeated brushing of her breasts against my arm, "that and the fact that we were manipulated into feeling that we were solving the case for ourselves, rather than just following a prepared script. It indicates to me that we weren't supposed to find out that this was all happening because Bev had it in for Nomura. Even if we did try to trace Bev, it should have been an impenetrable dead end. David does not want to be tied to this case in any way, so he has something nasty to hide."

"You're assuming that he's hiding from us," I objected. "He could be moving slowly and cautiously because he's afraid of Nomura: she's a nasty piece of work and I certainly wouldn't want to be identified as somebody scheming against her, somebody who could put her on death row."

"She was a nasty piece of work," my boss corrected me in a typically pedantic manner, "and certainly not someone to treat lightly. But look at the gratuitously complex manner in which this case developed: our opponent is very smart and extremely self-confident, which matches well what we know of McNeill. Do you really think he would be frightened of Nomura or worried that this scheme would backfire on him?"

I pondered this while I finished my beer. "No, I suppose you're right. We have completely destroyed the supposedly untouchable Nomura and, if we had kept a lead role in the investigation, would spend years tracing the spider's web of connections between homicides, illegal gengineering, police bribery, corruption and God knows what else. Nobody would be thinking about who stood to gain from this all."

"Exactly, exactly, you're not just a pretty face, lad," she patted me on the thigh in congratulation. "What did David get out of Nomura's downfall and why does he need to stay hidden to benefit from it?

So, that's your job. In the interim, however, you can get me another beer - maybe I'll try a Carib this time."

I had the feeling that I'd be playing barman for a while before I got a chance to start on my impossible task but, at least, the view would certainly compensate for my menial role.

***

After four beers, I was already beginning to feel somewhat spaced out, which I blamed on the combined effects of alcohol and jetlag. By four thirty the sun was beginning to sink towards the horizon and Koide had decided it would be a good opportunity to catch some last rays. We were lying side-by-side on loungers on the stern deck, myself stripped down to a pair of small briefs, due to the fact that I had forgotten to pack swimming trunks. My boss had stripped off completely, her uniform tan indicating that this was not an uncommon event. She was certainly aware of how disconcerting I found this - and completely unbothered by it.

David's villa was located on the hill overlooking the marina. The grounds actually looked quite modest, but Koide had determined that he actually owned all the surrounding properties, which provided luxury accommodation for his staff. Apart from the buffer zone these represented, high resolution satellite images showed sinister black posts encircling the estate, which must be part of some kind of security system. On the basis of this, I considered our chances of breaking into the house to be negligible and was very happy that this was not my job.

I closed my eyes to remove the distraction of a couple of nipples that resembled large brown acorns and considered how I could possibly find out more about what the secretive McNeill could be up to. Openly accessible databases showed only that he had joint UK and Antiguan citizenship and gave his current address. Instead of tax records, it was noted only that he had negotiated a fixed annual payment of one million EC per year in lieu of all local and national taxes and costs of supply of services. I was surprised to discover that, in fact, this was not an unusual situation for the rich ex-pats who provided a major source of revenue for the island.

As far as UK, Swiss and US records were concerned, he was a ghost. Passport details, school qualifications and traces of his time studying at Stanford and Cambridge or working in Zurich could be found, but links that should have provided further personal details always petered out or were defunct. Japanese immigration records showed that, after his first degree in the States, he had been a regular visitor to the land of the rising sun. Length of stays varied between a week and almost three months, but were never long enough to require a work or residence permit.

Interestingly, he had always given *Hotel in Tokyo* as his address during visits, but there were no records of anyone with his name staying in any such hotel over the time periods identified.

In the absence of a better idea, I had initiated a brute force approach, using the dates of his last three entries to Japan and his passport photograph to pick up the images of him arriving in Narita from the airport security camera images - fastidiously archived like all such material in Japan. This then acted as a seed for an expert system to search connections to other video archives, gradually building a summary of his movements within the country. Despite the massive computing power at my disposal, this would take a very long time, so I was not holding my breath for input on this during our stay on the island.

The other potential thread involved his activities in Antigua, but here we were inherently limited by the general lack of surveillance monitoring: usually limited to banks, liquor stores and the like, which were not likely to be frequented by our target. Further, such records were rarely archived, being discarded or over-written after a few weeks or, at most, months. Nevertheless, I initiated an image search based on all monitors that we could access via the Antiguan police network.

My final option would involve investigating Chrissy's account in the First Caribbean International Bank in St John's, but this would require footwork as, other than a description of their services, nothing was available online.

I was roused from my reverie by a creak as weight shifted on the neighboring lounger. "Wakey, wakey, Watson! Must be about time for a pre-prandial libation."

I opened my eyes and turned my head to admire the statuesque form beside me, noting that my boss had turned a little towards me with her upper knee cocked. This presented me with a better view of her depilated pussy, being deliberately provocative I was sure.

"I'm not sure that I need a pre-dinner drink, considering that we've been knocking back beers all afternoon," I replied, forcing my eyes upward to look directly into her face.

"So, if not a drink, what do you fancy doing between now and dinner time?" she enquired archly, opening her legs further to reveal a gold ring which adorned her clitoral hood.

My intake of breath - and probably also my increasing obvious erection - caused her to smile. "Mmm... , so you like piercings do you?" she teased me. "Would you like me to put rings in these?" She stroked a pair of erect nipples with the tips of her middle fingers.

My hard-on was now threatening to poke out of my pants. "A drink sounds good," I stated, assuming that these were rhetorical questions. "Better get some trousers on," I bounced to my feet and set off for my cabin, trying to decide what was really on offer and how I intended to respond to it. The taunting laugh that followed me did nothing to help resolve my confusion.

***

We had pre-dinner drinks in a restaurant called Jasmine's, which was located on the upper floor of the wooden building housing the Marina office. The restaurant had just opened for the evening and we were the first customers, allowing us to select a table on the patio which had a prime view over the harbor. Our waitress wore tiny white shorts and a restaurant logo vest which showed off her flawless mahogany skin. As she departed with our order of a bottle of New Zealand Sauvignon Blanc, Koide gave me a lecherous grin. "Very pretty, don't you think? Her skin color just goes perfectly with her heavy yellow gold jewelry. Do you think she'd be up for a bit of menage a trois?"

I struggled to dispel the resulting image that immediately appeared in my head, concentrating on the choice of seafood available on the menu. "What do you fancy eating?" I asked, attempting to change the subject.

"I would have gone for oysters, but they don't seem to be available. Very good for the libido, you know," she grinned, mischievously, evidently determined to maintain my level of discomfort.

I refused to rise to the bait and returned to perusal of the menu while my boss waxed lyrical on the benefits of marine fare for enhancing one's love-life. To my great embarrassment, this monologue continued while the waitress returned and served our wine.

I glared at my boss, but this acted only to encourage her to be more outrageous. "Give me a break," I hissed as soon as the girl was out of earshot. "Could we just discuss something other than sex for a bit?"

"We're supposed to be a married couple," she reminded me, "so I was getting into my role."

"Hardly the way that I imagine a wife to behave," I complained.

"Well, it would be if we were newly-weds on honeymoon," she grinned.

"Where did you get this newly-weds on honeymoon bit?" I inquired, suspiciously.

"It's all in the profile that I created for Mister and Missus Hamilton," she laughed. "It seemed like a good idea at the time."

I groaned in defeat and let the blonde outline the benefits of this cunning deception, which focused on our freedom to disappear off at any time with the pretense of having sex.

The waitress returned to take our orders, both of us starting with gazpacho, then mahi-mahi carpaccio for me and grilled lobster for Koide. By this time, another two couples had joined us in the restaurant, also sitting at tables on the terrace. The younger of these could well have been honeymooners, I guessed, from the way they stared into each other's eyes and touched at every possible opportunity. My companion clearly spotted this and started to copy them to my further annoyance.

"You said that we could add on a bit of holiday here," I tried yet again to find a neutral topic of conversation. "What did you have in mind?"

"Apart from screwing like rabbits, you mean?" again she herded me back into her chosen line.

"Well, I took that for granted," I decided to play at her own game. "You must have something else in mind though. I hear that this is a popular place for scuba: maybe we could have a go at shagging underwater?"

"That's a really good idea, you know," she responded with a straight face, "I haven't had underwater sex for ages. I'm certainly up for that if you are!"

I rolled my eyes and gave up, concentrating on my food and letting my boss's fantasies of underwater intercourse flow unimpeded over my head.

***

I was all for an early night when we returned to the boat, but Koide insisted on a nightcap. "You should try some of this," she recommended, pouring a very generous measure of XO cognac into a snifter the size of a goldfish bowl.

"Not for me," I demurred, selecting a small bottle of Wadadli and pleased to be finally able to make my own choice in something.

I had just started to sip the beer directly from the bottle when my boss started to undo her blouse, causing me to choke on the drink. "What the fuck are you doing," I spluttered.

"Just showing you that I did as promised," she replied as she opened the shirt, pulled it free of her shorts and removed it completely. I could now see her breasts straining against a silky white bra which seemed to have been dimensioned for considerably smaller mammaries. I stared like a rabbit in headlights while she unclipped a catch at the front and the bra exploded open. I hardly noticed the garment drop free, hypnotized by the sight of the gold rings that now adorned her prominent nipples.

"Umm, very nice... " I wittered, unsure about where this was going, but aware that my earlier tiredness had vanished completely.

"You think?" she flicked the rings in turn. "How would you like to give these a lick?" she licked the tip of her finger and proceeded to moisten a large brown areola. "Or would you like to start a bit lower?" She kicked her sandals free and started to undo the belt of her shorts.

"You can't... We can't... " I stuttered. "Isn't there some regulation about fucking your underlings?"

"There certainly is," she now started to unzip her shorts, showing the first glimpse of a small white tanga, "but we're undercover now and have to do whatever is required to conform to our specified identities: the legend I believe it's called in the trade."

"Shit! I'm sure this is beyond the call of duty." Her shorts dropped down and were kicked loose, quickly followed by her underwear.

She sat on a bar stool and coolly took a sip of her drink, totally unconcerned about her nakedness. "OK, Watson, your turn now. Let's see what you've been hiding under those baggy pants."

I swithered, seriously considered making a run for my cabin and locking the door. Koide smiled at me as if able to read my mind, then slowly opened her legs to allow me an unimpeded view of another gold ring.

"Fuck it!" I groaned. "I'll do the strip tease bit, but I'm not going to screw my boss!"

"We'll just have to see about that, won't we," my boss grinned, clearly convinced that she had already won this round.

By the time I had undressed to the point of exposing an erection like a bowsprit, I realized that she was probably correct.

Chapter 14

I awoke to early morning sunshine, which was filling the cabin with golden light. I turned my head to look at the naked body sprawled beside me on top of the rumpled sheets. The curvaceous blonde was lying on her back with her head wedged into my armpit. I lay for a while just listening to her gentle snoring, admiring the rise and fall of her gigantic breasts and thinking back over the previous evening, which had involved the wildest sex that I had ever experienced.

It had started in the bar, after I had been goaded into licking Koide's pierced nipples - which rapidly progressed further to cunnilingus as I explored my boss's lower piercing and brought her to the edge of orgasm. I had then been unceremoniously shoved down onto a thick pile rug and straddled, my dick vanishing into her soaking wet cleft as she bounced on top of me. I was not sure who came first, but I was certainly spent when the large frame flopped forward onto my chest, panting and slick with sweat.

I would have been happy to drift off into post-coital slumber there and then, but, after about five minutes, Koide clambered up and pulled to me my feet. Despite my protestations, I was dragged along to her cabin and pushed onto the bed. She then clambered over me into a sixty-nine position and took my flaccid, sticky dick into her mouth. I initial protested, assuring her that there was no way that I could respond a second time, but again I was proven wrong as tumescence slowly built up, in line with my own interest in the cunt that began thrusting against my face. I licked the gold ring, rubbing it against a completely exposed clitoris while my fingers stroked her swollen labia, occasionally thrusting deeply into her wet vagina.

Time seemed endless as our sex play continued, very slowly increasing in intensity in line with the rapidity of our breathing. I was rubbing my moistened finger against her anus when she pushed back and my finger entered, exactly at the point when she stuck a finger into my arse. Both penetrations got deeper and deeper as the heavy body bucked on top of me until, with a groan from me and a scream from my partner, we came almost simultaneously.

***

I glanced at my watch and saw that it was just after six am local time, which would be about eight in the evening Japanese time. Despite the time difference and the long air trip, I felt fresh and wide awake. It seemed that shagging one's brains out acted as a cure for jetlag - something that I would be happy to try again in the future.

I gently prized myself loose and rolled off the bed, noting from the flickering of her long eyelashes and small twitches of her fingers that she appeared to be dreaming. Looked like an interesting dream, I guessed, if her erect nipples had anything to do with it.

I wandered through to the bar area, retrieved my scattered clothes and then padded to my own

257

cabin for a shower. My skin was sticky with dried sweat and other bodily secretions, which triggered further memories of last night's encounter although details seemed increasingly surreal. In any case, I resolved to make a copy of the appropriate section of the ship's security video log - and then delete the original before it shocked any innocent viewer.

After a quick shower, I dressed in my rather crumpled shorts from the previous day and a clean sports shirt and then, barefooted, set off in search of breakfast. Adjacent to the dining room and bar area, I found a small but very well equipped galley, where I set a pot of coffee on to brew and put some fresh-bake croissants into the oven. I then took a large glass of grapefruit juice with me and settled into a comfortable chair at the head of the dining table.

I slaved the comm on my belt to the yacht's system and displayed the holo case file, checking for any other links between Tokyo and Antigua that I might have missed. Everything was circumstantial and, in particular, the motive for David to develop and implement a plot of such intricacy was completely missing. My assigned task was not going to be easy.

I retrieved the croissants and their smell joined that of the fresh coffee wafting through the ship. I had left the door to the master cabin ajar and the aroma was probably what had awakened my boss. "Breakfast in bed would be fine," she shouted, "soon as you like, Watson." Our intimacy in bed had clearly not altered our master - slave working relationship, I was unsurprised to note while I found

258

a tray and began to set out a morning repast to replace the calories that she had burned the previous night.

Koide was sitting up in bed, now underneath the sheet that was pulled up to her waist. Her fine boobs were still on display, but I noted with disappointment that the nipple rings had been removed. "Work time now," she grinned, seeming to read my thoughts, "so you need to have as few distractions as possible. However, if you play your cards right, we might have an action replay before we head off home."

She reached for the tray causing the sheet to slip and giving me a quick glimpse of the cleft between her thighs. "Maybe fewer distractions in the dining room," I commented as I hurried out, closing the cabin door behind me.

***

After breakfast, Koide joined me for another mug of coffee while we confirmed our plans for the day. These were constrained by typical Caribbean island time, which meant that banks and many shops were open only during daytime, five days a week - a dramatic contrast from the twenty-four/seven commerce of the Shinjuku SAR. Thus, today being a Saturday, we would not be able to visit Chrissy's bank for a couple of days. However, the massage parlor run by David's sister was open and we were able to make a booking for the both of us to be treated together in the mid-afternoon.

For the morning, we intended our first foray against David's villa. Satellite images showed a conspicuous network of security cameras around the estate. In contrast to the minute monitors normally used elsewhere, these were heavy-duty installations, designed to function even during the heavy rainstorms and regular hurricanes that were characteristic of the island. Image analysis indicated buried cables connecting these to the main house, rather than solar power and wireless that might otherwise be expected.

We dressed for our role in swimwear - or, in my case, a pair of underpants that looked the part - t-shirts and sandals, with wide-brimmed hats and large sunglasses that would hide our faces. Both of us carried rolled-up beach towels and I had a backpack over my shoulder. It was just after nine when we set off, but the sun was already hot and I immediately broke out in sweat, which was soon dripping from my nose. Koide, by contrast, seemed unbothered by the heat, probably reflecting her past acclimatization in Australia.

We departed the marina area and turned left, heading along a quiet street which mainly comprised closed restaurants on our right, facing onto a large car-park opposite. Amongst the restaurants was the Titi car rental place that Captain Kempf had mentioned to us. At a T-junction we turned right into English Harbour, following signs for Nelson's Dockyard. Before we reached it, a sign for Pigeon Beach directed us right, up a steep hill which passed an old stone rainwater catchment tank, which must have been contemporary with the Dockyard.

Unlike the potholed roads of the rest of the island, this hill had been recently surfaced with smooth black tarmac, which made the heat even more intense. My t-shirt was entirely soaked and even the blonde had damp patches under her armpits in the couple of minutes that it took to reach the summit. This was already bordering David's estate, which stretched off to our right. As we passed the third streetlight, which incorporated one of his security cameras, my boss leaned against it while I bent down to remove her left sandal, shaking it as if to get rid of a piece of gravel. This ruse allowed Koide to surreptitiously place a small package the size of a matchbox on the backside of the pole. This was another bit of her military-spec kit, an electronic leech which would, hopefully, allow us to tap into David's security system.

We then continued downhill to Pigeon Beach, found a table shaded by a roof of palm leaves to dump our stuff on and went for a swim. Even though it was the weekend, the beach was populated by only two other couples, clearly tourists as indicated by their patchy sunburn. I could also make out someone swimming further out in the bay, probably from one of the yachts anchored there.

We walked down the soft sand, burning feet that were quickly cooled when we waded into the clear water. I carried swimming goggles that I rinsed out when I was thigh deep, this allowing me to admire the form that waded past me, clad in a minute black bikini and still wearing her hat and sunglasses. Despite this headwear, Koide launched into a powerful breaststroke and headed off towards the far end of the bay. I couldn't help comparing her to a fat English woman who was chatting to her partner at the water's edge; she was probably about the same age and weight as my boss but was at least forty centimeters shorter with her mass predominantly in the form of lard. Her shapeless black swimsuit looked like it had been stuffed with potatoes, I thought unkindly, as I lowered my goggles and set off in the wake of the blonde amazon.

While I swam in a relaxed crawl, I wondered if the tools at our disposal would really allow us to hack into David's stand-alone server. My boss seemed very sure of herself, but would not provide me with any further details, probably saving this for a future quiz, I guessed.

After swimming the length of the bay and back, a distance of about a kilometer, we dried off and lay to catch some rays for about twenty minutes, before being driven into shade by the power of the sun. It was now ten fifteen and Koide decided that it was time for beer, leading me off to a nearby beach bar called Bumpkins. There were no other customers as we settled into a shady veranda that offered a view over the bay. Without consulting me, Koide ordered Banks beer for both of us and turned down the offer of a breakfast menu. It was now three hours since breakfast and I was beginning to feel peckish, but I decided to just go with the flow, feeling island lethargy descend upon me.

Koide ignored the glass that had been provided and took a swig from the frosted bottle, which was followed by a sigh of pleasure. "OK, Watson, how do you think today is going to play out."

My sigh reflected confirmation of my forebodings and I concentrated on pouring my beer while I struggled to organize my thoughts. Koide must also be moving onto island time, I mused as I sipped a mouthful of beer while she waited patiently for my response.

"OK, tapping into David's system is a reasonable start, but I can't see that he won't have firewalls to handle anything that you can throw at him. You'd really need a backdoor into his main system to set up a syphon for the material you want to access."

"Absolutely correct, you're getting the hang of this kind of stuff." The complement would have been better if not accompanied by a look of surprise. "So what about the rest of our day?"

"Again approaching the sister is one of the few options that we have of sniffing around David's fortress of solitude. But it seems very risky: if I was him, I'd have spotted that this was a vulnerability and planned accordingly."

"Right again," another look of surprise was followed by a smile that took the bite out of it. "OK, you seem to have the essence of how things are going to play: get that beer down your neck and we'll head back to our place for a shower before lunch."

I did as commanded, bemused by my boss's lack of concern about the serious flaws in her plan that I had pointed out.

***

Back on board, the CI busied herself with a couple of heavily encrypted mails back to Shinjuku while I showered and changed into typical tourist ware - my own shorts and sandals complemented by a t-shirt from a local dive shop that I found in a drawer of my cabin, presumably abandoned by a previous resident. She looked up when I returned to where she was working - a luxurious lounge at the bow of the cruiser, lying directly above Koide's bedroom - and smiled. "Soul Immersions," she read from the logo on my chest, "sounds very Zen and somehow fitting to your quest."

"What quest is that?" I wondered, not quite seeing her point.

"Your fantasy about fucking me underwater," she grinned, "don't you remember?"

"I thought you were supposed to be avoiding distracting me during work time."

"True, true. I suppose I shouldn't ask you to wash my back in the shower then?" She heaved herself up and headed off to her cabin.

I took this to be yet another rhetorical question and set to work checking the link to the bug that Koide had placed.

I had no idea where she had obtained this tool, but it was capable of inductively coupling to the monitor power supply and using this to access any

264

other equipment using the same electrical input. As David's estate was supplied by its own generator, this trick could not be played using the island mains electricity network, hence the peripheral monitor that we had targeted.

The principle was fine but, so far, the associated hack expert system had managed to access only the controllers of domestic appliances: washing machines, refrigerators and the like. A host of other equipment had been registered, but the associated firewalls had resisted all attacks so far. All in all, pretty much as I had expected.

"Feeling vindicated?" the voice immediately by my ear caused me to jump.

"Well, I don't know how you would interpret it, but to me it looks like the hack is going nowhere fast."

"Yes, that's true," she responded with an enigmatic smile, "exactly as planned. Anyway, let's off to lunch!"

Despite my bafflement, I was resolved not to chase her on this and just keep an eye open to find out what could be behind her cunning plan. "Where are we going anyway?" I asked to change the subject.

"A wee place nearby, just beside the marina office, where we can sit at the waterside. It's called *Skulduggery*."

"Couldn't be a better place for my conniving boss," I muttered sotto voce as I scurried after her towards the gangplank.

***

After our early lunch - cheese and onion toasted sandwiches and more Banks beer - we killed time back onboard with mail and routine admin. I occasionally checked progress with our hack, but it had plainly stalled and looked unlikely to make any further progress without external help. Just before three we set off for the short walk to our massage appointment.

It took only ten minutes to walk to Nelson's Dockyard where, as tourists residing locally, we were granted free entrance. We passed a hotel with a very plush looking waterside restaurant and bar which incorporated strange stone pillars that I took to be part of the infrastructure of the old dock services. Immediately thereafter, we came upon the massage parlor, which comprised the upper floor in an old wooden building to our right, apparently a reconstruction of an old carpenters' shed.

We climbed a rather rickety wooden staircase and pushed through a glass door into a reception area that seemed incongruously modern and was air-conditioned to the point of almost being chilly. A young, thin, black woman wearing a loose white smock sitting behind a desk smiled at us. "Mister and Missus Hamilton, I guess?"

"Yes, indeed. We're here for the parallel massage at three."

"Perfect timing," she rose to shake our hands. "My name is Varry and I'll be one of your therapists today. We can go directly into the spa area where Kat, your other therapist, is waiting for us." The willowy girl led us towards another glass door, which opened at her approach.

The large, windowless room that we entered was a little warmer and lit only by candles, which were scattered around two solid wooden massage tables covered by thick, cream-colored mattresses. "Hi, I'm Katrina, how are you today?" The voice from the gloom drew my attention to a small, slightly chubby, middle-aged, Caucasian woman clad in a similar smock who was standing behind the furthest away table.

We moved forward and shook hands, introducing ourselves. "You sound like you're originally from England , maybe somewhere in the North?" Koide added.

The woman smiled in a way that lit up her face and caused her eyes to twinkle in the flickering light. "Right, well spotted: Yorkshire, on the Dales."

"Very nice," my boss smiled back, "but a bit of a contrast to here."

"You can say that again! Lucky that I like the heat. Anyway, you can take off your clothes there," she pointed to an alcove with a table and a couple of chairs, "and there's a shower if you want to use that first," this time indicating an open cubicle next to a rack of towels. "You can also wrap one of those towels around yourself if you're more comfortable with that."

"We won't need towels," my boss announced for both of us, "but my husband could do with a shower, he breaks into a sweat as soon as he walks outdoors here." She nudged me in the ribs and then led the way towards the changing area.

267

I carefully avoided looking at the CI as I stripped, worried that the sight of her naked body, or the memories that it invoked, would lead to a very embarrassing arousal. Showering in open view of the three women was also rather disconcerting, but the rush of cold water certainly helped to kill a developing erection.

By the time that I had dried off, Koide was already lying face down on a table, with Kat slowly rubbing oil into her shoulders while the two women discussed the relative advantages of England and the Caribbean. Varry patted my bed and I clambered on, quickly adjusting my wedding tackle so that I could lie comfortably on my stomach.

I closed my eyes as warm oil was rubbed onto my back, shoulders and buttocks and immediately felt myself start to relax for the first time in weeks, soothed by soft background piano music.

The massage was quite hard, causing grunts of pain as my knotted muscles were eased out. Varry initially checked that the pressure level was OK, but Koide answered before I could, assuring the masseuse that a bit of pain would do me the world of good, a recommendation which she seemed to take to heart.

After about twenty-five minutes I was turned onto my back, by which point I was on the edge of dozing off. Some painful manipulation of the front of my thighs brought me wide awake, but I was heading again for the land of Nod when Varry moved upwards to my arms, chest, belly and, finally, head and face.

When the masseuse bent over me and whispered something in my ear, I caught only *happy ending* and assumed that she was asking me something about the boat that we were living on. I was vaguely aware of my colleague answering on my behalf and drifted off again into a light doze.

When I first felt an oily hand caressing my penis and testicles, it seemed like some kind of daydream. Then my left hand was moved up a silky thigh and placed against wiry pubic hair. My entire body tensed with shock, causing the manipulation to pause. I slowly opened my eyes and looked down to see the black hand with a pink palm that was now recommencing its slow, sensuous motions.

I shot a glance over towards my boss and again tensed when I saw that she was receiving the same treatment from the older woman, who we knew to be David's sister. At this moment Koide turned towards me, looked into my eyes and gave me a conspiratorial wink just before her head rolled backwards, her back arched and she gave a low, feline moan. My masseuse's grip now tightened, her movements quickened and, before long, my own back was arching as I was masturbated to orgasm.

I could feel myself being cleaned off with a damp cloth, but felt too embarrassed to open my eyes. This condition was resolved by a playful slap of my flaccid willy. "Come on, hubby, you can't fall asleep now. He's always this way after sex," she added, causing the two therapists to chuckle.

I rolled to my feet and beetled off towards the shower, avoiding looking at anyone but feeling their eyes upon me. After a very quick splash, again with cold water, I grabbed he towel that I had previously used and confirmed out of the corner of my eye that Koide was sitting naked on her table, chatting animated to the other women. Her glance flickered to me a couple of times while I dressed, still damp from my rushed and largely ineffective toweling.

After I was ready, she bounced down from the table and stretched in an unselfconscious manner that I could not help but admire. She then showered, facing our masseuses and continuing to chat. After rubbing her front with a fresh towel, she chucked it to me and had me dry her back without a halt in the conversation.

Only when my boss had dressed did it slowly dawn on me that the conversation was all about different massage options and the preferences of the crews of the different luxury yachts who were the main clientele of this establishment. When Kat opened a cupboard to show off a collection of vibrators of different dimensions and Koide wandered over for a closer look, I decided the time was right for me to beat a hasty retreat, which seemed to go completely unnoticed.

***

I was waiting in the shade of a facing wooden shack that seemed also to have something to do with ship carpentry when the tall blonde finally emerged about ten minutes later. "You set that up, didn't you?" I started accusingly as soon as she was in earshot, causing a group of tourists emerging from a gift shop to look in our direction.

"Don't get your nickers in a twist," she responded coolly, "it's just all part of my cunning plan. Let's get over to that bar that we passed and then we can see if you can work it out for yourself."

I fumed as we walked back to the bar and selected a shady table as far as possible from the other two groups who were drinking in the bordering restaurant area. After we had ordered - both of us going for bottles of Wadadli - I couldn't restrain myself further. "For Christ's sake, I thought we were going to a massage parlor, not a fucking brothel."

"Well it was a massage parlor," she pointed out pedantically.

"But one offering special services! I've never been wanked off during a massage before!"

"You just haven't been going to the right places - or probably asking for your treatment in the wrong way. There's nothing particularly unusual about the services on offer there, especially in a port like this."

"But you didn't warn me about it!" I started to rant, but shut up quickly as our waitress approached.

My boss took advantage of this to pose a question. "Do you know what a nano-needle is?"

I was still angry, but the strange question diverted me. "It's a nanometer dimensioned filament that can be used in a wide range of applications. I don't know how they work, but they're widely used in medicine for directed drug delivery," I racked my brains, "and also in environmental monitoring."

271

"OK, keep that latter application in mind," she instructed me when the waitress disappeared. "Let me also provide you with a bit of background. It was important that we make contact with David's sister, because she lives in the same house as him. We've started an external hack, but it can't be completed until we open a door to the server from inside the estate. So how does this hang together?" She sat back with a smile and sipped a mouthful of beer.

I rolled this input over in my mind, trying to see how it might be connected with our treatment in the massage parlor. "The ideal thing would be to have Kat carry a trigger into the villa, slipped into her handbag or stuck to her clothing, but there's no obvious way to do that. It might also be picked up be any scanners they have at the entrance to the estate."

I quickly gulped down some ice-cold beer and went on, effectively musing out loud. "A nano-needle, however, would be almost undetectable, especially if it was passive or could be activated only when within the house."

"For example, by a signal sent over the site electrics," she confirmed, encouraging me to go further.

I went over the events of the previous hour in my head. "You shook Kat's hand, didn't you... ," I scratched my head as I searched for inspiration, "I guess you could have injected a subcutaneous nano-needle then. It would, of course be completely painless."

"Yes indeed, they're just loosely bonded to this membrane," she scraped the tip of her right index finger with her opposite thumbnail, removing an almost transparent film. "The back of her hand was a default option, but it has an associated risk of rapid loss if she washed her hands hard." She looked at me expectantly as she had another sip of beer.

"But you also knew about the special massage options," I realized as the jigsaw pieces began to fall together.

"Indeed: it's all information available on her website if you know the code-words to look for and spot images that make it clear that Varry and Kat's smocks reveal that they're not wearing underwear while working."

I had looked at that site, but had not noticed anything of the sort. Then I spotted that I had been given another hint. "You made sure that you were the one being massaged by Kat and, while you were being frigged, you had access to her naughty bits."

"More precisely her clitoris, clitoral hood and between her lips... between her labia," she clarified noting my momentary look of confusion. "Much less likely to be displaced."

"Jesus, how the hell did you come up with a plan like that?" I asked, amazed yet again at my boss's cunning.

"Just assessed the options that were available and came up with an optimal solution," she replied with a smug grin. "Just think what we'd have had to do if Kat had actually been running a brothel!

Anyway, let's get back to home, home on the waves."

I was starting to get diverted by consideration of brothel variants, when the final problem that I had identified came back to mind. "A good plan, but what if David is monitoring his sister's establishment? We were fully exposed there... " I dried up, uncomfortable about what exactly my old uni pal may be looking at in the near future.

Koide reached over and snaffled the last mouthful of my beer before replying. "I'm sure that he has got some kind of monitoring in place that will spot us, either there or somewhere in the vicinity. I mean, we're almost on his doorstep."

"But that gives us away, makes it even harder to hack into his system."

"Mmm... , you're not quite getting the point. It does, actually, make it almost certain that he'll hack everything he can get from our case files asap. He'll want to know what we're doing here and how it relates to our murder investigations."

"And that'll help us how?"

"It'll ensure that he picks up a Trojan that I've inserted into the case model and supporting files. This won't do much on its own, but opens a link to the nano-needles... "

"Which can open an internal backdoor to your power-line leech! Fuck, but you're clever!"

"I am indeed: did you ever doubt it?" she preened visibly.

I was still uncomfortable despite this bolt from the blue. "This gives us access, but puts him onto us. He hasn't held back in the past and I'm sure that he would be prepared to knock us off if he thought that we were any risk to him, especially as we've already served our purpose by taking down Nomura."

"Yes, that's the last part of my cunning plan. Any active attack on us provides further evidence of his involvement and allows us to respond appropriately."

"Jesus suffering Christ all bastarding mighty!" I groaned, as I struggled to my feet and followed the confident blonde out of Dockyard. Just as I was beginning to finally relax, I was back in the fucking firing line.

***

As we strolled back towards the Falmouth Harbour marina, Koide filled me in on her discussion with Kat and Varry. It seemed that the CI had sold us as swingers who were looking into the island *alt sex* scene, which fit well with her advance booking of a happy ending to our massages. It also fit with us staying on drug-dealer Halliday's yacht; his arrest had been kept under wraps by Interpol, in collaboration with the US DEA, and the woman assumed we were part of the wild, decadent crowd he usually associated with when in Antigua.

I groaned theatrically when my boss informed me that she had booked a further massage for Monday, for which Kat had promised us something special as an extra treat.

Apart from the vicinity of a couple of the all-inclusive resorts like Sandals, contact clubs were rare on the island and, in the Falmouth - English Harbour region, action seemed to focus predominantly on some of the larger visiting yachts and a few of the large, foreign-owned villas.

"This all gave me a chance to ask if Kat had a partner who was into this scene. She confirmed that she was single although, strangely enough, said that she lived with a sister. I couldn't push too much, but she certainly didn't mention a brother."

"Yes, that's a bit weird. I've gone over all we can find on David and this indicates that he and his sister have no other siblings. Admittedly, given how well he has removed electronic traces of his past, the existence of a sister isn't impossible."

I noticed Koide frown as she mulled over this situation. "The other interesting thing is that the sister seems to be called Dee... "

I felt as if a light-bulb flashed over my head as odd observations began to connect up. "... and this Dee could be our David, also known as Beverly! I always felt that he was a bit effeminate and took this as an indication of a possible closet shirt-lifter, but a budding transvestite would fit the bill just as well."

"It does make some kind of sense," she agreed, "and might give hints of what the link between David, Nomura and Chrissy could be."

We pondered this in silence the rest of the way to our mooring. As I looked around I noted how quiet the area was, typical off-season with most of the berths free and little sign of life on the boats that were present. "You know, boss, we're a bit vulnerable out here if the last part of your cunning plan comes off."

"Don't be such a wuss! It'll probably be a day or two before David has identified us: depends how often monitor footage from his sister's place is scanned. Then he would need to order a hit on us, which won't be as easy here as it was in Tokyo, with all kinds of yakuza links already in place."

"So we have a couple of days to organize some protection from the local police," I suggested, hopefully.

"Last thing we're going to do," she dashed my hopes with a smile. "David had moles in our precinct house, so he'll certainly have them throughout the island force. Our police contacts here so far are limited to Kempf and Scott, who both seem completely sound. We don't want to tip our hand here, so we'll just set up something to handle things on our own. If you're so scared, you can start on it tomorrow, after we get all of the hack tools up and running."

"Does that mean I get access to all your secret hardware?"

"Tell me what you want and I'll check to see what I can get a hold of."

"It'd be a hell of a lot easier if you told me what was available," I pointed out, rather petulantly.

"It would indeed," she grinned, "and that's exactly why I'm not telling you!"

I glared at her back as she boarded the boat, but realized that further remonstration would be pointless.

Chapter 15

While Koide was carrying out searches to check if David could actually have another sister, I spent a couple of hours tracing the progress of Koide's electronic leech, checking interconnections between all of the appliances accessed to date and other equipment in the estate. In most cases, these were the couplings that would be expected: cooker, refrigerator, deep freeze, pantry, wine cellar and a central kitchen management expert system that autonomically organized external purchases of food and drink. Unfortunately for us, the various expert systems that supported the household were located on a stand-alone server that was completely independent of David's own computing system.

I was just about to give up when, right at the bottom of the alphabetically ordered list, I hit a link to *Zenit Entertainment System*. This managed the multi-room, surround sound, music, video and holo available in the villa. Although most connections were standard and managed by the isolated expert system, a link labeled *XXX* hit an impenetrable firewall.

"I think you should see this, boss," I shouted from my location in the dining room to the CI's preferred work area in the upper lounge. I had already frozen all other activity and concentrated the hack entirely on this link when the CI appeared at my shoulder.

"That's the one we're looking for," she confirmed after I had summarized my work and we had hacked the entertainment system specs from the management server. "Perfect!" she pointed out the connection overview. "Shielded cables entirely in house, but wireless for the external speakers around the terrace and pool. That's our access point."

I watched as the CI called up an app that I hadn't seen before and reconfigured the leech's operational modus. "That'll do it now, we just need Kat to wander within range of the wifi and then we're cooking with gas!"

"So what do we do now," I wondered aloud.

"Now, Watson my lad, we get into our drinking clothes and head out for a celebrational libation prior to a hearty steak dinner."

"Sounds good to me." I stood, stretched and headed off to change into more appropriate clothing.

***

We walked back in the direction of Dockyard, but, before reaching it, Koide decided spontaneously on an Italian restaurant called *Abracadabra*. As we shared a bottle of Gavi de Gavi, we looked through the menu and agreed that the choice had been serendipitous, with suckling pig a specialty that seemed to be renowned amongst the local foodies. "That's the very job for us," she decided unilaterally, thoughts of steak abandoned.

After we had quaffed half of the bottle of excellent wine, she ordered, including an antipasto plate as a starter. I managed to talk her into a single portion size, which I was very glad of when the large platter of nibbles arrived. While we grazed on this, Koide discussed wine with the waiter, finally deciding on a Sicilian Nero d'Avola to accompany our main course.

The suckling pig was truly excellent - tender, juicy and tasty - and went very well with our rich red wine. The perfection of the meal was, however, rather spoiled by the noise from both inside and outside the restaurant. The former was caused by a group of six rowdy Americans who, based on the logos of their matching baseball caps, were crew on a large yacht that had newly docked, not far from our own boat. My boss was unamused and commented on the boorishness of noisy Yanks and the basic ignorance of anyone who wore hats indoors in a voice loud enough to carry to their table. This caused a couple of turned heads, but I was pleased that nobody seemed prepared to face up to Koide's fierce glare and the din did actually decrease, although not by much.

The external racket came from a couple of cars with mounted loudspeakers that blared some form of political propaganda related to an upcoming election. Apart from being so loud that I would think that it would deter rather than encourage voters, the Caribbean accent was so thick that it was difficult to be sure that the barrage of verbosity was actually in some form of English.

After polishing off our piglet, we declined the desert menu and paid, deciding to head back to the quiet of our ship. As we passed the table of mouthy matelots, one made the mistake of looking belligerently at the tall detective. "You should cut us some slack, lady, we've been at sea for a fortnight," he drawled in a southern accent.

"You should stop acting like a bunch of cunts or fuck off back to sea with the rest of your fucking bum-chums," she exploded.

For the first time since they arrived, the Americans were silent as Koide stormed out of the restaurant.

***

Back on board, we first checked on progress with the hack. To my surprise, the access firewall protecting the link between David's private server and the entertainment system had been successfully undermined and his records were now freely available to us. The problem here was simply the size of his database, which was measured in huge numbers of Exabytes. Our leech was inherently limited by transmission rates over the wireless - power-cable link, which was in the glacial tens of Megabytes per second range. A complete system copy would thus require thousands of years.

Contained files were neatly structured into nested folders, which indicated a meticulous approach to database management. However, as the number of folders exceeded a hundred thousand, this did not help us a lot.

"What do you think, Watson, where do we start?" I was sure that my boss had a good idea, but was again using this challenge to test me.

"How about searching for Nomura as a keyword?" I suggested.

Koide set this up and, despite the size of the database, the summary appeared within seconds: just over eighty million hits. She opened the first listed file, dated only yesterday, which turned out to be an accounts sheet for Nomura Holdings covering the past year. It had multiple links to the next file on the list, a draft of the internal annual report for the entire Nomura empire. These rather small files were copied over as we found them, which would allow more detailed study later.

"Why the fuck David has this stuff is beyond me," I muttered.

"More to the point, how the fuck did he get hold of it? This has got to be ultra-top secret commercial stuff. Anyway, this is strengthening the circumstantial links to our case, but doesn't directly tie him to any serious crime."

"Well, the link to the entertainment system was labelled *XXX*, so what if we find this subdirectory," it appeared as I talked, "and search it for Nomura... "

The results appeared instantly: *no hits*.

"Jesus, that's weird," Koide opened the *XXX* subdirectory to list the folders therein in order of last time opened. The top folder was labeled internet porn and opened to show it contained a dozen folders with titles indicating their content: lesbian, swinger group, S and M,... "What do you think?" she asked as she returned to the subdirectory contents and slowly scrolled down the hundred or so folders it contained.

Suddenly one of these caught my eye. It was one of the largest in terms of size and simply labeled *Carol*.

As I selected this, my boss looked at me quizzically. "Just one of the pieces of trivia that I remember from Nomura's file," I responded to the unspoken question. "The times that she got into trouble in the States were associated with an unacceptably revealing Cosplay costume, representing the character Carol... from the manga *Chirality* as I recall."

The folders therein were ordered by age and the oldest was *Carol in California,* which contained several dozen files: *C1, C2, C3...*

I opened the first, which was an old, low-res, two dimensional video. Koide dimmed the cabin lights to improve contrast and we leaned together to watch the action. A slim young Japanese woman was lying on a bed with an occidental transvestite, stroking his growing erection. As she started to lick the tip of his penis, I zoomed in. "Shit, it's Nomura-san. Much younger, but no doubt about it."

"Yes, definitely, but who's her partner?" The video was focused on the girl and so the face of the transvestite was blurry: but appeared to be an attractive woman with paged blond hair and delicate features. Koide fast-forwarded to a point when Nomura was straddling her partner's face, groaning as he tongued her engorged clitoris. Now his face was sharply focused.

"Jesus fucking Christ, it's David!" I gasped. "Well he certainly didn't have tits like that when I knew him - and didn't wear makeup either - but I'm sure it's him."

We watched the short video until its end, after David had climbed on top of Fumiko and shagged her to a noisy mutual climax. It froze on the final image, showing the little Japanese licking the juices off a slowly deflating dick.

I was about to close the file when my arm was grabbed at the elbow. "Wait a minute, zoom in on this!"

The picture quality was poor, but sufficient to show that this fellatio was accompanied by Nomura stroking the lips of an open vagina. David - or Dee - was evidently a hermaphrodite.

***

I fetched us occasional beers while we worked for three straight hours on the video files. In chronological order they documented David's relationship with Nomura, from an intensive affair in California, through occasional weekends or even weeks of passion during his times in Switzerland and the UK, to a fixed partnership in Tokyo. Although the earlier videos showed the pair alone, later ones increasingly included additional sex partners, who were predominantly young Asian women. Men appeared only in the last two videos of the *Carol* series, both shot in an S and M dungeon.

After the shock of finding the truth about David, the barrage of porn had begun to have its natural effect and I had become increasingly aroused. The site of the dungeon was, however, like a dash of cold water as it reminded me of the atrocities committed by Nomura and her evil partner. I thus wasn't paying the attention that I should have and it required Koide to point out that the masked dominatrix who appeared in both of these was Michiko Saito.

There was a gap of almost two years before the date of the last folder, labeled *Chrissy*, which seemed to record all sessions at Pleasure Doubled involving the evil lesbians plus Chrissy, either alone or together with other hermaphrodites or transvestites.

"Well, Watson, what do you make of this little lot?" Koide meshed her fingers and stretched, causing her knuckles to crack loudly.

"I'd guess that David met Nomura at a Cosplay event while they overlapped at Stanford. They had a close relationship during this time, which continued on and off thereafter while they were living in different continents. They seemed to be a couple again in Japan, then maybe split up before he headed here to Antigua. He seems to have maintained links via his internet Beverly persona, but I'm not sure that Fumiko was aware who he really was."

"Yes, it seems to hang together, doesn't it. The split up in Tokyo matches the establishment of the relationship between Nomura and Saito... "

"... linked to Fumiko's increasing involvement in extreme S and M," I added.

"So David is shy and, unsurprisingly, unsure about his sexuality. In Fumiko he finds someone who loves him as he is or, in any case, certainly fucks him enthusiastically. I would hazard that a hermaphrodite might also tick a lot of boxes for a lesbian who likes penetrative sex."

"So this encounter could also start Nomura on her herm-cloning project, which seems to fit with her nature. David might be smitten, but Fumiko is a control freak: she would want to have her hermaphrodite on tap. Indeed, with a fully functional herm, she has a dream sex toy and also the womb to carry the cloned fetus aimed to establish her idea of the dynasty that will be her legacy."

Koide looked grim. "So David is spurned and plots the downfall of his former lover. He's fully aware of her murder spree, but spends years building this complex plan that destroys her and her partner, while concealing his involvement. He must also have established contact to Chrissy at an early stage, at the latest when she first came to Tokyo, but I suspect before that. He was playing both sides: encouraging Chrissy to stand up to Nomura and setting up her murder at the same time. He really is a total cunt."

"So this is all just about revenge?" I wondered aloud.

"I think there may be more to it than that," Koide mused. "David is a whiz-kid accountant and has a pile of stuff on Nomura Industries, some of it very difficult for even a hacker of his standard to get a hold of... "

"... unless he was actually working for the company," I finished the sentence, suddenly seeing where this line of thought was going. "This might fit in with his move to Japan... "

"... joining his lover and working for her company," the blonde grinned and opened the case file in parallel to the ongoing hack. "Let's just start syphoning off the material on David's server that we picked up using the Nomura keyword and also, in parallel, see what we can hack from Nomura Industries directly. We can set up an expert system to look for links between the two."

"And what'll we do in the interim," I asked, glancing at my watch and surprised to note that it was already past midnight.

"This'll all run happily on its own, so I intend to take you to bed and shag your brains out." To emphasize the point, she started to unbutton her blouse as she headed off towards her cabin.

"Whatever you say, boss," I happily agreed, unbuckling my belt as I followed in her wake.

Chapter 16

Koide had been as good as her word. Although it was hardly needed in my case, the blonde decided to spice things up by playing a recording of her PD encounter together with Toyota-sensei while we lay together side by side, exploring each other with our fingers.

This commenced after Jasmine had been interviewed and, at this time, she was clothed in a black negligee, looking for all the world like a beautiful young woman. She sat on the edge off a bed, facing the tall blonde cop and the dark-haired professor, who were sitting together on some kind of padded table. The soundtrack was switched off, so I couldn't determine what initiated the action, causing the petite hooker to pad over and pull Toyota to her feet, running her tongue over her lips before kissing her deeply. Koide then joined them, towering over the others as the trio exchanged kisses and started to undress.

I couldn't help gasping as Jasmine's huge erection was revealed, completely incongruous compared to the rest of her body. My boss's grip on my own erection tightened at that point and I struggled to prevent premature ejaculation. I managed to hold out until the action moved to the bed and Toyota mounted Jasmine. Koide zoomed in to show herself shifting her oral administration from the professor's clitoris to Jasmine's labia and anus. I came with a jet that reached the middle of my chest and could tell from her groaning noises that my partner would not be far behind.

We lay together afterwards, sweat drying on our bodies while we watched the different permutations of the trio, Koide now whispering a commentary in my ear, describing what it felt like to be part of this uninhibited threesome. Although I would not have thought it physically possible, I was soon erect again and happy to follow my partner's encouragement to move into a soixante-neuf position. As I sprawled under the weight of her heavy body, she licked my sticky belly before taking my dick in her mouth, while I used my tongue to toy with her genital jewelry.

I was just about to come, when a beeping noise caused my boss to roll free with a grunt. "Fuck!" she muttered as the video disappeared, replaced by a view from external monitor cameras.

"Fuck!" I echoed as I struggled to the edge of the bed, realizing that this was a warning that Koide had programmed into the boat's security system. I grabbed up my underpants and struggled to get them on, hampered by my still-throbbing erection. The CI had ignored her scattered clothes and was rummaging in her luggage, providing a somewhat distracting view of her bare backside.

I peered at the monitor feed, which showed five black men crowded around the gate to the gangplank while a sixth was working at a nearby box, which I knew controlled the external services to which the boat was hooked up when docked.

Then the image vanished and with it room lights, plunging us into darkness.

"They've taken out external power," I reported as phosphorescent green emergency lights flickered on and then flared and died.

"Now probably overloaded the ship's electrics and fried everything," Koide mumbled, still sorting through her suitcase. My eyes slowly adjusted to the light from the surrounding marina and an almost full moon which seeped in the cabin windows, to the point that I could clearly discern my boss's big bum, just before she straightened up and moved to my side. "Did you notice, had they image intensifiers?"

I strained to recall. "The five guys at the gate all seemed to be wearing glasses, so could be."

"Five, that's all there were?"

"There was another guy who knocked our power out, but I didn't get a good look at him," I replied.

"They'd maybe keep someone as a lookout anyway, but let's assume six to be on the safe side. Keep count as we take them down." At that point the room was lit by a narrow beam of light, which showed that the tall blonde had strapped on a minute head-torch. She mutely passed me its twin, which I fumbled to adjust with the torch centered on my brow.

"Just how are we going to take down a mob like that?" I enquired, noting a quiver of fear in my voice and realizing that my erection had gone completely. "I don't suppose I have to remind you that you're buck naked."

"Not a problem for me, so you just need to keep your eyes off my delectable arse and we'll be fine." I couldn't see her face, but could detect amusement in her voice, How could she possibly be so relaxed, I wondered.

I heard a distant crashing noise. "I guess knocking out the power left all external doors locked, so that'll be the heavy team on board now. What do we do now?"

"I don't suppose we have external communication?"

I located my comm unit from under a pile of discarded clothing and saw that, for the first time that I could ever recall, a symbol was displayed to indicate a complete absence of all wireless links. "Nothing at all," I confirmed.

"Down side of being on a high security drug-runner," she sighed, "Faraday cage to block all external scanning, with links to the external world only via the ship's own radio and satellite dish." To my amazement she sounded as if this was merely a minor inconvenience, rather that the catastrophe that it seemed to me.

"OK, Watson, listen at the door and wave to me when you hear them coming along the corridor. They're bound to have seen the cabin lights, so they'll know where we are. Give me an open hand signal when they approach our door, then make sure that you look away, into the cabin."

I moved to comply and felt her breasts against my back as she adjusted me into a position to the right of the door. "Don't want you in the way when I open it," she explained in a whisper. "Now put these on," I looked to see that she was handing me a pair of black gloves, matching those that she already had on. "Electrodes in front and tips of fingers, switch on back," she pointed these out on her own gloves. "They're good for about half a dozen shocks, but need about thirty seconds between uses to fully recharge."

"Are you sure that these'll work?" I whispered back.

"Make any contact with bare skin and the bastard will go down," she assured me, "so just don't fiddle about with yourself when they're switched on!"

We stood in silence for about two minutes before I heard footsteps coming along the corridor and the sounds of the doors to neighboring bedrooms being opened. There was a bit of a delay, which I assumed would be inspection of the room that I had been using, then progress resumed until they were right outside our door.

As my hand cut down, I saw Koide wrench the door open, throw something out and then slam the door shut. There was a loud pop, then the room was lit by an actinic flash. It was clear to me that, given that this was light had penetrated the gaps around the closed door, the flare must have been like a supernova, even without the amplifying effect of night vision goggles. The screams of anguish confirmed this.

Koide now pulled the door open, allowing a tall, Caribbean man who appeared to be wearing a black tracksuit to fall forward into the room. He had pulled his glasses loose and sobbed as he rubbed his eyes, hampered by the huge machete in his hand. The naked blonde hit him in the throat with a straight-fingered blow from her right hand that causcd him to fly backwards into the man who was crowding behind him.

The CI stepped confidently into the corridor, clearing the collapsing body of her first victim by an elbow to his ribs. The next attacker in line was now backing away, waving his huge knife blindly in our direction as a form of defense and with his goggles still clutched in his other hand. I watched in silent admiration as she caught his wrist with her right hand then slipped forward to jab two fingers into his eyes. I had no idea about the others, but the burning smell made it clear that this was certainly one man who would never see again.

Koide now stood to one side to allow me to pass her while her gloves recharged. By the time I had clambered over the two bodies, only one man remained in the corridor, crawling on his hands and knees and mewing like a kitten. I guessed he may have been looking directly at the flare when it went off, so it may have been a kindness when I kicked him over onto his side and rendered him unconscious with an open-handed blow to his face.

I slid towards the end of the corridor, hearing crashing noises from someone who had blundered into the bar. I cautiously glanced into the dining area, then jerked my head back as a blade cut down savagely, swishing past within a centimeter of my nose. "Fuck!" I gasped as I threw myself forward in a roll that brought me to my feet in the middle of the large cabin with my foe caught in the beam of

293

my head-torch. The man was huge, well over two meters tall and built like a body-builder, the black tracksuit tight over his massive frame. His dark face was framed by dreadlocks and his incongruously delicate features were contorted by a glare of pure malice. He held a huge machete in his right hand and, while I watched, quickly stooped to grab a second weapon that must have been dropped by one of his companions.

The continuous sound of breaking glass from behind reminded me that he was not the only threat in this room. Keeping my attention on Goliath, I carefully stepped backwards until I passed the other man, who was now caught up in some bar stools, dropping him with a hard slap to the side of his face with my fully-charged glove. Although I could now focus on a single opponent, I now saw that I could retreat no further as the area behind me was covered in shattered glass and I was barefoot. The large Rastafarian was also clearly aware of this situation as he moved confidently towards me, both machetes raised and a wide grin on his face.

I leaned over to the bar counter and grabbed an empty beer bottle and hurtled it at his face. His grin only widened as he swatted it with a knife, sending shards of brown glass back in my direction.

I directed the beam of my torch directly into his face, causing him to squint his eyes while I frantically tried to figure a way of getting close enough to use the gloves, assuming that I could last out long enough for them to recharge.

"Boss, I could do with... " I started to shout when, to my amazement, the giant's head fell from his shoulders and I was drenched in a gout of blood as his corpse toppled forward towards me.

The beam from my torch was now ruddy from its film of gore, but clearly showed the naked blonde and the dripping machete that she held in a two-handed grip. "What was it you were wanting, Watson?" she enquired coolly as she stared down at her victim. "Anyway, that's five - any sign of number six?"

I carefully worked my way to the external door, which was now smashed and hanging loosely on one hinge, trying to avoid the broken glass that was scattered about and cursing every time I stood on something sharp. I peered carefully out and heard the *phut* of a silenced pistol at the same time as a crash from the room behind me indicated that the shot had gone wide.

I ducked back in. "Shooter out here somewhere around the stern," I called to my boss. "Either he's a totally crap shot or maybe partially blinded by the flash. Despite that, I don't think rushing him would be a good, idea, so we're pinned down at present."

"Leave your torch there by the door and come back here," she commanded in a low voice.

I complied, using the light from Koide's torch to avoid the worst of the glass although I stepped on a couple of sharp shards and could feel my feet now sticky with blood.

As I reached her side she whispered, "You OK?"

"Apart from my fucking feet," I muttered. "How about you?"

"Completely unscathed," she confirmed. "Only blood on me comes from the bad guys. Anyway, we need to get rid of number six ASAP. It isn't outwith the bounds of possibility that he's called for backup and we won't get off as easily a second time."

Despite the fact that I would hardly call this fracas getting off easily, I remained silent as my boss continued. "I noticed something at the back of the boat, one deck down."

"The stern;" I corrected pedantically, "it's a diving platform. I seem to remember from the ship plans that it can be accessed from stairs down from the sun deck or from the lower deck via an equipment room. That door there," I indicated with my head a door to the left of the corridor leading to the bedrooms, "opens to stairs to the lower deck; fore to the engine room and aft to the diving equipment."

"That's exactly as I remembered it," she stated confidently, making me wonder why she had asked the question in the first place: unless it was another one of her annoying quizzes. "You stay here and move this about a bit," she handed me her head-torch. "Listen out for me; I shouldn't be long." With this she opened the door to the stairs and vanished into the darkness.

I moved to the dining table and sat on a chair, using the torch to examine my torn feet. There were about a dozen cuts of various sizes on each, but none of them seemed particularly serious. Several did contain shards of glass, which I attempted to scrape out with my fingernails. This operation was continually interrupted as I paused to listen for outside sound and flashed the beam of light around to assure myself that nobody was near the door or that there was no sign of our electrified attackers regaining consciousness.

I guessed it was about ten minutes after Koide's departure when I heard an odd *twang* followed by a scream of pain. "Fuck, man, fuck! I's going to fuck'n kill you!" The shout caused me to rush to the door leading to the stern, completely ignoring the glass this time.

I glanced around the door jamb and saw a squat man crouching by the Jacuzzi and aiming a gun held in his left hand towards the stairs that led down to the diving platform. "Fuck, fuck, fuck!" he continued to swear and I spotted that his right hand was clutching a metal shaft that had penetrated his left side and guessed the sound had been that of a spear-gun. At that moment he appeared to sense my presence, warned either by the sound of my approach or the light leaking from the torch at my side and started to turn towards me.

Without thought, I threw myself at him, barreling into his chest just as he completed his turn. My right hand caught his left wrist, forcing the gun to the side just as he fired and my left grabbed his right, which had clamped onto my throat. He continued to scream a litany of *fucks* as we struggled and I could feel my eyes begin to bulge from his strangle hold. Although wounded, my opponent was clearly much stronger than me.

Just as I felt that I was about to black out, I managed to get a knee up high enough to press against the haft of the protruding spear. His body tensed with pain and his grip slackened, allowing me to use my knee again with more force. A third knee to the gut and he staggered backwards, giving me the leverage for a push that sent us together into the Jacuzzi.

The thug had gone in backwards with me on top of him, losing both the gun and his grip on my throat. I was now trying to force his head underwater while he writhed about and slammed punches into my ribs. I grunted in pain as I felt a rib crack and redoubled my efforts to hold him under.

Suddenly there was an almighty splash and wet skin pressed against mine. Koide had arrived and jumped in, both feet on top of the gunman's head. I don't know if his neck was broken or if he was simply knocked out, but his struggles ceased immediately. Nevertheless, the statuesque blonde knelt on his chest for five minutes, ensuring that he had certainly drowned.

Quite a way to go, I thought irreverently after I clambered out of the pool and looked down at his dead face, which was staring up directly into the detective's gaping vagina.

***

Despite the noise of combat, our remote berth meant that we seemed to have disturbed nobody: maybe deliberately selected on this basis for drug-dealer Halliday's dubious dealings. I retrieved the robust little torch, which had been dropped during my rush at the gunman and was still our main source of light. As we worked our way back to

Koide's cabin, via the lower deck to avoid the glass-strewn dining room, I felt strangely exposed, conscious that my underpants were the only piece of clothing between the two of us.

Before ascending the stairs to the upper deck, the CI quickly popped into the engine room to pick up a couple of large torches from a conspicuous, red-painted emergency supplies cabinet. In her cabin she reconfigured the torches to act as lamps and set them on the cabinets at each side of the bed. I started to assemble my scattered clothing, but she pushed me towards the bed. "Get your arse down on that!" she commanded.

"Hardly the time or place," I protested, concerned that her rigid nipples were an indicator of her intentions.

"Don't be a tit, Watson, I'm just going to have a look at your fucking feet" I could hear humor in her voice as she spotted my mistake.

"Don't you think you should put some clothes on first," I suggested.

"There's nothing on view that you haven't seen before, if not licked or stuck your dick in," she pointed out with a smile, "so do as you're told and sit on the fucking bed."

While I complied, the CI padded off into the en-suite bathroom and returned with a damp towel that she used to gently wash the soles of my feet. "Doesn't look too bad," she commented, "but still a few bits of glass still in there. Need a bit more light!" She donned the head-torch and set it to a narrow, intense beam before pulling a compact first aid kit from her Tardis-like luggage.

"You're such a poofter that you'll probably need this," she commented, spraying my feet in turn with an analgesic that immediately blocked all pain from the multiple cuts and made the subsequent probing for buried glass with a scalpel and tweezers a somewhat surreal experience.

"It'd probably be worth getting this looked at by a doctor at a later stage," she concluded, "but it should be OK for now." She finished by rinsing my feet again with the towel and then spraying a coating of synthetic skin over them.

"So, what're we going to do now?" I enquired and stood gingerly, before I walked around the room to check that my feet seemed, amazingly enough, to be in perfect order. I was, however, heavily bruised over the ribs on my left side and touched them gingerly, wincing from the pain. "You should keep in mind that I've probably got a busted rib or two."

"Jesus, what a fucking drama queen!" she muttered, prodding the area around the bruise, completely unimpressed by my squeaks of pain. "Bruised or cracked at worst," she concluded, "so I'll just strap them up for you." An elastic bandage was produced from her kit and the job was soon done.

"Anyway, to return to your original question, what to do now: what do you think we should do?"

"Well number one would be to contact Captain Kempf and get a load of uniforms here PDQ."

"That'd certainly be an option," my boss sounded skeptical, "but how do you think David would react then?"

"I suppose it would depend on whether he spotted our hack or not," I mused aloud. "If not, I'll bet there'll be no connection between him and the bodies that we have strewn about the boat."

"The approach used for the hack is subtle, but it also means that this gives us only access, without the tools that would allow our activities thereafter to be covered up. If he had any suspicion that we were in, it wouldn't take him long to trace everything that we've done," Koide expanded, confirming my suspicions.

"How do you pick up the signal from your database leech?"

The CI smiled at my question, indicating that I was going in the right direction. "Direct encrypted beam to my comm via the boat's radio mast; we'll have lost everything since the shipboard power was fried."

"But if the leech is still running, it's good evidence that our hack hasn't yet been spotted. All we need is some way of picking up that signal."

Koide rummaged in her luggage and then gestured with a small box that looked like a twin of the leech itself. "It just so happens that I have just the very thing," she grinned smugly.

"And how come you just happen to have exactly the tool we need?" I enquired suspiciously.

"I had no idea what equipment we would have on this island, so I brought a receiver for the leech. It transpired that the ship's communication system was ideal, so I didn't need it - until now that is."

"So all we need to do is get outside this Faraday cage and we can check immediately."

"Yup! Up by the radio mast would be ideal," her grin widened, "but maybe some clothes would be an idea first."

***

Although my boss was unmarked, she made first use of the shower to remove a general coating of gore. I then dumped my blood-soaked pants and rinsed myself down in the last trickle of cold water that emerged from the shower in the absence of power. After dressing, we used the lanterns to find our way to the wheelhouse on the top deck, from which a ladder led to the base of the radio mast. Koide slapped the little box against the base of the mast, while I monitored the response on my comm, to which it had been slaved. It took only moments for synchronization to be completed. "Still churning away nicely," I reported, pumping a fist in triumph.

"OK, that makes things a lot easier. Leave your comm here to maintain the link to the case file in Shinjuku and we'll use mine as needed."

"I hadn't realized that you were copying everything directly to the case file," I said as I followed my boss back down towards her cabin. "Isn't that a bit dodgy for an illegal hack?"

"Not really illegal, more not yet fully authorized. The hacking kit is registered with Interpol and automatically requests authorization when first switched on. This is linked only to GPS coordinates and details must be combined with a warrant within seven days or else all material obtained must be deleted. So we've plenty of time."

"I didn't know we could do that," I commented in surprise.

"Only works if we can show that internal police security is compromised and the process of obtaining a warrant would tip-off the perp."

"Can we do that?" I wondered.

"I really fucking hope so, or else all of this effort will have been for nothing."

I was pondering this as we settled down side by side on the disheveled bed, aware of the dull ache from my ribs and wondering what further cats my devious boss had to pull from her sack.

Chapter 17

The first order of business for me was to immobilize the four unconscious attackers, a couple of whom were now beginning to stir. I used zip-locks to bind their wrists and ankles, trying to ignore the smell in the cases where the shock had caused loss of bowel and bladder control. While I was doing this, Koide downloaded the video records from the two head-torches and marched off towards the stern, searching for an area outside of the boat's electromagnetic barrier.

I had just finished repacking our luggage when my boss returned. "That's things sorted out with Kempf," she reported. "It seems that our attackers are well known members of a drugs gang from St John's: suspected enforcers who have reputations as hard men."

"Any links to David?"

"I didn't ask, as I don't want to tip our hand here. Although Kempf and Scott seem to be straight enough, I'm pretty sure that David will have a mole or two within the Antigua force."

"So what did you tell the Captain? I mean she's smart enough to know that this attack could hardly be coincidental."

"I let her know about Chrissy's bank account and implied that we suspected that someone with knowledge of the murders might live in the vicinity of St John's. This would explain us being in English Harbour, to reduce the risk of being spotted; a ploy that has clearly failed."

"And you think this information will leak?"

"I sincerely hope so, as this may divert David for a bit, decreasing the chance that he'll spot our hack. We've also got new digs sorted out. It's a rental villa not far away, near Pigeon Beach, where we lunched yesterday. It's supposed to have a reasonable security system and we'll have a couple of uniforms providing protection, so it'll be more of a challenge to organize another hit."

"You think he will?" I enquired, not liking the way that my boss's eyes seemed to gleam in anticipation.

"Don't you think so?" she responded.

I brooded on this rhetorical question in silence, wondering when our luck would finally run out.

***

Fifteen minutes later our Antigua Police contacts arrived, ahead of a posse of further police cars and ambulances that appeared over the next half hour, flooding the marina car park in a sea of flashing blue and red lights. Despite the late hour, rubberneckers were beginning to emerge from surrounding bars, requiring a cordon of crime scene tape to be set up to keep them back.

Koide walked the Captain through the attack, linking off-shot action to that already transferred from our head-torch records, while Scott and I trailed silently in the wake of the disparately sized women. The main gap in the records involved the take down of the gunman and here the CI was rather economical with the truth, failing to mention the step that she took to ensure that our attacker was dead. It was evident, however, that the Antiguan woman was completely in awe of the tall blonde and was more concerned by her own failure to warn us about the hit than our lethal response to it.

Immediately after this formality was completed, Kempf led us to her car and we drove off, bracketed between police cruisers in front and behind us. I was amused to note that our route took us directly past the gates of David's fortress and wondered what he would be making of all of this. He must now know that his attack had failed, but the fact that we were remaining in the vicinity should surely confuse him. I know that it was confusing me.

***

Ten minutes later we were ensconced in our new accommodation, a large villa with a faded wooden exterior that contrasted markedly with its chrome, steel and marble interior, which seemed to feature the best of every luxury mod-con. Provisions were limited to those abandoned by the previous tenant, but would be restocked in the morning Kempf promised before she drove off, leaving one of the police cruisers prominently parked to block the driveway. I yawned, beginning to feel physically wiped out as the exertions of the night caught up with me, but somehow still mentally wired by the remnants of the adrenalin rush.

Koide annexed the single bottle of Wadadli that she found in the large fridge, while I poured a small measure from a bottle of fifteen year old *English Harbour* Rum that I found at the back of a drinks cabinet. While we sat in the lounge together, facing the picture window that looked onto the mast lights of small yachts moored in the bay, the CI checked the link to my comm and confirmed that the data upload was still running.

"Well, I was caught a bit flat-footed last time, but that's not going to happen again," she announced, accessing the villa security cameras and initiating upload of a series of apps of her own to increase the sophistication of the system. "I also checked that this place has its own power, so I'll throw the breakers on mains power," the lights flickered as she spoke, "and now there is no chance of that power-surge trick being played against us for a second time."

"So what else do we need to do?" I enquired as I sipped my drink, feeling my body slump with fatigue.

"Nothing more at the moment, just unpack and hit the sack."

"Which bedroom do you want: there seems to be five of them?"

"They're all in a row, facing the bay, so we'll take the middle one."

"We? I'm fucking dead on my feet," I groaned in protest.

The CI laughed and I realized with annoyance that I'd again misunderstood her meaning. "I may decide to give you a good shag in the morning, Watson, but it's painfully obvious that you're fuck all use to me as you are at present. I do, however, want to have you in reach when David mounts his next attack."

I was relieved that my boss didn't expect me to perform now and the idea of a morning shag was definitely attractive, but I really didn't like the sound of that *when*!

***

Despite the fact that it was almost two o'clock before we finally got to bed, I woke up at six to the sound of heavy rain battering down on the patio that ran the length of the house outside our bedroom window. Stentorian snoring betrayed my partner's presence even before I turned to look at her, typically sprawled on her back on top of the single sheet covering the bed. I silently observed the rise and fall of her large breasts for about five minutes, fighting the urge to stroke or lick the prominent nipples. Noting the twinge of a developing erection, however, I decided that discretion was the better part of valor and slipped carefully from the bed.

I donned the y-fronts that lay on the floor at my side of the bed and padded barefoot through to the large kitchen that lay at the back of the house. The windows looked onto the driveway and I could see that the police car was still there. After a search, I eventually found a tin of coffee beans in the double-door refrigerator, a box of filters in the larder and a grinder under the work top. I set a pot of coffee on to brew and then switched off the security locks and wandered through a door from the cool lounge into the Caribbean heat of the patio, the rain shower having already passed, leaving the decking steaming as it dried. I leant on the rail, spotting an oval swimming pool set in a lower terrace that I hadn't noticed when we first arrived.

I scanned about to confirm that the pool was not overlooked, then walked down the steps, dropped my pants and lowered myself carefully into the blue water, aware of a dull throb from my bandaged ribs. The first shock of the temperature difference made the water seem cool but, after a few lengths of breast stroke, the feeling was more refreshing than anything else. After 15 minutes of relaxed swimming I clambered out, only then realizing that I had forgotten to bring a towel with me. I stood in a sunny spot until I had dried a little and then, underwear in hand, ascended to the patio and walked along to the bedroom nearest the lounge and entered it through sliding doors. Confirming that the bathroom was stocked with towels, I treated myself to the luxury of a hot shower, soaping myself down twice to remove any traces of gore accumulated in the battle which, I now noted, had occurred only little more than six hours previously. I dried myself cautiously, again favoring my damaged ribs, and then pulled on my underwear and headed back to the kitchen.

To my surprise, my boss was already there, sitting naked at the breakfast bar as she sipped a large mug of coffee. "You snuck off before I could give you your promised shag," she noted with a smile, "but you can have a rain-check on that. I guess we need to get our plans sorted out before

Kempf gets back. She said about eight, but I wouldn't be surprised if she was early."

"A plan would definitely be a good idea," I agreed as I poured a coffee for myself. "What do you think we should... "

My question was interrupted by a loud buzzing noise from the lounge, causing me to over-fill my mug as the CI raced to investigate. "Fuck!" I cursed as the hot coffee burned my hand, before I hurled the cup in the direction of the sink and ran after her.

The CI stood beside her comm, which sat on a desk at the side of the bright, sunlit room. She swiped the alarm off and looked grim, making me fear that another attack was underway.

"Shite!" she grumbled as the case model expanded, showing us that the alarm had been triggered by the feed from our hack being cut off.

My first reaction was one of relief; I wasn't going to be immediately fighting for my life. Then I remembered that this also meant that our nemesis would now know everything that we had hacked from his computer and must be aware that we were presently an even bigger threat than we were before. We might not see combat this morning, but the threat to our lives had certainly not diminished; if anything, it had probably increased.

**

"Now what do you suggest, Watson?" I had been waiting for this question for the entire time it had taken for the CI to confirm that the hack had been blocked at source and that it hadn't been some kind of equipment failure. She had also double checked the buffer store where hacked material was quarantined while it was scanned by our anti-virus apps. The last three files uploaded had contained both time-bombs and depth-charges, programs that would activate after a specific time or as a result of processing steps and completely destroy all accessible memory or data storage. To be on the safe side, she physically isolated the quarantine buffer while debugging took place on a stand-alone computer.

"It's a bit tricky," I responded thoughtfully, "as it depends whether he thinks we have a case against him and what options he has already in place to bail out of here fast in case of trouble."

"I'm sure the choice of Antigua was carefully made, because this place doesn't have an extradition treaty with Japan." She tapped her lower lip with her right index finger while she pondered this puzzle.

"So you think he may try to tough it out here? Of course, being the arrogant sod that he is, it may never have occurred to him that he could ever be threatened, so might not actually have an escape plan."

"Let's first have a look at what the expert systems have been able to do with David's Nomura material and the stuff that we were able to dig from the company web site." A few waves of her hand and the appropriate section of the case model appeared. "Well, that's interesting... "

I screwed my eyes to examine the linked argumentation blocks, then gave up and found the controls that polarized the windows, making the hologram stand out more clearly in the subdued light. "David was Nomura's chief financial officer for a while: we knew that already."

"But look at the links generated from David's files, he's been involved with Namura continuously since he went to Switzerland, I'd guess in some consultant capacity. The anomalies here are clear, don't you think?"

I peered at the summaries of the material that we had obtained, presented as chronologies of both file production and last time opened. These were color-coded in terms of identified content, with about sixty percent being financial documents of some kind or other. "Almost all the files are financial before he went to Tokyo," I mused, "which could be consistent with him doing small consulting jobs for his beloved Fumiko. Thereafter, they're a bit more diverse; I suppose that's consistent with his CFO job."

"But, in terms of Nomura divisions and daughter companies, a rather noticeable concentration on Philippines and Nomura Life Sciences," Koide pointed out.

"Well, yes. Accessed since he went to Japan, but tracing back all of Nomura-san's cloning work," I commented, now seeing the pattern that my boss had identified. "So, whether his lover told him about it or not, he was presumably well aware of Chrissy's origins."

"We can look at this stuff in detail later, but this is just adding to our circumstantial case for his development of the intricate plot against Fumiko and her new bed-mate. It's gratuitously intricate, but I guess he was intending to kill several birds with one stone: destroy the lover who spurned him together with the woman who replaced him, while manipulating Nomura into eliminating her own pet project, Chrissy, along with her dreams of her own special dynasty."

"It all hangs together," I agreed, "but still isn't the hard evidence that would allow us to build a case against someone who appears to be a successful businessman, without any record of previous criminal activity. He used Nomura's account to commission the attacks against us in Tokyo, but our chances are one in a million of finding any evidence to support that using this undirected data piracy approach."

"Very much less than one in a million," the naked blonde automatically corrected me in her usual pedantic manner. "Nevertheless, I've got a feeling that there's even more to it. The very first file that we opened during the hack has been bothering me... "

"What, you mean the draft annual report?" It took only a few gestures to uncover the link that opened this document.

"That's the one. If he had that while he was CFO, it wouldn't be surprising; but, even if he is a top-level consultant, he shouldn't have access to that kind of extremely sensitive internal material."

"Well, we know how good with computers David is," I pointed out, "so it would be quite plausible for him to have built in a back door during the time he was employed by Nomura."

"Exactly! And if he had that kind of access, what would he do with it?"

I couldn't quite see where my boss was going with this. "I don't know, but it would certainly put him in a good position for a bit of insider trading."

"Right on the button, yet again! This is the final part of his plot, the bit obscured by the other, more obvious, stuff. He wanted to take everything from Nomura, ruin her completely... "

"So this included also possession of her family company," another loose end was suddenly tied into the case argument's logical structure. "With the publicity associated with Fumiko's high profile arrest, the company management will be in chaos. Just the time for someone with inside knowledge to make a killing."

"OK, Watson, let's chase that up a bit further. You dig through everything we have in David's Nomura files and I'll check with the UN and Interpol on the regs for handling major international insider trading scams. Maybe we'll be able to do an Al Capone on his arse."

"An Al Capone? I don't get it,"

"Al Capone: the US gangster from prohibition times. The police couldn't nail him for a load of mob crimes including the Saint Valentine's Day massacre, but he was eventually banged up on tax evasion," my boss explained.

"Do you think insider trading would be enough to do the trick?"

"I think so, as long as it is big enough."

"Well, based on David's past record, he doesn't seem to do anything by halves. In any case, I think I know what I'm looking for now," I confirmed.

"Great, so I'll get started on my bit - but, first things first."

"Put on a pair of nickers?" I guessed.

"Not at all," she grinned, "first another cup of coffee!"

***

I was far out of my depth with the financial information that we had ripped off, but the Interpol commercial crimes expert system that Koide's comm could access did all of the heavy lifting and quickly outlined the essence of the malpractice involved. Although there was clear evidence of only two cases of insider trading, this must be the tip of an iceberg that had allowed David to amass almost twelve percent of the conglomerate's shares, with a total book value that was eye-wateringly huge. With all the bonuses involved, David's various jobs and consultancy work had made him a millionaire several times over, but the manipulation of Nomura stocks placed him well into the billionaire category.

I had just completed integrating a summary of the expert system output into the case model when my boss reappeared, wearing relatively demure navy shorts and an uncharacteristically baggy white smock. "Better get into something more than those budgy-smugglers, Watson, the captain should be here soon."

I was surprised to note that I had been working for just under an hour and that it was now almost eight o'clock.

By the time I had dressed, Kempf has already arrived and was sitting drinking coffee with the CI, both women munching large croissants. I drained the coffee jug to derive a half cup for myself and then joined them. "Have one of these, they're really good," Koide offered me a paper bag containing several more croissants.

"They be's from a likkle bakery at de Dockyard," the captain explained as I took one, "that's why I's a likkle bit late."

"Actually you were bang on time, and even if you had been late, it'd have been worth it for these," my boss finished her pastry and helped herself to another. "Anyway, as we were discussing, the attack last night suggests a link to a local resident living on the hill above English Harbour. We would appreciate if you could help us ensure that nobody leaves the premises for the next twenty-four hours, while we put a warrant together."

The dusky policewoman looked uncomfortable. "I's suspected dat dere was more to you's visit dan de Saint John's stuff, but I guess you was't able to pass it on to us."

"I knew that you were smart enough to work that out for yourself," Koide smiled in a most disarming manner, "but I wanted your records to show only the bank link."

The captain now frowned. "So, you tink dere's a leak in my department?"

"I'm fairly sure of it, just like there were at least two moles in my own." This admission caused the Antiguan to relax a little. "We have a suspect here who we are convinced has links to both our Tokyo mass-murderers and also commercial crimes in the multi-billion EC scale."

This information seemed to remove Kempf's misgivings and she unclipped the small comm unit from her belt. "OK, what I can do first is put a no-fly zone over English Harbour; the estate has a helipad which might offer an obvious escape route. I'll need to put in a better justification later, but for now I can just link that to investigation of the attack on your boat. Ditto for restrictions on sailings from both English and Falmouth Harbours. We can use the coastguard to search any ship that attempts to leave. Who is it that we're actually looking for?" I was amused to note that, as she moved into work mode, her thick Caribbean accent vanished and was replaced by something more reminiscent of Oxford English.

This was the tricky question, but Koide was evidently prepared for it. "Brother and sister, David and Dee McNeill. I'm afraid we have only a couple of old images," head and shoulder shots appeared above Koide's comm, which was sitting between the women on a low coffee table, "but I'll transfer these over to you now with the other descriptive details that we have. There is also another sister who is resident there and works as a masseuse in Nelson's Dockyard. We have no evidence that she is complicit in these crimes, but we would certainly also want to hold her for questioning."

"Okey dokey," she smiled, showing off her perfect, pearly-white teeth. "Anyting else you's wantin'?" The thick accent had slipped back immediately we went back to conversation mode.

"Just anything that you can get on those guys who were sent to take us out. Although they're evidently local hooligans, the tool they used to take out the ship's power must have been quite sophisticated, as all backup and emergency power was also fried."

"Dat's a good point, I'll get de guys to have a look into dat."

"I've got an app that could help there," Koide offered as she waved her hands over her comm, flicking through nested menus, "I'll just transfer it over to you now."

"Tanks fo'dat," the captain said cheerfully as she bounced to her feet. "I betta hit de road."

We shook hands and said our goodbyes, standing at the door until the captain's car vanished and our guard's cruiser was back in place, blocking the drive. "That app that you gave Kempf... " I started.

"Yup, also automatically transfers all case details to me," she grinned in a conspiratorial manner. I wondered if the captain would have been as cheerful if she had known this.

***

Ten minutes later Scott arrived, together with two uniformed constables who ferried a half dozen boxes of provisions from the back of his SUV and stocked up the larder, refrigerator and deepfreeze. I noted that this included a couple of cases of beer, a half dozen bottles each of white and red wine and bottles of rum and gin. It looked like enough to keep us going for about a fortnight. Except, possibly, in terms of booze, I reflected, considering the rate at which my boss put it away.

After confirming that there was nothing else that we needed, Scott departed with our guards of the night before, the two replacements taking up their positions in the police cruiser. The CI then headed off wordlessly to our room, returning shortly thereafter wearing nothing but a sun hat, a large white towel over her shoulder. "May as well catch some rays as we work, so get into your sunbathing togs," she commanded as she headed off in the direction of the patio.

I changed into the smallest pair of briefs that I had, grabbed a towel and joined her poolside, where she was already sprawled on a lounger. "Why don't you get some sun on your parts?" she enquired cheerfully as she patted the deckchair beside her.

"A sunburned willy is just what I don't need," I replied grumpily, trying to keep my eyes averted from her naked body.

"Whatever. Anyway, now to work. We've got all the information that we're likely to get from David's database and blocked all his escape routes. However, we need to make a case tight enough that he can be arrested without risk of being granted bail. Thoughts?"

I spread my towel on the indicated seat and slowly settled myself into it, feeling the heat of the sun batter down on my head. "Need to watch it," I muttered, "more than half an hour of this and I'll be down with sunstroke."

She tossed me a large tube that I had not previously noticed. "Here, slap on some of this stuff. You can also do my back afterwards," She rolled onto her stomach, presenting me with an only slightly less distracting view. "And you can talk to me while you're doing it."

I rubbed cream onto my head and face, struggling to find something sensible to contribute. As I moved onto my neck and shoulders, I could sense my boss getting restless and decided to play for time. "Right, we've got hard evidence of two cases of insider trading and good indications that this has been carried out on a massive scale. Based on this, we should be able to get an international arrest warrant that'd also allow us to search his place. Get a hold of his complete database and Bob's your uncle."

"... and the problems with this little scheme are?"

I stood up and then knelt at the far side of her lounger, squeezing a blob of sun-cream between her shoulder-blades. "Well, David's now forewarned that we're going after him. In his shoes, I'd bury anything that I need to keep and set up an auto-delete on my entire stand-alone system."

"... and how would you make sure that we couldn't recover anything at all with the forensic tools at our disposal?"

I thought hard as I dreamily massaged the cream into her smooth olive-tanned skin. "Well, electronic reformatting together with complete physical destruction of all memory units would be best - sort of belt and braces approach."

"Ouch!" her entire body twitched as my thumbs hit a knotted muscle. "Yes, well we can assume that he'd prepare something like this anyway, probably with some kind of dead-man's switch that would trigger it even if we could take him down quickly."

I worked on the knot, causing further twitches and groans of pain, which I enjoyed in a definitely sadistic manner. "The buried backup is maybe his key vulnerability," I suggested. "If he was convinced that we had bested him, he'd just scrub everything immediately, regardless of its value to him. But he's not like that, I'm sure. He'll be convinced that there is some way that he'll be able to win out in the end."

"I'm sure that you're right, certain of it," she squirmed as I moved lower, rubbing cream into her buttocks and thighs, admiring the view as I spread her cheeks and slid my thumbs deeply into the exposed cleft. "OK, all we need to do now is work out how we find out where he has his cache hidden."

I finished working on her legs in silence, both of us deep in thought. While settling back into my deckchair, lack of sleep beginning to make me feel weary, an idea sprung to mind. "If we think about how convoluted David's planning is, maybe we should consider that, despite his megalomania, he may have actually planned a backup from the start - when he first came to Antigua. Even if he considered that he was too smart and careful to be hacked, we are in the Caribbean and devastating natural disasters can't be precluded: hurricanes, earthquakes, volcanoes, tsunami... "

"... yes and also not so natural disruptions; we lie under a flight path, civil disruption or war is always possible... " my boss added, leaning on her elbows to look at me.

"So an ultra-robust data cache would be a sensible precaution," I concluded. "In fact, he would already have had experience with such systems."

"Where?" Koide was clearly racking her brains to see what she could have missed.

"Switzerland!" I answered quickly, to ensure I got this out before she caught up with my line of thought.

"A private Swiss bank!" she rolled to her feet and strode off in the direction of the house, abandoning her towel. "It'd certainly have an atom-bomb-proof vault with copies of all key files. We need to get a hold of any plans we have of the buildings on that estate, any construction or renovation records and multi-spectral satellite scans."

I trotted in her wake, revitalized by this progress and my mind flooded with possible ways in which we could benefit from David's vulnerability. However, my brain still had space to admire the sway of the tall blonde's buttocks as she climbed the steps in front of me.

***

The next couple of hours were filled with detective grunt-work. We first contacted Kempf to arrange access to all government planning and building records for English Harbour, which were available as digital records since the start of the century. A problem was that the seven original houses that were now integrated within David's estate were significantly older than this and Scott had to be dispatched to a document archive in Jolly Harbour to dig out and scan paper copies of relevant material. While this was ongoing, we started to trace details of rebuilding, modification and renovation of these properties, integrating openly available material with any required hacks into the companies who carried out the work.

In general, Koide's tools cut through any firewalls on the databases of local contractors like a hot knife through butter, but external specialist companies required a bit more effort: especially, as would be expected, those responsible for site security installations. The only complete failure involved a Swiss-based firm responsible for David's computer system. Government records showed a series of import licenses for hard- and software over the last two decades, but nothing else could be found on it because the company kept all records off-line in a stand-alone system. It was notable that major customers of this firm were predominantly banks.

While my boss focused on these aspects, I concentrated on synthesis of all aerial and satellite images of the area, searching archives going back five decades. Especially for earlier material, it needed to be recovered from ancient file formats and then images rescaled and reoriented to allow a multispectral analysis of the evolution of the site. When this was complete, an app summarized it in form of an animation, which was integrated with all of Koide's material and automatically assessed to determine any inconsistencies or incompatibilities.

"So, Watson, got anything useful?" The question made me aware that the CI was standing behind my shoulder and had finally deigned to get dressed, although the small while tanga nickers and tight, semi-transparent vest did not leave much to the imagination.

"Nothing definite, but the villa that David lives in was completely rebuilt when he first bought the estate twenty years ago. The nearest house to it, which was built last century by the then Governor General, has also received a lot of work. Interestingly, this is recorded as the residence of his sister, although she told us that she lives with her sister in the big house."

"How does it look in terms of security layout?"

I called up the appropriate overlay for the most recent satellite image. "There's a primary external ring of intrusion detectors that encircles the entire site, complemented by a second internal system for each individual house. Additionally there is a third system which encloses these two houses and a path between them, which I guess would make sense if his sister actually did live in the smaller villa."

Links to the material that Koide had dug up appeared as summary text boxes as I spoke. "So David bought all this property two decades ago, when his sister moved to the island. She then stayed in the smaller villa - called Harbour Hill - while another villa, then called Hummingbird House, was pulled down and his grandiose mansion was built. He moved to join her five years later, when the name of the new villa was changed to The Promised Land."

I flicked open a side window to a wiki-cheat, feeling slowed down without the apps on my own comm unit. "*To the promised land*: that was the title of the first volume of the manga Chirality, the one that featured Carol."

Koide rolled her eyes and groaned theatrically. "Another one of these stupid fucking comic links! What is it with this guy? Anyway, it's time for lunch: why don't you rustle up a couple of sandwiches for us and we can munch them out on the veranda."

I stood and stretched, preparing to do as told, but was surprised to see my boss pulling her top over her head. "What... ?" I started to ask.

"May as well catch some rays while we eat," she explained, throwing the garment carelessly onto the coffee table and starting to pull down her pants.

"Jesus!" I rolled my eyes and I padded off into the kitchen.

***

During a lunch of cheese and salami baguettes, washed down by copious quantities of Red Stripe lager, we puzzled over the possible location of the vault holding David's backup database. Koide suspected that it had been built into The Promised Land during its construction: plans showed a basement level below the entire villa, containing a large garage, a wine cellar and a battery room, which complemented the array of solar panels that provided dedicated power for the house. There were also two huge freshwater storage tanks: one filled by rainwater captured on site and one topped up with water pumped from a central tank in the grounds of Harbour Hill, itself filled by a dedicated desalination plant because, even now, there was no mains water supply to this part of the island.

Unlike other houses on the island, The Promised Land did not possess a hurricane shelter: the villa was constructed in such a robust, over-engineered manner that it would be able to easily withstand anything that the forces of nature could throw against it.

Although I could not flaw my boss's arguments, I had a feeling that this was too pat a solution; it just did not fit with the additional complexity that my old university pal seemed to build into everything that he did. I remembered the specs for the armored glass used for all windows: these would not only resist a class five storm, but would require specialist armor-piercing rounds if you wanted to penetrate them using a bazooka.

"David's place was built to withstand a siege," I muttered aloud, causing the CI to pause with a beer halfway to her mouth. "From the moment that he decided to destroy Miss Nomura, he must have been aware that there would be a possibility of his plan being found out. Even if he considered the probability remote, he'd still put appropriate defenses in place."

Koide absentmindedly rubbed the frosted bottle against her left nipple as she picked up on my thoughts. "If Fumiko had even the slightest inkling of what David was up to, she would have had him eliminated immediately. With her yakuza links, organizing a hit team here wouldn't be a great problem."

"Probably not even a straightforward assassination either," I added. "She and her equally sadistic bed-mate would haul him off into a dungeon and pull out all the stops. David knows what that pair are capable of and there's no way that he wouldn't have something in place to neutralize any potential threat."

"So this would explain the extra layers of security and the almost impregnable fortress that he's built," she agreed, moving the ministrations to her right nipple. "OK, playtime's over, time to get back to work," she looked in my direction but gave no indications of moving herself.

"Sho' ting, boss," I tugged an imaginary forelock and pushed up from my deckchair.

"Actually, just before you go, you could give my front a coat of that sun stuff," she requested, linking her hands behind her head as she closed her eyes.

I searched around the decking for the tube of sun cream, picked it up and then knelt by her naked body: this wasn't going to be the worst job in the world.

327

When I returned to the case model, I saw that the scanned documents had now been uploaded and I quickly looked over all new material on Harbour Hill. "Yes!" I muttered to myself as an application for construction of a hurricane shelter opened; this would be exactly the kind of thing that would suit David. I pulled together all linked records, spotting that the owner at that time was Swiss, which might explain why the specifications of the construction looked like those for a nuclear bomb shelter.

I overlaid the basement plans on my site map and saw immediately that the emergency escape hatch from the shelter - provided for the case that the overlying house had collapsed - lay directly under the path connecting this property with David's new house. Now that I focused my attention on it, I noticed that the path was dead straight, which must be almost unique in an island where every road and pathway snaked through the countryside.

I reviewed the animation of the site evolution, zooming in on this path, and further anomalies emerged. The path had been laid after Hummingbird House had been torn down, but before construction started on The Promised Land. It had been a far from trivial job as, in order to establish its linear route, several large trees had to be removed.

My suspicions now aroused, I then listed all further work carried out in and around Harbour Hill at that time. The main items identified were installation of high performance solar panels and the desalination plant with associated water storage tank, the latter replacing an older tank that had been previously filled by water trucked from off-site. I pulled up the desalination plant construction details and then the picture became clear.

"Boss, I think you should have a look at this," I called out as I quickly produced the required links within my site development animation.

A bare breast pressing against my back announced Koide's arrival. "What've you got for us, Watson?"

I started the animation and talked though my findings. "We got to the point of linking the possible location of David's backup database archive to what was probably his major concern: an attack from his ex-lover. His new house is, indeed, like a fortress; but what if someone did manage to break into it? I can't find any indications of a panic room, somewhere he could tough it out until external help arrived."

"There is, however, exactly such a facility at Harbour Hill," I opened the link to the old plans, "which might actually be linked to his choice of this site for his little empire. This vault is ultra-hard and would be extremely difficult to penetrate, even if his opponents were able to find it in the first place. An existing escape hatch needs only to be linked to a tunnel to the basement of his new house, which would have been constructed while the house was being built."

"So this is just a panic room, that's all?" the formidable blonde sounded unconvinced.

"Yes, you're also getting a feeling for the way David does stuff; that was a question I immediately asked myself," the link to the desalination facility construction opened. "The basement at Harbour Hill also holds the desalination plant, which treats seawater pumped from Falmouth Harbour below. The pump-house at the waterside doubles as a garage and is just beside the private jetty at which his yacht is moored."

"It's a bit arse to tit," the CI noted, pointing to the plant outline. "Putting the reverse osmosis unit in the basement means that seawater needs to be pumped up and brine pumped back, whereas, if this plant had been located below, where the pump-house is, you'd need only to pump freshwater up to the storage tank."

"Indeed! The tunnel containing the required pipes was constructed from below and, based on the license for spoil disposal, must be around two to three square meters in cross-section."

"Right, Watson, great job!" She slapped me heartily on the back. "David has both a bolt-hole next door and also an escape route, which could allow him to get away by road or sea."

"Actually, the tarmac parking area beside his jetty would also be ideal for landing a helicopter," I pointed out.

"Excellent! David may just have outsmarted himself by undermining his own stronghold. We just need to get hold of an appropriate petard."

And assure that we're not inadvertently hoist by it, I silently added.

Chapter 18

The basis of Koide's plan was quite straightforward: have Kempf obtain a search warrant for David's estate and then serve that at The Promised Land. Using this as a distraction, we would hack our way into David's escape tunnel and either intercept him if he tries to bolt for it or else break into his hidden database. The tricky bit would be the hacking, as we knew how good David's security is.

I thought about this and immediately identified a serious problem. "I don't know what else will be built into the firewalls, but biometric identification would probably be the core of it. In fact, given that we have no recent images of him, a regularly updated biometric access key would be virtually un-crackable."

"And also have the advantage that it'd be extremely fast and fool-proof in an emergency situation," she agreed.

"But virtually un-crackable," I reminded her.

"But that's only if we haven't a recent image."

"We haven't, that's the problem." I really could not see where this discussion was going.

"So we need to get one," she grinned at me. "That's your job."

"How the fuck do I do that, give him a call and ask for a recent photo?" I asked, sarcastically.

"Exactly!" her grin widened. "Actually, all you need to do is get the call through; I'll be able to do the rest."

I could guess how one of the CI's smart apps might be able to grab a high resolution video image, but had no idea what I could say to the man that I knew only briefly as a student. Or, even trickier, the woman that he now appeared to be.

***

I hit the i-skype link on the website for David's sister's massage parlor. Moments later Kat's image floated before me, the high resolution hologram uncannily realistic, as if the woman's head and shoulders had been lopped from her body.

"Ah, Mister Hamilton. I guess that you and your wife are looking for another massage, the one with special services included," she gave me a sly wink.

"Yes, indeed, how about tomorrow," I ad-libbed, a little caught out by this question.

"You're lucky that it's low season now. We could fit you in at three, four or five."

"Three would be great."

"OK, I'll book that in."

"Actually there's one more thing," I interrupted before she could sign off. "You mentioned your sister and it occurred to me that I may actually have known her from university."

"I don't know about that," she sounded skeptical, "Dee doesn't have many old friends."

"Could be someone else with the same name," I agreed, trying to be as disarming as possible, "but could I possibly have a quick word with her?"

Kat shrugged her shoulders. "OK, I'll give it a try. We'll see you tomorrow afternoon in any case. Bye for now." Her image vanished as was replaced by a rotating three-D i-skype logo.

I waited on hold for about five minutes until the upper torso of a middle-aged woman with large blue eyes and short red hair appeared. She was small, almost elfin and her fine-boned features made her face pretty, even with minimal makeup. She was clad in a tight lycra top which showed off her well-formed, taut breasts.

We stared at each other in silence for a few seconds before I gasped, "David, is that really you?"

"Hello Jimmy. Sorry I took so long to answer, I'd been working out in the gym. It's nice to see you after all this time. You haven't changed a bit." Her smile transformed her face from being pretty to really beautiful.

"Well, I can't really say the same, can I?" I couldn't suppress a grin. "Do I call you David or Dee?"

"I'm Dee now - and have been for a number of years. It's a bit complicated, though, as I go through short David phases now and then."

"I guess that could make your life complex," I admitted.

"Anyway, I'm sure you didn't make contact just to discuss my sexual orientation. To what to I owe this pleasure?" From her smile I got the distinct impression that Dee was toying with me.

"I just wanted to really confirm that it was you," I looked directly into pale blue eyes that twinkled with amusement.

"Did you really have any doubts?"

"Not really," I confessed, "but I did hope that we might be wrong. I quite liked you at Cambridge."

"Yes, but not quite enough. For a while I really fancied you, Jimmy. But it was very clear that you weren't interested - and definitely would have been frightened off if you found out the truth about me," she responded, somewhat sadly.

I found this admission uncomfortable, but realized that the analysis was spot on. "You're probably right. Anyway, I wish you had never been involved in all this shit - and that you hadn't maneuvered me into it. Why did you do that, anyway, why involve me?"

Dee´s grin could have been used to epitomize smugness. "You'll never get it, because you've never been truly rich - with the ennui that comes with vast wealth. Why do anything, if it isn't fun to do? I can't even spend the money that I have, so why do I spend time getting more? Like all rich people, I do it because it amuses me. If I'm going to do something awesome, why not bring all my buddies into the game, include all my cosplay hobbies, see how many birds I can kill with one stone - just to prove to myself that I can."

"You're actually a bit of a sad case," I responded, actually feeling a bit sorry that the oddball student that I knew had turned into this softly spoken monster. "You don't have any buddies and even Nomura-san was probably using you only for your physical attributes. You weren´t even able to kill some of the birds using a lot of stones, so we're going to take you down."

My words wiped the grin off the beautiful face and it was a grim Dee that responded. "I know what you've ripped-off my server, but I really don't think it's going to do as much as you think. I learned a lot from my Carol, how the rich and powerful put themselves above the law. I already have a team of top lawyers working on the case, who will block any attempt that you make to prosecute me. With the stuff in your case file, I'll die of old age before you can get me near to a jail."

Dee's confidence worried me and I wondered if she had managed to hack into the server holding our case documents. "Well, we'll just have to see about that. I think that we have everything that we need and I've only one question, for my own personal interest. After you split up with Fumiko, you helped her build that fucking torture chamber in Kabuki-cho. Why was that?"

I thought that I had pushed too far but, after a moment of reflection, Dee slowly answered. "If someone you loved dropped you for a truly fucked-in-the-head psycho, you might let them have free rein in the expectation that increasing depravity would eventually bring your lover to her senses. Of course, that presupposes that your lover isn't also fucked-in-the-head," this accompanied by a sad shrug of the shoulders.

I was struggling to think of a way to continue the conversation when Dee continued. "I think we're finished now, Jimmy. You may have hoped to get me to say something incriminating, but that just isn't going to happen. I don't much like games but, if I play, I never come second. This is something that your fuck-buddy, Chief Inspector Stella Koide, is just going to have to learn."

I broke the connection and looked over to my boss, who was sitting out of view of the holo camera. "How the hell does she... he... whatever the fuck it is, know that I'm shagging you?"

"You're not," she grinned at my look of confusion, "it should be very clear that it is I who am fucking you!"

I groaned and rolled my eyes. "Anyway, do we have all you need?"

"Absolutely, very high res images and enough text to synthesize anything that we need to say."

"As long as we don't need fingerprints," I pointed out.

"We won't," the blonde winked at me, indicating confidence that I certainly did not possess. "Right now, Watson, time to gird up our loins and prepare for a bit of breaking and entry."

***

It was five pm by the time that we had everything organized. The material downloaded from our electronic leach during its search for access to David's internal server included a complete map of his security sensor coverage, which allowed us to identify a flaw in the perimeter around the pier-side entry to his escape tunnel. Detectors were set up to be triggered by any approach by road, foot or boat, but the cordon could be breached by a diver who surfaced inside it, under the jetty.

Captain Kempf herself picked us up and drove us to Halliday's Happy Endings, with the two small rebreather units that we had requested thrown into the back of her SUV. We took these with us, while Kempf headed back towards The Promised Land. There she would rendezvous with Scott, who had the search warrant that they were going to serve. There was no way that David could prevent formal delivery of a hard copy of this document, but we were sure that he would have already managed to implement the legal defenses needed to block or, at least postpone, the search itself. In any case, it should provide the diversion that we needed.

Ducking under the crime scene tape that still cordoned-off the yacht, we proceeded directly to the dive equipment room, where two black one-piece suits had already been left for us. These were designed for use in iron man triathlons in cold conditions and so fit like a second skin and dried almost immediately after coming out of water. We stripped and pulled these on, helping each other with the zips that ran up the back of the suits. Weight belts had also been set out for us, calculated somehow from the biometric data that Koide had provided, and we buckled these on before strapping on the rebreathers and picking up fins and masks.

I had protested to my boss when she informed me of her intrusion plan, due to the fact that I had only once tried scuba and that time was with conventional compressed air. Her response was typical: "I haven't used such kit either, but it's just falling off a boat and remembering to keep breathing: how difficult can that be?"

Koide's comm was sealed into a thick waterproof bag that clipped to her weight belt and she strapped a small dive computer to her wrist, which was slaved to an auxiliary waterproof comm on her belt.

Thus prepared, we slipped onto the dive platform and lowered ourselves gently into the crystal clear water, which was still lit by the golden glow of a sun that was approaching the hills on the other side of the bay. At first contact the water seemed cold, but the LED display in my mask indicated that it was actually twenty-eight degrees Centigrade. We slowly dropped near to the sandy bottom, which was about ten meters deep, clearing our ears as we had been instructed by the expert system that set up our dive profile and facilitated buoyancy control.

As we finned our way towards our target, following the route indicated in our masks' head-up display, I couldn't help being diverted by the great diversity of small, brightly-colored fish that seemed to congregate around any feature of the bottom - rocks, coral and the bottles, cans and other jetsam from the boats using the marina. We had almost reached the jetty when I was startled by a sudden cloud of sand from which a strange alien shape emerged. I had started to head for the surface in a panic before I recognized it as a small stingray and forced myself to calm down as I descended back to my previous position, following close to the CI's heels.

At the jetty, we swam beneath the pilings until the water was knee deep, when we cautiously stood and peered around to confirm that the area was completely clear, with no signs of life. We then divested ourselves of our diving kit, dumping it at our feet before carefully pulling ourselves onto the decking of the pier, my boss carrying the bag containing her comm. From the position of the black poles housing the motion detectors, we could see in the increasingly ruddy light of the setting sun that we had popped up as planned, about two meters within the security perimeter.

I followed Koide as she strode confidently towards the blocky building facing us, feeling the sharp edges of gravel through the thin fabric of the integrated bootees of the triathlon suit. The seaward side of the pump-house had both a normal-sized door to the left and a wide roller door to the right that accessed the garage area. The CI stood in front of the former, which featured an old-fashioned looking keypad where a handle would normally be. She tapped in ten digits and a red light turned green and the door silently opened. "I hacked this from the company that services the desalination kit," she explained, entering as internal strip lights flickered on to illuminate the windowless room.

A glass partition to the right separated the pump-room from a garage that contained two large SUVs and a panel van. Apart from a gently humming pump, the left wall was lined with racks which appeared to store diverse equipment for David's yacht. In the middle of the wall facing us, which backed directly onto the hillside, was the steel bulkhead door that we were looking for. As we neared it, we could see that the door itself was completely featureless, but to the left of it was a circular smoked-glass panel of about two centimeters diameter, which was roughly level with my shoulders.

My boss looked determined as she extracted her comm from the waterproof sack, which she chucked carelessly into a corner. "Right, let's see if this is going to work." A holo image of Dee appeared in front of the panel as her synthesized voice commanded "Open!" and the door slid silently aside.

Koide turned to me and grinned smugly. "What did I tell you, it's a piece of piss!"

I still had great doubts about this, but kept them to myself as I followed the tall blonde into the stairwell that was now exposed.

***

The tunnel was circular in profile, the walls coated by rough shotcrete. Two, five centimeter diameter pipes were bracketed onto the left side and a continuous light tube ran along the center of the roof. Concrete steps alternated with paved ramps as we followed its snaking path up the hillside. After about a kilometer, we came to another bulkhead door, but this opened automatically as we approached. We had now reached the basement of Harbour Hill.

I looked around the large room, which was dominated by the reverse-osmosis unit. The two pipes that we had been following led into one side of it, while a single pipe from the other side connected it to a huge steel storage tank, which I guessed must have had a capacity of about fifty cubic meters. The unit was completely silent, but a panel with flashing green lights and two rows of slowly changing digits indicated that it was operating.

"Rather dusty," I commented as we walked together towards the door into the panic room, "I guess this basement is rarely visited."

"Shouldn't need to be. These desalination units are designed to run for decades without maintenance. Could well be that nobody has been here since it was installed."

There were certainly no indications of footsteps in the dust or indications that the bulkhead door leading to the house upstairs or the thick concrete door to the panic room had been opened recently.

The door to David's retreat reminded me of those I had seen in the atom bomb shelters still found in older Swiss houses, except that the large levers for manual operation were replaced by an electronic drive system that was somewhat reminiscent of bank vaults. I had no doubt that physical intrusion would require major industrial equipment or military-grade explosives.

I followed my boss to the glass panel to the left of the door, an identical clone of the one in the pump-house below. Again the holo of Dee was created by Koide's comm, but this time there was no reaction at all. "Fuck!" Fucking, cunting, bastard!" she cursed, shaking the comm as if this would help in some way. "What the fuck is going on, it worked fine already."

"Well, if I was David, I'd have even higher security for this vault," I mused.

"Yes but, as we discussed, access has to be fast and fool-proof. A regularly updated biometric profile does that - and worked downstairs."

"I kind of expected something like this," I ventured, hesitantly. "Can I use the voice synthesizer?"

The CI passed me the comm and Dee's voice emerged from it, "Shiori!" With a snick of locks disengaging and a groan of heavy duty motors, the door slowly opened towards us.

"How the fuck did you do that, Watson - and what the fuck's a Shiori?"

I was actually very surprised that this had worked, but tried to hide it by an attempt to mimic the smug grin that my boss so regularly sported. "Just based on something that surprised me when I was talking to David - or Dee - earlier. He referred to Nomura-san as my Carol, which seemed to be rather intimate for someone who he has cold-heartedly destroyed. Maybe he still yearns for the Fumiko he used to love, personified by the manga character Carol that she dressed as at Cosplay... "

"And this is going where?" Koide interrupted impatiently.

"I just remembered how David dressed at Cosplay conventions, which made his contact with Fumiko almost inevitable. It was Carol's manga lover... "

"Shiori?"

"Exactly, Shiori!" I felt very pleased with myself. David had brought me into this game to solve the clues that he had fed us, which would allow us to finally nail down Chrissy's murder and end the lesbians' ultra-violent killing spree. However, these very clues had also inadvertently provided insight into how his mind worked and hence his approach to setting security passwords. He had, indeed, been hoist by his own petard.

***

Unlike most Swiss bomb shelters, which are now used as wine cellars or a kind of lumber room, the vault was actually set up as an emergency refuge, complete with stores of food and drink, bunk beds and a chemical toilet. An escape hatch on the opposite wall presumably provided access to the tunnel leading to David's house. The only other furnishing was a desk and leather swivel chair, which looked strangely out of place in the otherwise Spartan accommodation. On the table sat an old-fashioned, anonymous, boxy laptop which was connected to a junction box on the wall by two cables; both the junction box and computer were linked to a small cube by a single cable in each case.

Koide moved her comm unit over the desk, allowing me to notice for the first time that a slim utility module had been added to it. "What've you got there," I asked as a holographic circuit diagram appeared in the air above this equipment.

"Room temperature squid," she muttered, clearly engrossed in the output of her tool.

"Squid... " I closed my eyes as I tried to recall what this was all about, "... S-Q-U-I-D; superconducting quantum interference device."

"Yes, it's a highly sensitive magnetometer that drives the neat little interpretation app that I have here. It shows, for example, that this is a trickle-charged backup power supply," she pointed to the small cube.

"OK, so these cables here are power supply and the other two must be data feed," I pointed at the wires to the cube and then to those connecting the laptop to the junction box.

"Yes, the uninterruptable power supply seems to be good for about a month and effectively isolates the computer from any mains surges - and also the kind of hack via mains power that we used on David's estate management system. The data feed seems to be via shielded, high-bandwidth, optical fibers. There are parallel optical convertors within the laptop, but the signals are identical, so I guess the data-feed runs with a backup, in case of any physical disruption of the main cable."

"Cables, optical fibers, that's a bit quaint," I commented, peering at the junction box.

"Yes, well it's a very secure option and any form of wireless is clearly out as this shelter includes two Faraday cages - internal and external," she pointed to a mesh of fine copper wires which I now saw were inlaid into all walls, the floor, the roof and the inside of the door.

"Certainly is belt and braces: this really would withstand a nuclear blast and the associated EMP."

"I don't think that even Nomura would consider using an atom bomb, but high capacity capacitors can generate a sizeable electromagnetic pulse that would be the kind of thing that any invaders of this estate might use."

I remembered the way in which our ship had been attacked and realized that this was defending against a version of the same approach: a high power electrical pulse to wipe out all electronic systems. "So, this must be his backup database, nicely protected from all potential disruptions."

"It certainly looks like it." Koide opened the laptop and the flat screen flickered on, showing wallpaper that I recognized as a cover image from the Japanese language Chirality manga, showing the naked bodies of Carol and Shiori in an intimate embrace. In the center of the screen a white bar showed a flashing cursor, evidently inviting a password to be entered. She pointed at the primitive keyboard and raised her eyebrows. "What do you think, Watson? Ready to do your magic again?"

I shook my head immediately. "I don't think that'd be a good idea; one mistake could screw up everything. I think we should just take the entire thing and leave it up to the experts to hoover off the database."

"I think you're right on that; let's see how it's hooked up," she waved her hands to pull up an exec sum of the power supply. Following the instructions displayed, she lifted up the laptop and wrenched off a panel in its base, exposing a battery pack which she removed. She then simultaneously pulled the power supply and both data feed cables free. The screen went black.

Following a gesture with her open hand, I closed the screen and tucked the surprisingly heavy computer under my arm. I then followed my boss's swaying hips as we hurried back the way that we had come.

***

We emerged from the pump-house into the last light of the setting sun, high altitude clouds still glowing a deep scarlet. I had picked up the waterproof sack that Koide had previously discarded and this now contained both her comm and the laptop. Dropping down under the jetty, we quickly located our diving kit and donned the equipment, switching on little torches that were integral components of our rebreathers. I clipped the bag onto my belt and slipped under, following the glow of Koide's light through the dark water.

The swim back seemed to take ten times longer than expected, reflecting how unnerved I was by the uncanny sensation of being underwater and able to see clearly only what lay within the cone of light from my torch. I was constantly startled by fish that darted by and, on one occasions, by the bizarre sight of a lobster marching out from a hole under a coral head.

The navigation system was invaluable as I was rapidly disorientated; nevertheless it brought us up at the steps leading onto our boat with centimeter accuracy. We stripped off fins and chucked them onto the diving deck, then clambered aboard and started to strip off the rest of our kit.

I had just unclipped the carry-sack and dropped my weight belt when a figure emerged from the passageway into the dive equipment room. It was David - or Dee - incongruously dressed in a short black skirt, pearl necklace and high heels that seemed more appropriate to a dinner party. Although clearly middle-aged, she looked very attractive, pinned in the beams of both of our torches. My attention was, however, completely focused on the heavy revolver that she held in her right hand, pointed directly at my chest.

"You're very good, Jimmy. Much better than I expected," her voice was completely calm, which made me even more frightened. "But you know that I can't let you steal my computer. If you just hand it over now, I won't need to kill you or your big, fat girlfriend." Although I could see her only out of the corner of my eye, I could sense my boss tense at this disparaging description of her build.

"So I hand it over and you just leave peacefully?" I asked, trying to imply that I was seriously considering this.

"As we discussed earlier, I can handle anything that you had on me up till now. If you don't have that archive, then I have nothing to fear from you - so why not let you go?"

"I'm not convinced: if you didn't fear us, why bother setting the heavy mob on us last night? I think you completely underestimated how good we would be and that this has backfired on you, showing that you're nothing like as smart as you think you are."

"Whatever," now her voice showed distinct traces of annoyance, "just hand over the fucking computer. Otherwise I'll just shoot you and take the fucking thing from your dead hands."

"I don't think you will," I looked directly into her eyes, hoping that I portrayed more confidence than I actually felt. "If you were capable of shooting someone in cold blood, you'd have done that straight away. You can give orders to have someone whacked, but don't have the guts to do it yourself. That's yet another way that you differ from your beloved Carol - and probably why she chucked you for the delectable Miss Saito."

"Fuck you!" Dee screamed. I saw her finger beginning to tighten on the trigger and instantly wondered if I had completely misjudged the situation. At that moment Koide threw herself forward, causing the gun to swing in her direction before it went off with a deafening *bang*.

Dee seemed shocked as the CI grunted in pain, her knees buckled and she dropped to the deck, her arms cradling her chest. Just then I realized that I was still clutching the sack and stepped forward, swinging it so that it smashed into Dee's face, toppling her backwards with her legs in the air. My opponent was squirming to bring the gun back towards me, when I kicked her between the legs with all the force I could muster. Although the impact was lessened by my soft foot-ware, it was sufficient to cause a howl of pain and enough distraction to allow me to drop heavily to my knees, one pinning her gun arm at the wrist and the other landing on her shoulder, causing it to dislocate with an audible *pop*.

I was now aware of my boss's shouts, which caused a flush of relief that she was still alive. "Fucking cunt shot me, fuck it's sore! Fuck her up for me, that's a fucking order!"

Ignoring a further litany of *fucks*, I looked into the pain-filled eyes of our nemesis and felt a moment of uncertainty. Then, with all the force I could muster, I chopped my hand down and smashed her windpipe. There was a distinctive crack that indicated that I had probably also broken her neck.

Although I was sure that we had nothing more to fear from the crippled woman, I grabbed the gun from where it had been dropped as I rolled over onto my hands and knees and crawled to my partner's side. She was still swearing like a trooper, but I was concerned to see that blood was seeping from between the fingers that were holding her side.

I quickly stripped off my suit and rolled it into a ball. "Press this against the wound," I commanded as I pushed it below her hands. I then crawled back to my victim, who was doubled up on her side, with her head at an unnatural angle as she choked. Retrieving the sack that was lying beside her elbow, I pulled Koide's comm out and, checking that we were outside the ship's Faraday cage, hit the panic button. "Officer has been shot and wounded, require emergency medical evacuation as soon as possible. Shooter is down and looks terminal; probably a hearse would suffice, so this is a definite second priority."

I returned to my boss, who was still swearing colorfully, describing what she had planned for Dee. "I'm afraid that won't happen, I smashed her throat really badly and I think both the trachea is crushed and probably neck as well. I could try to provide some kind of emergency support but, to tell the truth, I really can't be arsed."

Koide forced a grin through her grimace of pain. "A good turn of phrase, Watson, as your arse is on show for all to see," she grunted before returning to a string of curses.

"Quite frankly I don't give a shit," I retorted, noting, to my surprise, that I really did not.

Chapter 19

I was still buck-naked, kneeling by my boss, when a US military medevac copter landed in the marina car-park about ten minutes later. Two paramedics raced towards us with large kitbags over their shoulders, while a third followed with a rapidly assembled trolley. I shouted them over and made way as they swarmed about the detective, first injecting an anesthetic and putting an oxygen mask over her face, before prising her arms free, cutting her suit loose to the waist and exposing an open wound in her side that showed traces of bone.

I used my torch to provide light until the trolley-guy set up a pair of lamps that flooded the entire area with a glare of actinic brilliance. "Bit of luck there," the medic who was evidently in charge commented, "but I'm not sure if it's good or bad. A centimeter to the left and the bullet would have missed completely, to the right and it would have caused really serious damage. As it is, it has scraped and cracked a rib, but these large caliber rounds pack a huge punch. I'm really surprised that this woman stayed conscious."

I hefted the gun that was still held loosely in my hand, noting for the first time how heavy it was. It was a snub-nosed revolver, possibly a Smith and Wesson magnum or something similar and looked old, maybe an antique. In any case, I was very glad that the slug from this brute had not caused more damage.

"Can you patch me up here?" Koide asked as she prized the oxygen mask loose, startling the

351

medic who had evidently considered her completely out of action.

"Well, theoretically... " the question seemed to put him at a loss for words. "We should evac you to hospital ASAP, you could go into shock at any time."

"I can assure you this isn't the first time that I've been shot," the CI protested. "Just bandage the hole up and get me on my feet again, I've got work to do.

The medic looked at me, clearly noting my bruises and the pressure bandage around my ribs. I simply shrugged. "Just drug her up to get her through the next twenty-four hours and then we'll take it from there."

He shrugged back. "Up to you two, but don't get into any more fights until you're both healed. And, also, get some bloody clothes on," he handed me a white towel that was just large enough to wrap around my waist.

While two of the paramedics worked on Koide, I led the third to Dee's body. "We just need a confirmation of death here," I said, waving over to Kempf who had just raced onto the jetty followed by a posse of police officers.

I started to explain what had happened to the captain, when we were interrupted by a shout. "Christ, this woman is still alive! Give me some help here!"

There were a couple of minutes of chaos, while I fought to ensure that one medic continued to work on my boss, while the others prepared to evacuate the person who had attempted to kill her.

Nevertheless, by the time that Dee was wheeled off to the helicopter, Koide was standing at my side, leaning heavily on my shoulder. Despite the seriousness of the situation, I could not help note that the towel that had been thrown over the buxom blonde's shoulders was doing a poor job of preserving her modesty and a brown nipple was exposed every time she inhaled.

"Let's get back to the villa, we can do the debriefing there if that's OK with you, Captain." When the policewoman nodded her agreement, the CI nodded her head in the direction of the sack that lay on the deck. "Pick up that stuff, Watson, together with the torches from our diving kit: they have integral cameras."

"And what about our clothes?" I asked as my boss let me go, holding on to a railing for support.

"Fuck the clothes, we can get them picked up anon. Captain, I wonder if someone could help me to your car." I grabbed the sack and rummaged for the torch in the scattered remnants of Koide's kit while Sargent Scott rushed to her side and they started to totter together towards the jetty.

***

Our route back to our accommodation took us past David's estate, where flashing red and blue lights indicated a couple of police cars at the main gate. "After this latest development, we can upgrade the warrant to include attempted murder of two police officers. With Miss McNeill out of action, I doubt that her lawyers will be able to stall us any longer."

"Hopefully, we'll have a lot more than that," my boss responded, without going into detail and causing a raised eyebrow from Kempf as she glanced at the laptop that the blonde was cradling in her arms.

At the villa I helped Koide stagger into the living room, where she collapsed with a grunt onto a sofa while Scott rushed to fetch her a footstool. I hurried into our bedroom, where I quickly pulled on shorts and a t-shirt, grabbing a loose, kimono-type robe for my boss. By the time I returned, Scott had downloaded and synchronized the low-res, two-D video records from our torches and scrolled through till images from both were frozen in parallel displays, just at the point where we were clambering onto the dive platform.

The CI unselfconsciously removed her towel and wrapped the robe around her battered body, seemingly oblivious to the shocked looks of the two police officers as her breasts were exposed in all their humungous magnificence. "The diving kit that you provided was just the job and our search for supporting evidence went completely to plan," she was clearly providing background to the action about to be displayed. "As I promised, we'll download a full report on this to both you and Interpol within the next twenty-four hours," she cocked an eye in my direction, indicating that this was a job for me.

"It was inevitable that our intrusion would be noted, but I hadn't anticipated that McNeill would be on our heels so quickly," she continued, with a look that indicated her annoyance at this lapse. "She must have followed us to the pump-house and might even have seen us swimming off. In any case, she must have driven round to the jetty, probably in the SUV that I noticed in the car park as we drove here, the one that was empty but with its lights on. She was thus on board before we emerged from the water."

The videos then started to play and Koide provided a background commentary on the action. To my great relief, I noted that there was no soundtrack, so that she was able to put a somewhat different slant on off-camera action, particularly at the point where I smashed McNeill's trachea, implying that she was trying to point the gun at me at that time, despite the fact that I knew that this had already fallen from her grasp by then.

After the quick debriefing, we called up a report on McNeill's current condition from the hospital on the outskirts of Saint John's where she was being treated. She was in a coma and had severe damage to her cervical spine. If she did regain consciousness, there was a high chance that she would end up quadriplegic. I felt a twinge of guilt, a feeling evidently not shared by my boss who I could hear muttering under her breath, "... evil fucking cow, serves her fucking right!"

We answered some basic questions on details of the encounter and then discussed further actions needed to wrap up the Antigua side of the case. After half an hour of this, the blonde's eyes began to droop and Kempf called a halt, promising to return with the prosecutor's team and some Interpol liaison guys in the morning. The Antiguans rose and I led them to the door while we said our goodnights.

No sooner had the door closed behind them when Koide made a miraculous recovery. "I don't know what those guys pumped into me, but, apart from a dull stiffness around my ribs, I feel fine. Grab me a beer and we can quickly check our swag here," she lifted the computer, which had been sitting on her knees the entire time, and started to examine it closely.

By the time that I had returned with a couple of bottles of Wadadli, the results of a scan by another one of Koide's special apps was displayed in the form of a rotating hologram. "Another bit of luck here," she explained as she took the beer from my hand, pausing to swig down half of its contents. "Despite your careless maltreatment of our key piece of evidence, it's military spec, so appears completely intact."

"Hardly careless," I objected, "if I hadn't hit that fucker Dee with it you might well be pushing up daisies by now."

"Whatever," she grinned, indicating that she was only teasing me. "I'll hook this up to the squid and let the big brains in Tokyo have a go at cracking it. If you dig out the inductive charger for our comms, this can be used as a power supply, so they can power up and rape this baby's brains as soon as any pitfalls and bear traps have been neutralized,"

I returned with the charger and silently passed it to her, easily able to interpret the command implicit in the empty beer bottle waved in my

356

direction. I groaned theatrically as I had yet to even taste my own first beer.

By the end of Koide's second beer, the kit was set up and a high bandwidth, encrypted satellite link to our forensic IT team in Japan established, allowing them full remote control of the hacking process. There was now nothing else for us to do but keep our fingers crossed. We had been playing fast and loose with the laws associated with legally obtaining evidence: if our case was watertight, this would be brushed under the carpet, but, if the laptop was fried, we were going to be in very hot water for rather blatant breaking and entering, theft and maybe even assault or homicide, if it could be argued that Dee was only attempting to recover something that we had stolen from her.

These concerns did not seem to bother my boss in the slightest. "We'll synthesize the new case input tomorrow and then the prosecutors here, in Japan and those with Interpol can start the bun fight to see who is going to take the lead on this. Thereafter we can keep our heads down and take a few days well-earned island R and R. In addition, Kempf is certainly going to want us to clear up the two serious assaults that we've been involved in during the short time that we've been on the island."

"You know very well that we could provide any input needed from Shinjuku," I objected.

"Of course," she smiled. "I know that, you know that, but our rather ditzy Commander hasn't a clue - so we can basically do as we want."

"So, what are we going to do while we're killing time here: just lie in the sun and work on our suntans?"

"That certainly," she grinned, "plus a lot of shagging. A complete shitload of passion and red-hot lust."

"I sincerely doubt that," I lifted my shirt to expose my bandaged ribs, "I'm completely buggered as far as red-hot sex is concerned."

"We'll see about that," she dropped her robe, exposing both her own bandages and her giant tits. "Let's adjourn to the bed chamber, compare wounds and see just what that leads to."

She proffered her hand and I dragged her to her feet, noting a small twinge of pain that was quickly hidden. I was not at all sure what was going to happen, but suspected that it might be painful for both of us. Despite that, I could not deny a thrill of anticipation as I helped her walk to our room.

***

I awoke with a feeling of déjà vu as I looked at the gently snoring form beside me. Last night had started in the shower, me helping my boss strip off the bottom of her triathlon suite, startled by the acrid smell of urine as I pulled it down.

"Tends to happen when you get shot," she explained with a wry grin, evidently unbothered by this sign of weakness, "but you don't see it in the movies, so nobody thinks about it. Just lucky that we had these triathlon suits: they have inbuilt absorptive pads. Guess these guys must piss themselves a lot if they're racing for hours. Something else the man in the street doesn't think about. Anyway, chuck that in the bin and get going with the soap!"

I certainly did not want to think about the physical reactions to being shot, but I could not help myself running my fingers between Koide's legs before I reached for the soap. It was impossible to tell if the wetness was due to piss, vaginal fluids or, maybe, both, but I could feel my erection stiffen in immediate response. Despite this encumbrance, I managed to soap and rinse the buxom blonde's body twice, until she was convinced that the job was complete. I then had to wipe her dry with a fleecy white towel before I was dismissed to my own ablutions while she headed for the bed.

Our love making thereafter had been gentle, reflecting the battered state of our bodies, but very satisfactory, nevertheless. I had fallen asleep immediately after my orgasm and suspected that my boss would have been just after me - if not before.

I started to caress a prominent nipple, then changed my mind, aware of just what this might lead to. "Discretion, the better part of valor!" I muttered to myself as I rolled off the bed, grunting at the jab of pain from my damaged ribs.

I padded naked into the kitchen and set coffee to brew, before venturing forth into the blast of heat from a cloudless Caribbean morning. My entire attitude to nudity seemed to have changed, I recognized, as I jumped into the pool and started to swim lengths of a slow breast-stroke. I felt, as the Irish say, good in myself. I had never worked on a case of anything like this complexity, but I had played an important role in cracking it. OK, I might have been manipulated into being involved in the first place, but underestimation of my capabilities had been the root of David's downfall. He had as good as admitted it himself.

My reverie of self-congratulation was interrupted by a shout from my boss, who was now heading in my direction, clad only in the bandage around her ribs. "Hoi, Watson, coffee and a croissant as soon as you like, please!"

I clambered from the pool with a muttered, "... and a very good morning to you too... ", and headed to the kitchen while my boss lowered herself gingerly onto a sun-lounger. The schadenfreude of knowing that my boss must be suffering a lot more than me made the ache from my own ribs seem much less of a burden.

It was less than ten minutes later when I returned with a tray laden with large mugs of coffee, grapefruit juice spiked with a trace of a naff-looking sparkly wine that had been left in the fridge and croissants with all the trimmings of butter, jams, cheeses and anything else related that I could find.

Expecting, even if not a rapture of praise for my efforts, at least some kind of acknowledgement, I was sorely disappointed. "Fine, Watson," she murmured without taking her eyes from her comm as she gulped the juice down in one. "That's OK, but just too small - get us another would you?"

I was about to explode but, instead, mildly returned to the house to fulfill my boss's wishes. I did mutter a series of comments on her extreme rudeness - but only well out of her hearing.

When I returned again with her drink, this time served up in a pint mug in an effort to make a point, it again was wasted effort. "Finally, a drink served as they are in the land of the amber nectar," she noted, before sinking half of it in an inelegant slurp - still without even raising her eyes towards me.

I sat silently, sipping my coffee, until she burped loudly and, finally, looked in my direction. "OK, lad, the good news or the even better news?"

"Cure for cancer, peace on earth?" I responded facetiously.

"Both better than that," she responded instantaneously, without batting an eyelid.

"Jeez - if it's all at that level, you'd better break me in gently with the good news."

"We didn't get our arses blown to fuck! Now, you've got to admit that that's better than a cure for cancer - at least, assuming that you don't actually have cancer."

"Could be," I conceded, "but I hadn't been aware that getting blown to fuck was a concern here."

"Yes, well, I've just been going through the feedback from the Tokyo hack team. Your buddy David doesn't fuck about, does he? That laptop has a layer of plastic around the memory chip."

"Plastic? That's supposed to scare me?"

"Plastique!" her exaggerated pronunciation made the meaning unambiguous. "Does that make it clear to you EU types?"

"Oh, yes, as in the high explosive stuff. That certainly is a way to ensure a complete memory wipe if required."

"Yep, that's the stuff - but at the very high explosive end of the range. It really was literal over-kill: had we even opened the laptop after a power down without first priming it with a radio-frequency password, we would have been jam - along with anyone else within about a ten meter radius."

"Fuck! That was very lucky that you've being doing all the interrogation passively, using your squid."

"That wasn't luck, that's just clever," she responded smugly while coating the end of a croissant with a thick layer of strawberry jam, which made me think again of the consequences of a misstep with this booby-trapped computer. "No, the real luck was the way in which we returned with our swag... "

I waited for more information, but Koide had gone into Sphinx mode, clearly waiting for me to decipher this clue. "Well, if I was David,... " I started uncertainly, but recognizing that this was the route leading to solution of most of these puzzles, "... I would want to ensure that only I could leave with this backup memory store. The secret escape route is a sensible precaution in case of some kind of disaster, but it's also inherently a vulnerability. As we have shown, even if unlikely, the possibility of theft has to be considered - which is the explanation for the inbuilt self-destruct. But this is deactivated by radio, so it could also be fired by a remote radio signal."

The look of surprise on my boss's face was comical. "Fuck me, Watson - you're bang on the button! And the luck was?"

I was sure that this was a further test to check that my progress so far wasn't a fluke. I grinned and hesitated for a moment as I suddenly saw the entire picture come together.

"I'd guess that we set off alarms everywhere when we grabbed the laptop and David would have checked the situation out before hitting the kill signal. Might even have waited until we had left the pump station, save himself the problem of having to cover up a large explosion, laced with our DNA, on his property. He would have panicked, of course, when nothing happened. This is why he had to go after us immediately, it looked like the trigger had failed."

"And it hadn't?" My boss was now clutching at straws.

"I think we'll find the trigger mechanism is intact. The luck was that we had the laptop sealed in the carry bag which, knowing you, is probably military spec. A layer of fine mesh for EMP protection and a radio signal wouldn't touch it."

"Jesus, Watson, where does this newfound brilliance come from?" A look of annoyance flashed over her face, probably in recognition that she was being too forthright in her praise. "Anyway, grab me another cup of coffee and then I'll tell you the better news," she recovered quickly, reverting to her usual commanding mode of address.

"That's OK," I replied over my shoulder, as I set off with the empty mugs, "I think I've probably worked that out as well."

***

I took my time fetching the coffee, wondering if I had maybe shot myself in the foot by gratuitously provoking my boss. Nevertheless, it had been worth it just to wipe the smug grin off her face for a few minutes.

I took a deep breath before descending to the poolside and placing a mug of steaming coffee on a small table by the side of the statuesque blonde. I calmly looked her over, noting now the gold rings through her nipples and wondering how I had missed noting them previously, because I was sure that they had not been in place when I was washing her in the shower last night.

"OK, put your tongue back in," she commanded, but with a different tone of voice to usual, "and stop playing hard-to-get. Let's hear the even better news - and see if you've really turned into a detective."

"Well, for me, even better news would be that the memory is intact and that we have a way of getting hold of it without taking any further risks by guessing passwords." My nervousness vanished as I saw the CI's evident amazement. "Because David's such a whiz at software, I'd even hazard a guess that this is a hardware option - probably physical removal of the memory chip."

Now I knew I had done my bit and did not need to fuck up by venturing into areas far beyond my ken. "I don't know exactly how we would do this - probably some smart trick with your squid, as that hasn't blown us up so far," I finished with a smile which, I am sure, matched my boss at her best in terms of smugness.

To my surprise, Koide giggled, making me wonder if I had somehow managed to miss something important. "Bloody good work, Watson. If you do want the details, the squid can actually be transmogrified to an active mode that will short the laptop's internal batteries and drain all power from backup capacitors." She glanced at her comm, clearly refreshing her mind on the procedure. "We then drop the entire thing into liquid nitrogen, crack open the carapace and then quickly remove the chip. All we need to do after that is insert it into a fast comm and then we let the Tokyo - Interpol bun-fight commence."

"So I take it the local fuzz are rustling up the required materials as we speak."

"They'd be lucky to get the chance. Interpol are already on the island and I'm sure that the locals have enough on their plate sorting out more bodies and GBH cases than I imagine that they normally see in a year. The Inters will actually remove the chip, but we have to oversee to ensure that it is first uploaded to Japan. Thereafter, Interpol can clone it and we take the original back to Japan."

"I thought we were hanging about for a holiday of sex and wild hot lust?"

"Well, you're certainly due a bit of leave, so why don't you just go for it?"

I tried to keep the look of disappointment off my face. "I don´t know, maybe... Let's see what it looks like after we've got the Interpol circus out of the way." As if on cue, the doorbell rang and I suddenly realized that we were sitting about in the buff.

"Fuck!" I jumped to my feet and sprinted towards my room as fast as my battered ribs would allow me.

"And pick up a robe for me!" I heard as I reached the patio door, accompanied by a delighted giggle, which highlighted the limits of my new-found body confidence.

***

Zoo might have been a better term than circus to describe the scene as our villa gradually filled with more and more computer geeks, international financial crime experts and top-level police brass from Antigua and also the surrounding tax havens. Serial killers and gruesome mass murders may catch the public eye, but the big crime-busting guns were reserved for this type of white-collar crime, involving manipulation of stock of a major multinational company. The concern that really had the bigwigs shitting themselves was the possibility that this case exposed fundamental vulnerabilities of international finance. We had nailed down the Nomura case and the link to Antigua, but there is no reason that David's ambitions could not have been much grander.

It was a measure of how seriously the teams were taking this, that even the initial presence of Koide clad only in a rather skimpy yukata caused little distraction. I suspect this lack of impact was the main driver for her to finally retreat from the fray and get dressed in a slightly more modest vest and shorts.

Although the Inters would have liked to have dismantled the laptop in one of their own labs, it had been agreed that it would be safest to avoid any further movement or delay, just in case there were any other triggers that David had managed to hide from our examination. I watched in amusement as a copper-wire cage was constructed in the kitchen and the worktop there converted into a blast-shielded cryogenic handling lab. The CI stood at my side as we saw the chip successfully extracted and, still coated with a layer of condensation, inserted into the ultrafast satellite upload comm.

Despite the high transmission speed, the upload took an hour and cloning the chip a further twenty minutes. There was then an air of ceremony, when the original chip was sealed in a special container for highly sensitive evidence and handed to Koide by the head of Interpol for the Caribbean and South America. By this time, despite high security, the villa was encircled by a cordon of local and international press - held back by what must be a large proportion of the total Antiguan police force.

The Interpol boss, an elegant grey-haired man in a tropical linen suit who looked more like a politician or diplomat than a policeman, tried for fifteen minutes to talk my boss into a press conference. Her insistence that this was set up by Interpol, but with a direct video link to Tokyo, initially surprised me. "This is your chance to make it clear what our role in this was, it'll be good for your career," I whispered into her ear.

She only smiled and whispered back. "Don't you worry, Holmes, our careers are made anyway - and this is the best way to milk this cow for all it's got."

I was so surprised by her response that I almost missed noticing how she addressed me. Almost, but not quite!

Epilogue: Hanoi, Vietnam

I awoke to the sound of traffic outside the window and gazed about, momentarily disorientated by the heavy wooden furniture and the old-world feel to the room. Slowly it came back to me: I was in the Hotel Metropole, built by the French in 1901. Apart from the external noise and the air-conditioned coolness, it seemed to have changed little in one and a half centuries. I looked at the depression in the mattress beside me - Koide had gone already, without even a goodbye. Typical!

I had to admit that, despite my sleuthing successes, the CI was still well ahead of me when it came to office politics - and also scheming in general. I had been convinced that her low profile approach to cracking the case, allowing others to bathe in the limelight while we kept our heads down, was missing out on a great chance. She had, of course, been correct: every one of the higher-ups who benefited from a share of the glory now owed the CI a favor. Our roles in the case were quickly known throughout the police grapevine, anyway, as was the fact the entire Tokyo police force had been praised by Interpol for both the quality of their work and their openness.

We had left Antigua the evening after cracking the case and flown to Haneda via London, where the chip was handed over to the Tokyo metropolitan police commissioner at a huge press conference held at the airport. Koide said little at this event, apart from thanking the SAR, metropolitan and national serious crimes unit for their critical support in this case. She then managed to look surprised when the commissioner praised her work effusively and announced that she would be promoted to head up a newly created unit that would support Interpol in major crimes in Japan and South East Asia. Almost as an afterthought, he also mentioned that I would be promoted to Chief Inspector - although it was clear that neither he nor anyone else in the audience had any idea who I was.

Immediately after the press conference, we flew directly to Hanoi - selected only on the basis that it was the first international flight leaving, which allowed no chance for any of the paparazzi to follow us. We had transferred directly to this bijou hotel and spent the entire first twenty-four hours in our bedroom - with lots of sleep, sex and cordon bleu room service but, amazingly, no electronic contact with the outside world. At first this just seemed like a dream come true but, having seen my boss surreptitiously checking the time with increasing regularity, I realized that there was more to this idyll that was evident on the surface.

I decided to take the initiative and, on the second evening, proposed that we adjourn to the poolside bar. My suspicions seemed to be confirmed by the way that Koide distractedly accepted this suggestion without comment.

Leaving the air-conditioning of the main building, the heat and humidity of the open bar hit me like a wall, causing me to instantly break into sweat despite the gentle air flow from the quaint, roof-mounted fans. Although a few pink tourists lay around the pool in the late sunset glow, we were alone in the bar. Without looking at the leather-bound menus and wine lists that were proffered by a rather camp young waiter, I ordered a bottle of champagne - now succeeding in attracting the blonde's attention.

"What's this in aid of lad?" she enquired, reminding me again that she no longer referred to me as Watson, although still avoided Holmes to the extent possible.

"I guess it's thanks for everything," I replied, trying to make this sound as cheerful as possible.

She grinned in delight. "I knew that you'd work it out: you are, despite my original impressions of you, a fucking good dick. Detective, that is, in case you're getting your hopes up!"

I grinned back. "Yes, that's a part of the problem, isn't it. The sex is still great as far as I'm concerned, but I get the feeling that your heart isn't in it. It's just something to do to kill time."

"A bit hard on yourself, but also a bit of truth there," she looked relieved when the waiter arrived with the wine, sitting back to consider how to go further while he poured the champagne.

Just as we were about to clink glasses, a buzz announced a message on Koide's comm. I froze in surprise, assuming that lack of action over the last day meant that it was switched off. Koide however, grabbed the machine from the pocket of her baggy cargo pants and scanned the incoming message.

Her face lit up as she punched the air in delight, surprising the waiter who was hovering behind her and causing him to scurry back to the safety of the cash desk. "Holmes, you fucking jammy bastard!

How did you manage to time the champagne like that?" She frowned in suspicion for a moment, then her grin returned. "Whatever the fuck, cheers!"

We clinked glasses and sipped the ice cold fizz, while I theatrically raised my eyebrows to encourage my boss to explain further.

"Well, that's it, we can come out of hiding now. The shit has hit the fan and we're still smelling sweet."

I waited for a moment, but it was clear that this was as much as I was going to get. These little games no longer fazed me, however. In fact, if I was truthful, I now rather enjoyed them. "OK, we cleared up the case and passed over all responsibilities to the Tokyo and Interpol brass - who thus now think the sun shines out of your arse. They have everything under control and we went off for a well-deserved holiday. But there must still have been an open end, something that could backfire on us and hence that we were well out of the way for."

The blonde said nothing, but gulped down her champagne and refilled her glass, topping up also for the little sip that I had taken from mine. I was definitely on the right track. I closed my eyes and visualized the case model that we had worked on together during the flight back to Japan, - upgraded to first class, no less, courtesy of Interpol.

"Yes! It's David or Dee or whatever the fuck we're supposed to call him or her. He was in a coma, but stable: not a problem for a quick euthanasia jab in Japan, but potentially a long, hard slog to take down in the Caribbean."

Koide was trying to keep a straight face, but with very limited success. "Psychopathic Miss Nomura might have decided to take the quick hara-kiri way out, but she wasn't one to let any enemy off the hook simply because of the fact that she was dead. She must have put a bounty on Bev as soon as it was clear that her virtual best friend was responsible for her downfall and the destruction of all her dreams. It might have been very hard for a yakuza hit squad to find David due to the way that he had covered his traces but, as soon as we cracked the case, it was inevitable that they would pick up the spoor."

"Of course," she grinned, "I even warned both Tokyo and Interpol about the risk. I was, however, pretty sure that they wouldn't take it seriously - too busy fighting for press time."

"So you just let the yakuza have a free hit, to clear up a loose end." I was disturbed by the thought, but not really very surprised.

"Not quite. I did insist that they used top-range surveillance kit to monitor David, so I'm fairly sure that the perps won't get off scot-free."

"But you knew it was bound to happen... " I ground to a halt realizing, in retrospect, that it should have been obvious. "You devious bitch!" I couldn't help smiling in admiration. "You get Brownie points for cracking the case, more points for keeping your head down and letting others share in the glory and now you'll emerge from your self-imposed isolation after the one failure of the system - but able to say that you did warn them in advance, so even more credit to you."

"... and, even better, without the risk of being embroiled in a long drawn out slog to ensure that David's wealth would not buy him a get-out-of-jail-free, in the unlikely case that he ever regained consciousness," I continued as the picture came together in my head.

I pondered this as the waiter silently topped-up our champagne flutes. "OK, that's our serendipitous reason for celebration cleared up, but I haven't forgotten that you were going to explain the recent change in our relationship."

The blonde was clearly still buoyed by her good news, which took a little of the bite from her words. "Yes, well that's actually the problem, lad. We don't have a relationship and never had, other than boss and underling of course. You have lucked out with a couple of good shags, but that just sex - nothing more. I have these little hetero flings now and then, just to remind myself that I made the right choice in terms of my orientation."

"... the right choice... " I broke in, feeling deflated.

"Yes, even you must have spotted that I've rather catholic tastes when it comes to sex... "

"To avoid confusion, I'm not sure that Catholic would be the term that I would use, but I know what you mean." I muttered.

"Anyway, that's sex. In terms of relationships, I definitely prefer women - and that's relationships with a lot of very wild sex," she clarified, to ensure that I got the point. "I guess I would call myself a lesbian with bi leanings, but it gets a bit complex if you try to use simple categories to classify something as complex as human nature."

"So the holiday is over, you go back to your partner and new job and I... "

"You get on with your life! Remember, you're also going back to a new job, with the dubious pleasure of taking on a useless underling to train up. I did say in the beginning that you'd learn a lot from this case and you certainly have. You've not only developed as a very fine investigator, you're also a lot more of a whole man... "

Koide suddenly stopped, as if aware that she had stepped completely out of character with her ebullient praise, but recovered quickly. "Anyway, Holmes, let's get this down our necks and I'll give you the fuck of your life as a going-away present."

***

Despite our bruised bodies and her confessed ennui with hetero sex, she had been as good as her word. I rolled off the bed and stretched cautiously, easing out residual aches and pains. The bedroom, which had seemed a bit cramped and over-furnished the previous evening, now seemed strangely empty without my larger-than-life bedmate.

All of Koide's clothing was gone, with the exception of a small pair of white tanga nickers that appeared to have been casually thrown onto a desk by the window. I was sure that this was deliberate, her way of leaving me a little memento. As I moved over to lift the pants, I saw that they were lying on a sheet of hotel notepaper. I lifted it and strained to read the scrawl: *OK, Jim, now a last one for the road. Got the report on D's murder. How was it done?*

I grinned in delight. Bloody typical, sneaks off but leaves me another of her fucking puzzles as a goodbye! "Well, how could I be expected to be able to work this out from scratch?" I murmured, as if I was responding to a spoken question. "Must be linked to Nomura's past murders - but torture would be fairly pointless for someone in a coma. Of course, she couldn't have known the shape that her victim would be in when her post-mortem revenge was finally implemented. But, somehow, the torture seemed to be something that she and her lesbian lover carried out for their own pleasure: not directly associated with targeted murder." I could feel I was getting close.

I stood in silence for a couple of minutes, but nothing else came to mind. "Just a shame that David wasn't in fit shape to eat a poisoned apple," I concluded in frustration, before deciding to cheat and turn over the sheet of paper.

I laughed out loud as I read: ... *drip containing cyanide-laced apple juice! Love, Stella.*

Well, it was not one hundred percent, but I was pretty sure that my ex-boss would have accepted my guess.

I now had to decide what to do with the rest of my two weeks of holiday. Maybe start off with a massage, I decided with a grin: now that I knew what to look for I could ensure that this would all have a happy ending!

Also by Ian McKinley
From Fiction4All
https://fiction4all.com

COF
What would it be like if you woke up tomorrow morning and all computing infrastructure had vanished? It's a scary thought! Now move forward three decades, when quantum computing and artificial intelligence prevents collapse as the result of unsustainable development of an over-populated planet. A hacker attack that destroys this isn't scary, it's apocalyptic! Billions die and survivors are thrown back to a Stone Age hunter/gatherer existence. Well, most of the survivors. Cof had created one of the few communities that retained technology and was set to be a center of a new renaissance. He would do anything to protect this commune and his plan for the future, including mass murder and use of weapons that would have convicted him for crimes against humanity in earlier days. But did the end really justify the means and would his leadership be accepted if anyone found out the scale of the slaughter that it was based on?

Emergence
Emergence is a science fiction thriller set in the near future, when supercomputers are ubiquitous and the knowledge engineers who manage them have inordinate power. Two such engineers, Fallon and O'Neil, are the main protagonists in a battle to control "backdoors" that allow computer systems to be hacked without trace. These are used by O'Neil

to combat the many threats to a grossly over-populated planet on the brink of environmental collapse, but initiate violent responses from the organizations hacked, which catch Fallon in the crossfire. Fallon's increasingly intimate use of a neural link to communicate with his computer when he is under threat - and to facilitate his sexual conquests - has the by-product of catalyzing emergence of a conscious artificial intelligence in his computer system. With such assistance, he has a hidden advantage that may allow him to take over O'Neil's invaluable hacking toolkit. Can a man like Fallon be trusted with such power and, indeed, could machine consciousness present a greater threat to mankind than any environmental hazard?